D[illegible]KULL . . .

Lu Thong turned to Mai Suphan and said, 'There are treasures, my dear, you cannot even begin to imagine – treasures so rare that they're often assumed to be legendary, rather than actual artefacts, but treasures that do actually exist and are so highly prized that only those with extraordinary determination – and, of course, the financial means – can possibly obtain them.'

'Such as?'

'The missing Lodestone from the Great Pyramid of Giza, said to be the Philosopher's Stone imbued with unearthly powers. The Excalibur Sword of King Arthur, also imbued with magical powers. The Holy Grail, which may or may not exist as a physical object. The coded manuscript from the church of Rennes-le-Chateau, said to reveal the location of King Solomon's treasure, the most fabulous in the world. The infamous *Necronomicon*, a book containing the secret code that can summon forth the Great Old Ones and enable the holder to take possession of the whole world. And, of course, the legendary Crystal Skull of the Mayans that is said to be able to conjure up all the hidden powers of the universe . . .'

Also by W. A. Harbinson in New English Library paperback

Projekt Saucer 1: Inception
Projekt Saucer 2: Phoenix
Projekt Saucer 3: Genesis
Projekt Saucer 4: Millennium
Revelation

About the author

W. A. Harbinson has been a journalist, magazine editor and TV scriptwriter. Born in Belfast, Northern Ireland in 1941, he left school at fourteen, studied mechanical engineering, then joined the Royal Australian Air Force. While serving in the RAAF, he drafted his first novel, *Instruments of Death.* In 1980 he completed *Genesis*, the epic novel of the world's most fearsome secret that became the inspiration for the whole *Projekt Saucer* series. Harbinson lives in West Cork, Ireland.

The Crystal Skulls

W. A. Harbinson

NEW ENGLISH LIBRARY
Hodder and Stoughton

First published in 1997 by Hodder and Stoughton
A division of Hodder Headline PLC

A New English Library paperback.

10 9 8 7 6 5 4 3 2 1

A CIP catalogue record for this title is available from the British Library

ISBN 0 340 67251 X

Typeset by Palimpsest Book Production Limited, Polmont, Stirlingshire
Printed in England by Clays Ltd, St Ives plc

Hodder and Stoughton
A division of Hodder Headline PLC
338 Euston Road
London NW1 3BH

For Miles & Suzanne Walker
&
Miles Jr.

AUTHOR'S NOTE

The Crystal Skulls is a work of fantasy and the fantastical should not be hemmed in by mere facts. There is, indeed, a Museum of Mankind in London, England, and it did, and possibly still does, display an early Mayan crystal skull.

However, the Museum of Mankind mentioned in this novel is purely a figment of the author's voluptuous imagination and the physical layout and security systems described herein bear no relation to those of the real Museum of Mankind and are not recommended to those planning burglary. Likewise, while there is a British Embassy in Bangkok, the British Consulate described in this novel does not exist in reality. The pursuit of fiction is not the pursuit of facts and *The Crystal Skulls* is entirely a work of fiction.

W. A. Harbinson
West Cork, Ireland
21st January 1997

CHAPTER ONE

The Great Pyramid of El Castillo at Chichén Itzá, Yucatán, was bathed eerily in the moonlight, under a star-filled sky, when two Mexican peasants, each using a hammer and chisel, chipped away the cement around one of the heavy stone slabs in the flat roof of the Shrine on the summit. Once the cement had been chipped away, they began prising the stone slab out of its ancient, dust-filled foundation.

Exposed to the chill night wind sweeping across the open-sided Shrine thirty metres above ground level, surrounded by the other Mayan ruins of this ancient site, the Mexican peasants were breathing harshly and sweating from their efforts to lift up a slab that had been embedded there for many centuries.

They were being watched intently, nervously, by a red-haired American with a scarred face who was dressed in a badly rumpled light tropical suit. Though normally a hard man, cold as ice, casually murderous, he could not help feeling nervous at the thought of what that equally murderous bastard Lu Thong would do to him if, after all this time and effort, he returned empty-handed to Bangkok. *Either Lu Thong or that psychopathic bitch Mai Suphan*, the American thought. *Neither will welcome me back with a smile if I return without what they sent me here for. I'll be dead meat for sure.*

Filled with dread at this thought, the American became impatient and, when the slab had been removed and set aside, he roughly pushed the peasants away and dropped to his knees to look into the dark rectangular hole. A few seconds later, when his eyes had adjusted to the darkness and he could see properly, he gave a low whistle of disbelief, then reached down into the hole and pulled out a macabre, eerily shining skull.

'Jesus Christ!' he whispered.

Holding the skull up in both hands, he turned it slowly in the moonlight shining obliquely under the roof of the Shrine. It was a life-sized skull, made of clear crystal, with a smooth, domed head, two gaping, empty eye sockets and parallel rows of perfect, exceptionally large teeth gritted together in a mouth whose upper lip merged with the cheek bones and the flat line of the nose. Everything – head, jawbone, eye sockets and teeth – was made from the same clear crystal and it appeared to have been carved from one solid block, being without the slightest trace of a seam, except for the hinges of the jawbone.

In the moonlight it gave off an eerie, unreal glow that only enhanced its dreadful, frightening appearance.

The two Mexican peasants had started gibbering fearfully the instant they set eyes on the crystal skull. But now, as the American examined it, helplessly filling up with awe and exhilaration, thinking *Even that bastard Lu Thong can't touch me now,* they looked at the roof of the Shrine and let out wails of absolute, inhuman terror.

Startled, the American also looked up and saw something that defied his comprehension.

Though the roof of the Shrine was directly above him, he somehow saw, as if seeing *through* it, an enormous, saucer-shaped, pulsating light, materializing magically in the moonlit darkness of the sky and growing wider as it descended silently upon him.

Still looking up, disorientated by what he was seeing, suddenly thinking that he was dreaming, he squinted against the light, tried to study it more thoroughly, and imagined that within its oddly pulsating brilliance he could discern . . . *stars*.

Not the stars in the normal sky – which had, in fact, been erased by the brilliant light – but much bigger, far closer stars that formed a slowly spinning, glowing whirlpool, now only a few metres above him and either melting, or somehow obliterating, the roof of the Shrine.

'Jesus Christ!' he exclaimed again.

The two Mexican peasants had fallen to their knees on the floor of the Shrine and were wringing their hands and gibbering even more fearfully, obviously offering up their prayers, when a much brighter light exploded out of that pulsating phenomenon – a blinding, scorching light that spread over the great temple – and the American was bathed in a wave of heat so fierce that it sucked the breath out of him and scorched him beyond the limits of pain.

He and his companions screamed dementedly as they burst into flames.

They collapsed on the instant, turning into three human torches, quivering in the spasms of death as they were covered in smoke. They were still burning, though no longer moving, released from pain through death, when the saucer-shaped light shrank back into the darkness, as if sucked up into a gigantic invisible funnel, letting the moonlight return and the roof of the Shrine reappear.

When the flames consuming the burning men finally died away, leaving only smouldering remains, the moonlight beamed obliquely on three hideously charred corpses . . . and on the miraculously untouched gleaming crystal skull that had fallen from the scorched hands of the American. Now it rested on its chin, its face turned to the east, on the windblown floor of the Shrine, on top of the ancient pyramid, high above the flat, moonlit earth, far below the stars in the heavens.

Had anyone been left alive to study the skull at that moment, they would have seen, inside it, another cosmos of stars that, glowing and pulsating oddly, were swirling like a slow, silent whirlpool.

Those stars vanished with the stars in the heavens when dawn broke over the ruins.

CHAPTER TWO

Dawn was breaking when Tom Powell turned off the Mex. 180 highway, heading for the ruins of Chichén Itzá. Twenty-nine years old, with a boyish, inexperienced face, unruly auburn hair and brown eyes that saw no evil, he was wearing rumpled blue jeans, a sleeveless photographer's waistcoat over an open-necked red-and-blue checkered shirt, and a pair of laced-up, rubber-soled canvas boots. He had left Mérida in the early hours of the morning with the intention of beating the heavy commercial traffic on the highway and now, as he left the main road and his rented jeep bounced over the rough gravel and potholes of the narrow track that wound through the soaring mahogany and dyewood trees of the rain forest, he felt proud of his initiative and was glad that he had decided to test his courage by coming on this trip alone. Indeed, he was deliberately taking this narrow back road to the ancient site as another test of his courage, determined, as he had been since leaving Mérida, not to be a normal tourist, resolved to shuck off the constraints of his past and to turn himself into a more worldly, independent man.

He was therefore very surprised when, mere minutes into the rain forest, he saw an attractive young lady up ahead, clearly Caucasian, wearing denims and shirt and with a rucksack on her back, frantically waving him down.

Tom carefully braked to a halt beside her.

'Hi,' she said.

Tom looked at her, speechless. He was often speechless in front of ladies. This one didn't actually look like a 'lady' in her denims and shirt, with her blonde hair pinned up on her head under a peaked cap clearly intended to keep the sun off her prominent nose and sunburnt pale skin. She had sharp green eyes and full lips that seemed curved in a perpetual grimace of mistrust, but her body was slim and full-breasted, supported on long, shapely legs.

'You dumb or something'?' she asked, sounding like a New York cab driver.

'Pardon?'

'I said, "Hi" and you're just standin' there gawpin'. The cat got your tongue or what?'

'Sorry,' Tom said. 'You just took me by surprise. What on earth are you doing here?'

She rolled her eyes. 'Bird watchin'.'

'Really?'

She rolled her eyes again. 'No, not really. I'm tryin' to get to Chichén Itzá, which is where this road leads to. You're goin' there, too, I guess.'

'Yes,' Tom said.

'So – are you gonna give me a lift or do I stand here an' fry in the heat when that sun rises properly?'

'Of course,' Tom said. 'Naturally.'

Before he could change his mind, she removed her rucksack from her shoulders and threw it into the back of the jeep, then she clambered into the seat beside him and strapped herself in.

'Great,' she said. 'Let's go.'

Disconcerted, wondering if he had done the wise thing in picking this young lady up, Tom started the jeep and drove off, making his way carefully over the potholes of the narrow track and trying to avoid the marshy ground around the trees on either side of his vehicle. He did, however, sneak a sideways glance at his passenger and judged her to be in her early twenties. She was attractive in a kind of rough-hewn way, but when she popped some gum into her mouth and started chewing – not bothering to offer him any – she seemed distinctly aggressive.

'So what's your name?' Tom asked.

'Molly Beale,' she replied, sighing as if aware that she would have to pay for the lift with forced conversation.

'American?' Tom asked.

'Yeah,' she said. 'From Brooklyn.'

'That's in New York, isn't it?'

Molly rolled her eyes again. 'Jesus Christ!' she said.

'I'm sorry. I'm not familiar with America.'

'So it seems,' Molly said.

Tom drove in silence for another minute or so, aware of the rising heat and humidity, then he broke the uncomfortable silence by saying, 'I just thought it odd that you'd be in the rain forest instead of hitching a lift on the highway.'

'What's odd about it?'

'The rain forest could be dangerous for a woman travelling alone,' Tom said.

'Dangerous? You gotta be kidding! What's dangerous is that fuckin' highway, I can tell ya. You hitch a lift and you've got hands crawlin' over ya like spiders – that's a fact of life, buddy.' Tom winced at the profanity, but Molly went on. 'Jesus! These Mexicans! They see a white woman alone and they practically come in their goddamned pants. After a couple of days of that, I'd had enough and decided to take the back route. I'd rather get eaten alive in this rain forest than deal with those bastids.'

Tom watched the road ahead, embarrassed by Molly's way of talking. The sun was clearly rising and, though he couldn't see it, he saw its light forming silvery striations between the tall trees, falling on the branches and green leaves, forming luminous pools on the forest floor. The heat was steadily rising.

'You've come from Mérida?' he asked her, not knowing what else to say.

'Been all over,' she replied. 'Hitch-hiking through Mexico and Yucatan. I've been here for ever.'

'You're interested in Mayan culture?' Tom asked her.

'Don't know anything about it,' Molly replied, 'except what I've read in my fuckin' guidebooks. I just wanted to get away, distract myself with somethin' different, and this place seemed exotic enough when I saw it on TV. So I said "Fuck you" to my boyfriend and packed my rucksack and lit out with no particular plans. So, here I am.'

Tom sneaked another sideways glance at her to see her blowing a bubble with her gum, then sucking it in again. She certainly had a prominent nose and, as Tom glanced at her, she tapped it once or twice with her index finger.

'You're lookin' at my hooter,' she said, 'so let's get it over and done with. I'm Jewish on my Mom's side. My Dad's a bog-Irish immigrant. Does that give you problems?'

'No, of course not!' Tom said, even more embarrassed.

'My Mom wanted me to be Jewish but Dad put a stop to it. He told me that I was a tart like all the others and didn't need no religion. That probably made it easier for him when he felt me up in my bed – at least until I'd had enough of his shit and lit out of there. He was a bit of a lush, I guess, an' used to beat up my Mom, so she disappeared when I was only twelve years old, leaving me with him. With her gone, he had to stick it somewhere, so he stuck it in me. He started when I was fourteen years old, but I lit out two years later. I moved in with some junkie friends to a dive on East Fourth Street on the Lower East Side. Winos and junkies in the hallways, stale beer and piss stinkin' up the joint, but even then it was better than home, so I stayed on for a while.'

'You poor girl,' Tom muttered.

'Not so poor,' Molly said. 'It wasn't all that bad. I didn't take junk myself – I mean, I wanted to live a life, not walk around like a zombie – but my junkie friends looked after me as best the poor bastids could. Then I got a job and, eventually, a boyfriend.'

'That must have been nice,' Tom said.

'A fuckin' nightmare,' Molly said. 'Brad Crawford. What an asshole! I was workin' in a supermarket, a checkout girl – fuckin' borin', I can tell ya – and he was workin' in the stock room, unpackin' the shit we sold, jet-black hair an' big brown eyes, sleeves rolled up, muscles ripplin', a grin most girls would kill for, an' he took me out for a beer an' charmed the panties off me an' of course we ended up in the sack an' it went on from there. Downhill from Day One.'

'Deary me,' Tom said. He didn't know what else to say. He wasn't used to this kind of conversation – the women he knew were not like this one – and it made him feel distinctly uncomfortable as he drove on through the forest.

'First mistake,' Molly said. 'I moved in with him, practically just around the corner, and his place was even worse than the one I'd been in. He hadn't cleaned it since *he*'d moved in and it was clear, from the minute I stepped through the door, why he wanted me there. I worked night and day to keep that fuckin' tip-heap clean, but he kept throwin' his beer cans on the floor and throwin' up on his moth-eaten rugs. Second mistake. I thought I could change him but he kept drinkin' like a fish, stayed out all night with his pals and other girlfriends, an' obviously kept his muscles in trim by beatin' up on wimmen. Naturally, since I was his woman of the moment, I ended up black and fuckin' blue. So between him an' my old man, I figured I'd had enough of men. What assholes they all are!'

She turned to glare angrily at Tom, obviously incriminating him in the crimes of all base males, making him nervously finger the collar of his shirt with one hand while continuing to drive with the other. Cobwebs glistened on the branches of the trees slipping past on both sides of him.

'Well, I . . .' he began.

'Fuck you!' Molly exclaimed. Tom nearly jumped out of his skin. 'That's what I said to that bastid. "Fuck you, I'm gettin' outa here!" And that's just what I did. I waited until he was sleepin' – drunk and snorin' like a pig. Then I stole his billfold and lit out of there, determined to be my own woman.'

She lit a cigarette without offering him one. Not that he smoked, but he would, at least, have appreciated the offer – as he would, indeed, have appreciated a piece of her gum to freshen his mouth, which was dry after his early morning drive. He thought this, with a little resentment, when he glanced sideways and noted that she was still noisily chewing her gum when not actually puffing out smoke from her cigarette. Fearful that she would see his sideways glance, he turned his eyes to the front again.

'I'd already thought of Mexico.' Molly certainly knew how to talk. 'I mean, I'd seen it on TV – and so, like I said, I stole his fuckin' billfold. And I took the cash he'd hidden under his mattress, too – 'cause he was tight as a drum but didn't have a bank account – an' rode a Greyhound all the way to Tijuana where I stopped for a while, tryin' to work out what I should do with my future.'

'By way of being your own woman,' Tom ventured.

'Yeah, right,' Molly said, then she turned to stare at him, incidentally blowing a cloud of smoke over him. 'Hey, you bein' sarcastic, or what? You Limeys are famous for that.'

'No! No!' Tom exclaimed, almost stuttering, meanwhile concentrating on the muddy track ahead which was, he realized, more narrow than he had expected it to be – and potentially dangerous. The branches of the trees were scraping the jeep and the ditches on both sides were filled with water. Tom was keen to test his courage in certain ways, but Molly Beale was distracting him. 'I merely meant—'

'Yeah, right.' Molly looked to the front and exhaled another cloud of cigarette smoke. 'Anyway, as you can imagine, between that bastid an' my Dad I wasn't exactly keen on men an' then, to make some bread, I took a job in Tijuana, selling cigarettes in a gamblin' casino.' She inhaled again. 'You know? Do I have to describe it? Black stockin's, stiletto heels, my tits bulging out of a bit of cloth that wouldn't have covered a postage stamp, an' I was told to lean real low, lettin' a bit of cleavage show, when those asshole gamblers asked for a pack an' leered at me like fuckin' serial killers.'

'How awful,' Tom said.

'An easy number,' Molly informed him. 'I mean, the tips were fuckin' gi-normous. Then, on top, you got all these invitations to all kinds of gatherin's – parties an' dinners an' breakfast in bed, champagne on tap, to round out the night – and *they* paid for everything! Then I made the mistake of fallin' in love again and that fucked me up again.'

'Oh, dear,' Tom said. He didn't know what else to say. He was shocked by her story, not to mention her vocabulary, and he was wondering if he'd be able to get rid of her when they reached Chichén Itzá. He sympathized with her, of course – her life had clearly been a nightmare – but he really just wanted peace and quiet, which was what he had come here for.

'A fuckin' gambler,' Molly said. 'I know how to pick 'em, right? He liked to gamble an' he was fifty-five years old an' he fucked very young girls.'

'And you are?' Tom asked.

'Twenty-three.'

'I see,' Tom said.

Molly sighed, exhaling more smoke, then blew another bubble with her gum and popped it and sucked it back in. 'He was nice when he won,' she said. 'Real generous with those greenbacks. There was nothin' he wouldn't give you when he won – but, oh boy, when he lost!' She inhaled and coughed raggedly when she exhaled, then waved the smoke away from her face.

'Fuckin' fists and boots,' she said. 'A real rave-up of despair. Accusin' me of bringin' him bad luck an' then makin' me suffer accordingly. Of course, I lit out. I mean, I'd been that route before. First my old man, then that bastid Brad Crawford, now this lunatic who lost more than he won an' needed someone to blame. So I lit out again.'

Tom felt that at this point he should make a contribution to the conversation, but when he glanced sideways at Molly and saw the grim set to her lips – full lips beneath a generous nose and, possibly, attractive when she smiled, which so far she had not done – his nervousness made him decide against it.

Instead, he returned his gaze to the front, concentrating on the narrow track, watching out for fallen logs or wild animals or, even worse, the bandits that he was convinced, despite his travel books, inhabited the forest. Though he had come here to prove his manhood, he still feared certain things.

'The same shit all over again,' Molly said, puffing another cloud of smoke and noisily chewing the gum that would have refreshed Tom's mouth and cleaned his unbrushed teeth. 'I took a job at the racetrack. Goin' back to my roots, you know? I'd had enough of the high-rollers, all those gamblers with greenbacks, an' thought I'd fit in better where the gamblin' was done by guys in coveralls. It could've been nice, really. I mean, I had a protective window between me and them. The mesh-wire with the small slot below an' they just slid their hands under it, handin' over their dollars. Unfortunately, I had a boss. He was broader than he was tall. He had a wife you would have died to avoid and his kids were real monsters. Frustrated, right? Wanted somethin' more to live for. Couldn't keep his fuckin' hand off my ass and breathed like a gorilla. Did I get involved? Yeah. I mean, I needed the job. So I ended up bein' screwed by him and pretendin' I liked it. Then his wife found out. I mean, she found us on his desk. We always did it on his desk 'cause he couldn't take me home and so she walked in when she wasn't expected and all hell broke lose. Of course—'

'You lit out again,' Tom said.

'Yeah, right. I lit out again.' She turned to glare at him, her lips grim, her green eyes blazing. 'Say, are you bein' sarcastic again? You bein' a Brit' an' all.'

'No! No!' Tom denied strenuously, his heart racing. 'I merely meant to say—'

'Yeah, right,' Molly said. 'Okay. No sweat, pal. Anyways, I just lit out of there and started travellin' again. Hitch-hiking, mostly. Not really knowin' where I was goin' and not really carin'. Hitched all the way through Mexico, enjoyin' the sights, and then bought myself a little guide book and let it lead me to here. Just wanted out, right? To be on my own, right? Thought I might as well see a bit of somethin' that I might never see again. Pyramids, old ruins – that kind of shit – so that's why I'm here. What about you?'

'Me?'

'Yeah, you. You think I'm talkin' about the man in the fuckin' moon? Where do *you* come from?'

'England,' Tom said. He didn't wish to discuss himself.

'England,' Molly said. 'Terrific. Now I know all there is to know.'

'I'm sorry. I didn't mean to sound so abrupt. It's just that I've little of interest to say. I'm just—'

'You're wearin' one of those photographer's jackets –

you know? That canvas number with all them pockets for lenses and things. Are you a photographer?'

'Well, no, not really,' Tom replied, embarrassed once more. 'I have a camera, of course – I mean, I take the odd picture – but I'm not a professional photographer. I only take photos for personal pleasure. The jacket—'

'Yeah,' Molly interjected. 'I noticed that all those pockets were empty. Just decoration. So why the hell are you wearin' that kinda number?'

'It seemed appropriate for tropical climates,' Tom said, trying to regain his dignity. 'I mean, it has lots of pockets—'

'All empty,' Molly reminded him.

'—which hold money and passport and various documents,' Tom continued doggedly, 'and, of course, though it's quite warm when one needs warmth, it doesn't have sleeves. So, though I'm not a photographer, it *did* seem like a sensible garment to wear on this particular trip.'

'Yeah, right,' Molly said.

Feeling humiliated, Tom decided not to respond and concentrated instead on his driving, taking note of the striations of sunlight now beaming down through the soaring trees and of the heat, which already was rising and making him sweat. He was also sweating because his heart was racing, but he tried to ignore that fact.

'So, come on, tell me!'

'Pardon?' Tom said.

'Tell me why you're here. Just tourin', is that it?'

'Well, yes, sort of,' Tom said, not wishing to discuss his personal life.

'Just touring?'

'Yes,' Tom confirmed.

'All on your little lonesome?'

'Yes,' Tom said.

Molly took a last drag on her cigarette and flicked the butt out into the rain forest, not concerned that she might set it on fire. She then turned to blow the smoke in Tom's face while offering a slight, sardonic smile.

'You speak really nice,' she said.

'Do I?'

'Yeah. At least to my ears. I mean, you sound really English, kinda posh, an' I'm not used to that.'

'Really?'

'Really.'

'I don't really speak posh,' Tom said. 'It's just normal English. But then, you *are* from New York.'

'Where we don't speak proper English,' Molly said.

'I didn't mean—'

'No, of course not.' Molly leaned back in her seat, blew a bubble of gum, popped it and sucked the gum back into her mouth before speaking again. 'So you're touring the Yucatan on your little lonesome. Why's that, may I ask?'

Tom didn't want to discuss it. It was still too painful for him. 'I don't wish to discuss it,' he said. 'It's a personal matter.'

Molly turned to glare at him, obviously outraged. 'You don't wanna discuss it? Oh, terrific! I mean, you don't mind askin' *me* a lotta questions, pryin' into *my* personal life, but now you don't wanna discuss your own business. Boy, that really does take the cake!'

Tom couldn't remember asking her any questions, but he didn't wish to say so in case she became even angrier. 'Well,' he said, hesitating, his embarrassment now acute, 'like you, I came to get away from things.'

'What things?'

'Well . . .'

'Yeah?'

'Actually, I've just been through a rather painful divorce,' Tom confessed, feeling ever more uncomfortable, not wanting to think about it, 'and I came here to put it all behind me and sort myself out.'

'Why here?' Molly asked, sounding none too sympathetic, which, given the life she had lived, might have been understandable.

'I've always been deeply interested in Mayan culture,' Tom explained, sounding rather portentous, perhaps because he was uneasy, 'and so I decided that coming here, seeing the ancient sites at first hand, as it were, would be a way of finding perfect peace as well as gaining some intellectual satisfaction.'

'That sounds like a right mouthful,' Molly responded, 'but if you've come to see the sights, here they are. What more could you want, pal?'

And they were, indeed, leaving the dark rain forest behind them and heading along an open road that led to the vast sprawl of Chichén Itzá, its great pyramids and ruined temples and soaring columns bathed in dawn's pearly light.

'Oh, how wonderful!' Tom exclaimed.

CHAPTER THREE

Though a nominal fee was normally charged for entrance to the site, there was no one on duty yet and Tom was able to drive right up to the low fence at the edge of the vast, smooth green lawns that stretched out in all directions around the ruins. Once there, he stopped the jeep, turned off the ignition, applied the handbrake and clambered out.

As he removed his camera from the bag in the rear seat and slung its strap around his neck, letting the camera rest on his chest, Molly clambered out of the other side of the jeep to yawn loudly and stretch herself. When she did that, the shirt tightened on her body and showed off her fine breasts. Tom felt a sexual stirring that he tried to ignore.

Instead, he let himself fill up with awe at what he was seeing. Molly, however, merely blew more bubbles of gum, her face a picture of cynical bemusement.

'Jesus, this is weird!' she exclaimed.

The ruins certainly looked eerie in the dawn light, with their Chac Mools, friezes of ancient warriors, carved jaguars, soaring columns shaped like serpent bodies, their heads at ground level, and great stone stairways with sculpted serpent balustrades. Immediately ahead, beyond the fence, was what Tom most wanted to see: the great pyramid of El Castillo, with its four massive stairways facing the cardinal points and leading up to the Shrine on the high summit.

Impressed by that sight, Tom clambered over the low fence, again followed by Molly, then went up to the great pyramid and started walking around its immense greystone mass, with Molly sticking close to him. Now feeling awestruck, he took in the pyramid's calendric-cycle panels and many terraces and steps, wondering at the ingenuity behind it all and wishing that he could view it alone, as he had planned originally. When he reached the north-west side, he stopped walking and just stared at the ancient temple in respectful silence.

'You look disappointed,' Molly said, having blown another bubble of gum, popped it and sucked it back in, clearly not as impressed as was Tom.

Understanding instantly why he had wanted to be here alone – and certainly without the presence of this bubblegum-chewing, cigarette-smoking New York floozie – Tom replied: 'I'm only disappointed because I really wanted to come here during either the spring or the fall equinox, in March or September, when—'

'The what?' Molly interjected.

'The equinoxes,' Tom explained. 'That's when the sun crosses the equator and night and day are of equal length in every part of the earth.'

'Big deal,' Molly said, 'but what's it got to do with that pile of fuckin' stones?'

Tom sighed. 'During the equinoxes, an unusual solar phenomenon, the interplay of light and shadow creates a sunlit serpent on this side of the pyramid. That serpent is about thirty-four metres long and it appears to slide down the building to join the head of the stone serpent at the bottom of the steps. As you can see,' he continued before Molly could interrupt him, waving his right hand to indicate the serpent-shaped columns and sculpted serpent balustrades of this and the other ruins, 'the serpent is very much part of the Mayan culture; so clearly, this temple was created very deliberately to have that sunlit serpent materialize, almost magically, during the summer and fall equinoxes. That's rather marvellous, don't you think?'

Molly stopped chewing, studied the north-west side for a moment, then said, 'Men need their little toys to play with, includin' their snakes, which probably made the Mayans think of their cocks. So what's all that other shit I see? All those panels an' things.'

Deeply embarrassed by her comment, but also shocked by what he viewed as its Philistine nature, Tom blushed and coughed into his clenched fist. Removing his hand from his mouth and wondering secretly how he could get rid of this crass creature, he said, 'The panels correspond to the number of years in the Mayan calendric cycles, so there are fifty-two in all, and there are eighteen of those terraces on each side, each side representing the eighteen-month religious year.'

'There are only twelve months in the year,' Molly said.

'Not for the Mayans,' Tom said. 'As for the steps,' he continued doggedly, 'leading up to the summit, upon which the Shrine is built, there are ninety-one steps on each side, adding up to 364, so if you add the summit, or the floor of the Shrine, which is treated as another step, you have 365, which is the number of days in the year. So the outside of the temple was created as a kind of religious calendar.'

'Gee whiz, you sure know your stuff.' Molly chewed her gum even more vigorously while studying the great pyramid, obviously trying to make sense of what she was being told. 'So is it solid?' she asked eventually. 'Or is there somethin' inside it?'

'Well, it *is* a temple,' Tom said, as if speaking to a child, 'so it would hardly be solid. Inside is the temple built to Kukulcán. It contains a jaguar-throne encrusted with seventy-three jade discs, representing spots and eyes, as well as a reclining Chac Mool monolith in an adjoining room.'

'A *Chac Mool*?'

'A statue of the Messenger of the Gods, formerly used as a vital prop in sacrificial rites.'

'What kinda sacrifice?'

'Human hearts, torn from the living flesh of the unfortunate victims, were flung, still steaming and beating, into the laps of the Chac Mools by knife-wielding priests as offerings to Kukulcán, the Quetzalcoátl of the Mayans.'

Molly shivered. 'Jesus!' Though obviously, like a kid at a horror movie, she enjoyed feeling shivery. 'So what's the Quetzalcoátl? Some kinda high priest?'

Clearly, she was at least listening to what Tom was telling her. 'Not quite,' he said. 'The Quetzalcoátl of the Toltecs was a legendary figure widely believed to have arrived as a god in the tenth century with the first wave of Toltec-Nahua invaders. The name means "plumed serpent" in both languages.'

'Back to phallic symbols again,' Molly said.

'Yes,' Tom said, determined to educate the brainless, possibly sex-obsessed creature. 'And while that mythical figure came to be thought of as the incarnation of the god, the real Kukulcán didn't actually arrive until the middle of the thirteenth century. He's been credited with founding Mayapán as the civil capital of the peninsula, though this place, Chichén Itzá, long remained as its principal religious centre.'

Molly nodded, then looked again, more thoughtfully, at the Castillo. 'So why's that pyramid called the Castillo,' she asked, 'when it was really a temple?'

Surprised and pleased by the percipience of the question, Tom gladly explained. 'Because the Spanish used it as a fortress.'

'That makes sense,' Molly said. 'Can we go inside?'

'Unfortunately, not yet, though I certainly plan to enter it later when they start selling tickets and the guards open the place properly.'

'So why'd you come so early?' Molly asked.

'I wanted to get here before the tourists arrived. I wanted to contemplate the place in silence.'

'Now you've got me makin' noise,' Molly said.

'I don't mind,' Tom lied.

Appreciating that she may not be as dumb as she sometimes sounded, he suggested that they explore the whole site.

'Sure, why not?' she said.

First, they walked the rest of the way around the great temple, with Tom taking photos of its four separate sides. When he was satisfied that he had seen enough, he led them on to the Ball Court. More than 500 feet wide, it had massive stone platforms on either end of its two great walls. As they crossed it in silence, with Tom taking more photos, he tried visualizing the young men of the mysterious Nahua and Mayan people playing their ball games right here.

'This is a kind of football pitch,' he explained to Molly who was glancing left and right with searching eyes. 'The game was called *Tlachtli* or, in the Mayan, *Pok-To Pok*—'

'Sounds like sex,' Molly interjected with a grin. 'You know? Have a poke!'

Tom ignored the saucy remark. 'From the written records,' he continued, 'it seems to have been a rather bizarre mixture of soccer, basketball and lacrosse. The object was to propel a solid *chicle* ball through high stone rings using only the forearms, knees and hips, all of which were well padded.'

'Not too dangerous, then,' Molly observed.

'It could be,' Tom replied. 'As you can see from the magnificent reliefs on those two walls, the losers were often sacrificed.'

Molly glanced at the two reliefs and shivered. 'Jesus!' he said again.

Halfway across the Ball Court, Tom turned north onto the *saché*, or sacred road, that ran for approximately 300 yards to what seemed like a solid mass of jungle.

'What the fuck are you going there for?' Molly asked. 'There's nothin' there but the trees.'

'Yes, there is,' Tom said.

He was right. At the end of the sacred road, they came abruptly, almost shockingly, to what seemed like a gaping wound in the forest: a vast hole nearly 200 feet across and dropping just over seventy feet to the surface of a darkly glittering jade-green pool.

'Oh, boy!' Molly exclaimed softly, her eyes growing big as she looked down.

'This is the *Cenote Sagrado*, or Well of Sacrifices,' Tom explained with satisfaction, noting the look of awe on her normally cynical face. 'The victims were hurled into that pool to propitiate the god Chac.'

'Virgins, no doubt,' Molly said. 'And thrown down by males.'

'Not only virgins, but children of both sexes, most of them under twelve years old.'

'The barbaric, fuckin' bastards.'

'Not really,' Tom said. 'It was a deeply religious rite. However, the pool was dredged in 1968 and they found not only the bones of those poor children, but also many artefacts – hundreds of tiny copper bells, gold ornaments, jade fragments. Not that this cleared up the mystery of the Mayans, since apart from some 1,200-year-old jade fragments and bits of pottery, most of the artefacts were from the fourteenth and fifteenth centuries and of Central and South American origin.'

'A real mystery, these Mayans, right?'

'Right,' Tom said.

Deciding that he was getting her serious attention and hoping that this would make his tour more enjoyable, he led her back along the sacred path to the *Tzompantli* and the House of the Eagles and Tigers, the first a large platform of human skulls, the second a smaller platform adorned with carved eagles and jaguars holding human hearts in their claws.

'A bloodthirsty bunch of bastards,' Molly said. 'You don't need a fancy education to tell that about 'em.'

'That's a simplified way of looking at it,' Tom said, offended by her crass comment.

'Oh, yeah?' Molly said.

Deciding that he may have been wrong in imagining that he was gaining her *serious* attention, Tom took some more photos, then led her to the magnificent Temple of the Warriors. As large as El Castillo, it was fronted with a colonnade of square columns carved with plumed warriors and dominated by a recumbent Chac

Mool, gazing towards the pyramid of El Castillo and flanked by two enormous serpent columns.

'More phallic symbols,' Molly said.

'Do you mind?' Tom responded, sounding like a stern headmaster. 'There's more to this architecture than—'

'Violence and sex,' Molly interjected. 'Torn-out hearts an' snakes. Don't give me any intellectual crap to justify your pitiful male ego. These bastards were just like all men an' their women were, as usual, victims.'

'That's ridiculous!'

'Oh, yeah?'

'It's a gross simplification. Clearly, you know nothing about the ancient religions or those who once practised them.'

'All men,' Molly reminded him. 'The women were sacrificed, remember?'

Outraged, Tom glanced south and east to see the Court of the Thousand Temples with its remaining columns, representing giant plumed serpents, rising out of the rubble.

Oh, God, he thought, *more serpents. She'll go mad if she sees them. Clearly, she's a deranged Women's Libber. How on earth can I lose her?*

'Can I just explain—?' he began.

'No, you can't,' Molly said firmly. 'These bastards ripped the hearts out of virgins and threw them into that fuckin' pool while raising monuments to their big cocks. What's that if it isn't male ego runnin' rampant as usual?'

Shocked almost speechless, Tom turned around and started walking back to his car.

'Where you goin'?' Molly called after him.

Tom turned back to face her, trying to control his anger. 'To my jeep,' he said. 'I have to leave now.'

'Already?'

'Yes, already.'

'I thought you wanted to see inside the temples.'

'I've changed my mind,' Tom said. 'I have to travel on to Uxmal and I'd like to go now.'

He hurried away from her, making his way back to the great pyramid of El Castillo, which in truth he had wanted to climb before the Visitors' Centre opened and more crass American tourists like Molly made his life a misery. Now, however, he was so angry, so determined to get rid of her, that he kept on walking past it – until stopped by the challenge in her voice, ringing out loud and clear from where she had come up right behind him.

'Hey, you!' she called out.

Tom stopped and turned to face her. She grinned and pointed up to the summit of the pyramid. 'Don't you want to go up there?'

'No.'

'Why not?'

'I've seen all I wish to see,' Tom said.

'You're lyin'.'

'I am not!'

'That thing up top, the . . . ?'

'Shrine.'

'Yeah, right, the Shrine. It has a great view of the Court of the Thousand Columns and the Temple of the Warriors. They'd make great fuckin' photos – and you know that if you don't take those photos, you'll always regret it. So why aren't you doin' it?'

'I don't wish to.'

'You do. It's just 'cause I'm here. If I wasn't here, you'd be climbing that thing and takin' photos from up there.'

'I would not.'

'Scared of heights?'

Tom sucked his breath in, trying to control his racing heart. She was, of course, correct. More than anything else, he had wanted to climb to the summit of the pyramid, yet he now found himself reluctant to do so, not only because she was annoying him but also, as she had clearly deduced, because, as he realized when he looked upwards, he *was* afraid of heights.

'Don't be ridiculous,' he said.

'You're afraid of heights,' she insisted.

'I am not!'

'You are!'

'If you're so damned smart, why don't you come with me?'

'I will,' Molly said.

Realizing that he was trapped by his own childish challenge, Tom strode resolutely to the massive steps of the pyramid, took a deep breath, and began the arduous, dizzying climb to the summit. Molly joined him, coming up behind him, soon catching up with him, and grinning when she saw him perspiring and heard his heavy breathing. He was breathing not only from exertion but from visible nervousness.

'Are you nervous?' Molly asked, when they were only halfway up and had stopped for a rest, though Tom pretended that he had done so to take photos of the surrounding landscape.

'Of course not,' Tom said, squinting bleary-eyed through the camera's eyepiece and thinking that he might faint, given the fact that the ground was already far below him. 'But if you're nervous, by all means go back down and I'll proceed alone.'

'No way,' Molly said. 'I used to keep pigeons on

my roof when I lived in Brooklyn. I've always liked heights.'

Defeated again, Tom clambered up some more steps, surprised to find how tall they were, but eventually had to stop for another rest while he took some more photos.

'So what's your fascination with Mayan culture?' Molly asked, glancing about her and squinting against the early morning's brightening light.

'Oh,' Tom said, surprised to hear an intelligent question from her and glad to be distracted from his fear of heights. 'Their . . . their mysterious origins, I suppose.'

'What's so mysterious about 'em?'

'Well . . .' Tom hesitated, wondering if he could manage to discuss such esoteric matters with her, but pleased to be talking instead of climbing. 'Well,' he began again, 'we really know so little about them. In fact, all we really know about them is what you see before you. We *do* know that the Mayan empire included present-day Guatemala, British Honduras, Honduras, Salvador and, of course, Mexico and Yucatán, but we only know that from the evidence of their great lost cities—'

'Like this, right?'

'Right. But we still don't know where they came from, why they periodically abandoned their great cities only to reoccupy them centuries later, and why their great civilization broke down and eventually dispersed even before the arrival of the Spaniards. So, given this, the Mayans are surely one of the most mysterious peoples on Earth, which is what makes them especially fascinating – at least to *me*.'

'I can tell you're an intellectual,' Molly responded,

blowing gum, making bubbles, 'but let me tell you somethin' about intellectuals: they all have holes in their brains.'

'Oh? How come?' Despite himself, Tom was becoming intrigued by this blunt-tongued young American lady. She had the confidence of all fools, he thought, and that lent her a certain charm.

'They can't see the wood for the trees,' Molly explained. 'I mean, these Mayans, they're probably just like the Indians – like, they've been here since time began, right? There ain't no mystery to it.'

'Ah, yes,' Tom said, glancing down upon the lawns far below and quickly looking away. 'That theory belongs to the "Independent Origin" school of thought—'

'Pardon?'

'Which holds that American Man – in this case, the Mayans – was here from the beginning. However, there *is* another school of thought, the diffusionist theory, which holds that a large body of evidence indicates that other races – Chinese, Etruscans, Negroes, Phoenicians and Jews—'

'Don't drag *us* into this!'

'—came here first and contributed elements of their own culture to the Mayans.'

'Just hold on there, pal. Regarding we Jews—'

'However,' Tom continued, now enraptured with his own thoughts, being distracted from the dizzying heights, 'wherever the Mayans came from, they were almost certainly in this peninsula as early as 1,500 BC and it's possible – only *possible* – that their many migrations were due to periods of drought. As to their disintegration and ultimate dispersal, it is possible – just *possible* – that during one of the many droughts the peasants revolted, slaughtered the ruling priests and nobles and thus, depriving themselves of their knowledgeable leaders, ordained their own destruction.'

'Possible,' Molly echoed him.

'What?'

'Only possible. You intellectuals don't know shit from shinola – you're just makin' guesses. With guys like you runnin' loose in Academia, I'm glad I didn't have a proper education.'

'Very funny,' Tom said.

She looked at him and grinned. 'You wanna start climbin' again?'

'Why not?' Tom said.

This time she took the lead and Tom, though resenting that he was behind and below her, could not help feeling comforted by her presence, which somehow seemed protective even though, when you really thought about it, he would have been more protected had she been behind him and below him, to possibly break his fall if he slipped. In the event, after more strenuous effort, he followed her up onto the flat roof of the pyramid, being the floor of the Shrine, which had its own roof, and gratefully crawled into its breeze-blown, cool, silent shadows.

That was when Molly screamed.

CHAPTER FOUR

In his palatial home in the rich man's quarter of Bang Kapi, Bangkok, Thailand, the wealthy and powerful criminal Lu Thong was having lunch in his luxurious Oriental lounge with the beautiful, diabolically evil Mai Suphan. Having just removed his golden, catlike body from his wide bed – not quite as catlike as Mai Suphan's, but certainly just as slim – he was seated at the bamboo table in his dressing gown of glittering Thai silk, handwoven and painted by the peasants whom he ruthlessly exploited.

'So my dear,' he was saying to Mai Suphan as he smoked one of the cigarettes that he was convinced, rightly or wrongly, would kill him sooner or later, though sooner, he often thought, might be better than later, 'what is the situation with regard to the pharmaceuticals?'

He spoke perfect English with an Oxford accent of which he was proud, having been educated at that excellent university. His father, a Bangkok businessman of dubious reputation, had wanted him to be a corporate lawyer, which would have helped the family business, but Lu Thong, perhaps taking after his father and certainly loathing the English weather, had, upon graduating with a Law degree, returned home to create a criminal empire based on drugs, prostitution and, more to his personal liking, the sale of stolen works of art and antiques. By 'pharmaceuticals' he did, of course, mean drugs and Mai Suphan understood this, being one of his most efficient lieutenants as well as his extraordinarily sensual, untrustworthy mistress.

'We have no problems,' she now told him, finishing off her caviar on toast and dabbing her luscious lips with a hand-painted paper handkerchief of the kind used only by the very wealthy. 'Every dealer in Bangkok is now under our control and the streets, it can safely be said, are ours to command.'

'I'm surprised you've had no problems,' Lu Thong said, exhaling a thin stream of smoke from his cigarette and fully aware that Mai Suphan, though his mistress, was not a girl to be trusted. Like many a Thai girl who had come up the hard way, she had very expensive Westernized tastes and she was, furthermore, as independent as a wild cat in the forest. Sooner or later, she would want to be her own woman and he would have to watch out for that.

'You mean those who refused to cooperate?'

'Exactly,' Lu Thong said.

'They're all either in their graves or went up in smoke,' Mai said, referring to the cremation of the dead, which was how most in Thailand preferred to go to their Maker. Most of the drug dealers, coming from traditional families, had gone up in smoke. 'Not one has survived.'

Lu Thong smiled. 'I'm sure you enjoyed that little task, my sweet.'

'I'm sweet because I enjoyed it.'

'Your pleasures run to the diabolical,' Lu Thong said, 'and I find that irresistible.'

They were both sitting on velvet cushions placed on the floor on both sides of the low table and Mai, wearing a skin-tight Malaysian *cheongsam* slit up to the thigh, curled her long, shapely legs beneath her, drawing his dark, glittering gaze to her silken skin and perfect ankles in stiletto-heeled shoes.

'You think I'm evil,' she said.

'I don't believe in the concept. I only believe in what men *do*. And men do what they need to do to survive – no more and no less. Moral judgement, the concept of good and evil, becomes redundant when a man knows only one way to survive and has no choice but to take it. My brigands in the jungle, cutting throats in order to steal, do so because it's all that they know and they think it perfectly normal. Indeed, they take their pride from how well they do it – and with nothing else to measure their actions against, why, indeed, should they not? As for our whores, they're in the profession because they don't have a choice, and if they ever think in terms of right or wrong, which I doubt, they would almost certainly take their pride from the fact that their whoring feeds their poor children. Where is the evil here? It has no meaning to those poor souls. The brigands cut throats, the whores whore, because it's all they can do. Morality, a religious concept, is the invention of those who have the leisure to dwell on such abstract matters. No, my dear, I do not think you're evil: I think you are as you were born to be – and you can't be anything else.'

'*I* think I'm evil,' Mai said, 'but I rather enjoy it.'

'I'm sure you do,' Lu Thong said.

He studied her face, which was beautiful beyond compare, and wondered how such beauty could mask a soul so utterly black. She did not have an evil face –

for, indeed, it was sublime: high cheekbones, enormous, liquid brown eyes, an almost perfect, piquant nose and the kind of full lips that made men imagine the most exquisite pleasures. It was also, however, a face that could become all things to all men by shifting through moods of darkness and light in a way that bordered on the prismatic. She was an actress at heart, only alive when playing games, the more dangerous and deadly the better. Certainly she was as skilled at melting a hard man's heart as she was at destroying the soul of a decent man or, if the occasion called for it, cold-bloodedly killing him.

Lu Thung understood this because he'd virtually created her, abducting her from her jungle *kampong*, rescuing her from the thatched shacks raised high on stilts, from the shit and piss in the open drains, from the squawking chickens and the goats, from the old men smoking opium and the women aged dreadfully before their time through endless labour and lack of hope. In fact, she had been abducted by one of his roaming gangs of brigands – the ones who regularly raided the *kampongs* and trading boats, pillaging and looting, killing all witnesses, and abducting young girls for the slave trade. Mai Suphan had been such a girl, a rare beauty in rags, and Lu Thong's brigands had carried her off in their boat and brought her, with other abducted girls, to one of Lu Thong's many Bangkok brothels. There he had seen her for the first time: her ravishing beauty and lust for life; her seductiveness and cruelty; the pleasure she gained from sex and violence, having been abused as a child, all of which made her a natural whore and a woman to reckon with. He had decided, when he was told about her and finally called her into his presence, when he had personally sampled her whore's artistry and was reduced to a quivering heap, that he could mould her into what he wanted her to be and then use her for better things.

This he had done. But she was even better than he had thought, a natural talent, an unscrupulous little witch who could never be trusted. It was no accident, therefore, that he had decided to train her, to refine her love of violence, encourage her lust for wealth and power, eventually turning her into his deadliest, most efficient lieutenant in his ever-expanding world of vice and crime. She was ideal as a tool for blackmail, for various forms of entrapment, and finally, when he had addicted her to drugs, as a killing machine. She was a cold, calculating, clever woman, dangerous even to him.

'Actually,' she now said, having learnt her English from him, 'I'm just a simple girl with a simple girl's needs, easily satisfied.' She raised her glass of champagne before her darkly radiant brown eyes, alight with self-confidence. 'Champagne and caviar and and great wealth. What else does a girl need?'

'Sex?'

'That's for the taking.'

'For your kind, that's true. I consider myself lucky to get you just by snapping my fingers; but I know you have others.'

'So do you,' Mai said. 'You've always told me that boredom kills lust, variety being the spice of life, and that I, like you, should take what I can where I find it. What you tell me, I practise.'

Lu Thong smiled again, amused by her impertinence. He had strangled other women for less than this, but Mai Suphan was a special case. Being dangerous, she kept him on edge and that was better than boredom. He had a low boredom threshold, finding most of life banal, and he needed the thrill of danger, high risk and conquest to regenerate his easily depleted spirit and strengthen his flagging will to live. He saw life as a sewer, a cesspit, and only the very greatest challenges could revive his interest. Mai Suphan was such a challenge, being treacherous beyond belief, but he still needed power beyond measure to keep him afloat. For that, he would need the Crystal Skull and it loomed large in his thoughts.

'You do what I tell you,' he said, 'because it gives you more freedom than you could possibly have otherwise. You do what I tell because I tell you to go out and fulfil yourself in every way possible, without guilt or remorse. You do what I tell you because it suits you, but when it doesn't, you'll stop.'

'And then?'

'Then we'll come into conflict and that will give us both pleasure.'

Smiling like a Cheshire cat, Mai Suphan placed her champagne glass back on the table, then leaned forward to sniff up the cocaine that lay like like snow on its surface. As she did so, the silk *cheongsam* rippled over her perfect body, outlining every exquisite curve and hollow, making Lu Thong breathe deeply. Hearing that sound, Mai Saphan straightened up again and said, 'You've just had me.'

'And will have you again if I so desire.'

'You're insatiable,' Mai said. She leaned back on her hands, letting her breasts thrust forward, the silk tightening across them, and her long black hair fell onto the cushions, spreading out like a rug. After inhaling the cocaine and sighing rapturously, she returned her gaze to Lu Thong. 'You're insatiable because you're restless,' she said, almost purring. 'Like a spoilt boy, you've smashed all your toys and need something new.'

'What toys?' Lu Thong asked.

Mai waved her right hand, indicating the spacious lounge with its rare paintings, glistening crystals and rare antiques, some bought legally but most of them stolen and all of them priceless. 'All of this,' she said. 'All the wealth you've acquired. You've got it because it was a challenge to acquire it and now it means nothing to you. What comes after this?'

What a smart bitch she is, Lu Thong thought. *Much too smart for her own good. I drag her out of the* kampongs, *I teach her everything she knows, and now she throws her knowledge back in my face. It's my own fault, of course.*

But he had to admire her for it, so he told half of the truth: 'I'm bored with drugs and sex – even with my wealth and power – but I'm compensating by reaching beyond the merely rare and priceless – the world's great paintings and antiques; those bought and sold behind closed doors – and am now striving to obtain only those artefacts that are not only rare, but possibly legendary.'

'What does that mean?' Mai Suphan asked.

Lu Thong offered a loud sigh, feeling oddly inadequate, and turned his head to gaze through the panoramic window that overlooked the sprawling city of Bangkok, with its 3,000,000 lost souls. They were all lost, of course, because this was God's wish (or so Lu Thong thought) and they included the wealthy of this very area, Bang Kapi, the squatters of Klong Toei, where Lu Thong's drug business thrived, and the tolerably poor of Din Daeng and Hua Mak, ghettoized in their welfare housing estates and more fodder for Lu Thong's pimps and drug traffickers. Most Thais called Bangkok 'Krung Thep' – the City of Angels – and Lu Thung, who was fond of the decadence of Los Angeles, always thought of that great American city where crime was richly rewarded when he considered the cesspit he now ruled. Down there, in the sweltering humidity, around the banks of the Chao Phraya river, the Chinese of Samp Peng, the Indians of Wang Burapha, and even the Westerners in the affluent eastern section of the city were all subjected, in one way or another, to the rule of Lu Thong. The city was overcrowded – thousands of one- or two-storey wooden structures packed close together between high-rise buildings and the equally ghettoized masonry homes of the foreign community; and blocked up with traffic, including the ubiquitous three-wheeled taxis – and this overcrowding, not unlike that of a bee's nest, was also honey to Lu Thong. He exploited not only the poverty but the gap between rich and poor, as well as the witless yearning of foreigners for exotic experiences. Thus, his nightclubs and restaurants, his bars and brothels, brought him excellent revenue. Nevertheless – and this saddened him – he could also see down there the many *wats*, or Buddhist monasteries, over three hundred in all, that upheld the values in which he had been brought up and now could not believe in. He was a religious man at heart – he felt that life must have some meaning – but until he could find something greater than life's banality, the meaningless crawl from birth to death, the demeaning need to make money or have power just to feel human, he would never be able to sleep well at night without his nightcap of opium. For this reason – to rise above the need for opium or other sedatives, including Mai Suphan – he required nothing less than the world's greatest treasure.

He needed the Crystal Skull.

Sighing again, turning back to the gorgeous Mai, he said, 'There are treasures, my dear, you cannot even begin to imagine – treasures so rare that they're often assumed to be legendary, rather than actual artefacts, but treasures that do actually exist and are so highly prized that only those with extraordinary determination – and, of course, the financial means – can possibly obtain them.'

'Such as?'

'The missing Lodestone from the Great Pyramid of Giza, said to be the Philosopher's Stone imbued with unearthly powers. The Excalibur Sword of King Arthur, also imbued with magical powers. The Holy Grail, which may or may not exist as a physical object but is widely believed to be the chalice used by Christ at the Last Supper and therefore capable of giving magical powers to he who possesses it. The coded manuscript from the church of Rennes-le-Château, said to reveal the location of the most fabulous treasure in the world – that of King Solomon. The infamous *Necronomicon*, a book containing the secret code that can summon forth the Great Old Ones and enable the holder to take possession of the whole world. And, of course, the legendary Crystal Skull of the Mayans – for, alas, there is more than one, though not all of them magical – that is said to be able to conjure up all the hidden powers of the universe, perhaps even reveal God and the devil. These are treasures so rare and valuable that even I, who have treasures many would die for, find them irresistible. In fact, these are the *only* treasures that will now satisfy me and I'm determined to find at least one of them – for indeed, if a man possesses even one of them, he'll have as much as any human being can handle. In fact, he'll be gambling with the Great Unknown – and that, my dear, I am convinced is the only challenge now worthy of me.'

'Are you serious?' Mai asked.

Insolent bitch, Lu Thong thought. *She can help me, but her time will surely come and I'll be there when that happens*.

'Yes,' he said. 'I'm serious. Even now I'm in pursuit of the legendary Crystal Skull of the Mayas – and I believe that it's at last within my grasp.'

'What makes you think that?'

Though Mai Suphar was clearly sceptical of what she had been told – she was an earthy woman, after all, finding gold in cesspits – she also respected Lu Thong's judgement and would, at the very least, give serious consideration to anything he told her could be valuable. If he thought that this Crystal Skull was valuable, then almost certainly it was – not, in her view, as a magical artefact, but almost certainly as a saleable item in the illicit international marketplace. She was interested because of that and that alone, so she wanted to hear more.

'You must know,' Lu Thong said, 'that if I do anything, I do not do it by halves.'

'Yes, I know that,' Mai said.

Lu Thong nodded his appreciation. Then, with a lazy curving of his index finger, he pointed towards the ceiling, indicating the upper floor of his palatial home.

'Up there,' he said, 'is Professor Paul Schwarz, an English expert in antiquities and the world's foremost authority on the ancient Maya. Learning that he had been hired by the Museum of Mexico to work in their library and update their records on Mayan relics, I offered him more money than he had ever imagined he would possess to use his own knowledge and, of course, the museum's considerable research facilities, to learn everything he could about the original Crystal Skull and pass that information on to me. Having being doing that on my behalf for the past couple of years, the good professor has finally come up with the information, strongly substantiated, that the only genuine Crystal Skull in the world – apart from the one held in the Museum of Mankind in London – is to be found in a specially carved repository – a kind of miniature tomb – in the roof of the Temple of the Warriors in Chichén Itzá.'

'No problem there,' Mai Suphan said.

'Exactly,' Lu Thong said. 'So a few days back – the same day, in fact, that Professor Schwarz brought me this news – I dispatched one of my best men, an expatriate American gangster, to go to Chichén Itzá and bring the Crystal Skull back here. And . . .' Lu Thong checked his international-time wristwatch, then looked up again. 'According to my calculations, he should have found it by now and will already be on his way to Mérida, en route back to here.'

'Sounds great,' Mai Suphan said.

'Are you being cynical, dear?'

'No,' Mai replied. 'I'm merely thinking that if your Yank gangster friend *has* actually found this Crystal Skull, then you're going to have to keep the matter secret until you decide what to do with it.'

'So?'

'So the only person who'll know about it – apart from

your Yank gangster and, of course, me – is that helpful American academic now resting upstairs. Namely, Professor Schwarz.'

'Ah, yes,' Lu Thong said. 'That fact is undeniable. Not that I hadn't thought about it, but it's nice to be reminded. He will, of course, be disposed of.'

'Don't do that,' Mai said. 'You're depriving me of my pleasure. Let Professor Schwarz return to his hotel. He won't last very long.'

Lu Thong smiled, knowing exactly what she meant, and said, 'He's all yours, my sweet.'

Returning Lu Thong's smile, Mai uncurled her delicious legs and stood up by the low table, stretching her fabulous, seductive body.

'You want anything before I leave?' she asked.

'You've exhausted me already,' Lu Thong said.

Smiling even more broadly, her cynicism obvious, Mai picked up her alligator-skin bag, slung it over her bronzed shoulder, then nodded and walked out of the room.

When Lu Thong heard the front door slam shut, he picked up his intercom, dialled a number, and told his goons to inform Professor Schwarz that he could pack his travelling bag and come down to the lounge. The professor arrived within minutes, his travelling bag on his right shoulder. Dressed in a light grey suit with shirt and old-school tie, he was slim, silvery-haired and still handsome, though clearly scared mindless.

'Does this mean I can . . . ?'

He had been invited here three days ago to convey his findings about the Crystal Skull over an unforgettable, wine-sodden gourmet meal. Once he had conveyed the news that Lu Thong so badly wanted to hear, he had been sent up to a guest bedroom with one of Lu Thong's exquisite whores. When the good professor awoke the next morning, he found the whore gone and, even worse, his room door locked. He had remained there, albeit with a luxurious *en suite* bathroom, for three lonely days, no doubt tormented by his knowledge of just who Lu Thong was and what fate might now be in store for him. So, having been released from the bedroom and allowed to bring his travelling bag with him, he was visibly relieved, though still not sure if he had good cause to be so.

'Yes, you can leave,' Lu Thong said. 'I *do* apologize, my friend, for having kept you here so long, but I had to be sure that your information was correct. Luckily for you, a call from my man in Yucatán confirmed that the Crystal Skull was indeed where you said it was and that he was going to the temple to collect it and bring it back to me. Almost certainly he will have done that by now – so you may leave. Please rest assured that you *will* be well paid.'

'I've been paid enough already,' Professor Schwarz replied, inching back towards the door of the lounge, obviously still not believing his good luck. 'But, of course, if you insist, a little bonus would be . . .'

'Appreciated,' Lu Thong said, completing the sentence for him, understanding that he had a dry throat and needed reassurance. 'You can be certain that you'll be paid more than you can imagine for what you have done. Thank you and good day.'

'Good day, Mr Thong.'

Breathing heavily, Professor Schwarz turned away and hurried out of the room. When Lu Thong again heard the front door slam, he sighed, smiled triumphantly, then picked up the telephone and asked for a number in Mexico City. The line was not good – there was an awful lot of static and the operator was an idiot – but eventually he managed to connect with his friend on the ground and asked if the Crystal Skull had been located.

The answer wiped the smile from his face and made him slam the phone down.

CHAPTER FIVE

Molly's frightened screaming tapered off as Tom straightened up and saw her at the other side of the floor of the Shrine, silhouetted by the brightening morning light. She was staring down, bug-eyed, at what looked like three piles of blackened rags scattered around a rectangular hole in the floor. One of the stone slabs, Tom noted, had been chipped free with a hammer and chisel, which he could see lying close to the hole. He was still wondering what had made Molly scream when he realized that the piles of blackened rags were actually the charred remains of three human beings. Discerning this, and then smelling the scorched flesh, he almost threw up.

'Jesus Christ!' Molly exclaimed, staring at each of the corpses in turn. 'What the fuck . . . ?'

Tom, holding his handkerchief over his mouth and nostrils, was still fighting to stop himself from retching. When he felt that it was safe to do so – when his heaving stomach had settled down – he removed the handkerchief from his face and forced himself to look at the three charred corpses. He did not look long. The sight of those burnt men was too awful to contemplate. Revolted, he turned his eyes away and looked out over the ruins in the Complex of the Thousand Columns, the nearby Temple of the Warriors, and, beyond it, the dense trees of what seemed like endless, almost totally flat jungle. Then, reluctantly, he turned back to Molly and her wide-eyed, disbelieving gaze.

'They're all burnt to a cinder,' she said, obviously regaining control of herself but still scared for all that.

'Yes,' Tom said, just as scared, or possibly more scared than she was but trying not to show it. 'Burnt to a cinder – quite so.'

'And you can still smell the poor bastids—'

Almost retching merely at being *reminded* of that fact, Tom placed his handkerchief over his mouth again.

'—which means that whatever happened here, it only happened a short time ago. But what the hell *did* happen?'

Managing to control his churning stomach once more, Tom removed the handkerchief from his face and said, 'They've been burnt to death. I should think that was obvious.'

'But how? And by *what?*'

'Pardon?' Tom was still too dazed and shaken to think straight.

'Look around you,' Molly said. 'What do you see? Those corpses have been burnt to a cinder, but nothing else here – not even the floor – has a mark on it. So what burnt these guys?'

'A flamethrower?' Tom ventured.

'A flamethrower would have burnt the stones of the floor or at least one of the walls, but the only things blackened here are the corpses. Now how the hell could that happen?'

'I'm sure there must be a logical explanation. I . . .'

'So look around you again.' Demonstrating, Molly turned slowly on the balls of her feet, intending to study every side of the Shrine, then she stopped and her eyes grew wide again.

'What . . . ?'

Tom followed Molly's downward gaze . . . and nearly jumped out of his skin when he saw, not far from the three dead men and also resting on the floor, a brightly glittering, life-sized crystal skull. Its empty eyesockets appeared to be staring at him.

'Christ!' Molly exclaimed.

'Deary me,' Tom said.

'What the fuck's *that*?' Molly asked.

'A skull,' Tom replied, stating the obvious.

'Not a real one, buddy. It's made of glass or crystal. It looks pretty damned valuable to me – and those guys there—' – she indicated the charred corpses on the floor – 'were obviously here to remove it from that hole in the floor.'

'Stealing it?' Tom asked, not being too bright right now.

'What the fuck do *you* think? It had to be hidden in the floor, under that stone that's been removed, and shortly after they took it from there they were charred to a cinder. But how? And by *what*?'

Tom started forward, intending to study the skull up close, but at that moment he was struck by two dazzling beams of light that shot forth from the skull's gaping eye sockets.

Molly screamed again.

Temporarily blinded, shocked by Molly's sudden screaming, Tom thought briefly of the three charred corpses on the floor and imagined that he was about to suffer the same fate – burnt to a cinder by that magical, dazzling light. Instinctively, as if attacking a dangerous beast, he jumped forward and kicked out at where he judged the skull to be. The toe of his boot connected with it and sent it flying away to hit the wall behind and, judging by the ringing sound it made, to roll over the floor.

When Molly stopped screaming, Tom opened his eyes again. Though surprised and relieved to find himself still alive, he was stunned to see that the interior of the Shrine was being swept by brilliant beams of light that were flashing on and off rapidly. Squinting between those dazzling striations and orientating himself by the sections of gloom behind them, which offered depth and definition, he saw that they were still beaming out of the eye sockets of the crystal skull as it rolled over the floor towards Molly's feet. The beams of light were blinking out when the eye sockets faced the ground and flashing again in sweeping, silvery striations when the eyesockets turned sideways and upwards, creating a bizarre *son et lumière* spectacle within which Molly looked eerily ghostlike.

'Let's get out of here!' she yelled, obviously thinking, like Tom, that the beams of light were the cause of the charred corpses around the hole in the floor.

With his heart racing and hands shaking, Tom needed no further urging to make his way across the floor to the steps and start down the side of the temple. Molly was doing the same when the skull stopped its rolling and the lights beaming from its eye sockets blinked out and did not come on again. On an impulse, Molly raced back across the floor of the Shrine, tentatively touched the skull with her fingertips and then, ascertaining that it wasn't hot, picked it up and carried it down the steps, hurrying to catch up with Tom. When she reached his side, he was still running towards the low fence and he saw the skull in her hands.

'What are you doing?' he shouted.

'We can't just leave it there!' she shouted back. 'It's too valuable to leave behind!'

'That's why you can't take it!'

'If I don't, someone else will. Now let's get the hell out of here.'

They clambered over the fence and piled into the jeep, then Tom drove away from the ancient site as fast as he dared, this time taking Mex. 180 and not really thinking about where he was going. He just wanted to get as far as possible away from Chichén Itzá and the horror of what he had experienced there.

'You keep driving,' Molly said as she leaned over the seat and carefully placed the crystal skull in her rucksack. 'Don't stop until we're really far from here. We don't want anyone following us.'

'Follow us?' Tom asked, still too shocked to think straight. 'Who would want to . . . ? You mean the crystal skull? You mean that someone might follow us because you stole that crystal skull? I mean, why did you *do* that?'

Though realizing that he was sounding hysterical, he could not help himself.

'I didn't steal it, you dumb asshole,' Molly said. 'I rescued it! Those guys were obviously stealin' it an' they were burnt to death when they were doin' it – don't fuckin' ask me how – so the skull must be pretty valuable and it's better that we take it than someone else.'

Trouble, Tom thought hysterically. *I knew that the minute I laid eyes on her. Every instinct told me so. Now she's encouraged us to leave the scene of a multiple murder and stolen that artefact into the bargain. Oh, dear God, this is serious!*

'It's theft!' Tom shrieked, more hysterical than ever.

'It's rescue,' Molly insisted. 'Those dead men were obviously stealin' it – that means they were crooks – so we simply rescued it from a bunch of goddamned thieves. We might get a reward.'

'*We*?' Tom responded. 'Please don't include *me* in this. You stole that crystal skull – I had nothing to do with it – so please do *not* use the word "we".'

'Watch your driving,' Molly said.

'Don't change the subject,' Tom admonished her.

'All them vultures liftin' slowly off the road,' Molly said. 'If you're not careful, if you don't watch those goddamned vultures, you might come across one too late and have to swerve to avoid it.'

'Please don't tell me how to drive,' Tom said testily. 'That's the absolute limit.'

'Okay,' Molly said. 'Fine.'

Tom was in fact driving at a dangerously reckless speed, either looking frequently in his rear-vision mirror to ensure that they were not being followed or glancing left and right at the vast Henequen plantations on either side of the road, half expecting to see a police helicopter lifting out of the trees to pursue him and bring him to justice. Realizing that he was suffering from acute paranoia caused by fear and disbelief, he tried to compose himself and turned back to the front just in time to see a vulture, bloated from having just fed on the body of a squashed, bloody chicken, rising awkwardly off the tarmac right in front of him.

He swerved to avoid it.

'Oh, fuck!' Molly exclaimed.

The jeep went careening to the opposite side of the road and almost struck a battered truck that was coming in the opposite direction. Swerving again to avoid the truck, Tom drove back to the right side of the road and went into a screeching, shuddering skid that almost had him falling out of the vehicle while Molly hung on with all her might, holding herself well away from the windscreen. Luckily, the jeep came to a rough, bone-jolting halt in a patch of dusty wasteground at the side of an oval-shaped building with a thatched roof and walls made of poles. Tom and Molly both coughed dust while vigorously waving swirling dust away from their faces.

'Bloody bird,' Tom muttered when the drifting dust had settled down.

'A vulture,' Molly corrected him.

'All right! All right! So it was a vulture. What's the damned difference!'

'I told you that if you—'

'Yes, yes,' Tom interjected, not wishing to be reminded by this stupid girl of just how stupid *he*'d been. 'Thank you very much, my dear, but I think it's time to get out of this jeep and discuss what to do next.'

Molly glanced sideways at the oval-shaped thatched building which looked like it was falling down, though it had an advertisement for a world-famous American beverage dangling over the front door. 'You mean over there?' she asked.

'Of course,' Tom replied grimly, already clambering down from the jeep and taking his travelling bag in one hand, being sensible enough not to leave it in the vehicle. 'Why not, may I ask?'

'That's just a shack,' Molly said.

'It's a *Posada*,' Tom informed her. 'That's a kind of cheap hotel. We should be able to get a drink there – and right now, I could do with one.'

'That's not a *Posada*,' Molly replied. 'It's just some kinda sleazy bar.'

'I would never drink in a sleazy bar,' Tom insisted, 'and right now I intend entering that *Posada* for a soothing libation.'

'It's just a sleazy bar,' Molly insisted, though she climbed down from the jeep and reached out to pick up her rucksack. 'You might get more than a quick drink in there. You might get your throat cut.'

'It's a perfectly respectable establishment,' Tom said, 'but if you're nervous, by all means stay in the jeep until I return. As for me, I am thirsty and can recognize a normal *Posada* when I see one, so I'm going on in.'

'Okay,' Molly said. 'Fine.'

Shrugging, she followed Tom across to the thatched building. When they reached it, Tom saw that the building was indeed in a very bad state of repair and that the door – or what he had imagined was a door – consisted of no more than a piece of sackcloth hanging down from an empty doorframe. Tom stopped instinctively, wondering what was inside, but then he felt Molly coming up behind him and had no choice but to go in. Pulling the cloth aside, he created another cloud of dust: when he entered and saw what was inside, he wanted to turn around and walk back out again. In fact, he started to do so, actually making a half-turn, but when he saw Molly staring directly at him, her steady gaze challenging, he took a deep breath, turned back to the front and stepped into the building.

The floor was bare soil, the bar was clearly the door torn out of the front doorframe and now resting on upright barrels, the few tables were made from chipped wood, and the paint had peeled off the metal chairs and left them all rusty. There were a few men at the bar, most of them short, brown-skinned and black-haired, most of them drinking either beer or the anise-flavoured liqueur 'X-Tabentum', none friendly as the Mexicans normally were. When taking a deep breath to regain his courage, Tom smelt stale piss and shit.

'Oh, Lord,' he whispered.

'A *Posada*!' Molly said, loud and clear.

'All right, so it's not a *Posada*.' Tom could scarcely contain himself. 'Now why don't you just take a seat and I'll get us a drink?'

Molly took a seat at the nearest table, placing her rucksack on the dirt floor at her feet.

'I respect my body,' she said, 'so nothing alcoholic for me – certainly not at nine o'clock in the goddamned mornin'. You wanna destroy yourself with that piss, go ahead. Get drunk before you even have breakfast. I won't even pass comment.'

'Oh, won't you, indeed?'

'No, I won't.'

'I'm so grateful,' Tom said. 'So what would *you* like to drink?'

'*Horchata*,' Molly said.

'Pardon?'

'*Horchata*. It's a non-alcoholic drink made from rice, sugar, vanilla essence and ice water. More likely to quench a thirst than alcohol, but don't you listen to me. I mean, what would *I* know? If *you* need a little shot of courage, then by all means have alcohol.'

'I do *not* need a shot of courage!'

'You don't have to shout.'

'I'm not shouting!'

'You are!'

'Oh, go to hell!' Tom said, then he spun on the heel of his boot and stomped to the bar, inflamed that a woman so immature could talk to him, a mature man of thirty, as if she was twice his age and, worse, cast reflections upon his courage. When he reached the bar and saw the unsmiling, unshaven faces around him, his courage sank to his boots, but he managed, with his basic Spanish and a great deal of confusion, to obtain the drinks and pay for them. Then, even more aware of the grim faces all around him, he returned to the table and chairs on their bed of dirt and sat down facing Molly. He pushed her glass of *Horchata* across to her, had a good sip of his *Montejo* beer, then slammed his glass back down on the table.

'Very good,' he said. 'Excellent.'

'Quenched your thirst, did it?'

'Yes,' he said. 'Perfectly.'

Molly had a drink of her *Horchata* and placed her glass back on the table with deliberate delicacy. Moistening her full lips with her tongue, she said, 'That's pretty damned good.'

'I'm pleased to hear that,' Tom said.

'No, you're not,' Molly said. 'You're so mad, you'd like it better if this was cyanide, but I won't hold that against you.'

'How kind of you,' Tom said.

'Hey, can we stop this? I mean, neither of us needs this. We've just shared an extraordinary experience, so let's talk about it.'

'Yes, let's do that,' Tom said.

Glancing left and right at the grim-faced denizens of this sleazy bar, all of whom were staring directly, antagonistically at him, he remembered how he had desperately wanted to get rid of this foul-mouthed American floozy. But now, he realized, given the company they were both keeping, he was reluctantly being comforted by her presence. She was tough, after all – she had *street cred* – and that was more than he had. What he had was good breeding and an excellent education, neither of which were likely to be very helpful in these circumstances. So in truth, though he was loath to admit it, he was starting to appreciate the fact that she was sitting there facing him.

He could get rid of her, after all, in the near future when life didn't seem quite so threatening. He could quietly slip away from her.

'So,' he said, 'where do we begin?'

'We begin with this,' Molly said.

She reached down to her rucksack and pulled out the macabre crystal skull. Shocked that she should be so stupid in front of what he assumed to be a bunch of Mexican bandits, Tom was about to protest when he heard from the bar behind him a series of frightened outcries that made him glance back over his shoulder. Most of the men at the bar – who had looked to Tom like fearsome bandits – were now staring fearfully at the crystal skull and speaking loudly amongst themselves. Even before Tom could get fully to grips with this, they hurriedly downed their drinks and raced out of the bar, glancing apprehensively at the crystal skull as they passed the table and then looking away again. When they had left, only the barman and one customer remained. Though clearly not as frightened as the others, they were whispering to each other.

'Well, really!' Tom said, turning back to Molly, who had placed the crystal skull on the table, holding it between her hands, and was staring directly into its gaping eye sockets. The light from the naked bulb above reflected off the clear crystal of the skull and made it seem to glow magically within. Molly did not reply. She appeared not to have noticed the men stampeding from the bar and was, Tom noted eventually, staring at the skull as if hypnotized by it.

After speaking to her a few more times and receiving no response, he realized, with a shock, that she *had* been hypnotized by the crystal skull and could neither see him nor hear what he was saying. Shocked and even more frightened, he reached across the table, gently slid the skull away until it was out of her line of vision, then gently shook her right shoulder. Her eyes opened instantly, but she blinked a few times and glanced around her, as if disorientated.

'What . . . ?' She rubbed her eyes as if they were sleepy, then stared at Tom as if seriously bewildered. 'What happened?' she asked.

'You were hypnotized by that crystal skull,' Tom told her. '*Really* hypnotized. Your eyes were wide open, but didn't seem to be hearing or seeing anything. Do you *remember* anything?'

'Yeah,' Molly said after a considerable pause, her eyes slitted to denote that she was thinking.

'What?'

'The last thing I remember is looking into the crystal skull and . . .'

'Yes?'

'It went all kinda milky – or cloudy – and then I saw . . .'

She paused, clearly reluctant to give credence to her own words.

'Yes?' Tom said again.

'Stars,' Molly said.

She slumped back in her chair, took a deep breath, glanced nervously at the crystal skull, then quickly looked away.

'Just stars,' she said, returning her gaze to Tom. 'Millions of stars in a galaxy. I felt myself floating into those stars . . . and that's all I remembered until you woke me up. Nothing but stars.'

They were silent for a moment, both trying to take this in. Then Tom repeated, 'You were obviously hypnotized.'

'Yeah,' Molly said. 'Right.'

Tom sighed nervously and glanced at the bar, where the barman and his sole remaining customer were staring steadily at him. Lowering his gaze and feeling clammy with unease, Tom said to Molly, 'So what do we do now?'

Regaining her courage, Molly glanced at the crystal skull which now, being away from the naked light bulb, was not shining quite so much. 'Christ,' Molly said, 'whatever that thing is, whatever it can do, it must be fuckin' valuable. I say we take it to a museum in Mérida and find out just what it is and, you know, find out just how valuable it is and if we can clean up by sellin' the fuckin' thing.'

'I suspect that selling it would be illegal,' Tom said.

'Oh, yeah?' Molly responded with a sly grin.

Realizing beyond any shadow of doubt that this young lady was not only street-wise but unscrupulous and could get him into a whole heap of trouble, Tom was about to make the retort of an honest man when the barman walked up to the table. After glancing very quickly at the crystal skull, then, or so it seemed, deliberately looking away, he said in faltering English, '*Perdóneme, Señor*, but where did you get that?'

'What?' Tom asked innocently, though Molly immediately reached across the table and slowly dragged the crystal skull towards her.

'That,' the barman said, nodding sideways to indicate the artefact without actually looking directly at it. 'That crystal skull on the table.'

'We bought it,' Molly said, lying, Tom noted, with practised ease. 'From a roadside trader.'

'*Perdóneme, Señor*, but you're lying,' the barman said. He was small like most Mexicans, but he was almost as broad as he was tall and his unshaven, swarthy face was threatening. Also, his hairy right hand was dangling over the knife tucked down behind his belt. 'No local trader would deal in such an object – not even an artificial skull. So, please, where did you get it?'

'We found it in a field,' Molly lied, this time more brazenly. 'So what's it to you?'

Shocked that Molly could be so insolent to this mean-faced brute with a knife in his belt, Tom was about to calm what he imagined would be troubled waters when the barman said, 'Please understand, *Señor*, I don't want the skull. I don't want it in this bar. I only want to know if you found it in Chichén Itzá. This is all I ask.'

'Yes,' Tom confessed, 'that's where we found it.'

'In the pyramid of El Castillo?' the barman asked.

'That's right,' Tom said. 'Why?'

The barman took a deep breath. '*Señor*, if you truly found that skull in the pyramid of El Castillo, you've come into possession of the legendary Skull of Doom.'

'Which is?' Tom asked innocently.

'According to Mayan legend, the Skull of Doom was hidden in the great pyramid by the priests of ancient times. They hid it because it has magical powers that can be used for good or evil and the priests, when they saw that their civilization was crumbling, did not want it to fall into the wrong hands. It is called the Skull of Doom because only the pure of heart can possess it without fear and so most of those who have found it, being mortal men with mortal weaknesses, have come to bad ends. So please, *Señor*, leave and take that crystal skull with you and do not return. That skull is a curse not only to those who possess it but also to those who gaze too long upon it. Please leave right now.'

'I'll just finish my drink,' Molly said.

'No, you won't,' the barman said, reaching for the knife in his belt. 'If you please, you will get up and leave right now.'

'Of course!' Tom said. 'Naturally! Come on, Molly, let's go.'

Though she grinned mockingly at him, Molly slid the crystal skull back into her rucksack and then pushed her chair back. As Tom did the same, preparing to walk out, he noticed that the sole remaining customer, still standing at the bar, was staring steadily, fearlessly at him with only one eye. His other eye, Tom saw, was made of glass and it seemed to glitter unnaturally.

Shocked by that sight, feeling as if he was dreaming, Tom hurriedly turned away and led Molly out of the bar. When they were both in the jeep, he drove off as quickly as possible, heading for Mérida. He was hoping for peace and quiet, for time to think, but Molly soon started talking.

CHAPTER SIX

All heads turned when Mai Suphan entered the busy lobby of the Oriental Hotel overlooking the Chao Phraya River. The child of a Thai mother and Chinese father, Mai was a truly exquisite combination of the two races with light brown, almost golden skin, heavenly brown eyes, long black hair that fell to her slim waist, small but perfect breasts, and long, shapely legs that were always emphasized by her high-heeled shoes and a skintight *cheongsam* of shimmering Thai silk, slit up to the thigh. When Mai strode deliberately across the lobby, her hips swinging sensually, tight buttocks quivering, the slit in the *cheongsam* repeatedly exposed each of her long legs in turn and caused most of the men present to suck in their breath.

The hotel was famous for having housed Joseph Conrad and Somerset Maugham, but Mai did not know that and would not have cared if she had. Her only interest in this opulent establishment was the fact that it was used mostly by Americans and Europeans, all of whom had more money than they knew what to do with. This was Mai's general interest and it was strictly professional; she usually came here to pick up clients and seduce them into selling their souls to the devil for ephemeral pleasures. Her particular interest this day however, was in seeing Professor Paul Schwarz who, after his brief taste of heaven, would be flung into hell.

Taking the lift up to the sixth floor, Mai walked along to the suite being used by Professor Schwarz, though it was, of course, being paid for by Lu Thong. When she rang the bell, the door was opened by Schwarz who beckoned her in so urgently that she knew he was embarrassed to be using the services of a whore, albeit high-class, which he assumed Mai was. Amused, Mai stepped inside, deliberately letting her breasts brush against the professor's chest. The suite was large and exotic, with french doors overlooking the river, Siamese-styled furniture decorated with lacquered Thai mother-of-pearl, exquisite Celadon lamps and Bencharong ceramics, and a magnificent four-poster, high-canopied double bed covered in a quilt finely woven by hill-tribe women. 'You *are*, I take it, the woman sent by Lu Thong?' Professor Schwarz said as he closed the door behind her.

'Yes,' Mai replied. 'Mr Thong told me to tell you that I've been sent here as a sign of his appreciation and to reward you for your services.'

'Do you know what those services were?' Professor Schwarz asked nervously.

'No,' Mai lied blandly. 'I'm just a call girl. Mr Thong hires me by phone to pleasure certain of his friends and associates. He never tells me their business. I'm just given their name and address and the date and time when I'm to visit them. When I'm finished, I invoice him by mail and he always pays quickly. It's as simple as that.'

'You speak perfect English,' Professor Schwarz said, clearly relieved by what she had told him.

'Thank you,' Mai said.

The professor was slim, silvery-haired and still youthfully handsome, with the slightly naïve air of a man who had spent most of his life in scholarly pursuits. Though wearing grey slacks and an open-necked shirt, his feet were bare.

Already prepared for bed, Mai thought. *Though he's nervous about it. This one should be easy.*

The french window gave a superb view of the river with its huge steel barges heavily laden with sand, old teak rice barges used as family homes, tugboats, longtail boats, fishermen's boats, bum boats, sampans, and ferries packed with vehicles and foot passengers. Glancing down, Mai saw some water-borne vendors cooking and serving noodles to those on the family barges while half-naked children dived off the sides to go for a swim in the filthy water.

I could have been one of those poor kids, she thought. *Rather them than me.*

Turning back to face the English professor, she noticed the up-and-down glance of his eyes, which were slightly dilated, having just taken in the length of her wonderful body. She also saw the bulge in his trousers and knew just what he wanted.

'Can I fetch you a drink?' Professor Schwarz asked. Mai saw a half-finished bottle of Singha beer and an empty glass on the bedside table. There was also a bottle of champagne in an ice bucket, with two champagne glasses beside it. Clearly, the professor, ill at ease in this kind of situation even while he desired it, had prepared for her arrival and was hoping to break the ice with alcohol. 'Some champagne, perhaps?'

'No, thanks,' Mai said, having drunk champagne earlier with Lu Thong and also wishing to amuse herself by playing on the Englishman's nervousness. 'Do you have Mekhong whiskey?'

Schwarz nodded: 'Yes.'

'Then that's what I'll have,' Mai said. 'With club soda and lime.'

'I've heard that Mekhong whiskey packs an awful punch,' the professor said. 'It could be too strong for someone with a delicate constitution.'

'So?'

'You're a woman. Mekhong whiskey may be too strong for your stomach.'

'Nothing's too strong for my stomach,' Mai replied, not referring to the drink but to the many dreadful things she had seen and done in her checkered past. 'So please make it a whiskey.'

'Sure,' the Professor said.

As he was pouring her the drink, she dangled her crocodile-skin shoulder bag over the arm of a chair, then sat on the edge of the bed, crossing her legs, thus exposing a good length of golden thigh. When the professor turned back to see her, that sight almost took his breath away and brought a blush to his pale cheeks.

Mai smiled. The professor stepped towards her and then stopped, holding a glass of whiskey in each hand but seemingly paralysed. Mai smiled again and patted the area of bed right beside her.

'Sit here,' she said.

Nodding obediently, the professor stepped forward again, handed Mai her drink, then sat beside her, quite close but not as close as she had indicated, clearly still feeling nervous. He studied his feet, then had a sip of his whiskey and raised his uneasy gaze to her.

'I was surprised to receive Mr Thong's call,' he said, 'telling me that he was sending a woman over.'

'He's a kind man,' Mai said, 'but he doesn't do it for everyone. He only sends me to those he feels indebted to. He must owe you a lot.'

'Not really,' Schwarz said. 'And I don't think he's quite as kind as you say, since he practically kept me prisoner in his home for three days and nights.'

'Oh? Why was that?'

'I gave him some information that I knew he desperately wanted and he said I had to stay there until he checked it out. He said that if it didn't check out, he was going to kill me – and I'm sure that he meant it.'

'He certainly did,' Mai said. 'On the other hand, he must have been satisfied with what you told him, once it *had* checked out. Otherwise he wouldn't have sent me to you. Aren't you *pleased* that I'm here?'

'Well . . .' Mr Schwarz looked at Mai, at her heaving breasts and gorgeous, almost fully exposed legs, and sighed with lust and embarrassment. 'Yes, I suppose so.'

Mai let him watch her drinking and held his gaze while she licked her lush, finely painted lips. The bulge in his trousers was still there but the glass in his right hand was shaking and his gaze seemed distracted. Clearly, he was stunned by her beauty and drunk on his lust. Mai was pleased to observe this.

'You're a very handsome man,' she told him.

'You don't have to say that,' he replied.

'I meant it,' Mai said. 'You're a very handsome man for your age, though you seem a bit shy.'

'I'm just not used to this.' He had another sip of his whiskey, then rested the glass on his right knee. 'I wouldn't do this in England.'

'You're married?'

'Yes.'

'Children?'

'Two.'

'You feel guilty?'

'Yes, I suppose so.'

'That's nice,' Mai said.

The professor thought she was being kind, praising him for being moral, but in fact she was taking pleasure from his suffering and playing with his emotions.

'Do you want me to leave?' she asked, deliberately crossing one leg over the other, exposing even more thigh to mesmerize his guilty, lustful gaze. 'You don't *have* to have me – though, of course, Mr Thong might be offended and blame *me* because this didn't work out. Nevertheless, if this is making you feel bad, I'll leave right this minute.'

'No, please don't,' the professor said.

Clearly, he was a decent man and this knowledge pleasured Mai even more. Imperceptibly, while crossing her gorgeous legs, she had moved closer to him. Now she turned slightly sideways, placing her breasts close to his chest, breathing deeply, sensually, her luscious lips slightly parted. He was aware of her closeness, of her heat, and his own breathing quickened.

'Do you love your wife?' she said, deliberately reminding him of that dear woman to torment him even more. 'I mean, is that why're you're feeling so guilty?'

'Yes,' he said, 'I suppose so.'

'That's nice,' Mai repeated. 'So what would you like?'

'Pardon?'

'I said, what would you like? There's nothing you can imagine that I can't do, but I have to know where you want to start.'

She had another sip of her whiskey, deliberately licked her wet lips, then placed her hand on his trembling knee and gave it a light squeeze. His knee trembled even more.

'Well,' he stuttered, 'I don't . . .'

'Know.'

'Pardon?'

'You don't know. You're a happily married man and although you love your wife there's a limit to what you've done together, so you don't know just what to ask me for. Well, what would you *like*?'

Now in as much pain as a man on a rack – growing guilt on one hand, helpless lust on the other, both encouraged by Mai – the professor had another sip of whiskey and blushed with embarrassment. When he shrugged, hardly knowing what to say, too inhibited to give voice to the wild, reckless desires that now filled his thoughts, Mai slid her hand higher up his leg, up to near where the bulge was, then spread her fingers and squeezed again. Professor Schwarz trembled visibly.

'Tell me,' Mai said, almost crooning.

'I . . .' The professor opened and closed his mouth, then licked his dry lips, but he didn't get further. Mai took hold of his free hand and placed it over her gently heaving breast, then pressed it down for him. He closed his eyes and breathed deeply.

'Look at me,' Mai commanded with quiet authority.

The professor opened his dazed eyes.

'Why don't I get undressed,' Mai suggested, 'and we can go on from there.'

The professor stared at her with dazed eyes, as if deaf, then he nodded, 'Yes.'

'Why don't you help me?' Mai said.

In fact, she wanted to undress because she couldn't

move too much in the skintight *cheongsam* and soon she would need to move a lot. Gently removing the whiskey glass from the professor's visibly shaking hand, she stood up, went to the bedside cabinet and put both glasses down, his and her own. Then she returned to sit beside him again, first touching her knees to his, then smiling at him and licking her luscious lips, then gently squeezing the bulge in his trousers, and finally, artfully, turning her back to him.

'Unzip me,' she whispered.

With trembling hands, the professor unzipped the *cheongsam*, running the zip all the way down to her spine. He sighed audibly at the sight of her flawless golden back, then, forgetting his guilt, driven helplessly by his need, he leaned forward to press his hot lips to the skin between her fine shoulder blades. Mai sighed and deliberately arched her spine to make him think she was loving this.

'Mmmm,' she crooned. 'Now peel the dress off.'

Breathing harshly, the professor tugged the shimmering dress off Mai's shoulders – works of art, as she well knew – and then peeled it off her perfect body, all the way down to her waist, groaning softly and repeatedly kissing her as he did so – the back of her neck, her shoulders, her shoulder blades, then down her back until he reached that juncture where the spine leads to the crack at the start of the rump. By this time, the professor was on his knees, breathing harshly and practically sobbing, his body shaking with need.

'Oh, God!' he groaned. 'Christ!'

He was tugging frantically at the *cheongsam*, trying to work it down further, but he couldn't do that until Mai stood up, which was what she now did. When she stood over him, gazing down upon him, he looked up with blind eyes.

'Take my shoes off,' Mai said.

Obligingly, she raised first her right foot, then her left, to enable the panting professor to remove the stiletto-heeled shoes while kissing her feet and sucking her toes and licking her ankles. When both shoes were on the floor, while the professor was still slobbering over her feet, she gently grasped his hair and jerked his head upwards to let his eyes crawl all over her like spiders.

'Now peel the dress off,' she whispered.

Still on his knees, practically choking for breath and trembling, the professor used both shaking hands to tug the *cheongsam* all the way down Mai's long, shapely legs and over her ankles. She helped him by raising each foot in turn and stepping out of the dress. Then she bent down to pick the dress up and lay it out neatly on the bed so as not to crumple it. This done, she turned back to face the professor, who was still kneeling on the floor, and spread her legs just in front of his face. She was wearing a push-up bra, though she did not normally need it, and panties so small they were hardly more than a piece of string. She knew that to the average man she would have looked no less than breathtaking. As for the professor, he was desperately trying to catch his breath even as his widening eyes travelled up over her.

'Now what do you want?' Mai asked him, looking down upon him with a small, deadly smile.

'Anything! *Everything!*'

'Then stand up,' Mai said.

Freed from her skintight *cheongsam*, Mai was all set to go; and when the professor stood up, breathing hungrily in her face, she kneed him in the groin, making him scream like a stuck pig, then karate-chopped him on the side of the neck, sending him flying sideways to land spreadeagled across the big four-poster bed. The professor lay there, groaning, hardly knowing what had happened to him, until Mai leaned forward and dragged him off the bed, then picked him up and swung him over her shoulders and slammed him into the wall. He hit the wall with a sickening thud, actually cracking the plaster, then fell to the floor in a cloud of dust and rolled onto his back. His eyes were dazed and only came back to life when he vomited over his shirt.

'You poor baba,' Mai murmured.

She leaned down to him, smiling warmly at him, then took hold of the lapels of his vomit-soaked shirt and hauled him back to his feet. He stood there before her, swaying groggily from side to side, blood dribbling from his nose, until she kneed him in the groin again, making him scream and jackknife. Then she karate-chopped the back of his neck, hammering his face into her raised knee, breaking his nose entirely, then flipped him over her outthrust right leg to slam him into the floor for the second time. He gasped and groaned miserably and threw up again. Then Mai hauled him back to his feet, spun him around until he faced her and used a jujitsu movement to roll him over her stooped shoulders and finally, straightening up, to send him hurtling bodily through the air. He smashed through the french doors, making glass explode in all directions, and fell screaming to the crowded sidewalk ten storeys below.

Even as the sounds of wailing onlookers and skidding or crashing cars came wafting up from below, Mai was slipping back into her immaculate *cheongsam* and picking up her shoulder-bag and walking out of the room, a big smile on her lovely face, her eyes bright with excitement. She walked along the corridor and stopped at the lift. When the lift door opened, a waiter from room service came out, bearing a tray of cocktails.

'For me!' Mai said. She picked up a cocktail, drained it in one gulp, placed it back on the tray, then gave the stunned waiter a glowing smile and took the lift down.

When she walked out of the hotel, a crowd of people was gathered around the broken body of Professor Paul Schwarz and the road was covered with shards of broken glass. Schwarz had crashed onto the bonnet of a passing car and dented it badly, drenching it in his blood as he bounced off it and onto the sidewalk, coming to rest between shocked passers-by. Some of those people were now sitting on the pavement, sobbing and being consoled by friends or other passers-by. Also, due to the falling body some cars had crashed into each other and the drivers were now violently arguing, each trying to apportion blame to the other. Satisfied with her evening's work, amused by what she was seeing, Mai called a three-wheeled taxi to the side of the kerb and let the *samlor* driver pedal her away from the chaos that she had artfully wrought. She told the *samlor* driver to take her to Bang Kapi, then sat back and enjoyed herself.

CHAPTER SEVEN

'All I'm sayin',' Molly was saying as Tom, who had dearly wanted peace and quiet, drove along Mex. 180 heading back to Mérida, 'is that those men were burnt to a fuckin' cinder, as if with a flamethrower, yet nothing else in the vicinity was scorched – so it couldn't have been a flamethrower or any other kinda weapon. You get my drift, pal?'

'I think so,' Tom responded, not wanting to recall the dreadful sight of those burnt men, let alone discuss the matter with the inexhaustible Molly. 'Perhaps it was a gangster-styled execution of the kind that one sees in the movies. You know? Someone pours petrol over some poor souls and then sets a match to them.'

'That doesn't wear with me,' Molly said. 'If that'd happened, there would've been burn marks on the stones around them. Besides, if someone had done that to 'em, they'd have done it to get their hands on the Crystal Skull.'

'Which sounds logical,' Tom said.

'Except they *didn't* bother to take the Crystal Skull. Now do you think it's logical for someone to set those three guys on fire and then not take what they came for? No way, pal. *No* way.'

Wishing that she would shut up for just a few minutes, though feeling obliged to respond to her, if only to hear his own, much saner voice, Tom said, 'I don't know why. Maybe in their haste to get away, they just *forgot* to take it.'

'They set three guys on fire to get it and then they just *forget* it? Gimme a break here! And besides, as I've just said, if those three guys had been torched with a flamethrower or set on fire with gasoline, there would've been burn marks on the floor, walls or ceiling – but there weren't. So that's the most mysterious part of the whole damned thing and it's sure got me thinkin'.'

She's thinking, Tom thought. *God help me. The poor dear imagines that she's thinking. The self-delusion is wonderful.*

He studied the scenery passing by, the endless rows of cacti in the Henequen plantations stretching out to the flat horizon in the brightening light of the morning. Eventually, returning his gaze to the road ahead, he said, 'So what are you thinking? I can't wait to hear it.'

'Sarcasm,' Molly said.

'I can't help myself,' Tom said.

'You're just tryin' to shut me up, but I won't shut up, 'cause this thing needs talkin' through.'

'It needs *thinking* through,' Tom insisted.

'I'm thinkin' aloud,' Molly told him. 'An' what I'm thinkin' is that somethin' really weird went on back there.'

'Weird,' Tom murmured.

'Yeah, weird.'

'It wasn't weird, my dear, it was horrific. Three men were murdered back there.'

'Right. But . . . *How*? And by *who*?'

'Well . . .' Tom began.

'We're agreed,' Molly continued, though Tom could not recall agreeing to anything, 'that they couldn't have been burned by a flamethrower or by having gasoline poured over 'em – 'cause nothin' else around 'em was scorched. Right?'

Tom sighed wearily. 'Right.'

'Which means we're dealin' with somethin' unnatural, right?'

'Something . . .' Tom was intrigued, despite himself. 'Something . . . *unnatural*?'

'Exactly! 'Cause how else could that have happened? An' if a human element was involved, they'd have taken the Crystal Skull with 'em.'

Tom glanced to the side and saw another Henequen plantation, with the cacti running in neat rows for what looked like miles and the odd thatched shack rising lonesome out of them.

'I'm afraid I can't accept that . . .'

'You ever hear of spontaneous combustion?' Molly asked.

'I don't believe so.'

Clearly, Molly was getting into her element and becoming excited. 'Spontaneous combustion,' she explained enthusiastically, 'is a mysterious phenomenon in which human beings spontaneously burst into flames for no known reason. And what's so weird about it is that though the people are burned all over, they seem to have burst into flames from within – like, from inside of themselves – and the burning is purely localized.'

Impressed that Molly would even use such a term as 'purely localized' but feeling that this line of speculation was well off the wall, Tom merely repeated, 'Localized?'

'Yeah, right. I mean, the victim might be sitting in a chair when he or she bursts into flames and is burnt to death – yet the chair won't have the slightest burn mark on it. Or the poor bastid's in the bath or on the can and he'll suddenly burst into flames and burn down to a cinder – just like those men we saw – yet there won't be a burn mark anywhere: not on the bath, not on the toilet, not on the walls around 'im, not on the floor or the ceiling. So, you know, it's just like what happened back there and I think that's real weird.'

'I'm sure there's an explanation,' Tom said.

'Yeah. Some people think it's caused by an unusual electrical discharge, though no one knows what kind it is.'

'I see,' Tom said. 'So you believe—'

'Right,' Molly interjected excitedly. 'Those guys were the victims of some kinda spontaneous combustion – but what caused it to happen simultaneously to all three of 'em? That's what *I'd* like to know.'

'Well, perhaps it *wasn't* spon—'

'—taneous combustion,' Molly reminded him. 'But it had to be. Nothin' else could explain why they were burnt so badly – they were no more than charred rags – and yet nothing near them was burnt at all. So it had to be some kind of spontaneous combustion. The only question being: How come all three bought it at once?'

'Well, perhaps . . .'

'And what *I* say,' Molly went on, growing more excited by the second, 'is that they were attacked by some kinda unnatural force that was protectin' the Crystal Skull. It killed those men but it didn't take the skull, 'cause it wasn't a physical entity – it was some kinda . . .' She stopped chewing her gum, had a good think, then shrugged in defeat. 'Some kinda . . . *alien* force. Maybe somethin' released by the skull itself. So that's what I think.'

Realizing that the sun was growing hotter and that he was actually very thirsty, perhaps because of his increasing tension, Tom pulled in when he saw what looked like a genuine *Posada* with a neatly thatched roof, rainbow-coloured beaded curtains across the door and, standing out front, a sign advertising a well-known American beverage.

'We're stoppin' already?' Molly asked as Tom braked to a halt in the dusty ground near the entrance.

'I'm thirsty,' Tom said.

'We should keep drivin',' Molly insisted. 'We should try to get as far as possible from Chichén Itzá before stoppin' again.'

'I'm thirsty and tired,' Tom said, clambering out of the jeep and reaching into the back for his travelling bag. 'I was out of bed terribly early this morning in order to get to Chichén Itzá before sunrise. It was a journey of nearly eighty miles from Mérida and that, plus the recent dreadful events, may perhaps have tired me more than normal.'

'You got outta bed terribly early?' Molly asked as she too clambered out of the jeep and picked her rucksack off the back seat. 'What time was that?'

'Five a.m.'

'Oh, big deal!' Molly exclaimed in disgust, falling in beside Tom as he headed resolutely for the *Posada*. 'You mean, you slept all night in a nice bed in a hotel in Mérida, but had to get up at five in the goddamned mornin' and the effort has practically killed you?'

'I am merely pointing out that—'

'Well, let me tell you, buddy,' Molly interjected as resolutely as Tom was walking, 'that I've been sleeping in fuckin' fleapits in Mérida and that I *hitched* all fuckin' night, riskin' muggin' and rape, to get to that site – so don't whine to *me* about how tired you are. Jesus Christ, what a wimp!'

'Must you always be so aggressive?' Tom asked rhetorically as he reached the front door of the *Posada* and parted the brightly coloured beaded curtains.

'I'm just tellin' ya what I think, is all.'

'Keep your thoughts to yourself, thanks.'

Tom passed through the beaded curtains and entered the gloom of the *Posada*, which was considerably better than the previous joint, though hardly of luxury standard. There were, however, tablecloths on the tables, chairs of varnished wood, and a bar of similar wood with decent bar stools. The barman was swarthy, plump-cheeked and round-eyed, colourful in his long-sleeved, open-necked *guayabera*. A petite and pretty Yucateca, dressed in an equally colourful *huipil*, a loose-fitting shift flowered about the neck and hem, worn over a lace-trimmed underskirt, was cleaning one of the tables. She glanced up when Tom and Molly entered and gave them a glorious smile.

'*Buenos días*,' she said.

'*Buenos días*,' Tom replied, placing his travelling bag by a chair at the nearest table and pulling up a chair. '*Habla usted Inglés?*'

'*Sí, Señor*. A little.'

Relieved that he would not have to resort to his Spanish phrase book, Tom asked Molly what she would like to drink and, being informed that she would like a coffee, ordered that and an orange juice for himself.

'Would you like breakfast?' he asked Molly.

'Are you treatin' me?'

'Yes.'

'Great.' Molly studied the menu, then ordered eggs Mexicana with French toast, bread rolls, a grapefruit juice, a second coffee with cream and a bottle of *aqua minerale*.

'For the road,' she explained regarding the latter.

'Naturally,' Tom said. He ordered toast with honey for himself and sat back to drink his orange juice, his glance automatically taking in the pretty waitress as she headed back to the bar.

'If your eyes were spiders they'd be crawlin' all over her,' Molly said. 'An' her just a kid an' all. God, you guys are pitiful!'

Blushing to his roots, Tom tried to hide his face with his glass of orange juice, but the drink didn't last long enough. Putting the empty glass back on the table, he felt his cheeks still burning and tried to distract Molly from the sight of them by saying, 'You don't have to be so sexually obsessed. I merely glanced at her. She *is* quite pretty, after all, as well as extremely charming. I wasn't exactly thinking of rape, which seems to prey on your mind.'

'That's all you guys ever think about,' Molly retorted, 'even when it's *not* rape.'

'Do you mind if we talk about something else?'

'Sure, fire away.'

Desperate to change the conversation and realizing that he was uncomfortably aware of how shapely *Molly* was, never mind the young Yucateca, he opened with: 'Well, I must say your theory about how those men died is intriguing, if not quite believable.'

'I'm not sayin' that my theory's a fact, but something *very* strange went on back there and it certainly wasn't natural.'

'I think we're in trouble,' Tom said. 'That crystal skull

is obviously a dangerous item, if only in the sense that someone wants it – which is why those men were there – to steal it – and *something* – some unnatural force, as you would have it – may be protecting it. Perhaps we should dump it.'

'No way,' Molly said. 'I'm going to get that thing valued if it kills me.'

'It just might,' Tom said.

Molly grinned. 'Scared, are you?'

'Let's just say that I have a healthy respect for my own skin and that when three men get killed over an ancient artefact, I'm inclined to be careful. Whoever sent those men to find the crystal skull might send another bunch to find us – so, yes, I'm concerned.'

'We're off and running,' Molly said. 'No way could they find us. They don't know who we are – they don't even know that anyone, apart from their own men, was there – so if they exist and if they try to track us down, they're not gonna find us.'

'I truly hope not,' Tom said.

Molly grinned again and finished off her coffee. 'So you study Mayan culture,' she said. 'You ever heard of the Crystal Skull?'

'A little,' Tom said. 'There are plenty of those artefacts floating about the world, but only two are considered to be genuine and of any real value.'

'What are the others?' Molly asked.

'The Zulu Skull, sometimes, like this one of ours, called the Skull of Doom, which was stolen from the Zulus many years ago and has not been seen since. The Masai Skull, stolen from the Masais, is also still missing. A so-called Berlin Skull, in the possession of the Gestapo during World War Two, remained hidden in Berlin until the mid-1980s and then was taken to

Italy; though its present location has not been confirmed, many believe it is now held in the Vatican. The Paris Skull, also known as the Aztec Skull, is kept in a collection somewhere in France. The Amethyst Skull, so called because it's made of pure amethyst, is in a collection in San Jose, California. Another, known as both the Southern France Skull and the Skull of the Light of Christ, is reported to have connections with the Knights Templar and to be in the possession of a secret society known as The Light of Christ and located somewhere in France. Finally, another Mayan skull, appropriately called the Mayan Skull, was looted from a tomb in Guatemala and is now in a private collection in Texas.'

'And you think those skulls aren't genuine?' Molly asked.

'Those in the know are convinced that they're not,' Tom replied. 'Most likely they're the fanciful products of old legends and myths, rather than actual ancient artefacts.'

'And what about the two genuine ones?' Molly asked.

'One is the Rose Quartz Skull, widely believed to be the finest and purest in the world. Though it's rumoured to be hidden somewhere in Mexico or Guatemala, its exact location isn't known.'

'Somewhere in Mexico or Guatemala,' Molly echoed him.

Tom sighed nervously. 'Yes.'

'Then we might have found the Rose Quartz Skull.'

Tom sighed again. 'Yes.'

'And the other genuine one?'

'The other one's on display in the Museum of Mankind in London. Known as the British Museum Skull, or the Aztec Skull – not to be confused with the Paris

Aztec Skull – its earliest known record is a listing with Tiffany, the renowned New York jewellers, who had it in their possession in the 1890s. Eventually – I don't know when – it was sent to the British Museum in London. How it got to Tiffany I can't tell you, but now, as I've said, it's on display in the Museum of Mankind, London.'

'Anything special about those two skulls?' Molly asked.

'I'm a little vague on the details,' Tom confessed, 'but the skulls *are* of unknown origin and are rumoured to possess unusual characteristics, including occult powers.'

'Including mesmerism?' Molly asked.

'I believe that power has been mentioned,' Tom said.

'Anything about seeing *stars* in the fuckers?'

Tom smiled. 'Lots of people have reported seeing lots of things in their crystal skulls – ancient buildings, dragons, underwater scenes, strange creatures, even extraterrestrials – but as only two of the skulls are known to be genuine, I think it's safe to say that most of what was reportedly seen was mere wishful thinking.'

'But the two genuine ones are rumoured to possess magical powers?'

'Yes,' Tom said. 'Though their origins remain unknown, the little evidence we have about them indicates that they may have originated with the ancient cultures of Central America – either the Mayans, the Aztecs or the Toltecs – and that they were used for rituals of worship or for esoteric rites. They are also believed to have been used to *will* death. Perhaps because of this – and *only* because of this – a widespread belief has arisen to the effect that the skulls possess magical powers that can be used either for good or for evil. This sounds like so much nonsense to me, but it's what is believed.'

'It could be possible,' Molly said, 'and I happen to think it is – because what happened back there in Chichén Itzá was pretty damned weird.'

'Inexplicable, certainly.'

'So we'd better get this goddamned thing checked out.'

'I think we should,' Tom agreed.

They talked around the subject until the waitress returned with their food and drink. When the waitress had departed, Molly raised a forkful of eggs Mexicana to her mouth, then stopped, placed the fork back on her plate, and thoughtfully pursed her lips.

'New York,' she said emphatically. 'We could take the Crystal Skull to Tiffany in New York and have it checked out by them.'

'That's too far to travel with it,' Tom said, distractedly spreading honey on his toast. 'Also, I should remind you that you're in possession of a *stolen* artefact and certainly cannot take it through Customs. My suggestion, therefore, is that we show it to a friend of mine, Professor Emilio Juarez, one of the world's leading authorities on ancient artefacts, who's now working in the National Museum of Anthropology in Mexico City. We'll let him examine the artefact and base our decision on what he says. I think that would be wise.'

'Wise, hell, he's a friend of yours!'

'I beg your pardon?'

Molly swallowed some of her eggs Mexicana and gave Tom a beady, suspicious look. 'This Mexican bastard's a friend of yours,' she said, 'and will probably say what you want him to say. Such as, leave it with me, folks, and you, Tom, my friend, can sneak back later for your little cut on the sale . . . Well, thanks, but no thanks!'

Outraged, Tom hurriedly swallowed his bitten-off piece of toast with honey, washed it down with a slug of coffee and said, 'Professor Juarez is *not* a so-called Mexican bastard! He's an eminent Mexican scholar, specializing in the ancient Maya. And I'm simply going to ask him to examine the Crystal Skull, tell us if it's genuine, if it's legal for us to keep it, and if it has any market value at all. After that, we'll decide between us what to do. It's as simple as that.'

'Oh, yeah?'

'Yes!'

'Okay, but just remember that *I'm* the one who had the presence of mind to actually grab this fuckin' thing and bring it down from the pyramid – so *I'm* the one who should be given priority with regards to its fate.'

'Which you will be,' Tom snapped, though he was outraged by the very suggestion that he was being dishonest. 'Now will you kindly drop the subject for now and let me finish my breakfast?'

'Oh, oh,' Molly muttered, freezing with her fork held to her lips and her eyes fixed on the front door, almost directly behind Tom's back. 'Don't look over your shoulder.'

Tom twitched with nerves when he heard the beaded curtain rattling and then footsteps coming over the wooden floor towards him. The footsteps stopped briefly behind him, then turned around him to go past him. He looked up from his plate to see a man walking away from him and taking a stool by the bar. He was wearing a checkered shirt, faded denims and high-heeled boots, with a knife sheathed at the big-buckled belt around his waist.

After taking the stool, he ordered a beer in Spanish, then swivelled around until he was facing Tom. He stared malevolently at Tom with one eye, his other eye being made of glass.

'Oh, Lord!' Tom whispered.

Molly leaned across the table towards him, clenching her fists in front of her face, and whispered, 'It's that one-eyed guy we saw in the other bar! That bastard's been following us.'

'Nonsense,' Tom said, though his voice was shaky.

'No, it's not,' Molly insisted. 'That bastard had his eye on our crystal skull and he's obviously been following us, probably intending to rob us.'

'Nonsense,' Tom repeated.

'Go challenge him,' Molly said.

'Pardon?' Tom responded in a panic.

'If you don't believe he's following us, go up to him and demand to know if he *has* been and let's see what he says.'

'Don't be ridiculous,' Tom said. He felt flushed and his heart was racing. 'I can't go up to a perfect stranger and ask him if he's been following us. He'll think I'm as mad as a hatter – and so will the barman.'

'He's followed us and you know it and so do I – so you go up there and tell 'im to get off our tail.'

'That man's a ruffian,' Tom said.

'That's why you've got to challenge him.'

'That man looks like the violent type and could explode if offended.'

'So offend him. Let's find out if I'm right. Go up and ask him if he's been following us and then, no matter what the bastard says, say you don't believe him and that you want him to get off our fuckin' tail 'cause if he doesn't, you'll break his balls.'

'Pardon?' Tom repeated, burning up in a fever of fear as his weak stomach heaved. 'I can't possibly—'

'God damn it, you're scared!'

'I am not!'

'Yes, you are!'

'All right, then, I'm scared. I don't want my throat cut. I'm going to pay the bill and get out of here and that's *all* I'm going to do.'

'Christ, you goddamned English wimp!' Molly snapped, then she grabbed her rucksack, pushed her chair back and stomped out of the bar.

Tom didn't go to the bar. He didn't have the nerve for that. Instead, he called the waitress over, quickly paid the bill and then, without waiting for his change, he pushed his chair back and stood up. He glanced briefly at the bar, saw the one-eyed man grinning at him, mockingly, malevolently, so he shivered, picked up his travelling bag and followed Molly outside. The man laughed hoarsely behind him.

CHAPTER EIGHT

As the *samlor* carried her back to Lu Thong's mansion in the hot and humid early evening, Mai crossed her long legs, giving an eyeful of thigh to the male passers-by, and gazed with her diamond-bright hard gaze at the sensuous feast of this most diverse of cities, with its golden-spired temples, *wats* with bell towers and monks, cells, canals shaded by drooping palms, towering skyscrapers of glass and stone, exotic, chaotic markets, beseeching sidewalk vendors and dense, roaring, polluting traffic. Here beautiful prostitutes in skintight revealing clothes, bare-footed, saffron-robed monks carrying alms bowls, distracted businessmen in shirts and slacks, bearded men wearing white prayer caps or turbans, and teenagers of both sexes in Westernized clothing, all walked casually side by side. Here Thais, Chinese, Indians, Burmese, Laotians, Vietnamese, Europeans and Americans – Buddhists, Muslims and Christians of all denominations – lived in a harmony only broken by the impersonal crime and mayhem common to most major cities.

Mai knew all about crime. As she sat in the *samlor*, her long legs crossed and exposed, watching her world pass by, sniffing the heady aromas of roasting chicken, the sweet incense smoke spiralling out of Chinese shrines, the seductive scents from the garlands of orchids overhanging the canals, and the stench of shit and piss coming up from the canals themselves, she thought of the man she had just killed, the man who had ordered his execution, and the life that she had led up to now.

It had been, for the most part, a life of profitable crime, really only beginning when she was fourteen years old and hardly worth considering before that. Though Mai preferred not to consider it, she nonetheless recalled certain things about it, notably that she had lived in a floating house in a badly depressed riverside village near Ayutthaya, north of Bangkok, and that her life there had been miserable and hard. The family toilet was a hole in the floating floor – you shat and pissed into the muddy river below, in the presence of the other members of your family – and her father fucked her mother on a mattress on the floor not a metre away from where Mai and the other children slept. In other words, given the total lack of privacy, there was little room for inhibitions and certainly Mai had never had any. As for her father, when not fucking her mother in full view of his children he was away from home a lot, spending days at sea with the other fishermen of the village, trawling for diminishing fish and shellfish and becoming visibly poorer by the year.

As Mai clearly recalled, she and her brothers and sisters (five in all, three girls and two boys) were made to work almost as soon as they could walk, usually helping their father to gut and pack the fish, then transport them in heavy loads to the nearest market town. Because of this, they never went to school, ran about barefooted and in rags, were often beaten black and blue, and harboured few hopes for the future.

Mai's only other recollections of the time before 'real life' began were that she, alone among her brothers and sisters, constantly burned with resentment and the need to escape; that before she was fourteen she was raped at least three times by strangers passing through the village; and that at some point she realized that the lust of men could be useful to her. She found this to be true when, at fifteen, she was abducted by some of Lu Thong's brigands and installed in one of his brothels in Bangkok. Her real life began from that moment on and she never looked back.

Rather than being shocked at finding herself working in a Bangkok brothel, the fifteen-year-old Mai, already sexually abused and generally hardened by life, viewed it pragmatically as the opportunity of a lifetime and took to it like a duck to water. Delighted to have escaped her poor riverside village, informed by the *mamasan* of the brothel that she was beautiful, and swiftly becoming one of the most demanded girls working there, she did all she could, without qualms or doubt, to make herself ever more popular with the customers. Luckily, most of these were American and European tourists, usually happy to slip her extra money in return for some tricks that the other whores could not, or would not, perform. Mai refused no request, no matter how perverse, viewing everything as experience, and between her growing bag of tricks and her ravishing beauty, she soon had customers queuing at her door and could hardly deal with them all. Then Lu Thong stepped into the picture and her life changed again.

She had, of course, heard about her unseen boss long

before he told his men to bring her to him. Lu Thong: the notorious Lothario who had been born with a silver spoon in his mouth, educated at Oxford, England, and returned to Bangkok to lend support to his father's criminal activities, including drug-running, organized prostitution, protection rackets, and a lucrative trade in stolen antiques and works of art, while furthering his sexual education in the fleshpots of Patpong and Sukhumvit Road. Lu Thong: the notorious criminal who had come into conflict with his own father, possibly had that father murdered, and took over his deceased parent's criminal empire to become the most powerful crime baron in Bangkok. Lu Thong: the notorious drug dealer and addict who had often been seen in the strobe-lit discos and videotheques off the Vipavadee Rangsit Highway or in the middle of rice paddies by the Pechburi Road, personally dealing in crack or Ecstasy or even more dangerous drugs, just as often seducing those he had addicted into dealing for him. Lu Thong: the notorious devil incarnate, who was rumoured to indulge in extraordinary sexual activities, both hetero and homo, with partners of all ages, and whose mansion in Bang Kapi was widely reported to be the scene of diabolical rites based on the most ancient and dangerous of the black arts. Yes, the notorious Lu Thong, who even owned the brothel that Mai was working in and, having heard about her remarkable sexual talents, eventually had her brought to his home in order to check her out personally. So Mai went there, knowing exactly who he was, not knowing what to expect.

At that first meeting, she was taken aback to see just how handsome he was and shocked at the harsh asceticism she sensed behind his exquisite, oddly tormented features. His face was stripped almost to the bone, all angles and flat planes, with the inner luminescence often seen on the dying; and his body, though as languid as a big cat's, was so undernourished that it seemed as insubstantial as a wisp of smoke. The unnatural glitter of his brown eyes was certainly due to drugs, but also sprang, Mai was convinced, from experiences so diabolical and extreme that few men would even have dared to consider them, let alone have survived them. In the event, when she came to know him better, she learnt that this was indeed the case and that Lu Thong was so easily bored that only the most extreme experiences could arouse his interest. He was a man who lived on the very edge and dared himself not to fall off.

During their initial encounter, he told her that he had heard about her and wanted to see her with his own eyes. He told her that she was even more beautiful than he had imagined and that such beauty, if combined with her reported sexual talents, could gain her much more than she would ever have if she remained in the brothel. He wanted her to work for him, he told her, to do more than just whore, though certainly that would be part of it, albeit in an elevated manner. He wanted to use her for blackmail, for smuggling and dealing, for seductions that would have a greater purpose than mere sexual pleasure. She would have her own place, he told her, a magnificent apartment in this very area, and, if she did what he said, she would end up with more wealth than she had ever dreamed of.

'I'll do it,' Mai said.

But first she had to prove to him that she was as good as he had heard – she had to show him what she could do – and this she did for the next five days, never leaving his house, rarely leaving his vast bedroom with its duvets of Chinese and Japanese silk, its exotic Indian carpets, its Laotian frog-drum tables, its bronze utensils stolen from the burial mounds of Ban Chieng, its erotic paintings and drawings smuggled in from the four corners of the globe, and its seemingly boundless supply of opium and cocaine. She performed in his bed, on the floor, in the *en suite* bathroom, first above him, now below him, next in front of him, then behind him, doing everything he asked, no matter how perverse it was, showing him some perversions that even he had not yet tried, and she did it all in a haze of opium dreams and cocaine fevers, until he was completely satisfied. By the end of that five days, she had turned into an addict – addicted not only to drugs, but also to extreme sensual experiences – and shortly after that testing, which she passed with flying colours, she moved into her own luxurious apartment located not far from Lu Thong's house. Lu Thong paid her rent.

Thereafter, he had used her for a wide variety of tasks, including the seduction of important men for the purposes of blackmail; the smuggling of cut jade from Burma, silver jewellery from Khmer, Lao and Shan, drugs from Cambodia and Colombia, and rare paintings, antiques and religious manuscripts stolen from ancient Thai temples; and, finally, the harsh disciplining of his whores, drug-peddlers or dealers in the fake antiques that were sold in Chiang Mai and Chatuchak Market. Though Mai excelled at all of this and certainly enjoyed doing it, she didn't really discover her true nature until, at Lu Thong's request, she killed for the first time.

'It's a necessary part of our profession,' he told

her, 'but that's not the only reason you must do it. To kill your fellow man in rage is a meaningless act; but to kill pragmatically, in cold blood, in full awareness of what you're about, is the ultimate high for creatures like you and me. As for you, with your lust for life, for the extremes of experience, drawing blood and watching your victims breathe their last will set you free and exalt you. More than sex, more than drugs, the act of cold-blooded murder will offer you transcendence to a state of being beyond good or evil – a state of *pure* being. When you kill, when you see the fear in your victim's eyes, you will come close to God.'

'Is that who you're seeking?' Mai asked him.

'Him or the devil,' Lu Thong replied.

'I think you *are* the devil,' Mai said.

'Who knows? Now go and kill for me.'

Mai's first victim was a Chinese drugs dealer who had been falsifying his financial records in order to retain more of his cut than was normally allowed by Lu Thong. As this was a crime punishable by death, Mai was sent by Lu Thong to kill the offender in his office in Wongwienai. When the well-fed Chinaman, dressed in an immaculate grey suit with shirt and tie, fell to his knees before Mai, tearfully begging for his life, his hands clasped under his chin, she felt more powerful than she had ever felt before. She then found 'transcendence' – to use Lu Thong's terminology – when she ignored her sobbing victim's entreaties and shot him between the eyes.

That killing was the first of many, each more exciting than the last, and over the years Mai became increasingly inventive, devising ever more novel ways of terminating her victims – by the gun and the blade, by smothering and strangulation, by the injection of lethal drugs and enforced feeding and poisoning – often taking as long as she could, mercilessly toying with her victims, tormenting them with the knowledge of what their ultimate fate would be, frequently physically torturing them, in order to prolong her own pleasure. She learnt through this that her soul was as dark as night and that the fear she instilled in others, the pain and suffering she caused them, gave her a satanic, sensual satisfaction. She orgasmed on blood-lust.

'You're my most exquisite creation,' Lu Thong told her eventually. 'A perfect killing machine. You could surely cross the face of the sun and not leave a shadow. You're hardly human at all.'

'That's why you're proud of me,' Mai said.

In fact, *he* was hardly human – or, at least, he didn't appear to want to be so – and the longer she worked for him, the more she came to understand this, seeing in his drug addiction, his bisexual extremism, his obsession with death and the occult all the passions of a man whose ultimate high could come only through some form of suicide. His opium dreams came from the dark side of the moon and he would go there some day. In his heart that was where he wanted to be – in eternal darkness and silence. He would sell his soul to the devil for that and he was working towards it.

When the *samlor* stopped in front of Lu Thong's home in Bang Kapi, Mai paid the driver, gave him a handsome tip, then pressed the bell on the electrified gates. Identified by the guard inside (he could view the grounds of the large house, including the front gates, on the TV monitors installed in his security booth), she was permitted entry and the gates swung open to give her access. Though Lu Thong was wealthy beyond imagining and the grounds around his house were extensive, lush with tropical foliage, the house itself was not ostentatious and in fact looked no different than the homes of the many Americans and Europeans living in the same area. It was, however, protected by high-tech surveillance systems and by the well-armed security guards who patrolled the grounds constantly.

Mai made her way up the driveway, under large drooping palms, passing rainbow-coloured orchids and other exotic fauna and flora, to the front door of the house where a barrel-chested, grim-faced security man, armed with a hidden Browning 9mm High Power handgun, was standing guard. The gorilla stepped aside to let Mai press the door bell, which automatically activated another TV monitor in the guard's room inside. When the guard recognized Mai for the second time, he spoke through the intercom, giving the gorilla permission to let her in. The gorilla opened the front door with his personal key. When Mai stepped in, he closed and bolted the door behind her.

Once inside the house, Mai went straight to the Oriental lounge. There she found Lu Thong seated at the glass-topped bamboo table, wearing only his dressing gown of shimmering Thai silk and looking as frail as someone at death's door. Nevertheless, he seemed to glow with an inner radiance, a magical, perhaps diabolical energy, and though his brown eyes were, as usual, brighter than they should have been, his gaze was steady and searching.

The devil thinks he's God, Mai thought as she sat on the cushions at the other side of the low table, curling her long legs beneath her, letting him see her perfect, golden thighs. *And I'm his dark angel. Sooner or later we'll turn against each other and then all hell will break loose. I look forward to it.*

'Welcome,' Lu Thong said, his voice eerily sepulchral, yet as sensual and seductive as the unnatural glittering of his heavy-lidded, long-lashed drugged eyes. 'What brings you back here, my pet? Have you some news to impart?'

'Yes,' Mai said. 'You can stop worrying about Professor Schwarz. He's just met with an unfortunate accident of a terminal nature.'

'Mmmmm. Did you say "terminal"?'

'I did.'

'And am I allowed to ask how this unfortunate termination came about?'

'Professor Schwarz threw himself out of the window of his room on the tenth floor of the Oriental Hotel and ended up like English jam on the pavement below.'

'Suicide, was it?' Lu Thong sounded sardonic.

'It could be viewed that way. After that kind of fall, it would be impossible to tell if he was damaged *before* he crashed onto the sidewalk or by the fall itself. Either way, the good Professor Schwarz is now out of the picture and your secret is safe.'

Lu Thong smiled bleakly. 'I trust you enjoyed your brief visit with him. I wouldn't like to think, my dear, that you were doing this *only* for me.'

'I wasn't,' Mai said, taking note of the sarcasm and realizing that he was angry about something. When angry, Lu Thong was a dangerous man, so Mai spoke up quickly. 'Is something wrong? Have I done the wrong thing?'

'No, my dear, you haven't done the wrong thing. But something *is* wrong.'

'Can you tell me about it?'

'I've already told you about it and a man has just died because I did so.'

'Professor Schwarz.'

'Correct.'

'That means you're concerned about the Crystal Skull.'

'Correct again,' Lu Thong said.

'So what's your concern? Professor Schwarz, being dead, can't tell anyone else what he told you. Your secret is safe.'

'Not any longer. I've just had a call from a friend in Mérida, telling me that—'

'The American gangster you told me about,' Mai interjected. 'The one who was on his way to Chichén Itzá to dig out the Crystal Skull and bring it to you.'

'No, not him,' Lu Thong replied, his beautiful eyes now glittering not only with cocaine but with rage and what seemed like confusion. 'Though certainly he's part of the problem.'

'What does that mean?'

Lu Thong sighed, as if wearied by life, which he often was. 'My American gangster friend is dead. A few hours ago, three corpses, all charred almost to a cinder, were found on the stone platform of the Shrine on the summit of the Castle, or El Castillo, in Chichén Itzá. As the platform of the Shrine is where Professor Schwarz insisted that the Crystal Skull was hidden, those three men – all burnt beyond recognition, thank God – were almost certainly my American gangster and his Mexican helpers.'

'And the Crystal Skull?'

'The charred corpses were found scattered around a rectangular hole in the floor of the platform, where one of the stone slabs had been removed. That hole had to be where the Crystal Skull was hidden, but according to newspaper reports of the incident, nothing was found in the hole when the charred bodies of those three men were discovered by the guards opening the site a few hours after when the fire was said to have taken place.'

'What kind of fire?'

'The newspapers didn't say. But according to my friend in Mérida, there was something strange about it. Reportedly, though those three men were burnt to a cinder, no damage was done to the Shrine itself.'

'That's impossible,' Mai said.

'That's the story,' Lu Thong said.

'And the newspaper reports made no mention of a crystal skull having been found at the scene of the incident?'

'No. Not a word.'

'Maybe it wasn't there in the first place,' Mai said. 'Maybe Professor Schwarz lied.'

'Professor Schwarz was too frightened to lie. If he said the Crystal Skull was there, it was there. Besides, someone obviously burned those three men to death and those murders must be related to the Crystal Skull. Whoever killed those men almost certainly did it in order to steal the artefact from them. So somewhere out there' – Lu Thong languidly waved his wafer-thin hand to take in the world outside his own home – 'somewhere, I'd say, between Chichén Itzá and Mérida, someone is trying to make his escape with the Crystal Skull. I want that person, or those persons, found and I want you to find them.'

'And if I find them?'
'Kill them and bring me the Crystal Skull.'
'I will,' Mai promised.

CHAPTER NINE

'I simply don't like embarrassing scenes,' Tom said, still trying to defend himself as he drove into the outskirts of Mérida. 'That's all there was to it. I mean, why make an unnecessary scene when one can simply walk out? Heroism is, after all, a fool's virtue and to confront that one-eyed bandit would have been tantamount to suicide.'

'That's a faggot Englishman's excuse for cowardice,' Molly retorted, then she turned her head away in disgust and let Tom drive on in silence.

In truth, he appreciated the silence because they had been arguing about his so-called 'cowardice' for the past forty minutes, ever since leaving the *Posada*, and he now felt exhausted by her constant abuse. He also felt guilty because, despite his repeated denials, he *had* been terrified of that malevolently sneering one-eyed bandit. Finally, he was glad of the silence because he wanted time to think, to work out his confusions, which were composed of his excitement at finding the crystal skull, his fear of the danger the skull might put him in, his frustration at having to deal with this highly strung, foul-mouthed American girl, and his growing awareness that despite his own reservations he was having sexual fantasies about her.

With regard to the latter, he was trying desperately to distract himself from his uncomfortable awareness of her close proximity, but each time he removed his gaze from the road ahead, his eyes automatically gravitated to the long, shapely length of her thighs as revealed in the tight denims, the fullness of her breasts as emphasized by her tucked-in shirt, and even the sensual lushness of her lips which, though too often curved in a sneer of disdain, made him burn in the lambent heat of lust. He had even found himself wondering, when glancing at the blonde hair piled up under her peaked cap, just what that hair would look when it came tumbling down. The very thought of it had given him an erection and now, in the growing humidity of late morning, he felt drowsy and even more sensual, too close to her for comfort.

As if knowing what he was thinking and deliberately tormenting him, Molly crossed one long leg over the other and then ran her fingers lightly over the raised thigh. Instantly imagining his own fingers doing the same, Tom blushed and quickly averted his hungry gaze.

'So where are we goin'?' Molly asked him.

'Pardon?' he responded, as he often did with Molly, this being a sign of his increasing disorientation.

'You deaf or somethin'? I asked where we're going to? I mean, I assume we're going to spend the night here, before driving on to Mexico City.'

'I suppose we must,' Tom said.

'Don't sound so fuckin' enthusiastic. I could weep, I'm so welcomed.'

'Sorry,' Tom said, trying to concentrate on his driving and wondering how he could possibly lust after this girl who was so obnoxious. 'I was just a little distracted.'

'So are we going to your hotel?' she asked him.

'*My* hotel?' Tom was embarrassed. The very thought of waltzing Molly into the neo-colonial elegance of the de luxe Casa del Balam hotel sent a tremor through him, though he wasn't about to confess that to her. Instead, he lied, practically stuttering: 'I'm afraid I booked out of my hotel when I left for Chichén Itzá and I really don't think I'll get back in, so I suppose we'll have to look somewhere else. Also, my hotel was rather expensive and . . .'

'You can't afford to put me up there as well.'

'Well, to be truthful . . . I mean, do you have *any* money on you at all?'

'Hitch-hiker's money. Not much. Just enough for basic food and amenities. I couldn't *afford* a decent hotel.'

'Exactly, so—'

'So you're goin' to treat me to a room, but you can't afford to do it where you were staying.'

'That *would* be a little expensive,' Tom managed, though he was writhing in discomfort behind the steering wheel.

'I understand that,' Molly said understandingly. 'So where were you staying, as a matter of interest?'

'The Casa del Balam,' Tom said.

Molly gave a low whistle of appreciation. 'Oh boy, that's a real five-star joint. Real de luxe, so I'm told.'

'I could only afford one week there,' Tom lied quickly. 'A sort of treat, as it were, before I moved on to somewhere cheaper.'

'Oh, yeah?'

'Yes.'

He was heading for the Old City, downtown, revelling in its remarkably clean pastel streets, its

Spanish–Moorish–Mayan architecture, its red-tiled rooftops, and its many *veletas*, or windmills, while driving even more carefully than normal (and he *was* a nervous driver) to avoid its many cars, pedestrians in *guayaberas* and *huipils*, and the ubiquitous pony-powered buggies known as *calesas*.

'You've got money, haven't you?' Molly said.

'Money?' Tom responded uneasily, since he had it but was prone to being careful with it.

'Yeah, money. The stuff you fill your billfold with. You stay in that hotel, even for a week, and that means you've got bread. So what do you do in England, pal? You haven't told me that yet. In fact, you haven't told me a damned thing about yourself, though you've let *me* talk my head off. So tell me what you do for a livin'. I'm dying to know.'

Taken aback, once more, by the crass young lady's assertion that he had somehow tricked her into talking, when in fact he had not been able to stop her tongue from wagging, Tom replied, 'Well, that's rather difficult to explain. I mean . . .'

'I can't wait to hear it,' Molly repeated, 'so just spit it out.'

'Well . . .' Tom always felt vaguely embarrassed to be talking about himself; more so when he was dealing with someone like Molly, to whom his background would be virtually incomprehensible. 'Well,' he said again, 'I'm a kind of a . . . perpetual student. I don't really have a job, as such. I mean, I've spent the past few years studying ancient civilizations, mostly through archaeology, which is why I'm now touring the Yucatán, but I only do it as a kind of hobby – to give me something to do, as it were.'

Having become lost in Mérida's dense traffic, he now

found himself in the immense *zocalo*, or Plaza de la Independencia, lined with Indian laurel trees, dotted with conventional benches and Victorian love-seats, and dominated by the Casa Monteja, the palace constructed by the younger Montejo in 1549. As he had already done his standard tour of Mérida a couple of days ago, he did not wish to repeat it and kept driving until he came to the beautifully weathered colonial structures of the Old City. Once there, crawling at a snail's pace, he kept his eyes peeled for somewhere to stay.

'You don't have a profession?' Molly asked him.

Tom sighed. 'Alas, no.'

'But if you stayed in the Casa del Balam hotel, you've obviously got bread and plenty of it. So how did you manage that?'

This was the part that Tom always hated, so he took a deep breath and let the words out when he exhaled. 'I inherited it,' he confessed. 'I don't like to talk about it, but my father and mother are English aristocracy. When my father died, which he did a few years back, I inherited his estate. We're not exactly the crème de la crème of the English upper classes, but I have to confess that we're well off and, once I'd completed my education at Oxford, I didn't have to work for a living. To you, this must sound terrible.'

'It sounds fuckin' wonderful,' Molly said. 'But who do you mean when you say "we"? I thought you'd separated from your wife.'

'I did. By "we" I mean the family in general, including my mother, who is alive and well and still living in Reigate, Surrey.'

'You've got one of them big fancy English castles?'

Tom couldn't resist smiling at the remark, even

though the thought of home, given his last few years there, was still painful to him. 'Hardly,' he said. 'Though it's certainly a large Georgian house with extensive grounds.'

'You live there all the time?'

'My mother lives there all the time and the house is open to tourists, which is the only way we can maintain it properly. My wife moved out when we divorced and returned to her own family, which owns an even bigger estate in Windsor.'

'Is that where the royal family live?'

'Correct.'

'Gee, this is really too much. I'm travellin' with English aristocracy! Damned right, you pay.'

'Pardon?'

'For the hotel.'

'Oh. Of course.' Landed with this, Tom kept his eyes peeled for some decent accommodation, but set his sights, as it were, even lower, which meant even cheaper.

'So where do you live? In the big house with your mother?'

'I go there most weekends,' Tom said, 'but when my wife moved out, I decided I didn't want to stay there with only my mother, conducting tourists around the place, so I moved into a small apartment in Mayfair, London.'

'I hear it's a great city,' Molly said, actually smiling and seeming to warm to him.

'It is,' Tom said.

'Is that why you moved there – to have a good time?'

'For the distraction,' Tom said. 'I was alone and I wanted lots of people around me, including my old friends from Oxford, many of whom now lived and worked in the capital. Also, London is a wonderful place for research and as a jumping-off place for worldwide travel; so when I immersed myself in the study of ancient cultures, which also involves lots of travelling, London seemed the sensible place to be.'

'Shit, man, it must be incredible to have all that bread at your disposal and be able to do what you want and go where you want without worrying.'

'It certainly has its advantages,' Tom said.

He pulled into the parking lot of a small, relatively modernized hotel on the Parque Cepeda, downtown, facing a busy *calesa* stand. It was an old colonial building recently modernized, with Indian laurel trees on both sides of the short driveway lending it a rustic, romantic appearance. Sleepless, and having drunk beer on an empty stomach, Tom was feeling much warmer towards Molly and thinking dangerous thoughts, including the thought that she seemed much warmer towards *him*. 'What do you think?' he asked.

'I think it's fine,' Molly said. 'It ain't exactly the Casa del Balam, but I suppose you don't wanna be embarrassed to be seen with me in a swanky joint like *that*.'

'Not true,' Tom diplomatically lied, applying the handbrake, clambering out of the jeep, and removing his travelling bag from the rear as Molly climbed down from the other side. 'It's just that I came here on a tight budget—'

'But you're loaded!' Molly exclaimed.

'—and having to pay for you will put a strain on it, so this place is a compromise.'

'You English are known to be tight-fisted bastids,' Molly said as she picked up the rucksack containing the crystal skull, 'but that's okay by me. I mean, beggars can't be choosers, after all, so I'm not about to complain.'

'That's terribly decent of you,' Tom said, then turned away to lead her into the hotel.

He heaved a sigh of relief to note that the hotel was as pleasant inside as it was outside, with old colonial furniture, floors of fine Carrara marble, potted plants and functioning air-conditioning. At the reception desk, which was manned by a genial Mexican wearing a brilliantly coloured *guayabera*, he ascertained that the place had a swimming pool, bar and excellent restaurant. Pleased, he asked for two single rooms.

'Sorry, *Señor*,' the desk clerk responded, 'but we are practically booked out, being always very popular, and so only have one single room left. Cheaper for you, *sí*?'

'I ain't sleepin' in any fuckin' room with you, that's for sure,' Molly said.

Blushing to have such foul language spoken in front of the amiable, polite desk clerk, Tom coughed into his clenched fist and said, 'Really, we would *prefer* separate rooms, so if you could—'

'Please, *Señor*,' the desk clerk interjected, shrugging and raising his hands pleadingly in the air, 'if I could help you, I would, but I only have one single room left.' He smiled seductively at Molly. 'And this young lady, I am sure, is understanding and will surely—'

'Share the single bed with him, right?' Molly said, staring the desk clerk down. 'Well, to hell with that, buddy. We're not here to have some hokey-pokey together – I mean, this is a *business* trip – so you fix us up sharpish with two rooms or we'll go somewhere else.'

'That would be difficult, *Señora*—'

'*Señorita*,' Molly firmly corrected him.

'—because this is the time of carnival and every other hotel in Mérida is booked out.'

'Except this dump,' Molly said. 'With its one remaining room and single bed. Thanks a lot, pal!'

'Well, really,' Tom said timidly, 'I do believe this fine gentleman is merely trying to help us and—'

'And get me into your goddamned bed. Thanks, but no thanks, pal!'

'May I suggest,' said the desk clerk, unperturbed and smiling, understanding that certain *gringos* could not be *seen* to be sleeping together, 'that we solve this little problem by putting an extra bed in the room? This, I fear, is all I can do for now, so I trust it's agreeable.'

'Well . . .' Tom said, embarrassed, but also helplessly thinking, in the back of his mind, that perhaps he and Molly would actually . . .

'I'm not wearin' it,' Molly said firmly.

'Either one room or we sleep in the car,' Tom said. 'It's up to you, my dear lady.'

'Don't call me "dear",' Molly said.

'Sorry,' Tom said.

Molly sighed and stretched herself, thus showing off the perfection of her breasts and the exquisite curve to her long legs. 'Okay,' she said. 'If we have to, we have to. But don't get any fresh ideas, pal.'

'I won't,' Tom promised solemnly.

He signed the register. Then, having been informed that it would take half an hour for the room to be prepared and the extra bed moved in, suggested that he and Molly retire to the restaurant for a spot of lunch.

'Great,' Molly said. 'I'm fuckin' starvin'.'

As both were reluctant to give up their bags, they carried them into the restaurant and placed them on the floor beside their chairs. It was a very pleasant, spacious, Mexican-styled room, filled with tourists here for the carnival. Tom was, in fact, too tired to eat properly and really just wanted a couple of drinks, but he dutifully ordered lunch – a filling *mucbil pollo* for Molly and a more modest *pollo pibil* for himself – and picked at his own food while managing to polish off a whole bottle of imported red wine. By the time Molly had enthusiastically devoured her large *tamales* stuffed with pork and chicken and drenched in *anchiote* sauce, Tom was into his second bottle of wine and seeing Molly in a very different light. Though he couldn't see her shapely legs, which were tucked beneath the table, he was increasingly mesmerized by her breasts, whose perfection was emphasized by the tightness of her open-necked shirt (he saw the hint of cleavage there), and by her full, always-on-the-move lips. As for her blonde hair, still piled up beneath her peaked cap which she had not removed, he kept imagining it tumbling down around her bared shoulders, onto her bare breasts, and the thought of this almost made him swoon.

They talked throughout the meal. At least, Molly talked and Tom responded as best he could until, when Molly had finished eating and Tom's second bottle was almost empty, she said, 'You sure know how to put away that hooch. You must be a sad sack.'

'Pardon?'

'A sad sack. I think you're still sufferin' over the break-up of your marriage an' that's why you drink so much.'

'Perhaps,' Tom said, hiccuping.

'So why did it break up?'

Tom shrugged forlornly. 'I don't know; it just happened. The marriage was practically arranged – in the sense that both sets of parents wanted it – and I guess we both slipped into it to please our parents. It wasn't that we weren't initially *fond* of each other or anything – certainly, being friends since childhood, we were – but we weren't really in love. So we were married and it didn't really work and we just drifted apart.'

'Lousy sex, eh?'

Even drunk, Tom was embarrassed. 'Not so bad,' he lied. In fact, the sex between him and Lucinda had been a disaster from Day One, which was why, he assumed, he was so sexually frustrated and presently lusting after the luscious Molly. 'It was more of an emotional problem. We simply didn't have much to say to each other and the silences became longer and, as it were, louder, until we just couldn't stand it. We separated by mutual consent and we still keep in touch.'

'Any kids?'

'No.'

'That was lucky,' Molly said. She finished off her glass of non-alcoholic *horchata*, glanced around the busy restaurant, then returned her gaze to him. 'How long will it take us to drive to Mexico City?' she asked him.

'About twenty-two hours,' Tom said.

'Christ,' Molly said, 'that's a long drive.'

'Yes,' Tom agreed. 'And I'm really feeling rather tired. So I suggest that we try to sleep this afternoon and then, if we feel up to it, commence the drive to Mexico City in the early hours of the morning. That way, we'll reach our destination in the daylight and find it easier to locate a hotel. We can then have a proper sleep tomorrow night and awaken refreshed the following morning. How does that sound?'

'Sounds fine,' Molly said, offering what seemed to be a warm smile.

'Excellent,' Tom said.

He signed for the meal, then left the restaurant with Molly, swaying slightly, being extremely drunk, and humming to himself. He dangled the room key suggestively from his index finger, swinging it to and fro like a metronome, as he made his way along the ground-floor corridors with Molly close beside him, squinting owlishly and grinning like a lucky man as he searched for their room. When Molly placed her hand lightly on his shoulder, obviously trying to keep him steady, he mistook her touch for affection and swelled up with emotion.

'Thank you so much,' he said.

CHAPTER TEN

The curtains had been drawn to keep out the sun and the room was in semi-darkness when Tom and Molly entered it. It was a very pleasant room, sparse but comfortable, with two single beds along opposite walls, a couple of comfortable armchairs and an antique writing desk by the window. Rather than draw the curtains, Molly turned the lights on, then she placed her rucksack by the side of one of the beds and Tom, given no choice, placed his dusty travelling bag on the other. Drunk, he was in a mood both amorous and mischievous, which was not his normal self, and so he threw Molly a big, flush-cheeked smile and said, 'Well, now, how cosy!'

'It could've been cosier,' Molly retorted, falling backwards to stretch out on the bed and stare at the ceiling. 'It could've been a fuckin' de luxe hotel – the one you'd have probably returned to if I hadn't been with you.'

'Not fair,' Tom said, smiling ever more broadly, letting his bleary gaze roam fondly along the length of Molly's slim body, from her feet in sandals to her flat, white belly (slightly exposed where the shirt had come out of her denims) and upthrust, intoxicating breasts, more prominent than ever under the tightly drawn shirt. 'Unkind, my dear. I merely felt that since I came here with a strictly limited budget, I would have to make some cuts if I also included you in my expenditure. It's as simple as that.'

'You're a tight-fisted English bastid,' Molly said. 'It's as simple as *that*. Either that, or you're embarrassed at the thought of being seen with me in a fancier joint.'

'That, also, is untrue.'

'Then you're just a skinflint. You're English aristocracy, fuckin' loaded, but your kind hates to spend it. I always heard that the English were like that an' now I believe it.'

'That's nonsense,' Tom said, feeling desperately in need of sleep but unable to take his eyes off Molly's supine body and therefore unable to bring himself to lie down. 'It's true that I have a certain amount of money back home – more than adequate, I confess – but, alas, it is there and not here; and I did, indeed, come here on a deliberately limited budget, so I have to be careful.'

'You're startin' to sound like a fuckin' English actor,' Molly said. 'All florid and plum-in-the-mouth, like.'

'Well, I'm terribly sorry if my way of speaking offends you, but that's how one speaks where I come from and one simply cannot help oneself. Do I complain about *your* manner of speech?'

'I speak perfectly fine, thanks. I don't come out with all that one-this and one-that shit. I say "me" or "I" like a normal person. I don't talk like I'm in an English TV series, wearin' a fuckin' top hat and tails. Anyway . . .' She turned her head to stare at him from her supine position on the bed. 'You're just changin' the subject and I still say you're a skinflint and you're also a disgustin' fuckin' lecher, at least judgin' by the way you're starin' at me. Why don't you stop ogling me, you poor bastid, and lie down and sleep?'

Now too drunk to be embarrassed and so opting for outrage, Tom straightened his shoulders, stared sternly at Molly and said, 'I wasn't *ogling* you, my dear. I am not the kind to *ogle*. I was merely giving you my attention as we talked, to let you know I was listening.'

'You were ogling,' Molly said. 'Admit it. Your eyes were poppin' out of your fuckin' head and crawlin' all over me – legs, belly and boobs.'

'That's ridiculous,' Tom said. 'You have a rich imagination. I've noted before, and have informed you accordingly, that you suffer from certain sexual obsessions of an unhealthy, or possibly egotistical, nature. If you're not being threatened with rape, you think you're being ogled. What absolute nonsense!'

'Just lie down and let us both have some sleep.'

'Certainly,' Tom said with dignity.

With a melodramatic sigh, he removed his shoes, switched off the lights and stretched out on his bed. The minute he closed his eyes, his head started swimming, so he quickly opened his eyes again and took a couple of deep breaths. That seemed to help. He closed his eyes again and this time his head didn't swim, but he felt that he was suffocating in the humidity and so he opened his eyes again. Turning his head, he glanced sideways at Molly, whom he could just about discern through the semi-darkness, and noted that she had closed her eyes and was either sleeping or simply breathing deeply. He suspected the latter.

Was it possible, he wondered, that she was thinking of him, just as he was thinking of her? No, of course not . . . But then again, you never knew . . . She was a healthy young lady with normal desires and she had smiled at him a couple of times, which was certainly hopeful.

Tom heard her even breathing, saw the rise and fall of her lovely breasts, and he filled up with drunken emotion, burned with sensual need. Sighing, he closed his eyes, hoping to find distraction in sleep, but instead her image swam around in his head to tease and torment him. She was silent in those visions, not whiplashing him with her tongue, and so he saw only what he wished to see, which was her soft, unclothed body. He saw himself on her bed, stretched out beside her, unbuttoning her shirt to expose the brassiere he had fleetingly glimpsed now and then. He saw her breasts in the brassiere, her denims slipping down her broad hips, exposing her white, flat belly (also exposed only fleetingly now and then) and then he saw her spreadeagled beneath him, stark naked and wonderful.

Groaning, Tom opened his eyes again, stared blindly at the ceiling, gradually returned to his senses and realized that he'd been sleeping and dreaming. Agitated, he glanced sideways to see Molly on the other bed, still outstretched, eyes closed, breathing evenly, almost certainly sleeping.

Even more agitated, feeling drunk and unreal, he swung his legs off the bed and stood up and went to the window. Standing there, he glanced sideways at the sleeping, evenly breathing Molly, at the mesmeric rise and fall of her breasts in the tight shirt, in the seductive semi-darkness. Then, in an attempt to distract himself, he pulled the curtains apart to look out.

He was surprised to see that it was dark out there.

Realizing that he had slept a lot longer than he had

imagined, he glanced again at the sleeping Molly and was consumed by the sight of her, so he gulped and looked out the window again, still seeking distraction. This room was on the ground-floor level, at the rear of the building, and pale moonlight was falling on a quiet road that ran alongside a park with trees silhouetted against a starry backdrop.

As Tom was studying the road, distracting himself by staring at nothing in particular, a red Ford Escort came into view and stopped by the rear garden of the hotel. Its headlights remained on. The driver's window was rolled down and the indistinct blob of a human face appeared and seemed to be staring straight at the hotel and, as Tom imagined it, straight at him.

The hairs on the back of Tom's neck stood up when he realized that the distant face was, indeed, staring straight at him – or, at least, at his room.

Even as he accepted this, the face disappeared back into the car, then the driver's door opened and the driver stepped out. Though Tom still couldn't discern his features, he could see clearly that the man was wearing a checkered shirt, faded denims and high-heeled boots, with a knife sheathed on the big-buckled belt around his waist.

Tom knew then, without doubt, that he was looking at the one-eyed bandit who had smiled malevolently at him in the last two bars he had been in.

Molly was right: the one-eyed man was following them.

Shocked back to sobriety and instantly scared, Tom watched the one-eyed man as he walked from his car to the fence at the rear of the garden. The man disappeared when he approached the fence, but a few seconds later his white knuckles, illuminated by moonlight, could clearly be seen where his hands had gripped the top of the fence as he prepared to haul himself up and over. Even as Tom guessed what the man was doing, the latter did indeed appear on the top of the fence, balancing precariously as he glanced left and right, checking that no one could see him.

'Oh, God help us!' Tom exclaimed involuntarily, his eyes almost popping out of his head as he stared at the man on the fence.

'What . . . ?' Glancing sideways, Tom saw Molly sitting upright on her bed and rubbing her sleepy eyes. She blinked a few times and stared at him. 'What the fuck's goin' on?' she asked.

'That man!' Tom exclaimed in a melodramatic whisper that sounded, to him, like a scream.

'What man?'

'That one-eyed man who was following us!'

'You insisted he wasn't following us,' Molly said.

'No, I didn't!'

'Yes, you did!'

'Well, he's following us,' Tom said, his whisper still resounding like a scream in his own head, 'and he's come to this hotel and right now he's clambering over that fence out there, about to drop down into the garden. *He's coming for us!*'

'Stop shouting.'

'*I'm not shouting!*'

'Yes, you are.'

'What's the difference? I'm telling you that that one-eyed man's out there in the garden and he's—'

'You said he was on the fence.'

'What's the difference?' Tom almost screamed. 'He's on the fence and he's about to drop into the garden and he's coming for us.'

'Not for us,' Molly corrected him. 'He's coming for the crystal skull.'

'What's the difference?' Tom repeated, panic-stricken. He couldn't believe how calm she was. 'If he's come for the crystal skull, he's obviously going to kill us to get it. He's—'

'He won't necessarily kill us,' Molly said.

'*What?* But he's . . .'

Tom turned back to the window and looked out just as the one-eyed man dropped off the fence, into the garden, briefly disappearing into the darkness of the lawn, then reappearing in striations of moonlight as he made his way at the half-crouch towards the hotel in general and Tom's room in particular.

He was carrying a pistol in his right hand.

'*He has a pistol*!' Tom bawled.

Instantly, Molly rolled off the bed, groped around in her rucksack, then rushed up to stand beside Tom and look out through the window.

She was holding a Browning 9mm High Power handgun in her steady right hand.

'That's a gun!' Tom exclaimed, staring at the weapon, shocked.

'Fuckin' right, it's a gun,' Molly said. 'So where is that bastid?'

'You can't shoot him!' Tom exclaimed.

'Wanna bet? Where *is* the bastid?' She was staring intently down through the window, trying to catch a glimpse of the man who had vanished into another patch of darkness. 'There he is!' she said excitedly and started opening the window while holding the handgun up beside her head and releasing the safety catch.

'Oh, my God!' Tom exclaimed. Looking down through

the opening window, he saw the one-eyed man emerging again from darkness, crossing a pool of pale moonlight, and rapidly coming straight towards the room.

When the one-eyed man saw the window opening, he stopped in surprise. Quickly recovering and, more importantly, seeing that Molly was aiming her handgun at him, he swung his own pistol up in the hope of firing first.

'Don't fire that thing!' Tom bawled at Molly.

Molly fired. The sound of the shot ricocheted in Tom's head. He closed his eyes in horror and opened them again to see that the one-eyed man had not been hit and was now running back towards the fence. Molly fired another shot. The noise almost split Tom's head. He closed his eyes again, but felt compelled to open them once more and saw that the one-eyed man was now clambering back over the fence. Once straddling it, he twisted sideways, took aim with his pistol, and fired a single parting shot. The bullet ricocheted off the wooden frame of the window, just beside Tom's head, making him drop instantly to the floor in fear of his life. Molly fired a third shot. Tom stayed there on the floor, keeping his eyes closed, until he heard the sound of the Ford car racing away, followed by Molly speaking.

'You can stop lickin' the tiles with your tongue,' she said. 'That bastid's gone.'

Tom raised himself high enough to glance over the bottom of the windowframe and confirm that the one-eyed man and his car had indeed vanished. When he stood up fully, though keeping well to the side of the window, Molly was sitting on the edge of her bed, putting more bullets into the magazine of her handgun. When she had finished, she applied the safety catch, then she slipped the handgun back into its leather holster and carefully inched the complete package down through all her junk, to the very bottom of the battered rucksack. She patted something inside the rucksack and then straightened up again. She gave Tom a big grin.

'Just thought I'd check,' she said calmly. 'The crystal skull's still there and in one piece. Don't know why I bothered to check. Just instinct, I suppose. Thought it might have vanished *without* that bastid's help. I'm superstitious that way.'

Tom stared disbelievingly at her, aware of his racing heart, then said in a shocked whisper, 'You're carrying a loaded gun!'

'Not much use if it ain't loaded.'

'A loaded gun! That's dangerous!'

'Only to the bastid it's aimed at – and it made that bastid run away.'

'I refuse to travel around the country with a woman carrying . . .' Tom began. But he was cut off by the hammering of knuckles on the door and a voice telling them in Spanish to open up. Even more shocked, Tom glanced at the door, then back at Molly. 'Oh, my God, is that him?'

'No,' Molly said calmly. 'It won't be him. It's prob'ly the manager. You better open the door.'

'*You* open it,' Tom said.

Rolling her eyes, Molly stood up and went to open the door. She was right. It was the manager. He spat a stream of Spanish at them, then reverted to English and demanded to know who had been firing a pistol in his respectable hotel.

'Pistol?' Tom said. '*I* didn't fire a pistol!'

'Me neither,' Molly lied, then she jabbed her finger

at the open window behind her. 'But we heard the sound of gunfire from out back and opened the window to look. There was somethin' goin' on out there. We think it may have been a robbery. There was a police car and the policeman was on the pavement and firin' at a man we could see running away from 'im. I guess that's what you heard.'

'The shots came from here, *Señora*.'

'*Señorita*,' Molly corrected him. 'And the shots didn't come from here, *Señor* – they came from out there. I mean, what kinda place are we staying in, if that kinda crap goes on at night? Is this a dangerous area?'

'No, no, *Señorita!*' The manager, who was tiny, with a face as round as his belly and large liquid brown eyes, waved his hands frantically in denial and took a couple of steps back. 'This is a respectable establishment in a *very* safe area. What you saw very rarely happens here and I must apologize for it. Our local police force, which is excellent, will surely catch the criminal intruder and in the meantime, *Señor* and *Señorita*, in recompense for your suffering, I offer you this room for free for the night. I trust this is acceptable.'

'Most kind—' Tom began.

'We could sue you,' Molly said. 'We've spent a fortune in your restaurant and were almost murdered in our beds by way of thanks. We could sue you for damages.'

The manager was aghast. 'I include the meal, *Señorita*. I throw in all your drinks from the bedroom bar and, of course, your breakfast. Also included will be a hamper of food to send you on your way in the morning. I trust this is acceptable.'

'Well . . .'

'We accept,' Tom said quickly. 'You're really too kind, *Señor*. Thank you and goodnight.'

'*Buenas noches*, my friends.'

With a quick, graceful bow, the manager departed and Tom just as quickly closed the door after him. He then turned to face Molly. His heart was racing and he felt his cheeks burning, but Molly was grinning with triumph.

'Pretty neat, eh?'

'*What?*' Tom exploded.

'The way I took care of that prick – *and* that bastid outside. Now we can stay here for free, eat an' drink all we want, and then light out of here tomorrow morning, before that one-eyed bastid comes back, which he surely will.'

'You're carrying a gun!' Tom repeated.

'You've already said that,' Molly reminded him.

'I refuse to travel with a woman – a mere slip of a girl – who's carrying a dangerous weapon in her rucksack. That's really too much.'

'A girl from New York doesn't travel through Mexico without some kinda protection. And if *I* hadn't been carrying a gun, you'd be dead meat, *amigo*.'

'Nonsense! I can take care of myself. I don't need some gun-toting American lunatic to come to my rescue. I could have dealt with the matter on my own, without causing mayhem.'

'Oh, yeah? How? Having a civilized English chat while that bastid shoved the barrel of his pistol down your throat and squeezed the trigger and ran off with the crystal skull? Don't come it with *me*, pal! Besides, you were face down on the floor while that guy was advancin', practically shittin' your pants, so don't tell me you know how to protect yourself. I protected you an' I got us this room for free, so why not show some gratitude?'

Tom turned away from her to sit on the edge of the bed and put on his shoes.

'What're you doin'?' Molly asked him.

'If, as you insist, that one-eyed man's going to return, I think we should leave here right now and put as much distance as possible between us and him.'

'He'll be out there right now,' Molly said.

Tom stopped tying his shoe laces. 'What does that mean?'

'He'll be out there right now, watching the entrance to this hotel, and he'll be delighted if we leave in the dark. In darkness, he can pick us off easier – and without being seen. So I suggest that we wait until morning and travel on in daylight. Of course, if you insist, we'll leave right now and . . .'

'No, no,' Tom said quickly, untying his shoe laces and kicking the shoes off again. 'Why not stay, indeed? It's not that I necessarily agree with you, but why waste a perfectly good room?'

'You're scared,' Molly said.

'I am not,' Tom said stoutly.

'You're scared an' you have a right to be, but you just won't admit it.'

'I'm really rather tired,' Tom said with a feigned yawn, 'and could do with another good sleep. Do you mind . . . ?' And, without waiting for his rhetorical question to be answered, he lay down, still fully clothed, on the bed and closed his weary, bloodshot eyes.

'Well, fuck you,' Molly said.

Tom pretended to sleep. He didn't want another argument. He intended keeping his eyes closed, even if he couldn't sleep, but when he heard Molly rooting about in her rucksack, he sneaked a sideways glance at her. She was sitting on the edge of her bed, her gorgeous legs crossed, and rolling what looked like an unusually thick cigarette. After lighting it and inhaling, she exhaled a cloud of smoke that Tom, though not a smoker himself, recognized by its sweet smell.

'Marijuana!' he whispered as he pulled his blanket up over his head. 'Dear God, what next?'

'What a wimp!' he heard Molly murmuring just before he did, indeed, slip off to sleep.

In his sleep, he had vivid erotic dreams . . . about Molly, of course.

CHAPTER ELEVEN

The Thai and Chinese girls on the stage in the middle of the noisy bar in Patpong Road were wearing either G-strings or see-thru negligees, with black stockings and stiletto-heeled shoes. Their breasts were bare. All were slim, smooth-skinned, long-legged and, in the subdued crimson lighting, irresistibly sensual as they gyrated their hips, rolled their bellies, shook their naked rumps, and writhed up and down the steel poles that rose phallically from the floor of the small, revolving, neon-lit stage, surrounded by tables packed with locals and tourists. The girls were dancing to a string of hit records and the volume was well up to challenge the din of wolf whistles, ribald remarks, drunken laughter and bellowed conversation.

Observing them as she drank her tall glass of bubbling vintage champagne, Mai Suphar's eyes gleamed with a rapacious light that Lu Thong knew only too well. Earlier in the evening he had taken her to the Thai boxing tournaments in the Lumphini Stadium on Rama 4 Road and she had, as usual, been stimulated by the violent spectacle. Certainly one of the fiercest sports ever invented (therefore Lu Thong's favourite sport) Thai boxing had originated in ancient days as a martial art, then evolved into a competitive fight in which not only gloved fists, but elbows, feet, knees and nearly every other part of the boxer's body could be used to kick, jab, chop and generally pummel an opponent into submission. Few things thrilled Mai more than to see two superbly fit, almost naked men inflicting ferocious punishment on one another over five three-minute rounds of nonstop, spectacular, brutal combat – and certainly she was excited sexually by it.

Lu Thong wanted Mai to be sexually aroused when he took her to bed later this evening for a drug-heightened orgy. Knowing that Mai, being bisexual, was also aroused by the sight of scantily-clad teenage girls performing erotic dances in the many strip joints and nightclubs of Patpong, he had deliberately brought her here straight from the excitements of the Lumphini Stadium. The combination of fierce Thai boxing between sweating men and the erotic dancing of these beautiful young women was having its effect and Mai, who also loved vintage champagne, was clearly becoming even more excited and repeatedly licked her moist, lush lips.

Remarkably, even when compared to the gorgeous teenagers on stage, Mai, in her short black silk dress held on by thin shoulder straps, her long legs in high heels, and her jet-black hair hanging all the way down her spine, was still the most beautiful girl in the place, drawing many a hungry glance.

Lu Thong himself was hungry for her and pleased that he'd brought her here.

'Would you like one of those?' he said, nodding to indicate the girls dancing on the revolving stage in visually enhancing crimson light.

Mai smiled. 'Why? Are you going to purchase one for me?'

'If you want one, I'll purchase one, my lovely. But, alas, not tonight. Tonight you're all mine.'

'So why did you suggest it?'

'Just curious.'

'About what?'

'Your preferences. Do you prefer men or women?'

'Women are less trouble,' Mai said, 'particularly when young and tender like those dancers. But men have their uses as well. With regard to what I prefer, it really just depends on my mood and you'll do for tonight.'

Lu Thong smiled at her insolence. He admired it, but he was also wary of it, knowing that it could lead to rebellion and, from that, betrayal. Mai, he knew, was capable of both and that made her dangerous. 'So what would you do if you had one of those young girls instead of me?'

Mai studied the girls on the stage, then licked her lips and looked dreamy. 'Assuming she was heterosexual – or at least thought she was – I'd take my first pleasure from seducing her and watching her shock and disgust change to rapture. Once she was mine, enslaved by my hands and tongue, I'd take more pleasure from showing her everything two women can do together, with and without my various aids, including dildoes and drugs. Then, having pushed her to the edge, beyond guilt or shame, I'd make her pleasure *me* in every conceivable way, doing things she could not have imagined herself doing just a few hours before. Finally, when she was addicted to me, thinking me to be her whole world, I'd persuade her to let me tie her to the bed. Once she'd done so, once she was helpless beneath me, I'd embark on the last stage, from orgasm to death. So that's what I'd do, my dear.'

'You'd kill her?'

'Very slowly,' Mai said, licking her lips and trembling with pleasure at the very thought of it. 'I'd tape her sweet mouth closed to prevent her from screaming and work tenderly and surely, with all the skill at my command, keeping her alive as long as possible, only ending it when I could no longer bear my own excitement and had to release it through orgasm. She would die in agony as I was dying from pleasure. That's my ultimate high.'

'It would not be the first time, would it, Mai?'

'No,' Mai replied.

Lu Thong studied her thoughtfully, then he smiled and glanced around the crowded, smoky bar. It was packed with a certain number of locals, but mostly with male tourists from Europe, America and Japan, all out for a good time and willing to risk AIDS to get it. They were also willing to conveniently forget their hometown morals when it came to what they wanted from Bangkok: young girls and young men, some hardly more than children, whose only means of survival was to whore.

As he studied the sweating, flushed faces of the other male customers, most seated at packed tables around the revolving neon-lit stage where the strippers and erotic dancers were still performing to pounding rock music, Lu Thong saw that most were sitting either with bar girls in miniskirts and hotpants or with handsome young Thai men in short-sleeved shirts and tight pants. A lot of hands were roaming under those tables, a lot of deals were being made, and the young whores, male and female, were mostly desperate enough not to think of the awesome dangers of their profession. In fact, young whores of both sexes disappeared every day in Bangkok and either were not seen again or were next seen, torn and bloody, in some grim hotel room or found floating face-down in the Chao Phraya river: beaten to death in drunken frenzies, stabbed to death by psychopaths, tortured to death by sadists, or overdosed, either accidentally or against their will, on lethal drugs.

Invariably, the perpetrators of these crimes were male clients, but certainly more than one death had been caused by the most beautiful woman in this room, Mai Suphan, who sought her highs from perverse sex, lingering torture and murder by the injection of lethal drugs that left no trace. Mai's preferred method was to bring her victims to the brink of orgasm and inject them just as they were coming. She came herself when that happened.

Now, turning back to his lovely companion, Lu Thong stared steadily at her and said, 'Don't get similar ideas about me. I would not be amused.'

'No, you'd be dead.' Mai's smile was as cold as ice. 'But, who knows? It might be the best way for you to go. You're a man drawn to death, possibly to suicide, certainly to the most extreme kinds of experience, so being taken from orgasm to death might be good for your twisted immortal soul. Try imagining it as the ultimate adventure – your last orgasm and your last breath simultaneously. Perhaps that's what you want, Lu Thong.'

'The ultimate adventure – death's doorway – yes, that's what I want. But not your way, my pet.'

'Then what way?'

'Magic. The occult. Power beyond what we can imagine. Perhaps a power that can only be purchased with death, which would make the dying worthwhile.'

'The kind of power said to be given to the one who possesses the Crystal Skull?'

'Yes,' Lu Thong said.

'Which is why you want one.'

'Yes.'

'Are you sure the skulls have magical powers?'

'I'm certain of it,' Lu Thong said.

'Why?'

'Because of their history,' Lu Thong said. 'Or, to be more precise, their strange lack of history, since in fact they're ancient artefacts with no verifiable history and therefore no historical references from which we could assess what they really are or where they come from.'

'But there must be clues.'

'Mostly conjecture,' Lu Thong said. 'There are those who believe that all thirteen of the known crystal skulls have magical powers and originated in Atlantis at least 17,000 years ago. According to this theory, Atlantis had thirteen so-called *healing* temples and one skull was utilized in each temple. Tenuous evidence links the skulls to Sha-Tree-Tra, a female priestess who was killed during one of the last earthquakes in Atlantis. The original skull of this priestess was transmuted into crystal through a process known as "morphocrystallic transformation" and that crystal skull is believed to possess the powers known to the priestess when she was alive.'

'Atlantis!' Mai exclaimed sardonically. 'It probably never existed.'

'Maybe not,' Lu Thong said, 'but the story is interesting, in that it at least gives a rough date for the origin of the crystal skulls. That date, give or take a few hundred years either way, was confirmed when one Francis Joseph, an historical writer researching Mayan civilizations, attempted to identify the race of the person who modelled for the skull – or the priestess whose original head was used for its morphocrystallic transformation – by reconstructing the face from a plaster mould of a skull.'

'I see,' Mai said. 'Please continue.'

After studying Mai through his beautiful, cocaine-brightened, dangerously perceptive eyes, Lu Thong continued: 'Frank Joseph called on the assistance of Peggy C. Caldwell, a consulting forensic anthropologist for the Smithsonian Institution, and Frank Domingo, a composite artist with the New York Police Department. Between them, using the plaster model and various photos of the skull, they came up with a drawing of the face of a young woman, seventeen to twenty years of age, with Oriental/Mongoloid features of a kind that linked her to early Mesaoamerican civilizations. Due to this, it's now believed that the crystal skulls are, if not human skulls *transformed* into crystal, certainly replicas of the head of an ancient Mayan high priestess, or goddess. It's also thought that they're made out of pure rock crystal because the Mayans believed that crystal has magical properties and used the skulls in their esoteric rites. It may be no accident, therefore, that the various owners of the skulls have reported that they could send them into trances, possessed healing properties, revealed secrets about the origins of mankind, and helped them communicate with other worlds.'

All that cocaine might have done his brains in, Mai thought, *but I might as well humour him. Besides, the skull, even if not remotely magical, is certainly valuable in the international marketplace, so it's well worth the having.*

'Such powers could be dangerous,' she said, determined to humour him until she found out all she needed to know.

'Yes,' Lu Thong said. 'Reportedly, the magical powers of the skulls can be positive or negative, used for good or for evil, to bless or to curse. Indeed, more than one owner of a skull has committed suicide after allegedly being cursed by it. However, it's thought that the awesome energy of the crystal skull, if harnessed correctly, could unleash the hidden powers of the cosmos, turning mortal man into superman.'

'But you don't know how to release that energy.'

'No,' Lu Thong confessed.

'So why do you want the crystal skull?'

'First, because it's one of the most valuable artefacts in the world. Second, because once it's in my possession, I can experiment with it and hopefully find out just how to arouse its forces, or turn on its energy. Others have done so before me, so I don't see why I can't do the same.'

'And if you do, what then?'

'It's believed that he who attempts to arouse the sleeping powers of the skull must accept that he is dealing with the unknown and gambling with his own life. It's that gamble – the ultimate gamble between life and death, between mortality and immortality – that I wish to make when I gain possession of the artefact.'

Mai glanced at the revolving stage, drinking in the sight of the tender young flesh – the perfect buttocks, the firm breasts, the flat bellies and long legs – of the young, eager dancers. She imagined the thin blade of her knife making crimson traceries upon its perfection.

She then recalled what it was like to have a hot young body beneath her, convulsing first in orgasm, then in death's frenzy, as she slid the needle containing killing drugs into her victim's neck. Mai almost swooned at the recollection, but controlled herself and turned away. She gazed into Lu Thong's beautiful wasted face, into the glittering depths of his brown eyes where the cocaine madness held sway, and wondered if what he was telling her was true and what it could mean to her.

Limitless wealth and power, at the very least, and that was well worth the risk.

'So what's happening in the Yucatán?' she asked him.

Lu Thong sighed and shook his head from side to side, as if quietly disgusted. 'The three who died at Chichén Itzá were supposed to have taken the crystal skull, when they located it, only as far as a certain *Posada* located on Mex. 180, about thirty minutes, drive from the site. There, the skull was to be passed over to a local hard man, a one-eyed former policeman and professional criminal named Emmanuelle Cortez, who was to take it in his own car to Mérida airport. There he would deliver it to another of my men, a Mexican working as a Customs official. Had he received the skull, that bent official would have smuggled it onto a flight to Los Angeles. From there, in the care of another bent official, it would have been flown on to me. In the event, my three men were burned to a cinder at Chichén Itzá and, as you know, the crystal skull wasn't found with the bodies.'

'Right,' Mai said. 'Someone took it. The question is: Who?'

Lu Thong nodded. 'I can tell you that Emmanuelle

Cortez was still in the *Posada*, wondering what had happened to the men who were supposed to bring him the Crystal Skull, when he received a phone call from a friend, another bent cop, telling him about the bodies found at Chichén Itzá and saying that no mention of a crystal skull had been made in the reports. Just as Cortez was about to leave the *Posada* to pass on this information to my man at Mérida airport, an Englishman about thirty years of age and an American girl about five or six years his junior entered the *Posada*. They sat at a table, ordered drinks, and then proceeded to study a crystal skull that the girl had pulled out of her rucksack. This took place hardly more than an hour after my men dug up the crystal skull and were fried to death – and after the skull went missing. And those two people – the Englishman and the American girl – had been observed by my one-eyed friend in the *Posada* to have come from the direction of Chichén Itzá.'

'So the crystal skull must have been there at the top of the pyramid, in the Shrine, when those two found the three charred bodies. They took the skull and fled.'

'Correct,' Lu Thung said.

'Do you know who they are or *where* they are?'

'Approximately. When they left the *Posada*, they took the crystal skull with them, but Emmanuelle Cortez kept on their tail. They drove straight to Mérida and booked into a hotel in the Old City. Flashing his old police identification at the desk clerk, Cortez learnt that the Englishman was called Tom Powell and that he was travelling with a British passport and using a rented jeep. Powell signed himself and the female in as man and wife, though the desk clerk was adamant that they weren't married and that the girl was an American hitch-hiker. Cortez then asked what room they were staying in. It turned out to be a ground-floor room at the back of the hotel.'

'Very convenient,' Mai said.

'I would have thought so,' Lu Thong said, 'but when, that evening, Cortez tried to break into the room in order to kill those two and recapture the crystal skull, he was shot at by one of them and had to make his escape. Returning to the hotel the following morning, again flashing his old police identification, he was informed that the couple had signed out, asking the desk clerk to recommend and book them into a hotel near the Zocalo in Mexico City. The desk clerk did so. We have the name of the hotel. They left for Mexico City early this morning, taking a free hamper of food with them, obviously intending to drive there without stopping. The drive takes at least twenty hours, possibly longer, but Cortez is following them all the way and, hopefully, will soon relieve them of the crystal skull.'

'Let's hope so,' Mai said. 'Particularly given what you've just told me.'

'What does that mean?' Lu Thong asked.

'If the skull has the powers you claim for it, those two could become more of a problem than you think.'

'You mean they could gain the powers of the crystal skull.'

'Exactly,' Mai said.

'They could, but it seems unlikely for now. The powers of the skull have to be aroused somehow – and it's the "how" that's the problem. If those two don't know that the skull has magical powers – if they're just running away with it because they assume it has fiscal value, which it certainly has – then the powers of the skull will remain dormant.'

Raising his eyes to the revolving stage in the middle of the crowded, noisy room, Lu Thong saw the flimsily clad teenage girls dancing sinuously to pounding rock music, rolling their groins, shaking their breasts, wrapping their legs around the phallic steel uprights and writhing against them. He was aroused by the sight, imagining them all in his bed at once, but he became even harder when he looked at Mai Suphan, at her exquisite, deadly beauty, and imagined her in bed with the same young girls, using her diabolical sexual artistry for pleasures beyond the pale. He almost gasped at the thought. He was on cocaine and his skin was burning. He wanted Mai Suphan, the young girls up on the stage, the male whores in the audience, anything and everything, but most of all he wanted the crystal skull and its hope of transcendence. Life was short and brutish, a sequence of couplings and disengagements, of petty desires and their disappointments, but the crystal skull could help him transcend the commonplace and replace it with magic. He needed that magic, the siren call of the otherworldly, and in the meantime he would try to lose himself in Mai's inventive, potentially deadly perversions.

Perhaps sensing what he was thinking, Mai turned back to smile at him. She leaned forward to slide her hand under the table and lay her calculating, expert, tormenting fingers on his pulsating erection.

'Let's go back to your place,' she said, her voice husky and sensual and also slightly mocking. 'You can test *my* magical powers. Then we'll discuss the Englishman, this Mister Tom Powell, and the American bitch he's running with.'

'Let's do that,' Lu Thong said, feeling breathless, sounding hoarse, and he stood up, not trying to hide what he was feeling, and left the bar with Mai by his side.

She's an angel from hell, Lu Thong thought, *and that's just where I'm going.*

The thought gave him comfort.

CHAPTER TWELVE

Tom and Molly had formed an uneasy truce by the time they completed the drive from Mérida to Mexico City, leaving the former just after breakfast and arriving in the latter early in the morning of the following day, when the normally dense traffic was relatively thin. This time, when they booked into their hotel – medium-priced and near the Zocalo, or main square – they were able to get separate rooms, which saved them both further embarrassment, though Tom also felt a disappointment that he could not admit to, now being tormented by sexual fantasies about this girl who annoyed him so much. He was also worried that she might lose the crystal skull or have it stolen from her in his absence.

'Perhaps I should look after the crystal skull for you,' he suggested anxiously as they were picking up their separate kit.

'No, thanks,' Molly said, slinging her rucksack over her shoulder and looking determined.

'I'm worried that we're still being pursued and that someone might attempt to take it off you.'

'I'm the one with the handgun,' Molly reminded him, 'so I'm the one who can look after myself *and* the crystal skull. Fat chance of that with you, pal, given how you performed back there in Yucatán.'

'You don't have to be insulting,' Tom replied, 'just because I don't happen to travel with an offensive weapon on my person.' In fact, he was thoroughly ashamed of the way he had acted in that hotel in Mérida, when the one-eyed man had come at them with a pistol and Molly had so successfully put him to flight. He had been shocked, certainly, to find that Molly had a pistol but was secretly grateful that this had been the case. He could not say that now, though. All he could do was fight to retain his dignity in the face of her onslaughts. 'Come to think of it,' he said, defending himself by taking the offensive, 'are you *licensed* to carry a loaded pistol?'

'That's none of your goddamned business,' Molly retorted. 'So what time do we meet?'

They agreed to sleep until lunchtime, then meet in the lobby for an early lunch and, hopefully, a visit to Professor Emilio Juarez in the National Museum of Anthropology, taking the crystal skull with them. Thus, in accord for once, they entered their separate rooms, one adjoining the other.

In his attractive single room of Spanish colonial design, Tom slept uneasily, being tormented first by his fear that the one-eyed man would come crashing through the door, wielding his pistol as he had done back in Mérida and, when he slept, by more erotic dreams about himself and a naked Molly in carnal embrace. He did, however, awaken feeling relatively rested and, after freshening up with a shower, phoned Professor Juarez at the museum. The professor, an old family friend who had helped Tom with Mayan research, was delighted to hear that he was in town and gave him an appointment for four that afternoon.

As he had plenty of time to kill and only Molly to kill

it with, Tom decided to be nice to her when he met her down in the lobby. She was wearing the same shirt and tight denims, but had a canvas bag slung on her right shoulder instead of her rucksack.

'Is the crystal skull in that bag?' Tom asked anxiously.

'What the fuck do you think's in it? My make-up?'

Determined to be nice to her, Tom ignored the remark and asked if she would like to go for lunch.

'Thought you'd never ask,' Molly said.

Tom tried to keep his cool, but their truce started breaking down first when they both started coughing and developed watery eyes from the intense pollution of the city, then when Tom suggested having Mexican food and Molly, perhaps feeling wan from the unusual atmosphere composed of a dangerous mixture of lead, sulphur and ozone, responded by saying she wouldn't touch 'that spicy greaser crap' and recommended dropping into a Burger Boys instead. Appalled by the very thought, Tom insisted that he would not eat that 'American filth'. They wrangled over it a bit and then compromised by having Italian in the form of a sit-down pizza in a Pizza Hut. Molly washed her ham-and-pineapple pizza ('Nothing spicy, thanks!') down with a strawberry milk shake, but Tom, disgusted at being forced to eat pizza in Mexico, insisted upon having a beer when the meal was finished.

'Yeah, right,' Molly said, 'you just go ahead and poison your system with more of that alcohol. I won't say a fuckin' word.'

Forcing himself not to make any retaliatory comment about, for instance, her marijuana smoking, Tom consulted his Fodor's *Mexico* and then led her along densely packed sidewalks, past endless streams of traffic pouring out more eye-watering pollution, to the highly recommended La Opera, described as 'a handsome turn-of-the-century bar' with 'lush Victorian décor'. His edition of Fodor's, though two years out of date, did not let him down.

'More authentic than a pizza parlour, don't you think?' he said to Molly while coughing to clear his throat, wiping his tearful eyes dry, and swigging his glass of wonderfully cold Bohemia beer.

'It's not bad,' Molly agreed reluctantly while also trying to clear her throat and clear her red eyes by sipping her iced lemonade speckled with tiny *chía* seeds.

'It was one of Pancho Villa's favourite hangouts,' Tom informed her, having memorized this detail from his Fodor's, 'which may explain why, up until a few years ago, women weren't even admitted.'

'You'd have liked it better then, wouldn't you?' Molly sneered.

'No, no,' Tom spluttered hastily to prevent another feminist tirade. 'I merely mean that this is a traditional establishment, so well worth the visit.'

'Yeah, right,' Molly said. 'Fuckin' Mexican male chauvinist bastards. Their time will come, pal.'

Ignoring her remark, Tom deliberately checked his wristwatch. 'Well,' he said, looking forward to some serious sightseeing, despite the awful air, 'we still have a couple of hours to spend, so let's go exploring.'

'I don't wanna see any boring churches,' Molly warned him. 'I wanna look at the shops.'

'Quite,' Tom said, his enthusiasm for sightseeing instantly dampened, though he was too gentlemanly to refuse her. 'I think you'll find those in the Zocalo – the main square – and it's not far from here. So, let's get started.'

He had really wanted to visit the Metropolitan

Cathedral, with its unique mixture of Ionic, Doric, Corinthian and Baroque architecture, as well as the National Palace, formerly the Palace of Moctezuma, then the headquarters of Cortés, but Molly had eyes only for the many tiny shops clustered together under the picturesque arches on the north side of the square. She depressed him even more by spending nearly an hour in the Monte de Piedad, or National Pawn Shop, known as the Mountain of Pity, telling him it was the 'most terrific pawn shop' she had ever seen and adding: 'Not that *you*'d be interested in somethin' like this, bein' filthy rich and totally removed from the real fucked up world.' When eventually he managed to drag her away from the hundreds of pawned items in the massive establishment, he tried sneakily to lead her across the great plaza to the Cathedral, but her voice, resounding firmly behind his back, stopped him dead in his tracks.

'No way!' she told him. 'We gotta go to the Zona Rosa. That's where it's all happenin' in this city an' I wanna see it.'

'Of course,' Tom said obediently.

The walk to the Zona Rosa took only minutes and led them to a lively neighbourhood packed with boutiques, art galleries, artists' studios, hotels, bars, restaurants, discothèques, sidewalk cafés with colourful umbrella tables, and shops selling everything from Mexican curios to eighteenth-century antiques. To his surprise, Tom actually enjoyed himself (the area was filled with pretty girls, most looking a lot happier than Molly) but eventually, with pollution exhaustion setting in, he insisted that they start off for the museum, even though they were still too early for his appointment.

'Yeah,' Molly said, 'right. Let's talk to this greaser friend of yours and find out what we've got here.'

There were plenty of taxis and white *peseros*, or minibuses, passing by, but all of them were full and after trying for about twenty minutes to wave one down, Tom decided that it would be quicker to walk. This turned out to be true, though the walk was quite dangerous, since the density of the traffic remained appalling, the fumes from its exhausts was dense enough to be sandwiched, and few drivers took any notice of pedestrians. The museum was located in the handsomely forested Chapultepec Park, on the west side of the city, and it certainly lived up to its reputation as the finest in the world. A truly magnificent building, it was constructed as a series of halls built around a patio, with at least six of the chambers devoted to the major pre-Columbian civilizations of Mexico, including the Toltecs and the mysterious builders of the Pyramids at Teotihuacán. Passing the huge statue of Tlaloc, God of Rain, which stood guard outside, they entered the building and spent the remaining twenty minutes studying murals and exhibits dealing with the history of Mexico and Meso-America and, in particular, the Mayans. While Tom found all of this to be fascinating, Molly's face was a picture of monumental boredom, her jaws working relentlessly on gum, her pursed lips blowing bubbles.

'Nothin' here about the crystal skull,' she noted sourly.

'No,' Tom replied. 'There wouldn't be. The true origins of the crystal skulls aren't known – though they're widely believed to be Meso-American – so they wouldn't be included here. Nevertheless, Professor Juarez has a particular interest in them, believing them to be of early- or pre-Mayan origin.'

Molly impatiently checked her wristwatch, then looked up, relieved. 'Time's up,' she said.

Tom told one of the uniformed guides that he had an appointment with Professor Juarez and was promptly led down the stairs to a room in the basement. Entering, he found the professor seated behind an immense cluttered table surrounded by archaeological rarities, ancient ceramics, faded manuscripts covered in hieroglyphics, other desks piled high with books and papers, and walls covered with maps. Juarez had a thick thatch of healthy grey hair, a neatly trimmed grey beard, and a surprisingly youthful good-humoured Spanish face. Standing up and coming around the desk to shake their hands, he revealed himself to be short and barrel-chested like most Mexicans, almost bursting out of his grey suit and buttoned-up waistcoat.

'*Buenas tardes*,' he said, vigorously shaking Tom's hand. '*Mucho gusto en . . .*' Then, breaking into perfect English, he continued, 'It is so good to see you, my friend. It's been so long . . . How long?'

'Five years,' Tom said. 'The last time you were in London.'

'Ah, yes, so it was. When your father was still alive. A good man, a great friend . . . But what can one say?' Seeing the shadow of remembered pain that flickered across Tom's boyish face, he emotionally threw his arms around his shoulders and hugged him, then turned to Molly and shook her hand also.

'And you are . . . ?'

'Molly Beale.'

'*El gusto es mio*,' the professor said, eyeing Molly up and down with undisguised macho appreciation. 'The pleasure is mine.' Molly glanced at Tom, a cynical glint in her eyes, while the professor indicated the two wooden chairs facing his large, cluttered table. 'Please, take a seat.' When Tom and Molly were seated, the professor sat opposite them, then clasped his hands beneath his bearded chin, raised his bushy eyebrows inquiringly, and said, 'So! What is it you wished to discuss with me?'

Tom explained what he and Molly had found in the Shrine of the Great Pyramid at Chichén Itzá. When he had finished, the professor nodded thoughtfully. 'So the men obviously removed the crystal skull from that hole in the platform of the Shrine before being burnt to death.'

'Correct,' Tom said.

'Well,' the professor said, 'I can certainly confirm that most of us in the field believe that there are only two genuine crystal skulls. One of them is in the Museum of Mankind, London, and the other – the so-called Rose Quartz Skull, reportedly the finest and purest in the world – disappeared centuries ago and was rumoured to be hidden somewhere in Guatemala or Mexico. It would seem to me, therefore, that if this skull is genuine, it's almost certainly the long-lost Rose Quartz Skull and has been buried in the platform of the Shrine for centuries. If it is, then your find is truly astounding – and the skull will be priceless.'

'Great!' Molly said.

Offended by Molly's mercenary attitude and hoping to receive something more from this than mere filthy lucre – perhaps his name in the history books – Tom asked of Professor Juarez: 'But can you prove if it's genuine or not?'

Juarez nodded. 'Let me examine it properly,' he said.

'You mean, we have to leave it here with you?' Molly asked with bald suspicion.

'No,' the professor responded with a knowing smile and not without taking another eyeful of Molly's long legs and firm breasts. 'Naturally, I understand your concern, but I can examine the skull right here, under your watchful gaze.'

Nodding and grinning, unembarrassed that the professor was aware of her lack of trust, Molly removed the glittering crystal skull from her shoulder bag, sat it on the base of its neck, and slid it across the table to him. He gave a low whistle of appreciation, then picked the skull up to turn it this way and that, studying it at length, causing the light from the overhead lamps to flash on and off it. After probing its empty eyesockets with his fingers, he opened the jaws as wide as possible to stare into the crystal throat.

'Mmmm,' he murmured. 'Fascinating!'

When he had seen all that he could with the naked eye, he studied the skull with a large magnifying glass, then under what looked like a combination of giant microscope and telescope, lit up inside with tiny bulbs.

'What's that?' Molly asked him.

'A binocular microscope that gives me a three-dimensional view of the skull. However, in order to see fully just how this skull was made, I have to complete another test.'

He carried the skull to a glass tank filled with milky liquid, placed it carefully in the liquid, then turned on the overhead lights. Instantly, the submerged skull took on an eerie luminosity that showed its interior in startling depth, making it seem much bigger than it was, revealing the hidden hollows, curves and joinings of its normally unseen structure. It resembled, to Tom's inexpert gaze, a large prism filled with darkness and light.

'This is a bath of index-matching benzyl alcohol,' the professor explained. 'By viewing the skull in the benzyl alcohol, under polarized light, I can determine whether it was cut from one chunk of quartz. I can also ascertain the angle it was cut relative to the natural axis of the crystal . . . Mmmm. Fascinating!'

Satisfied, he removed the skull from the benzyl alcohol, dried it, then placed it under what looked like an electric drill. However, the bit did not revolve but merely applied electronically controlled pressure to the top of the crystal skull and recorded some kind of measurements on an electric graph. Satisfied, the professor returned to his seat and placed the skull on the desk.

'It's certainly rock quarz,' he said, 'rating seven on Mohs' Scale of hardness.'

'Which means?' Molly asked.

'That it's very hard indeed. Diamond, for instance, is ten. So a Mohs' rating of seven makes this skull remarkably hard – certainly harder than any we know of today.'

The professor stared thoughtfully at the skull for some time, then again clasped his hands under his bearded chin. He took a deep breath.

'The tests,' he said, 'confirm that both the skull and the jawbone were cut from one single chunk of quartz, albeit of rare size and quality. Indeed, I think I can say with confidence that given a crystal of the same size, our foremost contemporary producers of cut quartz could not produce a skull of comparable quality. Indeed, it's my carefully considered opinion that it would have taken centuries of work to produce a skull of this quality; and, as I've said, I don't believe that it could be produced at all in this day and age.

My deduction, therefore, is that this skull is genuine, ancient, remarkable and absolutely unique.'

'Why unique?' Molly asked with a percipience that again took Tom by surprise and made the professor smile. 'I mean, what makes it so different from the other crystal skulls you've examined?'

'Well, apart from the quality of the cut, as I've just mentioned, it has a remarkable set of optical properties carved into it. Look here.' He held the skull up, opened the jaw and turned it in the artificial light to let them see inside it. 'Halfway back in the roof of the mouth here . . .' he indicated with his index finger '. . . there's a broad plane that acts like a forty-five degree prism, directing light from beneath the skull into the eyesockets. This means, for instance, that if the skull were placed in front of some kind of fire or light – say, an altar with a light concealed behind it – that light would be visible through the eyesockets as if it was actually inside them. This means, in turn, that a fire projected through the eyesockets in that way would create an extraordinary flickering light-show that would impress the unknowing.'

'Amazing!' Tom exclaimed softly.

Molly threw him a sardonic glance, but turned her attention back on Professor Juarez as the latter continued: 'Also, placed next to that prismatic plane, there's a ribbon-thin surface that acts like a magnifying glass. Finally, behind the prism, which to all intents and purposes that plane is, there are convex and concave surfaces that gather more light and direct it out through the eyesockets. More ingeniously, the back of the skull also acts as a kind of camera lens, gathering light from behind itself and projecting it through the eyesockets.'

'Extraordinary!' Tom exclaimed.

'Weird,' Molly said flatly.

'I haven't finished yet,' Professor Juarez told them. 'Another unusual aspect is the zygomatic arches carved next to the cheek bones.'

'The *what*?' Molly asked.

The professor smiled at her again. 'Zygomatic arches. Arches formed by the joining of the malar bone and the temporal bone of the skull.'

'Oh, right. Keep goin', Professor.'

'The zygomatic arches carved next to the cheek-bones have had a narrow space of crystal material removed from them to enable light from behind or underneath to flow through and into the eyes again. Even more ingenious effects are then produced when a light source behind the skull is moved about or flickered on and off.'

'What kind of effects?' Tom asked.

'All kinds of vague or ghostly images. Here, let me show you.'

The professor dimmed the lights in the room, plunging it into semi-darkness, then he turned on a small, brilliant light that was concealed behind the upright skull. His first adjustment of this light made dazzling striations pour out of the large, empty eye sockets. When the hidden light was moved again, the striations pouring out of the eyes flashed up and down the walls, floor and ceiling, then criss-crossed each other and, being refracted off the different planes and lenses inside the skull, formed startling, shadowy images that changed constantly as he kept changing the position of the light behind. Those shadowy shapes merged with faint colours to produce even more startling effects and shapes, with the latter looking in turn like the silhouettes of misshapen humans and bizarre animals, shadowy whirlpools, pools of silvery light, stars within patches of pitch darkness, and even enormous, glistening spiders' webs formed by the play of light and darkness.

It was a bizarre, disorientating *son et lumière* spectacle that almost mesmerized Tom. In fact, he was starting to feel faint and dizzy when the professor turned the hidden light off and switched the room lights back on. Tom heaved a sigh of relief.

'Jesus, that was weird,' Molly said.

'Quite remarkable,' Tom said.

'Even more remarkable,' the professor said, 'is that there are two holes here—' he picked the skull off the table and turned it left and right to show them the barely perceptible holes, one at each side of the base '—both invisible when the skull is stood upright. However, if you insert two thin rods into the holes – rods so thin they would not be seen in semi-gloom or darkness – they support it at a perfect balance point that enables it to be rocked to and fro. So! Observe!'

He inserted two thin steel rods into the holes, dimmed the lights in the room again, then lifted the skull slightly off the table and tapped it gently to make it rock to and fro, thus throwing more fantastic light images onto the walls, ceiling and floor.

'This, as you can see,' he continued, 'produces even more frightening effects.'

The extraordinary combination of light-and-shadow effects did indeed produce even more lifelike moving images that grew and shrank dramatically as well as taking on many different shapes and oddly glowing colours.

When he was satisfied that they had seen enough, the professor turned the room lights back on and switched off the light hidden behind the skull.

'It's like having a bad dream,' Molly said.

'That was probably the intention,' Tom said. 'Can you imagine those effects working on the imagination of primitive, deeply religious Mayans who believed everything their priests told them? Certainly, they would have been very impressed.'

'And probably scared shitless,' Molly said.

The professor glanced at her, startled at her obscenity, then he quickly turned his gaze upon the embarrassed Tom.

'Finally,' the professor said, holding the skull close to them and vigorously working the jawbone and the skull itself, 'the jawbone fits perfectly into two polished sockets, which means that the top of the skull can be moved up and down on the jaw, and vice versa. By turning on that light behind them – or, in the case of an ancient temple, some kind of fire or concentrated flame – the effects you've just seen would emanate from the jaw as well as the eyesockets. And if the priests decided to produce vocal effects, the skull would appear to be speaking in a rather hollow, ethereal manner.'

'Oh, boy!' Molly exclaimed.

They were silent for a moment, watching the professor as he carefully placed the skull on the table and turned back to face them. He smiled but said nothing.

'So who do you think made it?' Tom asked him to break the lengthy silence.

'It's my belief,' the professor said, 'that this particular skull is, indeed, the long-missing Rose Quartz Skull, one of the two which were rumoured to have been carried by an ancient and mysterious race, before the Mayans or Aztecs, in a legendary migration across the earth, from the west to the east, at least 3,500 years ago.'

'What race?' Tom asked.

'Well,' the professor said tentatively, 'we only know that a chain of mysterious remains of ancient civilizations stretches between southern Asia, across various Polynesian islands and Easter Island, all the way to Meso-America – the name given to the ancient American cultural region that extended from Chichén Itzá in northern Yucatán to the southernmost outposts of the Inca civilization in what is now Chile.'

Obviously pleased to be talking about this, he turned away from them, picked up a wooden pointer, and tapped it against the large map of the world spread across the wall directly in front of them, indicating certain places as he talked.

'It's not known if that ancient civilization followed the trade winds from east to west, or whether the ancient cradle of humanity, Asia, sent emissaries of its culture with the seafaring Polynesians as far as Easter Island and still further eastward.' He tapped the location with his pointer. 'However, it *is* believed that the fabulous forbidden city of Angkor, now in Cambodia, in the Khmer Republic, here—' he tapped the location with his pointer '—would probably have been the first stop on the eastward journey. The once-sacred lagoon city of Ponape, in the Polynesian Islands, here, would have been a halfway house. On barren Easter Island, here, the ancient travellers certainly left their fabulous monuments, in the shape of the giant sculptures still there today. The next stops, therefore, would have been Yucatán and British Honduras – here and here

– which suggests that the mysterious travellers had to be pre-Mayan.'

'What about the other crystal skull?' Tom asked. 'The one in the Museum of Mankind, London.'

'Since that other crystal skull was originally found in British Honduras, and since it's been assessed as approximately 3,500 years old, it almost certainly belonged to that same mysterious race of early Mayans. And with this second skull being found on top of the Great Pyramid in Chichén Itzá, it seems likely that both skulls were left behind by that same ancient race as it moved on from the Yucatán peninsula to Peru, where it finally came to rest, creating the holy city of Tiahuanaco.'

'Do we have a means of proving that?' Tom asked.

'Yes, by showing this skull to my British counterpart and friend, Professor Julian Weatherby, presently working for the British Museum, London. Julian's the foremost authority on the crystal skulls and can tell you all you need to know about this particular one.'

'Well, I'm on my way home anyway,' Tom said, casting a nervous look at the suspicious Molly, 'but I doubt that we can get the skull out of the country without being stopped by the Mexican Customs.'

'Then let's make it official,' Professor Juarez said. 'To let this priceless artefact fall into the hands of Customs officials, Mexican or otherwise, would be tantamount to giving it away. May I suggest, therefore, that you let me send the skull with other artefacts from this museum to the British Museum in London, which is preparing an exhibition of rare Mayan treasures. Once in the possession of Professor Weatherby, the skull, accompanied by a personal letter from me, detailing your involvement, will be separated from the real exhibits and kept under his personal supervision until your arrival. Once you've met him and talked, learning all you need to know about the skull, you can then decide what you wish to do with it.'

'Excellent,' Tom said.

'How can we trust that Limey professor?' Molly asked.

Tom winced with embarrassment, but Professor Juarez merely smiled, obviously admiring a woman of spirit, and said, 'As Professor Weatherby would have problems in explaining how he came to be in possession of this particular skull, I think you can take it as read that he won't try to keep it. Apart from that, he's an honest man and dedicated academic, devoted to his work. He does not steal ancient artefacts of any kind, so your skull will be safe with him.'

'Okay, I'll buy that,' Molly said. Then, bold as brass, she turned to Tom and said, 'But if you go to London, I go, too, and you'll have to pay. Otherwise, this skull goes with me to New York.'

'I won't be able to get it into New York,' Professor Juarez said, either telling the truth or slyly taking Tom's side.

'*I*'ll get it in,' Molly said. 'At least, I'll damned well try – I'll run the risk of being caught – rather than let him' (nodding at the embarrassed Tom) 'go to London without me and maybe set up some deal between himself and your Limey professor friend. I mean, money talks, right?'

'Well, *really*!' Tom exploded. 'The very idea that I would stoop to—'

'I go to London with you,' Molly interjected bluntly, 'or the crystal skull comes to New York with me.'

'Oh, all right,' Tom snapped.

'Great,' Molly said.

'So you want me to ship the skull to London?' Professor Juarez asked.

'Yes,' Tom said.

'Yes,' Molly said.

They glared at one another, then Tom turned away and wrote down the details of Professor Julian Weatherby as dictated to him by Professor Juarez. He then thanked his old friend, shook his hand and embraced him. Finally, gratefully, still burning up with embarrassment and leaving the crystal skull on the table, he led Molly out of the office and then out of the museum.

Though no longer in possession of the crystal skull, they still had each other.

'God help me,' Tom said.

CHAPTER THIRTEEN

'*What's* that?' Molly said as they left the museum and again tried in vain, while coughing and wiping eyes that were watering from the city's polluted atmosphere, to wave down a taxi.

'Nothing,' Tom said. 'I was just thinking aloud.'

'You said "God help me", right?'

'Well, yes, but I just meant . . .'

'Thinkin' about bein' stuck with me, right?'

'Well, not really. I . . .'

'Why're you stuttering?'

'I'm not stuttering! I'm merely feeling a little . . .'

Hitching her almost empty bag onto her shoulder, Molly turned to face him on the sidewalk. 'Listen, you little prick, let's get a couple of things straight *right now*.'

'By all means,' Tom replied, desperately looking up and down the road for an empty taxi and feeling mortified by Molly's fresh outburst. He hated scenes and Molly sure knew how to create them, so now he was burning with embarrassment, as well as suffering from the pollution – parched lungs, dry throat and watery eyes – and wanted to disappear in a puff of smoke.

'First,' Molly said, raising her index finger and burning holes in him with her bright gaze, 'you can stop bein' so superior just 'cause I'm a woman and younger than you and not too well educated. *I'm* the one who had the presence of mind to grab that crystal skull at Chichén Itzá when all *you* could think of doin' was gettin' the hell out of there. I'm also the one who protected us from that one-eyed bandit when all *you* could do was fall to the goddamned floor and bury your head in the fuckin' sand. Second,' she continued, raising another finger, 'I have more right to that crystal skull than you and that entitles me to speak my own piece about what we should do with it. Third,' she went on, raising a third finger, 'the only reason you're havin' to pay for my expenses regarding hotels and our flight to London is that *you've* decided we're going to London instead of New York and I don't have the bread for that kind of trip. Fourth,' she climaxed, raising a fourth finger, 'I may not be as educated as you, but that doesn't mean I'm not intelligent and can't think for myself, so you can stop all this English condescension crap and talk to me like we're equals, at least when it comes to decisions about the crystal skull – which is what we should be doin' right now. Agreed?'

'Agreed,' Tom said. 'Oh, look, there's a taxi!' Amazed to actually find an unoccupied taxi in Mexico City and relieved to see it pulling in towards him, he continued, 'You're absolutely right, Molly. I take all of that on board. I didn't mean to be condescending – I was just overly anxious and said the wrong thing – but I certainly feel that you're an equal in this matter and will be careful to treat you correctly in the future. I think we're in danger, Molly – *real* danger – and I'm concerned for the both of us. By all means, let's discuss this, but please *do* bear in mind that I have my own sensibilities and that your constant abuse, including many obscenities, pains me deeply and has possibly caused what you think is my condescension. It's not that, really. I'm just trying to defend myself. And I'm very easily embarrassed by scenes and don't know how to deal with them. I'm not used to women who talk like you do and so I say all the wrong things. Can we forgive and forget?'

Molly stared at him, half touched, half amused, then, grinning slightly, said, with a shrug, 'Well, okay, then.'

Like a gift from God, the taxi pulled in and they both clambered into the rear. After giving the driver the name of their hotel, Tom settled back in his seat and was instantly aroused by the closeness of Molly beside him: her long legs outlined in the tight denims, one crossed over the other; and the heat of her body, either real or imagined, permeating his left arm and thigh. He distracted himself by gazing out the window, beyond the dense, chaotic stream of cars, streetcars, trolleybuses, motorcyles and *peseros*, at the city's extraordinary architectural mixture of old churches, Aztec ruins and modern buildings of steel and glass. It was hot in the back of the taxi and he felt himself sweating.

'So,' Molly said eventually, breaking the uncomfortable silence, 'why do you think we're in danger?'

'Well, that's obvious, isn't it?' Tom replied. 'It's perfectly clear that we're being pursued by that one-eyed bandit – and that man had a pistol.'

'That was back in Mérida,' Molly said, 'and I don't think he'll have followed us all this way. He was probably just some local hoodlum who happened to see us examining the crystal skull in that bar and decided to steal it. He didn't look to me like he was exactly rolling in bread, so I doubt that he'll have followed us all this way, even if he knew where we were staying, which is highly unlikely.'

'I trust you're right, Molly, but he could have been *hired* by someone, in which case he's professional and could still be pursuing us. So that's one of the dangers.'

'And the other?'

'The crystal skull itself. If, as Professor Juarez suspects, we're in possession of the Rose Quartz Skull, we could be in personal danger from its legendary magical powers.'

'*What?*' Molly glanced sideways at him, a sardonic grin on her face.

'The two genuine skulls,' Tom explained, 'including the one we possess, are believed to have remarkable parapsychological powers that can be used for good or evil. Those powers include the ability to mesmerize, to will illness or death, to look into the future, and to create all kinds of magical phenomena – spirit beings or the manifestation of creatures from the subconscious. I know it sounds crazy, but there are countless recorded examples of people going mad and committing murder or suicide after coming into possession of one of the two genuine skulls. Many examples, Molly. Many! And while I'm not saying that the skull *definitely* has those properties, I *am* saying that we should be particularly careful when dealing with it or handling it.'

'Those stories are probably all bullshit,' Molly said, swearing again but this time not offensively. 'I mean, you saw what the professor did back there with the skull – all those incredible images he created just by playing with that light he placed behind it – and the stories you've heard probably came from people seeing similar effects. As your friend the professor said, the effects produced by the skull were probably used by the priests of ancient times to scare the shit out of their subjects; but they *were* effects, no more and no less, and the stories that came down through history doubtless came from the primitives who witnessed those light effects and didn't know they were being conned by the priests. That skull isn't magical or dangerous – it's just incredibly valuable as an artefact – and that's exactly why we'll make a lot of bread once we've proved that it's genuine.'

The taxi had just entered the Zocalo and Tom glanced out at the immense square dominated by the Cathedral and the National Palace. The shops beneath the arches were packed with tourists, shoeshine boys were vigorously polishing the black shoes of men seated at the outdoor bars and cafés, and people were cramming onto the trolleybuses, holding on for dear life. The sun was going down, though the light was still bright, and it created ever-changing, shifting shadows across the great plaza.

'Well,' Tom said, speaking with particular care as his loving gaze took in the Cathedral's baroque mixture of architectural styles and reminded him of the glories of history, 'that *is* the question, Molly. Do we think of the skull in purely mercenary terms or do we consider its immense historical value?'

Molly threw him a glance of dark suspicion. '*What?*'

'I merely meant . . .'

'You want to give it to some fuckin' museum or art gallery? Is that what you mean?'

'Well, it *did* occur to me that . . .'

'Oh, fuckin' great!' Molly exploded. 'You're an English aristocrat and you've no money worries, so you're gonna ask *me* to give up the only chance I've ever had in my life to make some genuine dough. Well, fuck you, I won't do it! If that thing's genuine, if it's worth a lot of bread, I'm goin' to get somethin' out of it.'

'Well, of course,' Tom responded, backing off instantly, not relishing another tirade, 'I appreciate your concern and was merely suggesting that . . .'

'Forget it, Tom,' she said, using his Christian name for the first time. 'Just *forget* it! If that skull's worth money, then I'm gonna make some and that's all there is to it. We can *sell* it to a museum, for Chrissakes! I mean, those museums have bread to burn. So don't even consider askin' me to give it away. I won't. And that's it, man.'

'Yes, Molly, of course. I understand your concern. If it's worth something—'

'It is!'

'—then I'll certainly ensure that you'll get it. I only ask that you let me find a good home for the skull, rather than sell it to just anyone.'

'A good home for it is the one that gives us bread. You find that and I'll sell the skull.'

'Understood, Molly. Naturally.'

Fingering the collar of his sweaty shirt, Tom was very relieved when the taxi pulled up outside their hotel. After paying the driver and giving him a lavish tip to avoid another argument, this time with the driver, who, being Mexican, was almost certainly volatile, he started towards the front door of the building. Then, drawn by some instinct he could scarcely comprehend, he looked across the car park, at his expensively rented jeep, and saw that it had been vandalized: all the tyres punctured and the windscreen smashed, with shards of glass glinting on the hood in the early evening's still pale light.

'Oh, God!' he exclaimed forlornly.

'What?' Molly asked.

Tom pointed at the car. 'It's been vandalized,' he said.

'Oh, the shits!' Molly exploded.

They both hurried across the car park to examine the vehicle and confirm that it had indeed been thoroughly trashed by some person or persons using blunt instruments that had done in the windscreen, smashed the headlights, battered all the doors and, as they'd previously observed, punctured all the tyres.

'Why the fuck would they do that?' Molly asked, glancing at all the other, untouched vehicles. 'I mean, they only attacked *our* fuckin' car. They touched none of the others.'

'Because they're not ordinary vandals,' Tom said, unable to stop the sliver of fear that slithered icily through him. 'Why pick this one car out? It's a jeep and it's open and there's nothing in it to steal. It was picked because it's *our* car and that means the person or persons who did it *knew* it was ours. This jeep's a mess – we can't possibly drive it – and that must be what they wanted. We're still being followed.'

They stared at one another, locked together in fearful silence, and then, for the very first time, even Molly expressed her fear.

'Shit,' she said, 'this is serious.'

'I think I need a drink,' Tom responded.

'So do I,' Molly said.

They hurried into the hotel and went straight to the bar. Tom ordered two whiskies and Molly didn't argue. When they had received the drinks, they sat at a table near the windows and stared out into the descending evening where a blood-red sun was casting its crimson glow on the car park and on their vandalized jeep. They both sipped at their drinks.

'Maybe we're just imagining it,' Molly said when she had taken the first sip of her whisky. 'It could have been vandals and they could have just picked our jeep by accident. You know? A bunch of fuckin' psyched-up kids wanderin' in an' hittin' the first vehicle they happen to see.'

'My jeep would not have been the first vehicle they saw; it's practically in the middle of the car park. They can't have picked it by accident.'

'Well, maybe . . .'

'There's no *maybe* about it. That jeep was smashed to make it unusable and it was clearly picked out specifically. We're being *followed*, Molly.'

'Yeah, right, well . . .' Her voice trailed off as her bloodshot eyes widened, staring at the bar across the large room. Following her gaze, Tom saw that familiar one-eyed unshaven face turned in his direction. The one-eyed Mexican was with some barrel-chested companions, all wearing worn denims and shirts, all grinning like hyenas as one ordered drinks from the barman and the others turned to leer at Tom and Molly.

'Oh, my God!' Tom whispered.

'Fuck 'em,' Molly said, reaching up to tug automatically at the strap of her shoulder bag. 'I've got my fuckin' pistol in here and I'm gonna challenge those bastids.'

'No, you're not!' Tom almost shrieked.

'We can't let 'em scare us,' Molly said, starting to rise out of her chair and swinging the shoulder bag around to get at it. 'I'm gonna brace 'em and if they make one false move, I'll waste the whole fuckin' bunch.'

'No!' Tom exclaimed.

'Yes!' Molly insisted. 'Either I do it or you do it, but one of us has got to face 'em down, so let's get the ball rolling.'

'No!'

'Yes!'

'That one-eyed man has a gun!'

'*I've* got a gun,' Molly reminded him, 'an' I know how to use it.'

'You can't!'

'I can!'

'I refuse to let you do this!'

'Then *you* do it,' Molly said, staring challengingly at him. 'Let 'em know you're not scared of 'em and threaten to call the police if they give trouble.'

'What good will *that* do?' Tom asked.

'Scared, are you?'

'Yes.'

'Then fuck you; I'm going to challenge those bastids.'

But when Molly started to stand upright, Tom leaned across the table and jerked her back down.

'All right, Molly, *I'll* do it!'

'Good. So get to it.'

Unable to ignore her challenge, Tom actually managed to stand upright in preparation for his march across the room. Just as he did so, however, the one-eyed man hooked a finger into his own eye-socket and popped out his glass eye, which landed, like a coloured marble, in the upturned palm of his hand. As Tom turned pale and almost dizzy with disbelief, the one-eyed man placed the glass eyeball on the table in front of him, then made it spin like a top. When it stopped spinning, its gleaming glass pupil was staring directly at Tom.

Shattered, he grabbed Molly and ushered her out of the bar while the hoodlums hooted with contemptuous mirth behind them.

'Jesus Christ!' Molly exclaimed as they hurried across the lobby, 'I don't fuckin' believe this.'

'I do,' Tom said.

'So what do we do now?'

'We go to our rooms and lock ourselves in,' Tom said, feeling positive for the first time in a long time, 'and then I'll book us on the first flight to London.'

'Right,' Molly said. 'Okay.'

Nervously hurrying upstairs, they went to the doors of their adjoining rooms.

'Make sure you lock the door,' Tom said. 'I'll call you as soon as I've booked the flight. In the meantime, stay in there.'

'Right,' Molly said.

Tom opened his door, stepped inside, and then closed and locked the door behind him.

'Dear God,' he whispered, glancing about him.

His room had been ransacked. The contents of his travelling bag had been upturned on the floor, the bed-clothes were scattered all around the bed, the mattress had been slashed to ribbons, and every drawer in the chest of drawers had been pulled out and also thrown on the floor with its contents distributed wildly around the room. Tom thought of that bunch of men down in the bar and his stomach turned over.

Someone knocked on his door.

Almost jumping out of his skin, he turned back to the door and whispered, 'Yes? Who is it?'

'It's me! Molly! Let me in!'

Tom let her in. She entered quickly, brushing past him, carrying her rucksack, still packed, in one hand. Tom closed the door and turned around to face her. She was staring, wide-eyed, at the devastation of his room.

'You, too!' she exclaimed.

'They ransacked your room as well?'

'Yeah, right.' She stared directly at him. 'We've gotta get out of here right now. You understand? *Right now!*'

'I agree,' Tom said.

Decisive as he had never been before, he picked up the telephone and rang the Aeropuerto Internacional to book the first flight out. He was offered the first flight out the following morning and gladly accepted. Putting the phone down, he turned to Molly and said, 'We leave at eight in the morning, but I think we should leave here right now and spend the night at the airport.'

'Fuckin' A,' Molly said. 'Except that your jeep's all clapped out. You'll have to call 'em and get 'em to bring another car around.'

'Good Lord,' Tom said, recalling the condition of the jeep and terrified at the thought of telling the rental company. 'I can't possibly do that. I mean, I can't let them see what's happened to their vehicle.'

'Why not? It's rented. That means those bastids are insured. Just ring up and tell 'em you've been vandalized an' need another car to get you to the airport.'

'They certainly wouldn't agree to that, Molly dear. In fact, they're going to be extremely incensed when they see the state that jeep's in.'

'Fuck 'em,' Molly said. 'What's their number?'

Tom gave her the number of the car rental company

and started picking up his strewn clothes as she went to town on the unfortunate on the other end of the line. Tom was impressed. Molly put on a great show of hysterics, wailing that the car had been vandalized and demanding to know what kind of town this was where any hooligan could walk into a hotel car park and do in a car rented to a tourist. She demanded compensation, threatened them with action from the American Embassy, warned them about possible repercussions from her lawyers and then slammed the phone down and grinned broadly.

'They'll be here in fifteen minutes with another car and that one's on the house. Come on, let's get out of here.'

Having finished his packing, Tom picked up his travelling bag and followed her out of the room, then back down the stairs. After glancing around the brightly-lit lobby and ascertaining that the one-eyed bandit and his leering companions were not present, he went to the reception desk and paid his bill. Then he and Molly went outside to wait for the new rented car, which arrived twenty-five minutes later. It was a battered old Volkswagen Beetle. Tom took the driving seat, Molly sat beside him, they belted up and then Tom took off, driving more recklessly than he had ever done before and feeling clammy with fear.

The sun had gone down and the town was lamplit, but the traffic in the city centre was still dense and chaotic, with mad kamikaze motorcyclists weaving recklessly between cars, taxis, streetcars, trolleybuses and the ubiquitous *peseros*. Though normally a nervous driver, Tom hardly noticed the noisy chaos around him and weaved his way through it with surprising skill in order to get away as soon as possible.

The long road out of the city centre took him past magnificent mansions built into landscapes of lava, rock and windblown foliage, backed up by the *ciudades perdidas*, where the poorest of the poor lived in their thousands of cardboard and sheet-metal huts. Soon, however, he found himself on the long straight highway that led to the airport, under a moonlit, star-filled sky, with the wind beating noisily against the car. The traffic here was less dense than in the centre of the city, but it was still surprisingly plentiful and dangerous.

'I've never seen you drive so well,' Molly said.

'Fear's a wonderful incentive,' Tom replied. 'And right now I feel fearful.'

'Why? We're well out of it.'

'I don't know. I just feel that we're not. It's probably my over-active imagination, but that's how I feel.'

'You're a real cute one, Tom.'

It was pleasantly reassuring to hear her using his name at last, but the feeling of clammy fear remained. As he drove along the highway, listening to the wind beating fiercely against the car, dazzled by the lights of the other vehicles racing up behind him to shoot carelessly around him, he was convinced that he was still being followed . . . by someone, or . . . *something*.

Certain that this was so, he repeatedly looked in the rear-view mirror, then up at the sky, and found himself wondering, in particular, why he was studying the latter. He lowered his gaze from the sky, concentrating on the road ahead, the rear lights of the other vehicles, then he glanced again in the rear-view mirror and saw the headlights of a car, a battered Mercedes Benz, that was travelling too fast even for this road – and it was catching up with him.

'It's them again!' he whispered, sounding strangled.

Even as he realized beyond doubt that he was being followed, the Mercedes caught up with him, its main beams on to dazzle him, and then bumped into the back of his Volkswagen, once, twice, a third time, making it jolt and almost go into a swerve.

'What the hell . . . ?' Molly exclaimed, glancing over her shoulder but forced to squint into the main beams of the Mercedes that was repeatedly bumping them from behind. 'Goddammit . . .'

Though already driving more quickly than he had ever done before, Tom accelerated to get away from the Mercedes, but it repeatedly caught up with him and bumped him again, making the Volkswagen jolt dangerously. Pulling on the steering wheel, Tom swept into the other lane and the Mercedes then raced up beside him and kept pace with him.

Glancing sideways, Tom saw the one-eyed man staring at him. His three hoodlum friends were in the car with him, all grinning wolfishly.

'It's him again!' Tom shouted. Then he saw the side window of the other car being rolled down and the barrel of a pistol aiming at him. 'They're going to shoot us!' he bawled.

He pressed his foot down hard and let the Volkswagen surge forward, leaving the other car behind temporarily. It accelerated immediately, racing forward to catch up, and Tom quickly pulled back out to the other lane, almost hitting the car ahead and causing a lot of drivers to hoot their horns.

Before he knew it, Tom found himself weaving desperately in and out of the fast stream of traffic, swerving and wobbling on screeching tyres, causing more horns to honk and other drivers to start doing the same. This did not deter the one-eyed man, who drove with reckless abandon, still trying to catch up and let his gunman get off a shot. When that first shot was fired, ringing out loud and clear above the bedlam of the swerving, now frantically honking cars nearby, Tom put his foot down to the floor and went barrelling onto the first slip road leading off the highway.

'Jesus Christ!' Molly wailed.

The car driven by the one-eyed man came barrelling down after them.

Tom kept going and found himself on a dark road that ran up into the hills of the shanty towns known as *vecindades*. The road soon turned into a potholed track that made the Volkswagen rock and roll, screaming and rattling dementedly. Another gunshot rang out and Tom glanced in his windscreen and saw that the car behind was catching up with him. He kept driving, wrestling with the steering wheel, desperately trying to avoid the potholes and ditches, the car being constantly whipped and scratched by the branches of Montezuma cypress trees, and then he came over the brow of a hill and found himself racing through a *vecindade*, past shacks with tin roofs and cardboard walls and dirt gardens, scattering the adults and children who had been squatting in the road, the car's wheels running through campfires and sending flaming debris flying, and then he plunged back into the moonlit darkness of another quiet road. He could see lights in the hills around him – the fires of other *vecindades* – and the streams of light of the vehicles on the highway, now far below him.

Suddenly the narrow track broadened and the Mercedes raced up beside them to strike them broad-side, trying to force them off the road. Tom clung grimly to the steering wheel and managed a quick glance sideways. He saw that glassy single eye staring at him and the barrel of a pistol aiming at him from a lowered back window of the Mercedes. That vehicle struck his Volkswagen again, making it lurch dangerously towards the edge of a ditch, and the pistol, mere feet away, roared sharply, followed by the high, keening sound of the bullet as it ricocheted off the Volkswagen's wing mirror and went whistling away into the dark night.

'Fuck 'em!' Molly wailed, then she whipped her pistol out of her rucksack and twisted sideways to take aim and fire a shot from behind Tom's head.

'Oh, God!' Tom cried out as the noise of Molly's shot reverberated through his head and the rear window of the other vehicle exploded in a glittering shower of spraying glass. Molly fired twice more and her bullets ricocheted noisily off the hood of the Mercedes, but then it suddenly raced on ahead to pull in in front of them. It started to slow down, braking steadily, forcing Tom to do likewise.

'They're gonna stop us!' Molly screamed.

At that moment, however, an eerie circular light appeared low above the road just ahead of the Mercedes, a mere pinprick at first, then rapidly expanding – as if flying out of the distance at a tremendous pace and growing bigger as it approached – and then suddenly it was an immense glowing circular shape, a ghostly, slightly transparent flying saucer, about thirty feet wide, that dropped vertically just ahead of the Mercedes and hovered there right in front of it.

Either blinded by the dazzling light, shocked by what he was seeing, or simply trying to avert a crash with that eerie object, the one-eyed man swerved violently and the Mercedes went off the road, crashed down into a ditch, flipped over, bounced a few times and then burst into flames.

Tom's car was racing towards that hovering, eerily glowing object and he thought he was doomed.

His car crashed into the object – or so it seemed to Tom – and he was dazzled by star-filled light and lost all sense of direction. But the Volkswagen kept going, as if travelling through the cosmos – a brief glimpse of distant worlds and double moons and pulsating suns – and then emerged to the darkness at the other side and raced on down the road.

When a disbelieving Tom and Molly glanced back over their shoulders, they saw the great glowing circular object shooting vertically skywards, shrinking rapidly as it ascended and soon becoming no more than another star in the vast, star-filled sky. Then it simply blinked out.

Hardly believing what he had seen, too speechless to speak, as was Molly, but now fully aware that they were both involved in a dangerous, possibly supernatural game, Tom glanced once more over his shoulder at the blazing car far behind, and then turned to the front, slowed his car down, and made his way back to the highway, this time driving with care. When the lights of the Aeropuerto International came into view, he heaved a sigh of relief.

The next morning, he and an equally shaken Molly were flown on to London.

CHAPTER FOURTEEN

Tom and Molly did not speak much on the flight to London, being too overcome with disbelief about what had happened on the road to the Aeropuerto Internacional in Mexico City and also trying to recover from the toxic fumes of that great but hopelessly polluted metropolis. Exhausted physically and mentally, they both slept throughout most of the flight, only being awakened by the enforced conviviality of modern air travel with its movies and duty-free goods and endless supply of meals that could not be refused.

More than once, just as they were both nodding off again, Molly would drift back to consciousness to find that her head was resting on Tom's shoulder, that she felt comforted by this fact, and that his snoring, his boyish face in the repose of sleep, made her feel soft and warm. He was a little English snob, born with a silver spoon in his mouth, but there was also something touching about him and he secretly touched her. She was surprised by this feeling, though it was undeniable and growing steadily, yet her own background, that hell of rejection and poverty in New York, made her mistrust it. Nevertheless, as she drifted off to sleep again, she kept her head on his shoulder. She had sweet dreams about him.

They both felt a lot better when they arrived at Heathrow Airport, rejuvenated by air only marginally less polluted, and as they were driven to London in a taxi paid for by the grumbling Tom, along a busy road lined with suburban houses, their throats cleared, their eyes dry, they fell into obsessive conversation about what had occurred.

'All I know,' Tom said, 'and I'll understand if you don't believe me, is that when driving us to the airport in Mexico City I was haunted by the undeniable feeling that I was being followed by someone or . . . *something*. Yes, someone or some *thing*. And, in the event, this turned out to be true. That someone was the one-eyed man and the *something* was that saucer-shaped light that came out of nowhere to make that Mercedes crash.'

'That thing looked like a flying saucer,' Molly said, recalling it vividly and immediately filling up with the kind of fear she had not known since childhood, 'but I don't think it was physical. I mean, it was like something I saw before, when I looked into the crystal skull. Remember? When I was hypnotized by it? That flying saucer was more like some kind of light and I noticed that it had stars and things inside it – big moons and stuff – like a scene from outer space. So I think it was some kind of . . . *substance* . . . maybe a spirit manifestation or somethin'. Anyway, that's what I think.'

'Correct,' Tom said. 'I agree entirely. I thought we were going to crash into it, but the car just passed right through it and, as it did so, I too saw what you saw: stars and great moons. A distant galaxy, maybe, or a parallel universe.'

'Shit,' Molly said. 'Jesus.'

'And, whatever it was,' Tom continued excitedly, 'it certainly made that Mercedes go off the road and then, when we drove right through it, it ascended and disappeared in the heavens. I still can't believe it.'

'Believe it,' Molly said, again vividly recalling that great saucer-shaped, oddly pulsating incorporeal light with stars visible inside it, racing at them out of the darkness, then hovering above the road, then ascending vertically back to the heavens. It awed and scared her to think of it. 'That light, that flying saucer thing, came down outta the sky and went straight back up into the sky once it had rescued us.'

'Rescued us? You think that's what it did?'

'Yeah, right. No doubt about it. It rescued us and then it took off again.'

To distract herself from the fear and awe, to bring herself back down to earth, she glanced out of the window of the taxi and saw that the nice suburban houses with leafy lawns had given way to increasing traffic and visibly polluted air – exhaust smoke from leaded petrol; more black smoke from industrial chimneys – on a road that ran between prefabricated factories, warehouses of steel and concrete, rows of crumbling council houses with clothes flapping in back yards, garages and supermarkets on pavements strewn with rubbish, and stores with plate-glass windows that reflected the snarling traffic that had slowed to a snail's place. Molly had been enthralled for the first twenty minutes of the journey into London, seeing in those comfortable middle-class houses with their leafy trees and green lawns all that she had thought England would be. Now, however, the scenery had changed dramatically and she recognized more familiar territory: dense traffic, polluted air and constant noise. It was just like New York.

'Jesus,' she said, 'I'm back home again!'

'Not quite,' Tom said. 'Anyway, what I'm trying to say is that if that saucer-shaped . . . *manifestation* . . . truly came down to rescue us from those villains, then I'm convinced it was a manifestation created by the crystal skull, which means that we're under its influence for good or for evil – and, frankly, that scares me.'

Molly didn't want to believe any of this – she was a practical-minded, street-wise lady – but when she recalled how the crystal skull had affected her when she looked into it, she, too, felt scared. She had been mesmerized by it, drawn into its darkly gleaming depths, and then found herself surrounded by unfamiliar stars and multiple moons, in a vast, teeming cosmos. It had been like a dream, a silent journey through time and space, and she had come out of it feeling distinctly strange, as if divorced from herself. Since then, she had relived that experience several times in dreams and she felt haunted by it. So maybe Tom was right – just maybe – and this thought was disturbing.

'Well, it scares me, too,' she confessed, 'but we may be imagining it. I mean, that manifestation *could* have been some natural, if unusual phenomenon – note the big words I'm using – of the kind you read about in UFO stories. You know? They're perfectly sane folk and they think that they've been harassed by a UFO, or flying saucer, and it turns out to be Venus or ball lightning or some other optical illusion caused by the atmosphere. That's what it *could* have been in our case – I mean, we *did* drive right *through* it – and the driver of that Mercedes, the one-eyed guy, just panicked and swerved to avoid it. That seems more likely to me.'

'Mmmm.' Tom pursed his lips, deep in thought. She thought he looked really cute and attractive in his sensitive English way. 'Perhaps. On the other hand, that one-eyed man and his friends were after the crystal skull – they assumed we still had it in our possession – and I think that may have something to do with it. Bear in mind, also, that those men on the platform of the Great Pyramid in Chichén Itzá were burnt to death in an unnatural manner – since nothing *around* them or *near* them was burnt – and that obviously happened when they unearthed the crystal skull. They were trying to steal it, Molly, and they were killed by an unnatural phenomenon to prevent them from doing so. From that we can but assume that some mysterious force was released by the crystal skull when it was unearthed – and whatever it was, it killed those men in the Shrine.'

'So how come it didn't kill us? I mean, *we* stole the crystal skull when we found it and we're not dead yet. Not only that, but we are, according to you, being protected by that very same force. That doesn't make sense, Tom.'

She liked speaking his name. It made her feel a lot closer to him and that surprised her as well.

Tom sighed and glanced out the window. The taxi had now entered London proper and was passing an area that looked, to Molly's urban eye, to be seedily sophisticated with the houses, formerly grand, now decaying. However, they soon gave way to a busy high street, shops filled with fashionable clothes, then a sidestreet lined with restaurants and more shops, then another busy main road. The traffic was crawling lethargically in smoky air, but few drivers were honking their horns. Clearly, the English were, like Tom, as polite as she had always been told they were.

'I don't know,' Tom confessed. 'It's a mystery to me.

All I can tell you is that the crystal skull is reputed to have unusual powers that can be used for good *or* evil. Perhaps, for some reason I simply can't fathom, it favours us over the men who were trying to steal it. So maybe we *do* have to give serious thought to what we should do with it. Indeed, maybe what we decide to do with it will decide our own fate. Please think about this.'

'You mean that if we sell it just for gain, its powers could turn against us?'

Tom nodded. 'Perhaps.'

'I think you're trying it on, pal.' Molly still felt the shadow of fear, but she had too much to lose here. She was fearful because she thought he might be right, but she couldn't be swayed by that. 'Listen,' she said. 'I've had enough hard times to last me a lifetime and I want no more. So if you're tryin' to con me into giving the skull away, believe me, you're gonna be disappointed.'

'I'm not saying that, Molly. I'm simply saying that we have to be very careful what we do with it. If we sell it, we have to make sure that it ends up in good hands. That's all I'm saying.'

'Well, we'll see,' Molly said. She glanced out the window of the taxi and saw that they were inching along a busy main drag packed with pedestrians and lined with elegant shops. As the taxi moved on, it passed the Ritz Hotel and Fortnum & Mason's. A uniformed doorman was standing outside the revolving doors of the latter and an old-fashioned horse and carriage was stationary by the sidewalk with another uniformed man in the driving seat, holding the reins. 'Wow,' Molly said, 'it's just like in the movies. Where are we now?'

'Piccadilly,' Tom replied, lost in thought.

'I thought that was a roundabout with a statue in the middle.'

'That's Piccadilly Circus,' Tom explained. 'This is Piccadilly.'

'Are we stayin' near here?'

'Yes, Molly. We'll be at the hotel in a couple of minutes.'

'Great,' Molly said, though she was wondering if she dared enter those shops in the rags she was wearing. She turned to glance at Tom, dishevelled and sleepy in his travelling clothes, and she felt a slight trembling within and a rush of warmth for him.

Godammit, she thought, *what's happening here? I must be losing my mind.*

The taxi turned left off Piccadilly and went up a narrow sidestreet filled with elegant Georgian buildings, black spiked railings around them, and lined with a lot of parking meters. A lot of the men on the sidewalks were wearing pinstripe suits and carrying briefcases and rolled umbrellas. The women all looked elegant.

'I'm gonna feel like a fish out of water here,' Molly said, 'in this crap I'm wearin'.'

'No, you won't,' Tom replied. 'The hotel you're staying in is nice but not that fancy and it's used by tourists who dress just like you. I *do* think, however, that you could do with some clothes more suitable to some of the places we'll be visiting, so I'm going to buy you some.'

'Ashamed of me, are ya?'

'No,' Tom said promptly. 'Those clothes are perfectly suitable for running around town, but you'll need more formal clothing for other occasions. Why feel like a fish out of water when you can feel perfectly comfortable?'

'Damned right. That's good thinkin'.'

She looked fondly at him, warming to his smile

and, yes, his consideration, as well as the fact that he had obviously been hurt by his broken marriage and was trying to mend himself as best he could while retaining his dignity. She could respect him for that. She also knew, from the way he looked at her, that he found her attractive but didn't quite know what to do about it. This, too, touched her secretly. In fact, given the men that she was used to, all the deadbeats she had known and suffered with, this nervous, rather formal English gentleman struck her as being special and unexpected.

'You know, you're not bad at all,' she told him as the taxi pulled into the kerb in front of a small, Georgian-fronted hotel. 'I don't really deserve you.'

'You're too kind,' Tom said.

He smiled nervously at her, then climbed out of the taxi and paid the driver as she slipped out after him.

'Where's this?' she asked him as the taxi driver was removing her rucksack from the boot of his vehicle.

'Mayfair,' Tom said.

'Swank territory,' Molly said, glancing up and down the street, taking in the elegant gentlemen and ladies wandering up and down under a leaden grey sky.

'Let's go in,' Tom said, carrying her rucksack for her and leading the way.

'Hey!' she called out to him, stopping on the first step and glancing back at the taxi, which was still parked by the kerbside with the driver reading a newspaper, clearly not going anywhere. She turned back to Tom. 'You've forgotten your travellin' bag.'

'I don't need it,' Tom said. 'Now let's get you signed in.'

Before she could say another word, he had turned

away and entered the hotel which did not, she noticed, have a doorman. Hurrying up the steps after him, she passed through revolving doors and entered a small reception area of darkly varnished wood and brass fittings. It was very English in an old-fashioned way, but seemed modest enough to prevent her from feeling out of place. Tom was already at the reception desk, her rucksack on the floor by his feet, and he was removing his credit card from his wallet while talking to the desk clerk. The latter was wearing a normal grey suit, with a white shirt and striped tie. He was pale-faced, black-haired, very formal and as thin as a rake.

'Hey,' Molly said again when Tom had finished his lengthy negotiations with the desk clerk and handed over his credit card. 'What do you mean, you don't need your travelling bag?'

Looking embarrassed, his eyes flitting from her to the desk clerk and back again, Tom replied: 'Well, I *did* say it was *your* hotel, Molly. I'm not staying here myself.'

'What?'

'I'm not staying here. I'm staying in my flat around the corner and it's too small for both of us.'

'Oh, really?' she said, burning up instantly.

'Yes, really.'

'You mean you don't want to share it with me.'

'I told you, it's too small.'

'Only one bedroom, has it?'

'Well, no, but . . .' Tom was blushing with embarrassment and distracted himself by signing the credit slip placed before him by the bland-faced but possibly intrigued desk clerk.

'So it has a spare bedroom.'

'Well, yes, but . . .' Tom finished signing the credit slip and slid it back to the desk clerk, who then pushed a registration from towards Molly.

'Could you please fill this in, Madam?'

'What?' Molly glared at the desk clerk, then at the form on the glossily varnished wooden counter.

'The registration form. We need your passport number and other details.'

'Yeah, right. Just a minute, bud.' She turned back to Tom, who was visibly wilting before her wrath. 'So it's got a spare bedroom,' she said loud and clear, making sure that the desk clerk could hear her, 'but you don't want me using it. Is that it?'

'Please, Molly, don't make a scene,' Tom said, squirming. 'It *does* have a spare bedroom, but the flat is rather small, fairly cramped, and so I thought—'

'Oh, it's too small, is it? Well, we shared a single room in Mérida and *that* wasn't too small!'

The desk clerk coughed discreetly into his clenched fist and Tom blushed again. 'Well, I just thought, Molly, that we could both do with a little privacy and my flat, though having a *tiny* spare room, is too small for us to feel really comfortable together in it.'

'Fuckin' bullshit!' Molly exclaimed.

The desk clerk, having already coughed into his clenched fist, now moved a little way along the counter, though not out of earshot.

'*Please*, Molly,' Tom said, 'this is really most embarrassing.'

'*Embarrassing*? Fuckin' embarrassing for *me*, I can tell ya! You lettin' that prick behind the counter know just what you think of me.'

'I think highly of you.'

'As long as I'm not in your fuckin' apartment. All

right! All right!' she added as Tom turned away to walk out. He turned back to her, his face burning with humiliation, and that made her feel bad. 'Let's forget it, Tom. Just tell me what we're doin' today and then I'll go to my room. What's the game plan?'

Relieved, though casting an embarrassed glance at the desk clerk, now studiously scanning some documentation on his desk though his ears were clearly flapping, Tom said: 'Well, I thought that perhaps we should both catch up on our sleep, have a decent lunch and then meet up again this evening for dinner.'

'Great,' Molly said. 'So what time's lunch?'

'Pardon?'

'Lunch. Are you deaf?' She was feeling angry again. 'What time are we meetin' for fuckin' lunch?'

Tom looked nervous again and glanced once more at the bland-faced, listening desk clerk. 'Well, actually,' he said, running his finger around the collar of his shirt as if he was strangling, 'that wasn't the plan at all. I thought we'd have lunch separately and then meet later for . . .'

'*What?* My first day in London and I have to have lunch alone? Christ, I've never been here in my fuckin' life, I don't know one street from the other, I don't have any fuckin' English money and—'

'You don't need money, Molly, and you don't need to know your way around. You can have your lunch in the restaurant of this hotel and just sign for it. Then I'll pick you up this evening and show you around.'

'Great. I eat alone in the restaurant. I sit there bein' gawped at by the fuckin' hoity-toity English, bein' treated as a freak because I'm stayin' all alone in this hotel and so I must be a whore. Thanks a million, pal!'

'I have to go now,' Tom said and turned towards the door, hoping to make his escape, though she soon jerked him back.

'So where are *you* havin' lunch?' she asked him. 'Are you cookin' for yourself in your nice apartment?'

'No.'

'So where are you havin' lunch?'

'Well, actually, I'm having it in my club.'

'What club?'

'A gentlemen's club, right here in Mayfair, just around the corner from my flat.'

'A *gentlemen*'s club?'

'That's correct.'

'So why can't I at least have lunch with you? Am I too common, or what?'

'It's not that, Molly.'

'So what is it?'

'My club, being a gentlemen's club, does not admit women as a matter of policy.'

'Christ!' Molly exclaimed, almost exploding. 'First I have to endure your snot-nosed English snobbery, now I'm suffering from your male chauvinism.' The desk clerk coughed again into his clenched fist, this time staring disapprovingly at both of them. Molly glared at him and then turned back to Tom. 'Well, go screw yourself!' she said loud and clear, making sure that the desk clerk could hear. 'I'll see you later this evening.'

'Right,' Tom said and turned away again to walk out. Molly tugged him back again.

'Do I at least get your phone number?' she asked. 'I mean, in case I get mugged, raped or murdered by some English psychopath.'

'Of course,' Tom said. 'Naturally.' Glancing despairingly at the disapproving desk clerk and blushing a bright red, he pulled out his wallet, withdrew his personal card and passed it shakily to Molly, who snatched it violently from his hand.

'Right!' she snapped. 'Have a good day!'

'I will,' Tom said.

He turned away and hurried out the door, back to his waiting taxi and travelling bag, actually making it this time.

Filled with fury, Molly turned back to the reception desk, scribbled her details onto the registration form, handed it to the bland-faced desk clerk and snapped, 'So, where's my goddamned door key?'

'Room 24, second floor,' the desk clerk said, handing her the door key.

'Enjoying yourself?' Molly asked him.

'Pardon?' the desk clerk said.

'Never mind.' Molly lifted her rucksack off the floor. 'You got a lift in this dump?'

The desk clerk nodded to the left-hand side of the lobby. 'The elevator is over there, Madam. Just press the button.'

'I think I can manage that much,' Molly said. 'Ya'all have a good day now.'

'Thank you, Madam. I'll try.'

Without another word, Molly turned away, took the lift to the second floor, and let herself into Room 24. It was a very nice room with a good-sized double bed, a dressing table of varnished oak, patterned curtains, a radio and a 21″ TV set, all surrounded by the framed prints of English landscapes that were hung on the walls. There was also a nice, recently renovated bathroom with a toilet and shower.

Still brimming over with anger and muttering dire threats against 'Mr Toffee-Nosed Tom Powell', she showered and slipped naked into bed, determined to have a good sleep. She was just getting cosy, dropping off, when the telephone rang.

Exasperated and perplexed, she picked up the phone beside the bed and gave the caller her name. There was a lingering silence, the sound of even breathing, then she heard Tom's soft voice.

'You know you really love me,' he said.

'Go to hell!' Molly snapped.

When Tom chuckled, she slammed the phone down and lay back on the bed, pulling the covers up to her chin. She stared grimly at the ceiling for a moment, wanting to kill the bastard . . . then she broke into a helpless smile and gratefully closed her eyes.

Tom was in her dreams when she fell asleep and so she slept like a baby.

CHAPTER FIFTEEN

The following morning, Tom escorted Molly to the British Museum in Great Russell Street. Molly was in a good mood again. The day before she had caught up on her sleep, had an excellent lunch in the hotel restaurant, albeit alone but treated with unexpected courtesy by the staff, and then, that evening, still amused by Tom's telephone call, she had met him in the lobby, as planned, to be given a tour of the West End.

Even before they left the hotel, she had asked him if he had meant what he had said on the phone and he had blushed, which he did easily, and confessed that he'd had some brandies in his flat and those, combined with lack of sleep, had made him drunk and mischievous. Nevertheless, she had sensed that if he didn't actually mean what he had said, he was certainly growing more fond of her and was even attracted to her, and so she had gone with him into the West End in an upbeat mood.

He had given her a great time – taking her on a roundabout route from Piccadilly Circus to Leicester Square, then up into Chinatown and Soho, then back to Trafalgar Square and along the Strand and up into Covent Garden. Molly had loved it, especially as the weather had improved dramatically since their arrival. While the tourist squalor of certain areas of the town had reminded her of New York, she had been enchanted with the outdoor cafés of Soho and the street performers in the Piazza of Covent Garden where, in the evening's summery warmth and dimming light, the outdoor tables of the restaurants had been packed. Later, Tom had taken her for a meal at Mr Kong's in Chinatown – an unpretentious restaurant where the food was divine – and followed it with a pub crawl through what he assured her were the best pubs in Soho.

They had talked a lot throughout the evening, without animosity for once, and he had loosened up and told her all about himself: his upbringing in his parents' stately old home in Reigate, Surrey; his education at Oxford; his marriage, virtually arranged, to a débutante, Lucinda Rees-Mannering, from Windsor, then the death of his father and his divorce from Lucinda mere months after the funeral, only two years ago.

It was clear from what Tom told her that he had, indeed, been born with a silver spoon in his mouth and, even better, to loving parents. While the family had neither a butler nor servants, as Molly had imagined they would, Tom had certainly been brought up with a variety of nannies and had never known the dread of insecurity. He had, however, been a delicate, nervous child – an only child – and the death of his father, whom he had worshipped, had, in his own words, 'devastated' him.

'He was a lovely man,' Tom told her. 'An astronomer with the Royal Society of Astronomers, well known in his field. A bit dizzy, perhaps even a little eccentric, but he had a head buzzing with ideas and he taught me all about the stars and, incidentally, stirred my interest in the nature of time and, subsequently, ancient civilizations. He gave me lots of attention and was always terrific fun, so when he died I took it very hard . . . and then my marriage broke up.'

The marriage, Molly deduced from what Tom told her, must have been doomed right from the start. While it had not actually been 'arranged', in the style of an Indian marriage, the young couple had clearly been pushed into each other's arms and their union was viewed as beneficial to both families. Shy and respectful, loving his well-meaning parents, Tom had simply let himself drift with the tide and it had carried him straight to the altar.

Lucinda Rees-Mannering had been something of a débutante, very pretty and dim, addicted to socializing, and no spark of true passion had ever been struck between her and Tom. Their sexual union was a disaster from the beginning and did not improve with time. Within a year, they had virtually stopped having sex and were living together more like brother and sister than husband and wife. For Tom, the relationship had been more than traumatic, shattering his fragile confidence, and then, when his father died unexpectedly of a sudden brain tumour, what little self-esteem he had left rapidly vaporized. Having not yet decided what he wanted to do in life, having been cosseted and protected from the need to have gainful employment, he had started drinking heavily, practically living in his various clubs in London, often staying overnight, and eventually, when this happened once too often, Lucinda filed for divorce. They were divorced eighteen months after the death of Tom's father and he was shattered again.

'Finally,' he told Molly, 'I managed to pull myself together by drinking a lot less and going back to my old interest in ancient civilizations. I became, in short, and as I think I've already told you, a perpetual student, and I remained far too timid for my own good. So while I then went to Mexico because of my continuing interest in ancient civilizations, particularly the Mayas, I also went because I knew that I was too timid for my own good, too protected by my sheltered upbringing, and I decided that travelling all alone might bring me out of myself. Silly as it seems, and probably is, I wanted to test my courage with the trip – and given the experiences we've both had, I think I *am* being tested. Perhaps it was preordained.'

'Seems like it,' Molly said.

He had finally dropped her off at her hotel just before midnight and she had slept like a baby for the second time. Now, as he walked her in the lazy light of late morning from Mayfair, back up through Soho, to Tottenham Court Road and Great Russell Street, she found herself thinking back on what he had told her about his life and comparing it with her own life in New York. For the first time she understood that she, too, albeit for different reasons, had been running away from her past. She had liked to think that she was tough, that she didn't need anyone, but now she saw, in the mirror of Tom's similar set of problems, that she had buried the pain of her childhood behind a front of indifference.

Brooklyn now seemed far away, but she still remembered her parent's squalid apartment above their grocery shop, her big, beefy father in his stained sweatshirt and loose pants, boozing, forever bellowing, beating up on her mother until, when Molly was only twelve, she'd had enough and ran away for good. Then the sexual abuse had started and Molly recalled that vividly: the sheer horror of lying there in the darkness of her bedroom, waiting in dread for the sound of her father's footsteps coming towards the closed door. She shuddered even to think about it: her shame and deep dread, her useless tears and entreaties, and even now she knew that she feared men because of what he had done to her. He had abused her for two years and she had fled home when she was sixteen, moving into that awful dive in East Fourth Street in the Lower East Side with a lot of winos and junkies. She had learnt to defend herself, to hustle for what she needed, and every experience that she had from then on had confirmed the need to do that.

She had seen life as a cesspit, men as brutes, herself their victim, and by the time she lit out for Mexico, she was as hard as a hammer. But that hardness was a front, her armour and shield, and now she realized that her growing feelings for Tom, her awareness of his innocence, had filled her with maternal concern and the need to show him some love. He was the first decent man she had ever met and he filled her with wonder. He frustrated her and often made her mad, but her rage sprang from love. She sensed this, though she could not quite accept it, but what she could not deny was that it was making her feel like a human being for the first time in her life.

'Is that it?' she asked, as they walked past the art shops of Great Russell Street and the black railings in front of a majestic colonnaded building came into view on her left. 'Is that the British Museum?'

'Yes,' Tom said, 'that's it.'

'It's Victorian, right?'

'No, Molly, not quite. Construction of the building began in 1823 and was completed in 1847. So it was *completed* at the beginning of the Victorian era, generally viewed as 1837 to 1903. A good try, though, my dear.'

Amused, he led her through the mass of tourists at the main gates, then across the crowded courtyard to the broad steps that led up into the museum. Tom had phoned the day before for an appointment, so once inside, he asked for Professor Weatherby and was directed through a series of hallways displaying antiquities of Egypt, Asia, the Orient, Greece and Rome, as well as the new and impressive Mayan exhibition, to an office located on an upper floor at the rear of the building. There they found Professor Julian Weatherby, another academic with grey hair and a short-trimmed grey beard, though Molly noticed immediately that he seemed nervous. Like his friend Professor Juarez, he was seated behind a cluttered desk and surrounded by packed bookshelves, old parchments, maps and graphs of hieroglyphics, many relating to Aztec and Mayan culture. When they had closed the door behind them, he immediately came around the desk, introduced himself and shook their hands.

'I'm so glad you could make it,' he said when the introductions had been completed. 'I was rather worried about having your skull in my possession and, frankly, surprised that Professor Juarez sent it with the other artefacts. He *is*, of course, Mexican and, though a dear friend, tends to liberal interpretations when it comes to little matters of legality.'

'What's that mean?' Molly asked, taking an instant dislike to Professor Weatherby.

'What it means, my dear, is that, technically speaking, we're breaking the law by allowing such a valuable artefact to be shipped into this country, unregistered, with our other, perfectly legal, artefacts. No matter, please take a seat.' When he indicated the two chairs facing his desk, Tom and Molly sat down. The professor then went around his desk and sat behind it and stared at them.

'You've got the skull?' Molly asked, feeling anxious.

The professor nodded. 'Yes.' He pointed to a large safe in one corner of the room. 'It's in there,' he said.

'Undamaged?'

'Yes. The skull is, after all, carved from quartz crystal and that's hard to damage. So what can I tell you before you take it away?'

Tom recounted what Professor Juarez had told him about the crystal skull and then asked if the information could be authenticated.

'Yes,' Professor Weatherby said. 'At my friend's written request, in a letter that came with the skull, I examined it thoroughly and can confirm that it's genuine in every respect. As we only know of two genuine crystal skulls – the others all being either fake or the products of wishful thinking – I must agree with my learned friend that this is the long-missing Rose Quartz Skull. Therefore it would, as Professor Juarez informed you, have travelled with that ancient race, pre-Mayan or pre-Aztec, on its great migration across the earth, from the west to the east, including a period in Meso-America and, of course, Chichén Itzá. Given that the second crystal skull – the one presently on display in the Museum of Mankind, here in London – was discovered in British Honduras and is approximately 3,500 years old, it seems likely that both skulls were left behind by that same mysterious race as it moved on from the Yucatán peninsula to Tiahuanaco in Peru. If this is so, I can confirm that your skull is an extremely valuable item, though I don't want it here.'

'Why not?' Molly asked.

'Because, as I said, it's been brought in illegally. Professor Juarez should have never sent it to me without proper clearance, but as he has, I'll simply return it to you and then conveniently forget that I ever saw it.'

'Before you conveniently forget it,' Tom said, sounding bolder than normal, 'can you tell us if you believe the skull has unusual characteristics?'

'It's unusual in every respect, as I believe Professor Jaurez has already told you.'

'By unusual characteristics, I meant remarkable, possibly occult powers. Do you think it has those?'

Professor Weatherby smiled cynically. 'Ah, yes,' he said. 'The occult powers of the crystal skulls, reported so often to have been used in esoteric rites by their original owners.' He leaned back in his chair and clasped his hands under his chin, distractedly stroking his grey beard. 'I've heard all the stories,' he said, 'and find them amusing, but personally I place no credence in them and certainly cannot substantiate them. The skull is remarkable because we don't know how it was made – nor, indeed, who actually made it – but that doesn't mean it's endowed with remarkable powers, supernatural or otherwise. My interest is antiquity, not magic, and I can't pretend otherwise.'

'What about the skull in the Museum of Mankind?' Tom asked.

'What about it?'

'Where did it come from?'

'I can only tell you that it was originally purchased, from an unknown person, by Tiffany's in New York, then brought back here by an Englishwoman: the daughter of Ronald Barratt-White, the famous – some would say notorious – explorer who found it in British Honduras in the first place. Lady Barratt-White gave it to the Museum of Mankind as a gift and there it remains to this day.'

'Why is Ronald Barratt-White thought to be notorious?' Molly asked.

'Because he was more of an adventurer than an explorer,' Professor Weatherby replied, 'and his interests were, to put it mildly, somewhat bizarre. He wanted to be taken seriously – and certainly he had a genuine interest in ancient cultures, particularly those of Central America, such as the Mayans, the Aztecs and the Toltecs. However, he was also a theosophist, a lover of mystical sciences, a member of various so-called secret societies, and an open believer in the legend of Atlantis. For this reason, and because Barratt-White liked to be seen as a swashbuckling character, there were many who believed that he did not in fact find his crystal skull in British Honduras, as he had claimed, but purchased it from someone and planted it in the rubbish of his excavation of the lost city of Lubaantun, in the jungle near Belize City, for his daughter to find.'

'Why would he do that?' Tom asked.

'In order to make himself famous and regain the legitimacy he had lost through his open support of outlandish theories.'

'Do you think that's true?' Molly asked.

'I've no idea,' the professor replied. 'I only know that the skull is genuine and that Lady Barratt-White, who was then seventeen and working on the site with her father, insists to this day that she was the one who actually found it and that the find was genuine.'

'Do you think there's a connection between the two skulls?' Tom asked him.

'What kind of connection?'

'A connection in the sense that though we don't know who actually made the skulls, it's now widely accepted, by yourself and others, that they almost certainly belonged to that mysterious pre-Aztec or pre-Mayan race, that they were both used in the esoteric rites of that ancient race, and that for unknown reasons they were both left behind in Meso-America, most likely in British Honduras and Yucatán. A connection in the sense that whatever they were used for, they might have been always used in tandem.'

'That's certainly possible,' Professor Weatherby said, 'but what's your point, Mr Powell?'

'My point is that the skulls may be a pair. Not just structurally similar, but somehow related to one another, perhaps working only in tandem.'

'Working?' the professor asked, looking bewildered.

Tom leaned forward in his chair, his gaze intense. 'If the crystal skulls do have unusual characteristics, or occult powers – and I appreciate that you don't believe this – they may communicate somehow with one another and need one another to function fully.'

'That's ridiculous, Mr Powell. Whether separately or together, the skulls have no supernatural powers. I can't believe that a man of your background would even consider such a ludicrous possibility. Such theories belong to the realm of cranks, along with UFOs and zombies. This is the *British Museum*, Mr Powell, and please treat it as such. We are interested in history, not in magic, so please desist from this particular line of reasoning, at least in my presence.'

'Sorry,' Tom said, though he did not, to Molly's surprise, look even remotely apologetic. Indeed, rather than looking as if had been reprimanded, he simply leaned back in his chair and offered a nonchalant smile.

'Is Lady Barratt-White still alive?' he asked.

'Yes,' the professor said. 'She's nearly ninety years old and seriously ill, but she *is* still alive. Why?'

'I think I'll pay her a visit,' Tom said. 'Can you give me her details?'

'She's in the phone book,' the professor replied, clearly wishing to involve himself no further in what he viewed as mere lunacy.

'Good,' Tom said, then he pushed his chair back and stood up. 'Thanks very much for your assistance, Professor Weatherby. Can we have the skull now?'

'My pleasure,' Professor Weatherby said. He went to the safe in the corner of the room, opened it and pulled out the skull, which was wrapped in cardboard and paper tied together with string. Placing the package in a British Museum shopping bag, he handed it to Tom. 'I can't believe you're going to walk out of here with that priceless item in a shopping bag,' he said, 'but I'm glad to be rid of it.'

'Thanks for looking after it,' Molly said.

'No thanks required,' the professor said. He then walked to the door and opened it for them, but stopped them just as they were leaving. He checked his wristwatch. 'Good Lord,' he said, 'it's lunchtime. Time for my pint. Let me walk you both down.' Together, they walked back through the great hallways filled with antiquities from many countries, then down the broad steps and across the great courtyard to the pavement. There, surrounded by milling tourists and snapping cameras, Professor Weatherby shook hands with Molly, then with Tom, and wished them good luck. They thanked him and were about to leave when he called out Tom's name. When Tom turned back to face him, the professor was looking extremely serious.

'One final thought,' he said. 'Much as I'm glad to get rid of this particular artefact, I have to say it grieves me that it's not in professional hands. Please be careful, Mr Powell. A lot of people would like to get their hands on that skull and some of them are the kind to be avoided. Be extremely careful about who you show it to, who you talk to, because otherwise you could find yourself in very serious trouble.'

'I'll be careful,' Tom said.

The professor nodded, then he crossed the road to enter the Museum Tavern on the opposite corner. Tom watched him disappearing inside the old pub, then he led Molly back along the crowded pavement of Great Russell Street, carrying the precious crystal skull in the museum's shopping bag.

'Let's have a drink and a talk,' he said.

CHAPTER SIXTEEN

Mai Suphar watched Tom and Molly until they had disappeared along Great Russell Street, then, with a chilly smile, she crossed the road and entered the Museum Tavern, which was busy and smoky and warm. Dressed in a long black coat over a skirt of black silk, with a snow-white blouse and red scarf setting off the golden skin of her lovely face and high-heeled black boots emphasizing her long legs, she was a picture of sophisticated elegance and heart-stopping beauty. While not actually stopping, more than one male heart fluttered when she walked in, as she could tell by the widening eyes of those who looked at her. She also saw, as she walked to the bar, that Professor Weatherby, sitting there with his pint and sandwich beneath a tinted-glass window and potted plants, was one of the gawkers.

Standing at the bar, with her leather bag slung over her right shoulder, she ordered a Campari with soda, speaking perfect English in a low, sensual voice and lowering her brown eyes as if shy. When the barman had served her, trying not to ogle overtly, though clearly he found this difficult, Mai shyly thanked him and carried her drink to the helpfully empty table beside Professor Weatherby's. As she sat down, crossing her long legs to let the black coat fall off them, displaying them, she glanced sideways at the professor and caught him hastily lowering his gaze to the newspaper spread out before him. He took another bite of his sandwich, as if distracted, though that distraction was caused by Mai, and she smiled slightly and then glanced about her as if, just like any other tourist, she found this old-fashioned English bar fascinating.

In fact, she was enjoying herself. She had never been in London before, had always wanted to visit it, and when Lu Thong had ordered her to come here, to pursue Tom Powell and the American girl, she had been delighted to do so.

According to Lu Thong, Tom Powell and the American girl, now known to be one Molly Beale, a nonentity from New York City, a hitch-hiker in Yucatán, had been pursued by the one-eyed criminal Emmanuelle Cortez all the way from Mérida to Mexico City. At that point, Lu Thong had been expecting a phone call from Cortez, informing him that the couple had been killed and the crystal skull regained; instead, he had received a phone call from another of his minions, informing him that Cortez and three of his hooligans had been found dead in their car, where it had crashed and exploded on a back road that ran above the highway leading to Mexico City's Aeropuerto Internacional. From this, Lu Thong had deduced that Cortez must have been pursuing the Englishman and his girlfriend to the airport, chased them off the highway, and then made some fatal error and crashed. Subsequent investigation by Lu Thong's minion had confirmed that Tom Powell and Molly Beale had boarded the first flight to London the following day.

'I have an informant at Heathrow Airport,' Lu Thong had told Mai. Lu Thong, it seemed, had informants everywhere and none of them would think to refuse him for fear of their lives. 'He checked the records of all those who had booked hotels through the tourist office at Heathrow during the morning of the Englishman's arrival and learnt that his travelling companion, this Molly Beale creature, was booked into a certain hotel in Mayfair, London. Powell personally made that booking, but didn't book himself in, which suggested that he was staying elsewhere, presumably at his own place. A check of the London telephone directory revealed that he does indeed have an apartment in Mayfair, just around the corner from the hotel. So we have his address and the name of that tart's hotel, which solves some of our problems.'

'What are the others?'

'It was not my belief that either the Englishman or his American tart could smuggle the crystal skull through Customs and that they must therefore have made other arrangements for its transportation to London. I checked my taped conversations with the late Emmanuelle Cortez, God rest his soul, who, when still breathing, was phoning me regularly from Mexico City with precise details of the movements of the frustrating twosome, and noted that they had paid a visit to the National Museum of Anthropology in Chapultepec Park. Visitors to members of the staff of that establishment have to sign the guest book. From that book we ascertained that Powell and his girlfriend had signed in for a visit to Professor Juarez, the museum's leading authority on Meso-American antiquities in general and the Mayans and Aztecs in particular. Since Cortez, God rest his soul, is no longer with us, I dispatched another of my men to the home of Professor Juarez and the good professor, having little resistance to pain, revealed, before dying in an unfortunate accident, that he had, with Powell's agreement, sent the skull, along with other, legally cleared Mayan artefacts to one Professor Julian Weatherby at the British Museum, London, with a note informing him that Powell would eventually collect it and would be requesting further information about it. Your job, therefore, is to wait until Powell and his floozy have visited Professor Weatherby, then find out exactly what he told them and what fate has befallen the crystal skull. When you find that out, please get rid of Professor Weatherby – we don't want him talking – and then collect the crystal skull, if he still has it, or, if it's back in the hands of Powell and Co., get it off them and then put out their lights. You leave for London tomorrow.'

In all truth, it was a job that Mai could not refuse and now here she was in London, sitting beside Professor Weatherby, having had all of yesterday to enjoy herself – seeing the sights, buying more clothes, enjoying the fine restaurants – before getting back to work.

To this end, she had conscientiously arisen early this morning and caught a taxi to Molly Beale's hotel. Taking a seat in the lobby while residents were still going into the restaurant for breakfast, she had waited patiently, chain-smoking cigarettes and offering a chilling, off-putting stare to all who glanced at her, until Tom Powell entered the lobby from the street. She recognized Powell from a blurry black-and-white photo taken off the video film routinely recording the movements of all passengers at the Aeropuerto Internacional security gates. Finally, when a young blonde woman emerged from the hotel's restaurant to greet Powell, speaking with a brassy American accent, Mai knew that she had to be Molly Beale. Thus, when Powell and Beale left the hotel and commenced the long walk to the British Museum, Mai knew exactly who she was following.

When they entered the museum, she followed them in. She lost them temporarily when they were escorted into an area forbidden to the general public, but she picked them up again when they emerged from that same area with the grey-haired, bearded Englishman, whom Mai could only assume was Professor Weatherby. Right now, the professor was sitting beside her, chewing on the last of his sandwich and, when not glancing helplessly at her, pretending to read his newspaper. He looked like an easy mark.

Mai waited until the professor had finished his sandwich and was sipping his beer while casting surreptitious glances at her. To keep his attention, she kept crossing and recrossing her fabulous legs and finally, when she sensed that he was already fantasizing about her, she turned towards him, as if to reach into her leather bag, now resting on the seat beside her, and deliberately knocked her glass over. When the drink spilled from the overturned glass and splashed onto her dress where it fell between her crossed thighs, she let out a girlish cry of despair and let her hands, with their exquisite fingers, flutter helplessly, as if in search of a napkin. Unable to find one, being a typical helpless female, she raised her gorgeous eyes pleadingly to the professor and he promptly leaned sideways towards her to pass her his napkin.

'Oh, thank you,' Mai said. Uncrossing her legs, she dabbed delicately at the slight stain on her dress, pressing the damp patch down between her thighs, thus making the dress tighten across both legs. Then, while the professor was staring wide-eyed at those legs, she giggled like an embarrassed schoolgirl and placed the damp napkin on the table. Turning back to the professor, breathing nervously, therefore deeply, pushing her breasts out, she gave the professor her most heavenly, though suitably embarrassed, smile. 'God,' she said, 'what a stupid thing to do. I feel such a fool. But thank you. That was kind of you.'

'Not at all,' Professor Weatherby said.

Mai sighed and breathed deeply, stretched her body, once more pushed her breasts out, then smiled again and shook her head ruefully, letting her long hair spill down her back like a shimmering black shawl. She fluttered her eyelashes a couple of times, spread her legs slightly to glance down at the small stain – which was now situated in the cleft between her thighs, precisely where the dress had tightened sexily across them – then giggled again and said, 'Oh, well, it's not *that* bad. I suppose I'll just have to stay here for a while until it dries out.'

The professor nodded agreement but was too shy to speak, so Mai sighed again, then reached into her bag for a cigarette. She also groped around in vain for a lighter, then shook her head and exclaimed softly, 'Damn!' Smiling girlishly at the professor, though giving him the full effects of her luminous brown gaze, she added, 'I'm not getting anything right today. Now I've forgotten my lighter. Do you happen to smoke?'

'A pipe,' Professor Weatherby replied, 'though never in public, since most people hate it. But I *do* have my matches.'

Pleased, Mai smiled at him, licked her luscious lips, slid the cigarette between them, then leaned close to the professor, her breasts practically touching him as her coat fell open, to let him light the cigarette for her. As he did so, his eyes were glued to her lips and they had a glazed look. Mai inhaled, which forced her breasts out further, then she sat back again, though she managed, in so doing, to inch slightly nearer to her new friend.

'Thank you,' she said.

'Not at all,' the professor said, placing his box of matches back into his pocket. Then, feeling more confident, he asked, 'Are you a tourist, by any chance?'

Mai nodded and brushed the hair from one eye with her beautiful fingers. 'Yes,' she said. 'I just arrived yesterday. It's a beautiful city.'

'You've never been here before?'

'No. But I've wanted to come here for years and, at last, here I am.'

She crossed her left leg over her right and the dress inched up her thigh, making the professor's eyes widen even more before he realized what was happening and graciously looked away. By the time he did so, Mai had moved even closer to him and was staring steadily, admiringly at him, like a young girl on her first date.

'You're here alone?' the professor asked.

'Yes, that's the worst part. I was supposed to come with my father, a bank executive in Bangkok, but his business here was cancelled at the last moment and so he sent me alone rather than disappoint me. Of course, I like it in a certain way – he's normally far too protective – but it's difficult when one doesn't know anyone. I mean, I really haven't travelled all that much and I'm shy of entering places alone.'

'You speak wonderful English,' the professor said.

'Do I? I'm so pleased. I was educated in an English convent in Bangkok, so that's why I speak as I do. And, of course, most of my father's acquaintances are in business and speak mostly English.'

'Your father must be well off.'

Mai nodded. 'He is. I suppose that's why I'm over-protected. I always had English nannies and later, as a teenager, when I was in the convent, the nuns were rather strict. So being here, I feel quite inexperienced, though I think it's good for me.'

'I'm sure it is,' the professor said, visibly warming to her for reasons both paternal and licentious. 'Can I buy you a drink?'

Mai acted hesitant, as if pondering the proprieties of this delicate situation. She glanced back down at the stain on her dress, pressed it lightly with her fingers, thus tightening the dress across her thighs even more, and finally, smiling, offering her innocent trust, she said, 'Well, since I can't leave until this stain had dried, I suppose I might as well have another drink. Yes, that *would* be nice, thanks.'

Two hours later, when the professor had downed three more pints and Mai had accepted some more Campari and sodas, they were sitting close together, no longer inhibited, talking with a great deal of what the professor, at least, thought was unusual intimacy. While conversing, Mai repeatedly giggled and let her hand come to rest on the professor's hand, as if doing it unconsciously, perhaps because of the alcohol, and the professor responded by doing the same to her in an avuncular fashion. Finally, when the professor had clearly forgotten that he was supposed to be back at work, Mai giggled like a naughty schoolgirl and confessed to her secret sin.

'Oh, dear,' she said, 'now that we know each other, I suppose I should confess at last.'

'Confess what?' the professor asked.

Mai giggled and shyly covered her mouth with her right hand, then removed it to let him see her flawless teeth, framed by pink-painted, luscious lips.

'I really can't!'

'Please do.'

'Well, all right, then,' she said. 'Actually, it's no accident that I have an interest in antiquities and now find myself sitting beside this lovely professor who works in the antiquities department of the British Museum. In fact, I saw your photograph in the catalogue of the Mayan exhibition and was struck by something in your appearance.' She shook her head from side to side, giggling again, as if deeply embarrassed. 'Don't ask me! I don't know what it was. I just saw something in your face that I seemed to recognize and then I desperately wanted to meet you and talk about the Mayans. Then, shortly after, when I saw you coming out of the museum with that young couple, I could hardly believe my eyes – or my good luck. So I have to confess . . .' Again, she covered her mouth with her hand in order to stifle a giggle, only continuing when she had managed to control herself. 'So I have to confess that, bold as it may seem, when you parted from the young couple at the gate and then entered this pub, I couldn't resist the temptation to follow you in and somehow arrange to meet you – which I did in the end . . . Now isn't that terrible?'

The professor leaned closer to her and patted the back of her hand, which now happened to be resting on his knee, the long-nailed fingers pressing gently, distractedly, as if the ravishing though seemingly immature young creature hardly knew, in her innocence, that she was doing it.

'No, it isn't terrible,' the professor said. 'It's my pleasure, I'm sure.'

'Anyway,' Mai said, now practically breathing into the professor's ear and occasionally dropping her head onto his shoulder, letting her long jet-black scented hair fall over him, as if she was drunk and about to fall asleep, 'who *were* they? Friends or relatives?'

'Just a couple interested in Mayan antiquities,' the professor replied, reaching up without thinking to stroke the hair on Mai's head and run his hand down it to her spine. 'They wanted some information.'

'About what?' Mai asked sleepily, as if just making small conversation.

'Oh, just some old artefact,' the professor said, placing his index finger under Mai's chin to push her head up and look into her ravishing brown eyes. 'Nothing important.'

'So what did they want to know?'

The professor smiled tenderly at her, breathing into her gorgeous face, then lowered his gaze from her eyes to her lips, which were opened ever so slightly, letting him see her pink tongue. 'Frankly, my dear – and please don't take offence – I spoke to the couple in confidence and don't feel I should break it.'

Mai pouted, disappointed, then gently poked her tongue out. The professor was mesmerized by that tongue as it trailed over her full lip.

'Well,' he said, breathing heavily and flushed more than he should be, but clearly concerned not to disappoint her, 'I suppose it hardly matters, what with you not being in the business and just here on a visit . . .' Mai's fingers were stroking his burning thigh in a touchingly innocent though certainly exciting manner. 'They came to collect a crystal skull and obtain some information about it. I told them what they wanted to know and then they left with the skull. That's all it was, dear.'

'A crystal skull?' Mai said. 'How fascinating! So what did they want to know?'

'Oh, just some rubbish, dear.'

Realizing that the professor was still reluctant to discuss confidential matters and was, indeed, becoming obsessed with the possibility of possessing her, Mai deliberately dropped her head onto his shoulder, squeezed his upper thigh with her fingers, and murmured huskily, 'Oh, dear, I think I'm drunk. I think I'm going to pass out.'

'Good God, don't do that, pet!'

'I think I'd better go back to my hotel now. Don't you?'

'You can't possibly go back in this state.'

'It's all right. I'll get a taxi.'

'You still can't go back in this state. You'd better let me go with you.'

Mai sighed and wearily raised her head to give him a dreamy smile. 'Oh, would you? You're so sweet.'

'Come, dear, hold on to me.'

More drunk than Mai, though he wasn't to know that, Professor Weatherby stood up with her, placed his arm around her waist, and led her out of the pub to catch a taxi. Twenty minutes later they were in Mai's room in the Savoy where (having been excited at the feel of her lying against him in the taxi, the skirt high up her legs, her breasts pressing against his chest as she seemingly slept on his shoulder) the professor stretched out on the double bed beside her, still wearing his suit and with Mai's leather bag resting upon the pillow just above his head.

The professor seduced Mai – or at least he thought he was doing so. He could scarcely believe that he was doing it – being a respectable married man with a loving wife and two good children, an academic of some standing, not *au fait* in worldly matters – but before he quite grasped how it had happened, her coat had been removed, her blouse had been unbuttoned, and her hand was pressing his hand onto her bared breast while she ground her hot belly against him.

'Just tell me,' she whispered, licking his ear with her tongue, inflaming his hardened organ with her writhing. 'I like to talk while I'm doing it. It's just something to talk about. What did that couple want to know and what did you tell them?'

'Oh, God,' the professor groaned, pressing his lips to her golden breasts, licking the nipples, gasping for breath, 'they wanted to know a lot of nonsense that I couldn't really help with, so now they're off to see an eccentric old woman who'll probably tell them what they want to hear. Oh, God, Mai! Oh, my love!'

'Yes, darling,' Mai crooned. 'Oh, Julian, that feels so good, so sensual, so exciting . . . What woman? I've got to talk, dearest. Who were they going to see?'

Professor Weatherby gasped and groaned. He was now licking Mai's navel. She was stretching out below him, one hand tugging his shirt open, the other flung in seeming abandonment above her tousled head, almost touching the leather bag on the pillow. 'Oh, God, Mai, you're so beautiful! Lady . . . Christ, Barratt . . . God, Christ, you feel wonderful! I've never known . . . *No, Mai!* Oh, God, *yes* . . . They were going to see . . . God, Mai, yes . . . Lady . . . what's her name? *Barratt-White.*

Another eccentric. Claims to have found the crystal skull now in the Museum of Mankind . . . Ah, God . . . may have done so . . . Oh, God help me, that's wonderful, so nice. Don't stop, Mai! *Please, Mai!*'

'Mmmm,' Mai crooned. 'Lady Barratt-White. Does she live here in London?'

'Yes, Mai! *Don't stop, Mai!*'

Mai stretched her gorgeous body, raising her belly to his face, and as his tongue frantically slipped into her navel, she groped inside the leather bag on the pillow and finally found what she wanted. It was a hypodermic syringe, filled with poison, ready to use. She simply prodded the plastic cap with a long fingernail and it silently popped off. She lowered the needle towards the professor as he rolled, groaning and gasping, between her legs; then, as he cried out, 'God, I want you!' she plunged it into his neck.

Weatherby's convulsions were not caused by orgasm, but by the spasms of death.

When he was dead, Mai kicked him off the bed and heard him thud to the floor. She then stood up, adjusted her clothing, fixed her hair, and finally, when she had picked up her suitcase, she walked out of the room. She went down to the lobby and checked out (having signed in under a false name) and then, feeling pleased with herself, she caught a taxi to another hotel.

She was not finished yet.

CHAPTER SEVENTEEN

Having phoned first for an appointment, Tom and Molly were greeted at Lady Barratt-White's front door by a maid almost as old as her mistress. The latter was, according to the data collected by Tom, eighty-seven years old this year. Lady Barratt-White lived in decaying elegance in a large apartment in Knightsbridge, not too far from Harrod's, and she received them in an expansive living room filled with Victorian furniture and an impressive collection of antiques from many parts of the world. The old lady was seated on a fading floral-print sofa under a large framed black and white photograph of herself with her father, the legendary explorer Roland Barratt-White, obviously taken when they were excavating the lost city of Lubaantun in the jungles of British Honduras, now known as Belize, in Central America. White-haired, her face deeply lined, she was wearing a loose-flowing Victorian floral-print dress that blended so perfectly with the sofa that it made her seem almost transparent, rather like a ghost.

The maid, also white-haired, wearing a black dress and white apron and stooping low as she walked or, rather, inched forward step by painful step, served tea and biscuits and then departed, leaving them free to talk.

'I must say,' Lady Barratt-White said, sounding terribly posh, though her voice had the shakiness of old age, 'that it was pleasant to hear you on the phone, Mr Powell – the perfect diction and proper grammar – instead of what I usually receive: occultists and flying-saucer fanatics with labourers' accents and vile colloquialisms. So what can I tell you?'

'We're in possession of a crystal skull,' Tom said, then nodded to Molly, who carefully withdrew the gleaming crystal skull from her shoulder bag and set it on the coffee table between them. 'And I wondered if you could have a good look at it and tell me if it's the same as the one reportedly found by you in British Honduras.'

The old lady stared at the gleaming, macabre skull, then raised her rheumy, though still perceptive, eyes to Tom.

'*Reportedly?*' she queried sharply. 'Don't disappoint me, Mr Powell. Surely you're not another of those tiresome creatures who has only come here to insinuate that I've been lying for most of my life. I found my crystal skull during the excavation of that lost city and my father swore to the day he died that he had not planted it there for me to find.'

'I'm sorry,' Tom said. 'I didn't mean to insinuate anything. I merely wanted to hear the story from you personally as I think it would help.'

The old lady nodded, then leaned forward to run her blue-veined, trembling hands over the crystal skull on the table. She studied it silently for a long time, then sat back again, breathing heavily. Her eyes flitted from Molly to Tom, then settled on the latter. She had a steady, bold stare.

'Your skull is genuine,' she said. 'There is absolutely no doubt about it. Where did you find it?'

'It was buried in the platform of the Shrine on the summit of the Great Pyramid at Chichén Itzá, Yucatán. Clearly it had been there for centuries.'

The old woman nodded again. 'The second skull – the lost skull – was known to have been buried somewhere in the land of the ancient Mayans, *somewhere* in Central America. What you have there is undoubtedly that lost skull – the so-called Rose Quartz Skull. You're a very lucky couple.'

'Is it the same as the one you found? Molly asked.

'Yes, young lady, it is.'

'Can you remind me of how you found your skull?' Tom asked, pretending ignorance in order to receive the unvarnished truth.

'I can,' Lady Barratt-White said, sinking back into the sofa, into the floral-print pattern, into the shadows falling over it, as if about to disappear into it. 'The word *Lubaantun* means "place of the fallen stones" and the existence of the lost city of Lubaantun, a true collection of fallen stones, was first reported to the British colonial government office in the late nineteenth century by inhabitants of the Toledo settlement, located near the site we excavated. We were not the first there, of course. The Governor of British Honduras initially commissioned Dr Thomas Gann to investigate the site. He began his excavations in 1903 and published his report in England the following year. In that report he stated that he had managed to excavate around the central plaza and concluded from his findings that the lost city had been very large indeed, with a substantial population. About ten years later, in 1915, Professor M. Merwin of Harvard University picked up where Dr Gann had left off and, after further excavations, uncovered a ball court and three carved stone markers depicting men playing ball games. My father arrived at the site almost ten years after that. Included in his expedition were the same Dr Gann who had first opened the site nearly two decades earlier, Lady Fiona Williams, my father's close companion and financier, and myself – then only fourteen years old.'

The old lady fell silent, lost in her memories. She glanced back over her shoulder at the large framed photo on the wall behind her, as if using it to jolt her failing memory. The grainy black and white photo showed the teenage girl and her famous explorer father, both wearing old-fashioned shirts, slacks and floppy hats to protect them from the sun, both standing in the rubble and ruins of the excavation site in British Honduras, surrounded by beaming Mayan workers. Sighing with sadness for the loss of her best times, the old woman turned to face them again.

'We worked there for three years,' she continued, 'digging, sifting and collating, gradually uncovering various parts of the ancient ruins. Then, on my seventeenth birthday, when I was helping to dig around a collapsed altar, I saw something glinting in the rubble. When I ordered my Mayan workers to dig it out, removing the last of the heavy stone slabs that had covered it, what I had in my possession was a life-sized crystal skull in perfect condition – the same skull that is now on display in the Museum of Mankind.'

'And this occurred on your seventeenth birthday?' Tom enquired sceptically.

'I know! I know!' the old woman snapped, shaking her head from side to side with frustration and turning red in the face. Eventually calming herself down and folding one blue-veined, trembling hand over the other, she coughed to clear her throat and continued. 'It was my seventeenth birthday, believe me. And that *is* an unfortunate truth, since I'm convinced that it was this simple fact that led to all the stories about my father having planted it there just for me to find – either as a kind of birthday present or to gain himself notoriety. But that's nonsense, Mr Powell. Believe me, it's rubbish. I repeat that to the very day he died, my father swore that this was not so – that he had never seen the crystal skull before and that the find was genuine.'

'What happened when you found it?' Molly asked.

The old lady picked up her cup and saucer, which rattled together in her trembling hands. She sipped some tea, then gently placed her tea cup back on the saucer and placed both on the table. Leaning back, she gazed at the ceiling and into her distant past.

'The Mayan workers were ecstatic when they saw it. Some of them actually performed a ritualistic dance around it and others bowed low to worship it. They stopped working on the instant and, instead, erected a crude altar to support the skull and insisted that they were going to pay homage to it every hour of every day. Realizing that work on the excavation would grind to a halt if the skull remained on the site, my father presented it to the chief of the local Mayans, telling him to keep it in the settlement, and after that, when they had the skull in their possession, the Mayans returned to work. A few months later, when our expedition was preparing to return to England – this was in 1927 – the Mayans gave the skull back to my father as a sign of gratitude for all he had done for them. So we returned to England, bringing the crystal skull with us, and my father kept it in our home in London until his death in 1959. He left it to me in his will and that, despite rumours to the contrary, is how the crystal skull came into my possession.'

'And eventually you presented it to the Museum of Mankind,' Tom said.

'Yes,' Lady Barratt-White replied. 'I was growing old – as you can see, now I'm truly *very* old – and so I thought it should have a proper home, which I hope it now has.'

Tom glanced at Molly and saw that she was sitting up very straight in her tall-backed Victorian chair, holding her cup and saucer in a steady hand and sipping more effetely than was her custom. Realizing that tight blue jeans and dirt-smeared tee-shirts were not quite the thing for a young lady to be wearing when visiting the likes of Lady Barratt-White, let alone when wining and dining in the kind of places he was accustomed to, Tom had taken Molly on a shopping spree along the better part of Oxford Street, encouraging her to select clothes that were neither too adolescent nor too sophisticated. Right now, with her blonde hair hanging down to her shoulders, she was looking, if not sophisticated, then certainly well-dressed and girlishly attractive in a thick bouclé shirt, cream-coloured shaped satin blouse, dark trousers pleated into an elasticated waist-band, and low-heeled black shoes. The outfit showed off her fine figure without being obvious.

'Did you learn anything about the crystal skull,' Molly asked intelligently, 'while it was in your possession?'

'No. In fact, I made a point of *not* trying to learn anything about it because I believe that the two skulls, yours and mine, the only two *genuine* skulls, can haunt those who look too deeply into them and have powers that can be unleashed in some as yet mysterious manner. Indeed, this is why I gave mine to the Museum of Mankind. And even there, so I am told, the skull is said to haunt those who clean the building. In fact, whether right or wrong, the staff are so convinced of this that they have insisted that each evening the crystal skull must be covered with a black cloth – presumably to ensure that they don't accidentally look into its dreadful eye sockets and become mesmerized by them.'

'I saw stars in that crystal skull,' Molly said, speaking with more care than normal, avoiding swear words, clearly determined not to offend the aristocratic old dear.

'Stars?'

'Yes, stars. I looked into it and was hypnotized by it and saw stars all around me.'

'Well, that's certainly possible. I *have* received many letters and phone calls over the years from people to whom I lent the crystal skull for the purposes of research. A lot of those people – indeed, *most* of those people – had serious problems in conducting their research because the skull affected them strangely. Some saw what you saw, others were hypnotized as you were, and still others became prone to serious hallucinations, suffered illnesses or even became suicidal. For this reason, most of my researchers returned the skull to me before they could complete their work on it. You can only handle the crystal skulls for so long, then they start playing tricks on you.'

'What about flying saucers?' Tom asked.

'What about them, dear boy?'

Tom recounted his and Molly's adventures, beginning with their discovery of the dead men in Chichén

Itzá and concluding with the saucer-shaped light that had seemed to come to their rescue on the road to the airport in Mexico City. When he fell silent, the old lady stared thoughtfully at him, then sighed and nodded.

'I believe you,' she said. 'The powers of the skull were obviously protecting you, even as they were turning against the others. Why this is, I can't say, though I would speculate that you're a good man with honourable intentions and the others were mercenary gangsters, intent on using the skull for evil purposes. That may explain it.'

Tom felt a sliver of fear trickle down his spine as he thought of what he had already experienced because of the crystal skull and what might lie in wait for him in the near future. When he glanced at Molly and saw how pretty she looked, even with her prominent nose and slightly hardened street-wise features, he realized that he felt something for her and was, despite his frequent frustrations with her, deeply concerned for her. He and she were in this together and now it seemed almost preordained. Wondering just where this was leading to, he turned back to Lady Barratt-White who, blending perfectly with the sofa, seemed even more like a transparent ghost.

'Did your father also believe that the skulls had magical powers?' Tom asked.

'Most certainly,' the old lady replied.

'What made him think that?'

'He had always been convinced that the original owners of the skulls were early Mayans – a most mysterious race, widely believed to have magical powers and to have practised esoteric rites. When he saw how the local Mayans behaved when we uncovered that crystal skull during our excavations of Lubaantun –

how they seemed to recognize it and worshipped it – he took it as proof that the skull originated with that earlier mysterious race of Mayans. Finally, because those early Mayans were said to have possessed magical powers, he became convinced that the two genuine crystal skulls – his own and the legendary, long-lost Rose Quartz Skull – could, when working in tandem, reproduce the magical powers of that ancient race.'

'Did you say in tandem?'

'Yes, young man.'

'What gave your father that idea?'

The old lady picked up her teacup, gazed down into it and saw that it was empty. Sighing, she placed it back on the table, then smiled sweetly at Tom.

'Mayan hieroglyphics found in my father's private collection of rare parchments suggest that the two crystal skulls were deliberately separated and hidden by the high priests of that ancient race with the intention that they would some day be found and returned to their source. Why they did this we cannot yet say, but certainly the two skulls have been found – one by me, the other by you two – and so they must soon be returned to their source.'

'But what source is that?' Molly asked, trying to sound well-spoken and academic.

'According to my father's reading of the hieroglyphics, they must be returned – and I quote – *to that majestic and long-hidden city that is linked to the stars*: unquote.' The old lady nodded affirmatively, her grey head bobbing in the shadows that fell over the floral-printed sofa and her floral-print dress and made her appear faintly transparent. Thankfully, she then leaned forward a little, letting Tom and Molly see her face again. She looked terribly serious. 'And until the skulls are returned to their source,' she said, her voice trembling and ethereal, 'the Earth's so-called hauntings will not cease.'

There was silence for a moment, only broken by the regular ticking of the grandfather clock, deeply varnished and decorated with gold-leaf motifs, that stood like a sentinel by the door.

'Hauntings?' Tom finally asked to break the silence. 'What hauntings would those be?'

The old woman shrugged. 'Ghosts, evil spirits, various inexplicable calamities – yes, even flying saucers and extraterrestrials – everything that torments us or haunts us. Such things will either come to an end or be resolved when the crystal skulls are returned to their source. Meanwhile, those who would seek to profit from the skulls will come to a bad end.'

Tom and Molly glanced at one another, both trying to be sceptical, yet both feeling uneasy. In that mood, Tom glanced around the spacious living room, at the many antiques collected from the four corners of the globe, found in various excavations, some of them almost as macabre as the crystal skulls. He thought of the great mysteries of human history and saw only a black hole.

'To get back to their source,' he said finally, breaking a lengthy silence. 'You mentioned a city linked to the stars. What could that mean?'

'According to the hieroglyphics, an ancient bridge between the east and the west – the legendary City of the Sun. In other words . . .'

'Tiahuanaco!' Molly exclaimed triumphantly, recalling what she and Tom had been told by Professor Juarez.

'Of course!' Tom said, also excited. 'The holy city on

the southern shore of Lake Titicaca in Peru. The site of the legendary Sun Gate.'

Lady Barratt-White smiled slightly and nodded, signifying agreement. 'So may I ask you what you intend doing about all of this?'

'Well . . .' Too confused to answer immediately, Tom hesitated and glanced instinctively at Molly. Turning back to the old lady, he said, 'Well, I don't know. I'm not sure. Right now, I only want to solve the mystery of the skulls – find out precisely what they are and where they came from.'

'And this need obsesses you?'

'Yes,' Tom confessed without thinking. 'It's come to obsess me.'

'It's obsessed me for years,' the old lady said. 'Alas, while all of my researchers were being foiled in *their* attempts to unlock the mystery, I grew too old to do anything about it myself. You've come to me as a godsend.'

'What?' Molly said.

'Pardon?' Tom added.

The old lady smiled sweetly at both of them, but then turned back to Tom. 'You're an honourable man, Mr Powell. I can see it in your face. You may have made a few mistakes in your life, but you're one of the pure in heart. That's why the skull has been protecting you while destroying the others. It senses the goodness in your heart and the purity of your intentions. You have a mission in life, young man, though you may not yet have realized it; and that mission is tied to the problem that's concerned me for years.'

'What's that?' Molly asked.

The old woman looked steadily at her, assessing her and eventually accepting her. 'As it was me and my father who removed that crystal skull from where the early Mayans had buried it, and as that skull, like the other, must be returned to its source, I feel personally responsible for finding out precisely *where* both skulls came from and then returning them to that sacred source. However, since I'm now too old to do this, you must do it for me. You can do it because you're both pure in heart and the skulls will protect you.'

Tom glanced at Molly and saw the wonder in her face: the realization that this old lady thought highly of her, which no one, apart from him, of course, had ever done before. His heart went out to her, combined with guilt at his own omissions, but he knew that he'd come as far as he wanted to go, that this was now far too dangerous. He was not pure in heart, as the old lady seemed to think; in fact, he was a pure coward at heart and now his fears were returning.

'It will cost a lot of money,' Lady Barratt-White said, 'but I'm dying and I have money to burn and want to put it to good use. I'll finance all your trips, pay for anything you need, then finally pay you a handsome fee, if you finish this for me.'

'I'm not in need of money,' Tom said abruptly.

'*I* am!' Molly declared. 'Excuse me, ma'am,' she went on, turning to Lady Barratt-White, 'for sounding mercenary, but I've never had any money in my life and so this means a lot to me.'

'I know that, my dear. I knew it before you came here. I've been waiting for you both to come along, though I didn't know precisely who you'd be. But I've seen you in my dreams, felt you deep in my heart, and I knew that you would come here to resolve this mystery and let me go to my grave in peace. Do this for me and you'll be richly rewarded. Why not discuss it between you?'

Obviously understanding that they were in conflict, she stood up laboriously, balanced herself on her walking stick and, smiling sweetly, left the room. 'I'll be back in a few minutes,' she said as she closed the door behind her.

Tom and Molly stared silently at each other, neither smiling at all. The silence stretched out forever.

'God damn you,' Molly said eventually to break the silence, 'I'm goin' to do this. I'm gonna go on a real fancy trip and get paid handsomely for it. Then, when I get back, I'm gonna get paid even more an' have a very nice future.'

'*If* you get back,' Tom said.

'I'm a survivor,' Molly retorted.

'You can't do this, Molly. You're exploiting that dear woman. She's obviously as mad as a hatter and you're taking advantage. I think it's shameless. Disgusting.'

'Mad as a hatter, Tom? Is that what you really think? No, it's not! You don't think that at all. You know she's as sane as we are, but you don't want to admit it. Yes, Tom, you believed her. Every fuckin' last word. You're just scared and now you're tryin' to say she's mad 'cause that lets you off the hook. Well, fuck it, get out! I'll do the rest of it myself. I'll take the skulls back to where they belong – which should satisfy you, at least – and then that old bird will pay me for my labours and I can live my own life. But I'm goin' and then I'm gonna come back to see the shame in your face.'

Tom knew it was the truth and he could have hated her for it, but when he thought of what she might have to brave in the future, he knew that he could not desert her now, no matter how scared he was. Besides, she had challenged his manhood and he couldn't let that pass.

'All right,' he said. 'I'll do it. I think we're both crazy, but I'll do it. Now finish your tea.'

After staring haughtily at him, Molly picked up her cup and saucer, her little finger raised, and finished off the last of her tea. She was just setting the cup and saucer down when Lady Barratt-White came back into the room, hobbling unsteadily on her walking stick, to sit again on the sofa.

'Well, have you decided?' she asked.

'Yes,' Tom said, 'we'll do it.'

'Excellent,' Lady Barratt-White said. 'Just get in touch when you need anything – plane tickets, money, introductions – and I'll do the necessary.' She looked flushed with excitement and waved her hands before her face. 'Oh, dear, I'm so thrilled! Alas, my heart is racing too fast, so I must go and lie down. Is there anything else, dears?'

'Yes,' Tom said. 'If the crystal skulls work in tandem, we have to take both of them with us. Do you think you can persuade the curator of the Museum of Mankind to hand over the other one?'

'I'm *sure* I can,' Lady Barratt-White said. 'I shall phone him as soon as I've had my sleep and tell him you'll be calling in to collect it, say . . .?'

'Tomorrow afternoon,' Molly said. 'That should give him time to remove it and wrap it up. So let's make it the late afternoon.'

'Wise thinking, my dear. And now I really must . . .' The old lady started rising from the sofa, wanting to show them to the door, but Tom, a gentleman first and foremost, motioned for her to remain where she was.

'We'll let ourselves out,' he said as he stood up, indicating that Molly should do the same.

'Thank you, dear. You're too kind.'

Molly stood up as well. She glanced at Tom, then smiled at the old lady and walked around the table to shake her hand.

'Thanks a million,' she said, then she placed the crystal skull back into her shoulder bag and led Tom out of the flat.

'Goodbye, dears!' Lady Barratt-White called out to them as they closed the front door.

It was raining outside.

CHAPTER EIGHTEEN

'Darling!' she said sarcastically into the telephone, speaking to Lu Thong in Bangkok from her new location in a suite in the Ritz Hotel. 'It's me, your beloved Mai Suphar, speaking from London where it's raining cats and dogs. How are you, my revered lord and master?'

'In a good mood, are you?' Lu Thong replied, his voice sleepily sensual from drugs and, no doubt, some other diabolical forms of self-indulgence.

'Yes,' Mai said, 'I am.'

She was stretched out on her large double bed, wearing a dressing gown of sky-blue Thai silk, her delicate feet in furred slippers, her precious body warmed in the British cold by an electric blanket purchased personally from Harrod's, and was idly scanning that morning's edition of the London *Evening Standard*, the first edition of the day, while holding the telephone to one ear.

The front-page story in the newspaper was about the mysterious death of the British Museum's leading authority on antiquities, Professor Julian Weatherby, who had been found lying on the floor beside the bed in a room in the Savoy Hotel, dead from an apparent heart seizure. Neither the professor's bereaved wife nor any of his associates could explain what he had been doing in a room in the Savoy, let alone at that time in the afternoon, though it was known that the room had been rented to a female tourist who had signed in under the name of Anna Chow from Singapore, Malaysia. Miss Chow had checked out some time before the body was discovered and, the story's writer hinted, might simply have fled in embarrassment after Professor Weatherby, almost sixty years of age, had his heart seizure during sexual intercourse. The Metropolitan Police were still trying to trace Miss Anna Chow, but so far no leads had come up. Though there was no suspicion of foul play, the case remained open.

'Mmmm,' Mai purred with satisfaction into the telephone, stirred by a rush of sexual heat to her loins at being reminded of her terminal grappling with the late Professor Weatherby.

'You're definitely in good mood,' Lu Thong said, audibly inhaling, probably sniffing up cocaine. 'So what's brought it on? Have you good news for *me*?'

'Yes,' Mai replied, reaching out to the bedside cabinet for her glass of bubbling Dom Perignon, sipping it and then resting the glass on her flat belly. 'As requested, I tracked down Professor Weatherby, had a lengthy discussion with him, and ascertained from him that your Mr Tom Powell and his American tart, Molly Beale, are indeed in possession of the crystal skull. It was sent to the professor, as you had suspected, and they paid him a visit, squeezed some information out of him, and then left, taking the crystal skull with them.'

'Do you know what the professor told them?' Lu Thong asked, his voice still sleepily sensual, though Mai knew he was just as alert and deadly as ever.

'Yes,' Mai said. 'It wasn't much but it was all that I need. He told me that they had asked him a lot of crazy questions . . .'

'About the magical powers of the skull.'

'Correct . . . and that they had told him they were going to visit Lady Barratt-White to find out more about it.'

'Lady who?'

'Barratt-White.'

'That name rings a bell.'

'She's the ageing daughter of Ronald Barratt-White, the famous, or notorious, explorer who discovered the crystal skull now on display in the Museum of Mankind.'

'Ah, yes,' Lu Thong said. 'And, in fact, it was his daughter, now Lady Barratt-White, who actually found the skull. Very good, Mai. So what's happening now?'

'I haven't finished yet,' Mai said.

'So sorry, my dark angel. Please continue.'

'Knowing that Powell and Co were going to see Lady Barratt-White, who is now nearly ninety and receives periodical visits from social workers, I bought some down-market clothes in that ghastly Camden Market – moth-eaten pants and jumper, a pair of shoes that looked like industrial boots, an old football scarf and a hideous beret – and then, looking like a classic ethnic lesbian social worker, paid the old girl a visit before our friends could get there.'

'Beautiful,' Lu Thong said.

'Lady Barratt-White is so old, she's nearly blind, so I flashed my old *Carte Orange* from Paris, which she mistook for a Westminster Council identity card, and told her I was the new health inspector and wanted to check that the pensioners under my wing were being treated okay. She invited me in and we had a good chat and I made her a good strong cup of tea. When her weak bladder gave out and she had to go to the toilet, as I knew she would, I planted a bug in her phone. When she returned, I kindly washed the dishes for her and then took my leave.'

'Pure genius, Mai, but from where did you listen in?'

'You gave me some names, remember?'

'Ah, yes, of course. Including the names of some bent Scotland Yard detectives who once specialized in high-tech surveillance of diverse insurgents in Northern Ireland.'

'Exactly,' Mai said. 'So they sat outside the old bird's apartment block in an illegally equipped surveillance van and brought the resultant tapes to me this morning.'

'I hear sweet music, my pet.'

'Sweet it was. Mr Powell and Molly Beale duly paid their visit to Lady Barratt-White and had a good conversation with her. To paraphrase, she's financed them to get hold of the other crystal skull, the one in the Museum of Mankind, and, once they have it, to take both skulls back to their original source.'

'Which is?'

'At this point, it appears to be the holy city on the southern shore of Peru – the site of the legendary Sun Gate.'

'Is that what they think?'

'So far,' Mai said. 'Naturally, that may change, but so far what they *do* know for certain is that the two crystal skulls can only be fully utilized when they're used in tandem. So Powell and Beale are now going to try getting their hands on that other crystal skull and, to this end, they have an appointment with the curator of the Museum of Mankind late this afternoon.'

'How do you know that?'

'Because Powell's telephone was bugged by one of your bent coppers masquerading as a meter reader for the electricity board. When he phoned the curator of the museum to make his appointment, we picked up every word. He was given an appointment to see the curator just after the museum closes for the day. That's perfect for me.'

'If I were capable of love,' Lu Thong said, 'I would love you, my sweet.'

'Maybe some day,' Mai said.

Lu Thong chuckled, then trailed off into a silence that lingered a long time. It was not complete silence: Mai could hear his distant breathing. He was breathing in and out, very deeply and slowly, inhaling cocaine or some other, possibly even more dangerous substance, risking his life in order to feel alive, which was all he could do these days. He sighed, as if exhaling the fumes of hell, and then blew her a kiss.

'I'm so weary,' he said.

'You have everything, Lu Thong.'

'That's why I'm so weary,' he said. 'I've had too much, too soon. I'm jaded with sex, with money, with earthly power; and now the only thrill I can imagine is braving the unknown.'

'You've been doing that since childhood,' Mai said. 'Living on the edge. You've pushed yourself as far as any human being can go and now, alas, you've nothing left to push against.'

'I've got you,' Lu Thong said.

'You can't be sure of that,' Mai told him.

'That's exactly what I mean. I'm so powerful, I

haven't even got an enemy who puts me at risk – only you, Mai. You can't be trusted, you're absolutely ruthless, you get your thrills out of causing wreck and ruin – and you'd love to ruin me. I taught you everything you know and you won't be happy until you turn those skills against me. You'd orgasm on that, wouldn't you? It would make you feel transcendent. You're the only worthy opponent I have left, which is why I adore you . . . but you're still not enough.'

'Then what is, my hero?'

'The ultimate risk. The only gamble worth the taking. The opportunity to see what lies on the other side of life and maybe even return from there. That's why I need the crystal skulls. It is *I* who must return them. Used together, they could release all the powers of heaven and hell. I have to know if that is so. To find out, I must risk all. I have to return the crystal skulls to their source and then see what happens. So get those two skulls for me, Mai. I don't care how you do it. Get them for me and then kill Mr Powell and his American floozy.'

'I will,' Mai said.

Lu Thong was silent for a moment, though Mai heard his heavy breathing, then he whispered, 'Ah, God, I am drifting . . . drifting, drifting away . . .' He went out on a lengthy, eerie sigh and the line went dead.

Realizing that Lu Thong had drifted into a cocaine stupor, Mai put the phone back on its cradle and finished her champagne. Licking the last of it from her lips, she rolled off the bed, letting her dressing gown fall to the floor, and then, naked, she went into the *en suite* bathroom to prepare for the afternoon.

Thirty minutes later, she emerged wearing a grey

windcheater with bulging pockets, a dark-green woollen pullover, blue denims and flat, rubber-soled black shoes. Her long hair was pinned up on her head and covered with a wrap-around scarf. She looked as normal as a woman with her looks possibly could.

Seeing that the rain was still lashing down outside, she removed a short-handled umbrella from her suitcase and then left the room. Once outside the hotel, she remained in the doorway until the uniformed doorman had hailed a taxi for her and, walking beside her, holding his own umbrella up over her, escorted her to the taxi and closed the door behind her.

'The Museum of Mankind,' Mai said curtly to the driver.

'It's only five minutes' walk from here,' the driver replied.

'You want my money or not?' Mai replied. 'Take the long way around.'

'No skin off *my* nose, miss.'

Even the long way around was a fairly short distance, but the dense traffic ensured that the journey took nearly fifteen minutes. Mai enjoyed the trip, settling in and gazing out, seeing the lights of Piccadilly and then Mayfair through the glistening rainfall. It was only five in the afternoon but the evening darkness was falling early because of the heavy rain, with the lights of the streetlamps and shop windows falling over the pavements. Mai liked London a lot and thought she might live here some day; find a nice house in Knightsbridge or Chelsea and then marry a rich old man whose sudden death from an unexpected heart seizure would seem perfectly natural. A woman could have a good life here, picking her victims up off the streets. London was a glamorous, lonely city where no one counted the missing. Mai thought of Professor Weatherby, of the sexual thrill his death had given her, and she looked forward to repeating the performance with Mr Tom Powell.

'Here we are,' the driver said.

Looking out, Mai saw the entrance to the Museum of Mankind, drenched and still being lashed by rain. She paid the driver, told him to keep the change, then dashed for the entrance of the museum without bothering to open her umbrella. Once inside, she strapped the umbrella to her belt and then walked to the reception, where she was warned that the museum would be closing in fifteen minutes.

'That's long enough for me,' Mai said.

Having already been given a map of the museum and been informed of the crystal skull's whereabouts, Mai walked up to see it where it was on display on one of the landings, at the top of the stairs, gleaming and looking suitably macabre in the overhead lights. Satisfied that it was actually still there, Mai explored the museum, checking out where the doors were, including the emergency exits, and then she wandered around, ignoring the many wonderful exhibits, in search of one of the cleaning women. Taking it for granted that the domestic wing of the museum would be on the ground floor, she went back down the stairs just as the attendants were calling out closing time and visitors were surging towards the entrance. Fearless as always, Mai simply stayed out of sight, while keeping the entrance in view, until she saw an attendant closing the front doors behind the last of the visitors. At that moment, she also saw a woman, obviously working-class and not here for the fun of it, passing around a wooden barrier at the end of a ground-floor hall and disappearing through the doorway behind it.

Checking that the attendants now gathering around the front doors to complete their last-minute duties and take their leave were not looking in her direction, Mai padded softly across the brightly-lit exhibition hall and then skirted around the wooden barrier to go through the doorway previously taken by the cleaning lady. The doorway led into a corridor that smelt of Lysol and detergents, with a series of storage rooms running along both sides. Mai saw the cleaning lady enter one of those rooms and, still padding quietly on rubber soles, she followed the woman into the same room.

The room was filled with buckets, mops, dustpans, brushes, detergents and all the rest of the woman's cleaning paraphernalia. As Mai entered, treading as quietly as a mouse, the woman had her back turned to the doorway and was shucking off her overcoat to put on the coveralls hanging from a hook on one of the walls. The woman didn't hear a thing as Mai stepped up behind her, withdrawing a length of fine cord from one of the bulging pockets of her windcheater. Stretching the cord taut between her two hands, she quickly looped it over the woman's head and pulled it tight before the woman even knew what was happening.

Mai pulled hard on the cord, crossing it behind the woman's neck and pressing her knee into the woman's spine as she jerked even harder on the cord. The woman gasped briefly, quivering like a bowstring, bent backwards against Mai's knee, but then the cord cut deeply into her windpipe and choked the life out of her. She quivered even more violently, but beyond that could not move, and soon her body went limp, started to sag and then collapsed against

Mai. The latter loosened the cord, but kept hold of the dead woman until she had lowered her gently to the floor and could let her go completely.

'Sweet dreams,' Mai whispered.

After carefully rolling up the cord and placing it back in her pocket, Mai removed the coveralls from the hook on the wall and put them on over her own clothing. Because she was still wearing her windcheater, the coveralls were tight, but apart from that they felt fine. Needing a good-sized bag for the transportation of the crystal skull, Mai looked around the room and saw a large canvas bag hanging from the handles of a wheeled trolley filled with more cleaning paraphernalia. Smiling, Mai removed the bag from the trolley and then went to the doorway. Sticking her head out, she looked left and right. Seeing no one, she left the room and walked back the way she had come, out through the door at the end of the corridor, back around the wooden barrier and then across the expansive hall filled with exhibits, only stopping when the entrance came into view. The entrance had been closed and all the attendants had gone home, though a security man was sitting in a chair close to the front door. When Mai approached him, he glanced up in surprise, relaxed when he saw her cleaning woman's coveralls, then frowned when he failed to recognize her, though by then it was too late.

Mai grabbed him by his hair, swiftly jerked his head down, brought her knee up into his face with remarkable speed and brutality and then, before he could even fall over, she chopped him across the back of the neck with the hardened side of her open hand. The man grunted and started falling, but Mai held him upright, not wanting any noise, then lowered him gently to the floor.

Reaching into another of her bulging windcheater pockets, Mai withdrew a hypodermic syringe of the kind she had used on Professor Weatherby. After glancing back over her shoulder to ensure that no one was coming, she removed the protective cap from the syringe, then plunged the needle into the side of the unconscious man's neck. When she removed the needle, the man went into violent convulsions, flapping his arms, kicking his legs, but eventually he died and was still.

Mai put the cap back on the needle, placed the syringe back into her pocket, picked up the canvas bag, then turned away and went through the doorway which, according to the map given to her by one of Lu Thong's informants, contained the main switches and burglar alarm system.

The informant had not been wrong.

Having been trained in the criminal arts by Lu Thong's best men, Mai knew exactly what she was doing and did it with all speed. Removing an all-purpose knife from one of her bulging pockets, she used a small screwdriver to short-circuit the electricity, plunging the building into darkness and aborting the burglar-alarm system.

Thankfully, no emergency back-up alarm bells started ringing.

Pleased, though knowing that there were other people still in the building, including other security guards and, possibly, Tom Powell and Molly Beale, Mai wasted no time in removing a torchlight from one of her pockets, turning it on and making her way up the broad stairs until she came to the crystal skull, which had already been covered in a black cloth. Just to be sure, Mai removed the cloth.

The skull gleamed in the light coming in through the windows and made her think of her bad dreams.

At that moment, she heard the shouting of various men – probably security guards – echoing around the darkened floors above her.

Being careful to avoid gazing into those gaping eye sockets, she slipped the black cloth back over the crystal skull, removed the skull from its tall pedestal, and carefully placed it inside the canvas bag. She slung the canvas bag over her shoulder and made her way back down the stairs.

The dead guard still lay on the floor near the entrance, but otherwise the ground floor seemed empty.

Satisfied, Mai made her way back across the darkened ground-floor hallway, guided by her torchlight, and then into the corridor at the back. Once there, she started running, holding tightly to the canvas bag, shining the torchlight on the walls, until she saw the dully gleaming steel bars of the emergency exit. She tried to open the doors, but they were locked, though even that didn't stop her.

Moving swiftly, she removed a small package from one of her bulging pockets. It was a simple home-made bomb consisting of Semtex explosive, an electric initiator and a blasting cap with bridge wire, wired to a remote-control firing device.

Using black masking tape, Mai stuck the bomb to the lock of the door, ran the detonating wire out about fifteen feet along the corridor, attached it to the remote-control device and then pressed the button.

It was not a massive explosion, but it certainly

sounded so in the confined space of the dark corridor, almost deafening Mai and dazzling her with a jagged sheet of flashing light that made her close her eyes briefly. When she opened her eyes again, she saw billowing smoke and the scorched, mangled lock clattering noisily across the floor to bounce off the opposite wall. While the shattered lock was still spinning on the floor, Mai made her escape.

She emerged to falling rain, to the early evening's gloom, to the bright lights and clamour of passing traffic and the many pedestrians passing by. Not wishing to take a taxi – the driver might remember her face – she unstrapped her umbrella, held it above her head and then, with the canvas bag still slung from her shoulder, she walked back to the welcoming grandeur of the Ritz Hotel.

CHAPTER NINETEEN

Entering the museum ten minutes before closing time, Tom and Molly gave their details at reception and were escorted through the building to a small waiting room outside the curator's office. There they were told to take seats and assured that the curator would see them in ten minutes or so, just as soon as the building was closed for the evening and his other administrative tasks were completed. Thanking the young lady who had showed them in, they watched her disappearing around the corner at the end of the corridor, then they sat there, side by side, on their hard wooden chairs, neither knowing quite what to say.

Finally, to break the silence, Molly said, in her admirably blunt manner, 'Okay, admit it, you're scared.'

'Of meeting the curator?'

'No. Of gettin' even deeper into this. You're scared of that and right now you hate me because I won't let you out.'

'Not true, Molly.'

'Yes, it is, Tom.'

'I, too, want to see this through to the end, to return the crystal skulls to their original source, where clearly they were meant to be, and to see what happens when we do so. If I'm scared – and certainly we both should be – it's not only for myself, but also for you. I care about you, Molly, after my fashion, and I feel concern for you. Those men who died at Chichén Itzá were undoubtedly criminals and the ones who followed us were clearly dangerous men and almost certainly not working alone. Whoever wants our crystal skull wants it badly and may not have given up yet. I think we're both in real danger.'

Molly turned to stare at him with eyes widening and brimming over with emotion. 'You care for me?'

'After my fashion.'

'What does that mean?'

'I care for you more than you might think and I have concern for you.'

'So what does *that* mean?'

Tom was uncomfortable. He found it hard to discuss such matters. The emotional world was very tricky and he wished to avoid it. 'I think you're cute,' he said. 'Too foul-mouthed, but good for all that. I believe the American word for you is "spunky" and I find that admirable. I've always lacked physical courage myself and you have it in bagfuls. Also, I happen to know that you've grown fond of me. Now why don't you admit it?'

'Gee whiz, the man's in love!' Molly was grinning, but her eyes were moist.

'I didn't say that, Molly. I said I cared. And that's just what I meant.'

'Oh, yeah?'

'Oh, yes. But of course I know that you've grown fond of *me*, so why not admit it?'

'Pompous little shit, aren't ya?'

'You don't have to be foul-mouthed.'

'I use the language that I learnt in the streets and

I can't talk with a plum in my mouth, but I get my meaning across.'

'You certainly do.'

'You love me,' Molly said.

'You love *me*,' Tom replied.

Molly chuckled and shook her head from side to side, filled with wonder and gratitude. 'The man loves me but he's too fuckin' English to express his true feelin's. Come on, Tom, why not say it?'

'You say it first.'

'I love you.'

'Really?'

'Yes, really.'

'You're a woman with surprisingly good taste.'

'Go fuck yourself, bud!'

Amused and blessedly distracted, Tom was about to offer a retort when the door to the curator's office opened and a man with a long, pale face and no hair whatsoever stepped out to stare at them. He was as thin as the stem of a lamp-post and wore a pinstripe suit with shirt and old school tie. He looked like a fairly decent man who had never smiled in his life.

'Mr Powell?' he asked of Tom.

'Yes,' Tom replied, rising to his feet and proferring his hand.

'William Postlethwaite,' the curator introduced himself. They shook hands and then Tom introduced Molly, who also shook the curator's hand.

'Please come in,' the curator said. When they were inside his office and seated in front of him, gazing at him across his surprisingly bare desk, he gave them the full blankness of his decent face and said, 'Before we go any further, may I just say that had it not been

Lady Barratt-White herself who called on your behalf, I would not have given you this appointment. I have a great deal of respect for Lady Barratt-White, but she *is* rather old now, not to say a little eccentric, and when she says she wants us to return the crystal skull to her and, moreover, hand it over to two perfect strangers, I'm bound to say in response that this is something that I, representing this museum, simply cannot agree to.'

'So why give us the appointment?' Molly asked tartly before Tom could even open his mouth.

'I gave you the appointment,' Mr Postlethwaite replied bluntly, being a decent and honest man, 'because I respect Lady Barratt-White, appreciate her great gift to this museum, and therefore felt obliged to at least see you.'

'Did you tell her you wouldn't let us have the skull?' Tom asked.

'No, I did not. I didn't wish to upset her. She's a dear old lady with not too long to live and I felt it best to humour her and, I must confess, to find out just why she felt the sudden urge to take the skull back and pass it on to someone else. May I ask who you are, why you want the skull, and how you came in contact with Lady Barratt-White? The world of antiquities is a small one and your name's not familiar.'

Taking a deep breath, aware that he was in tricky waters here and unwilling to let the upright Mr Postlethwaite know that he and Molly were in illegal possession of the second crystal skull, Tom thought hard before exhaling. Then he plunged in: 'Well, Mr Postlethwaite, while I'm not professionally involved in the world of antiquities, I've been studying the subject for some years and have a particular interest in early

Mayan culture in general and your crystal skull in particular.'

As Mr Postlethwaite raised his left eyebrow progressively higher in increasing disbelief, Tom, hardly aware of what he was saying, but instinctively leaving out any mention of his experience at Chichén Itzá and his possession of the Rose Quartz Skull, managed to explain, with a few little embellishments, how he had come to see Professor Weatherby in the British Museum, been 'recommended' by him to Lady Barratt-White, and been 'encouraged' by the latter into returning her crystal skull, the one in this very building, to its source in Tiahuanaco, Peru.

When Tom had finished, wiping sweat from his brow with the white handkerchief he always kept tucked into the breast pocket of the pinstripe suit he had worn since returning to London, Mr Postlethwaite raised his left eyebrow to its maximum altitude, then lowered it and practically quivered with outrage.

'Are you some kind of crank, Mr Powell?'

'Hey, watch your mouth!' Molly exploded.

'Please, Molly,' Tom said, then turned back to Mr Postlethwaite. 'No, I certainly am not!'

'Yet you believe the crystal skull has to be returned to its original source in order that its magic powers might be released?'

'That's correct,' Tom said.

'That's ridiculous,' Mr Postlethwaite retorted. 'I'm embarrassed to even hear it. I cannot believe you can walk into this museum and tell me this rubbish straight-faced.'

'Lady Barratt-White agrees with me,' Tom said, 'which is why she wants *me* to have the crystal skull.'

'As I said before, *sir*,' Mr Postlethwaite said, placing

an emphasis on 'sir' as if it was a dirty word, 'I have the utmost regard for Lady Barratt-White, but she *is* rather old now and, like many people her age, perhaps not all there in the head and so susceptible to the blandishments of charlatans. As for . . .'

'Hey, watch your mouth!' Molly exploded again.

'As for your supposed visit to my former colleague, the late Professor Julian Weatherby, I would like to know when you made that visit, since Professor Weatherby, God rest his soul, was found dead in suspicious circumstances in a room in the Savoy Hotel where, to the best of my knowledge, he had no business being. So when did you visit him?'

Shocked to hear this news, which really was news to him since he hadn't read a newspaper since returning to London, Tom felt himself dropping into a deep well of fear. Glancing at Molly, he saw that she felt the same way. Then he managed to regain control of himself and boldly faced the curator's accusing gaze.

'If you're suggesting that I had something to do with Professor Weatherby's death,' Tom said, 'just because I happen to have paid him a visit, I would just like to say that—'

He didn't finish the sentence because the room was abruptly plunged into darkness.

'What . . . ?' Mr Postlethwaite's voice resounded eerily in the sudden silence, then Tom heard a clattering sound as something on the desk fell over, obviously knocked over by Mr Postlethwaite's groping hand, and then he heard the telephone being picked off its cradle, followed by the sound of it being dialled. 'This is the curator,' Mr Postlethwaite said. 'My lights have just gone out.' A brief silence descended as Mr Postlethwaite listened to the voice on the other end of the line, then he said, 'A power failure? The whole building? Surely that's not possible. We have override switches to avoid that kind of incident, so the lights should have come on automatically.' He went silent again, obviously listening to the bad news, then said, sounding shocked, 'The burglar alarm system as well? But surely *that* isn't possible! That system has its own override facility and can't just . . . Pardon? *What?* You believe both systems must have been *sabotaged?* Oh, my God! Then . . .' But instead of finishing his sentence, he slammed the telephone down, kicked his chair back and stood up.

Tom's eyes were adjusting to the darkness as Mr Postlethwaite groped about frantically in a desk drawer, then the beam of a flashlight split the darkness and Mr Postlethwaite, carrying the torch in one hand, ran out of the office.

'Let's go!' Molly said.

Hurrying after Mr Postlethwaite, they followed him along the darkened corridor to the stairs leading down to the lobby. As they chased him down the stairs, guided by the frantically wavering beam of his torchlight, they could hear the panicky shouting of security guards echoing eerily around the other darkened exhibition halls. Mr Postlethwaite had just reached the bottom of the stairs leading to the ground floor when the lights came back on and revealed a body lying rigidly on the floor close to the front door. The man seemed to be dead.

'Oh, my God!' Mr Postlethwaite wailed, freezing near the dead man and glancing frantically left and right, his decent face pale and shocked. Tom and Molly stopped behind him, hearing footsteps running down the stairs behind them and more panicky shouting.

Before Mr Postlethwaite could make another move, a security guard came running through an open door, practically skidded to a halt, glanced down at the dead man on the floor and turned to face Mr Postlethwaite.

'He's dead,' the security man confirmed.

'Oh, my God!' Mr Postlethwaite exclaimed again, blinking repeatedly like someone in deep shock.

'I've just been to check,' the security man said, flushed with too much excitement for one evening, 'and the mains electric and the burglar-alarm systems have both been tampered with.'

'You mean . . . *sabotage?*'

'Yes. I've just turned the back-up generator on, which is why we have lights now.'

'But my telephone was working!'

'A different system,' the security man said. 'That's pure British Telecom. I've already called the police and . . .' He nodded towards the front door, which was being opened by another security guard. 'We're opening the doors to let them in.'

'But what . . . ?'

Another security guard came running across the exhibition hall to their right and stopped breathlessly in front of Mr Postlethwaite.

'There's a dead woman back there,' he said. 'A cleaning woman – Mrs Branson. The poor bitch has been strangled.'

'Oh, my God!' Mr Postlethwaite exclaimed, glancing about him as if expecting to be attacked by a gang of armed robbers. 'I just can't . . .'

There was the sound of advancing footsteps behind Tom and Molly, then another security guard ran around them and stopped breathlessly in front of Mr Postlethwaite.

'The crystal skull's been stolen,' he said.

'*What?*'

'I said—'

'Let's go!' Molly snapped. Then she grabbed Tom by the hand and raced him to the open front door where she rudely pushed the security guard aside and made her escape. 'Keep running!' she bawled.

Tom felt his heart racing as he followed Molly along the street, dazzled by the street lamps and the brightly-lit shop windows, drenched in slanting sheets of rain. When they had turned up a side street, out of sight of the museum, Molly slowed down to a walk, released Tom's sweaty hand, and raised an umbrella over their heads.

'Walk as naturally as possible,' Molly said, 'and stop lookin' so scared.'

'I can't help it,' Tom said.

At first, he didn't know where she was leading him and he didn't really care, being too frightened to think straight, but he soon recognized the area that he lived in and then they came to the hotel he had booked for Molly.

'We've gotta talk,' Molly explained.

When they entered the hotel, she shook the rain off her umbrella, folded it up, went to the reception desk for her room key and led Tom to the lift. They went upstairs and entered her room, where Molly immediately turned the light on and then carefully locked the door. Tom glanced at her bed and then looked away, feeling distinctly, oddly uncomfortable. His racing heart was gradually settling down, but he still felt very nervous.

'You wanna drink?' Molly asked.

'Desperately,' Tom said.

'You don't mind if I use this bar at your expense?'

'Of course not. That's the idea.'

Molly knelt in front of the refrigerated bar, then opened the door and looked inside. 'We've got whisky and brandy and . . .'

'Brandy. I could do with a brandy.'

'I'll try that,' Molly said. After removing two tiny bottles of brandy from the bar, she kicked the door shut and handed one of the bottles to Tom. As he was unscrewing the metal top, she fetched two glasses and handed him one of those as well. She sat on the edge of the bed while he took the only chair in the room. They both drank and then stared at one another, temporarily speechless.

Eventually, Molly brushed her damp hair away from her forehead and crossed her long legs. They were very nice legs.

'Why did you run us out of there?' Tom asked. 'You shouldn't have done that. Now they'll think . . .'

'That we had something to do with the theft of the crystal skull and, even worse, with the death of Professor Julian Weatherby? They'll think that anyway, Tom. That's *why* I ran us out of there. We were there when the lights went out, when the crystal skull was stolen. We also saw Professor Weatherby the same day he died, probably murdered, and that curator was already very suspicious about that and was about to ask questions. Then the lights all went out and the crystal skull was stolen, so he's bound to think his suspicions were correct. He'll tell the cops about us – and about our visit to Professor Weatherby – so the cops are gonna wanna talk to us. We have to leave London, Tom.'

'Leave London? You mean *now*?'

'If not now, pretty soon. Before the cops track us

down. We might as well take our skull to Peru and see what happens there.'

Tom finished off his brandy and helped himself to another. When he had poured it, he sat back in his chair and had a good slug. It warmed him and went to his head and made him feel a lot calmer, if decidedly unreal.

'The police won't have too much trouble finding me,' he said. 'I'm listed in the phone book, after all, and that's the first place they'll look.'

'Then we have to leave as soon as we possibly can, preferably on the first flight out tomorrow.'

'We can't,' Tom said. 'We have to take *both* skulls with us. One skull may be useless without the other, so we have to find out who took the other one and then take that as well.'

'That may not be possible,' Molly said.

'Perhaps, but we have to try.'

'We have one day – maybe two or three – and then we have to go, even if we go with only one skull. Anyway, think about it, Tom. Whoever wants that skull wants it pretty badly – he's willing to kill to get it – so he probably knows as much about it as we do. And if that's the case, then he knows it's gotta be returned to its source if it's to have any value. Given this, I say that if we take our own skull to Peru, the other guy—'

'It could be a woman, Molly.'

'It's a figure of speech, Tom . . . Anyway, the other guy, or gal, will probably know that we've no choice but to go to Peru and so either he'll follow us or, willy nilly, take his own skull to the same place. Either way, those two skulls are going to meet up, sooner or later.'

'Then we'll be killed and robbed of our own crystal skull.'

'Not necessarily. You heard what Lady Barratt-White said. For whatever reason, we're bein' protected by the magical powers of the crystal skulls while the others are bein' attacked by those same powers. Maybe it was *destined* to happen this way – so I say we've got to go.'

Tom thought about it, filling up with dread again, but realized that he didn't have a choice. 'All right,' he said, 'we'll go. But I need a few more days. I need to find out more about the crystal skulls and I know just the man I want to ask – an old friend of mine. Also, since this old friend is in the business, he might pick up some news about the whereabouts of the stolen crystal skull.'

'Fine,' Molly said, 'but you only have a few days and in the meantime you've got to move out of your apartment and stay somewhere else.'

'I'll move into my club,' Tom said. 'It'll take the police a while to find out I'm a member.'

'Good thinkin',' Molly said. She leaned sideways to place her glass on the bedside cabinet, then, with a sigh, she fell back on the bed, stretched out, breasts upthrust, with her legs dangling over the mattress and her feet on the floor. She looked voluptuous and irresistible lying there and Tom was embarrassed. 'God, I'm pooped!' Molly exclaimed.

Aware that he was sexually aroused, Tom felt even more embarrassed, so he stood up and placed his glass on the dressing table, saying, 'Well, I think I'd better get going.'

Molly sat upright again. 'So what happens tomorrow?'

'Meet me in the Museum Tavern,' Tom said. 'The one facing the main gates of the British Museum. We're going to visit that friend of mine at his very strange shop in Covent Garden. How about noon?'

'Great,' Molly said then she pointed to the bag containing the crystal skull. 'What about that?' she asked.

'What do you mean?'

'Someone murdered Professor Weatherby over that crystal skull, which means they must want it pretty badly. Is there anywhere safer than this room we can hide it?'

'Yes,' Tom said. 'In the safe in my club.'

'Then you'd better put it there.'

'Right.' Tom picked the bag up, hoisted it onto his shoulder and then, still embarrassed to see her on the bed, he turned away and opened the door, preparing to leave. Molly, however, jumped off the bed and rushed up behind him. Taking hold of his shoulders, she turned him around to face her. Before he knew what was happening, she kissed him full on the lips. When he stepped back, she grinned at him.

'Ah, ha!' Tom said, covering his embarrassment. 'It must truly be love!'

Before she could see the tenderness in his face, he turned away and walked out.

CHAPTER TWENTY

That evening, Tom moved into his elegant gentlemen's club in Mayfair where, as a guest from out of town (his formal address being his Reigate estate) he was allowed to stay a maximum of three nights each month. Though planning to go to bed early and be fresh for tomorrow when he would, he was convinced, be a bundle of nerves, waiting for the police to catch him, he was surprised to hear a knocking on his room door. Already in his pyjamas and dressing gown, he was embarrassed to open the door and even more embarrassed when he did so and found a beautiful Eurasian girl standing there. Taken aback, not expecting to find a woman, other than staff, in the building, he just stared at her in open-mouthed bewilderment.

'Mr Powell?' Her voice was low and sensual but sounded desperate.

'Yes,' Tom said.

'I know I'm not supposed to be here, but please invite me in. It's really dreadfully urgent.'

Glancing nervously up and down the corridor, all varnished oak beams and dust-covered chandeliers, to check that no members of staff were in sight, Tom nodded and stepped aside to let the young lady in. She brushed hurriedly past him and he closed the door quickly behind her, then turned to face her.

Again, he was struck by how beautiful she was and only then did he recognize her as a native of Thailand. Her face was truly lovely, with large, luminous brown eyes, long black eyelashes, a perfect nose and very full, crimson-painted lips. She was wearing an expensive black gaberdine, belted tightly at the waist, and high-heeled black leather boots. Her hair, which was as black as her coat, hung to her waist.

'Since it's so late,' she explained before Tom could ask the obvious question, 'I just lingered outside the entrance to the building where I could see the male receptionist, then, when he left his desk for something or other, I hurried in and managed to get up the stairs without being seen. I know it was an awful thing to do, but I'm absolutely desperate.'

She burst into tears.

'There, there, dear girl,' Tom said, instinctively reaching out to squeeze her shoulder and reassure her. 'Please be seated and let me fetch you a glass of water. Here, this chair here.'

Still sobbing wretchedly, she sat in the hardbacked wooden chair, dabbed her eyes with a handkerchief and then, seemingly without thinking, untied the belt around her black gaberdine and took a deep breath just as Tom was hurrying back with a glass of water. When he handed her the glass, the gaberdine fell open, hanging down to the floor, revealing a breath-taking figure in an elegant, tight-fitting black dress. The gorgeous creature was wearing expensive jewellery and clearly had class.

'Drink it up,' Tom said, indicating the glass of water. 'I'm sure it will help. Then tell me what you're doing here. I mean, I could get into trouble if you were found here, so . . .'

'I know! I know! That's why I feel so bad. But I just had to come. I *had* to!' And she started sobbing again.

'There, there,' Tom said again, compassionately patting the poor creature on the shoulder and, uncomfortably aware that he was wearing only his pyjamas and dressing gown, trying to stop himself from staring at her superb, trembling figure. When she had managed to control herself again and was dabbing the tears from her lovely, long-lashed eyes, Tom sat on the edge of his bed and stared sympathetically at her.

Returning his smile with a smile of her own – a smile so glorious that Tom, despite his new feelings for Molly, felt his heart lurching – she said, 'I'm a friend of Lady Barratt-White's, a dear woman, and I'm in trouble and went to see her this afternoon. When I told her the kind of trouble I was in, she recommended that I come and see you immediately.'

'Me?' Tom responded, surprised. 'Why me? I've only met the dear lady once and . . .'

'Yes, she told me – and told me why you had gone to see her. Which is why she sent me to you. My name, by the way, is Mai – Mai Suphar. I'm so pleased to meet you.'

Tom leaned forward off the bed to shake her hand. 'My pleasure, I'm sure.'

Mai smiled. It was a ravishing smile, but quite shy, which only made it all the more heartwarming. She dabbed at her still moist eyes with the handkerchief, sniffed pitifully a few times, then confessed, 'I did a terrible thing.'

'Oh, what was that, dear?'

Mai took a deep breath and held it in, thus emphasizing her wonderful breasts. Then, like a woman in deep despair, she let it out again as she spoke. 'Earlier this evening, under pressure from an extremely dangerous person, I stole a crystal skull from the Museum of Mankind.' And she burst into tears again.

Instantly, Tom jumped off the bed and took the two steps that carried him to her. He reached down with one hand to squeeze her shoulder reassuringly. Seemingly without thinking, for all the world like a hurt child, she pressed her forehead against his stomach and clutched the side of his dressing gown, to pull him protectively against her. Tom was shocked by the sensual warmth that flooded through him, but he was also filled with sympathy for her. Aware of these contradictory emotions, he squeezed her shoulder again and gently disengaged himself to sit back on the bed. Mai managed to control her sobbing again, dabbed at her wet cheeks with her handkerchief, then took another deep breath – Tom could not ignore those heaving breasts – and raised her head to stare solemnly at him, her brown eyes filled with shame.

'You stole the crystal skull?' Tom asked incredulously.

'Yes,' Mai said. 'I stole it. I was given no choice. That's why I went to see my dear friend, Lady Barratt-White, and why she then sent me to you. She said that you had an interest in that skull, desperately needed it, and that any information I could give you would be helpful to you. By giving you this information, she told me, I would pay for my sins. That's why I'm here, Mr Powell.'

Hardly knowing what to say, feeling naked in his pyjamas, Tom ran his fingers through his ruffled hair and managed, 'Oh, dear. Well, what can I say? I mean . . . You *really* stole that crystal skull?'

Mai nodded, staring soulfully at him with her big brown eyes, drawing him towards her like a moth to the flame, filling him with contradictory emotions, including compassion and lust.

'I think you'd better explain,' he said.

Mai nodded again, dabbed delicately at her wet eyes with the handkerchief, then took another deep, breast-enhancing breath, and looked up again.

'Mr Powell, please understand that life in Bangkok, where I come from, is very different from life here in England.'

'Well, I'm *sure* it is,' Tom said, trying not to stare at her, but drawn helplessly to the soulfulness in her brown gaze, as well as to her perfect breasts and slim waist and broad hips and long legs and swan's neck and delicate wrists. The more he tried not to stare, the more he stared, not knowing where else to look.

'For most poor people, Mr Powell,' Mai continued, 'life in Bangkok is very hard.'

'I'm *sure* it is,' Tom repeated.

Mai nodded affirmatively. 'I come from a very poor family in Wat Dusit, near the railway station. As you probably know, Mr Powell, there are so-called red-light districts around the railway stations of most major cities and it was in such a district that I was born and grew up.'

'You poor thing.' Tom said, feeling even more compassion for her.

'Yes,' Mai said, clearly grateful for his compassion. 'And at a very early age, my mother was forced into prostitution. Then my sister, too, was forced into the streets, to the despair of my father, who then killed himself.'

'How dreadful!' Tom said.

'Yes,' Mai said, looking as if she was about to cry again, but managing, with some more dabbing at her moist, fluttering eyes, to control herself. 'I only avoided the same fate,' she continued, 'by marrying a wealthy Chinese businessman and moving with him into the Bang Kapi district, where we lived very happily for a short while.'

'A *short* while?' Tom asked.

The poor girl started sobbing again, though this time she did so silently, merely letting the tears roll down her golden cheeks while nodding and saying, 'Yes, a short while. In marrying my dear husband, I angered a man who had wanted me for his mistress: an evil brute named Lu Thong, the very same pimp, drug addict and murderer who controlled the red-light district around the railway station and who had turned my mother and sister into prostitutes.'

'Oh, you poor thing. How horrible!'

Mai nodded her agreement, gave him an anguished, though ravishing smile, dabbed at her wet eyes again and continued: 'Yes, that same Lu Thong, that monster, was terribly angry when I married my dear husband and swore that he would get me in his bed, one way or the other. Then . . .' Unable to contain her grief, she burst into tears again and was only able to continue when Tom had jumped off the bed, fetched her another glass of water, given her a compassionate squeeze and returned to his awkward position on the side of his bed. 'Then,' Mai continued tearfully, 'only six weeks ago, my dear husband was killed in a hit-and-run accident; and, though the driver of that vehicle was never traced, Lu Thong let it be known to me that he personally had organized the so-called accident. He then said that something similar would happen to me if I did not relent and become his mistress.'

'Dreadful!' Tom exclaimed, now positively overwhelmed by compassion. 'Absolutely horrendous! You poor, haunted child. What on earth did you do?'

Mai raised her head to stare at him with a pride that went straight to his heart. 'I refused him,' Mai said. 'I told him that I would rather die than be his mistress – and I meant it, Mr Powell, I really did. I would have died first.'

'Most admirable,' Tom said. 'But then how come . . . ?'

Mai burst into tears again, was rescued again by Tom, gave him an instinctive, grateful hug and only continued when he had managed to wriggle free and sit back on the bed.

'Knowing that I would willingly die,' she said tearfully, 'rather than become his mistress, Lu Thong did something even more dreadful . . .'

'No!' Tom exclaimed.

'Yes!' Mai looked at him with luminous, tearful eyes. 'He told me that if I didn't become his mistress, he would kill my poor sister – and I knew that he meant it.'

'The vicious brute!' Tom said.

'Yes,' Mai agreed.

'And you . . . ?' Tom couldn't bear to ask the question.

'Yes, God help me – and to my eternal shame – I became that monster's mistress . . . and that's why I'm here.'

Tom thought that this was the most dreadful story he had ever heard in his life and he wanted to step over to the poor child and embrace her and hug her. However, the knowledge that he was wearing only his dressing gown and pyjamas, coupled with his frustrated desire for Molly and helpless sexual attraction towards this astonishingly beautiful, haunted creature, prevented him from doing so. Instead, he listened with a breaking heart to the rest of her tragedy.

'It was Lu Thong,' Mai explained, 'who first told me about the crystal skull. He's obsessed with it, Mr Powell, believing it to have magical powers and determined to have those powers for himself and use them for his own evil purposes.'

'Typical!' Tom interjected passionately.

'Yes, typical. Typical of such a monster. And so he told me that the crystal skull was in the Museum of Mankind and that he was sending me to London to bring it back for him. He did not tell me, however, until I arrived in London, that he had arranged for some of his thugs to sabotage the electrical wiring and burglar-alarm systems of the museum and that I personally would have to enter the building as a tourist, hide away until the building was closed and the security systems had been aborted, and then steal the crystal skull from its pedestal and then somehow spirit it away. When I told him, by phone, that I was frightened of doing this, that I could go to prison for it, he put my sister on the phone and she sobbed and told me that he had a knife to her throat at the very moment and was preparing to use it. So I did it, Mr Powell. To my eternal shame, I did it. I stole the crystal skull and made my escape by an emergency exit at the rear of the building. Now I'm a criminal, Mr Powell, and I feel like killing myself.'

'Oh, don't do that, my child!' Without thinking, Tom

jumped off the bed again and advanced the couple of steps that took him to her. When she burst into tears again, clearly moved by his compassion, he had no choice but to place his arms around her and let her rest her forehead on his stomach while clinging to him and sobbing. Tom stroked her smooth, sweet-scented hair and patted her trembling spine. 'There, there,' he said. 'You poor child. But it's all right. I'm here.' Then the heat of her body flooded his loins and he stepped back again, though this time not as far as the bed. He just stood about a foot away from her, gazing down upon her. When she stared up at him, her eyes widened even more and he almost drowned in their dark, beckoning depths.

'But what can *I* do to help?' Tom asked. 'Why come to *me*?'

'Because Lady Barratt-White, that dear woman, my good friend, told me about your interest in the crystal skull, insisted that you had to have it, and asked me to tell you of its whereabouts. She said that you would attempt to get it back—'

'*Me?*' Tom interjected.

'Yes. And now that I've kept my part of the bargain with that monster Lu Thong, thus saving my sister's life, I'm happy to give you the information you need in order to get it back.'

'Really?'

'Really. As Lu Thong won't know that I gave you this information, when you manage to steal the crystal skull back from him, my sister won't be endangered and I will have the pleasure of seeing his evil desires thwarted.'

Though his heart raced with panic and the blood rushed to his head, Tom managed to croak, 'I have to get the crystal skull back from Lu Thong?'

'Yes,' Mai said. 'At this very moment, the crystal skull, secured in a Thai Embassy diplomatic bag, is being flown back to Lu Thong in Bangkok.' She reached into her black leather shoulder bag and pulled out a neatly folded piece of paper, which she handed to Tom. 'This is Lu Thong's address, Mr Powell. The rest is up to you.'

Now feeling almost faint with fear, as well as dizzy with desire, Tom glanced at the piece of paper but was unable to focus upon it, so folded it again and placed it in the pocket of his dressing gown. When he gazed down at the lovely Mai, his desire briefly overcame his fear and made him feel disorientated.

'I have to tell you,' he said, trying to get a grip on himself and not be swayed by tender emotions, 'that tragic though your story is, and much as I would like to get my hands on that crystal skull, I really don't think that I'm equipped, either mentally or physically, to fly all the way to Bangkok and face up to a professional criminal and murderer like that swinish Lu Thong. No, my dear, I'm afraid not. My friend, Molly—'

'Yes, Lady Barratt-White told me about her,' Mai interjected, 'and clearly she's a most admirable young woman.'

'Indeed,' Tom said. 'Admirable – absolutely. And certainly mad enough to do as you suggest. Molly would. I wouldn't. I'm so sorry, but that's all there is to it. I simply won't do it.'

Mai lowered her head and crossed one leg over the other. Those legs, in sheer black stockings, flowing down from the hem of the tight, shimmering black dress, were truly a spectacular sight. 'I understand,' Mai said.

Tom sat on the edge of the bed again, feeling cowardly, generally confused and far too emotional. When Mai raised her head to gaze at him, he was mesmerized by her brown eyes.

'You really won't do it?' Mai asked softly.

'No,' Tom said. 'I'm sorry.'

'But you think Molly would?'

'Yes.'

'Would you mind if I went to see her?' Mai asked.

'That's your choice,' Tom said.

Realizing that this timid but rather cute Englishman meant what he said and would not fly to Bangkok, which meant that he was redundant, Mai decided to have a little pleasure by seducing him and then putting his lights out. To this end, she sighed mournfully, then pushed her chair back and stood up. Before Tom knew what was happening, she walked up to him where he still sat on the edge of the bed, and gazed mournfully, yearningly down at him. His eyes were as large as two saucers when he raised his head to look up at her.

'I understand perfectly,' Mai said, speaking softly, caressingly, 'and would like to thank you anyway for your kindness. You're a good, thoughtful man.'

Leaning forward, she placed her hands on his shoulders and kissed him on the cheek. Her lips lingered. She was breathing into his ear. Her body, she knew, was irresistible to most men and Mr Tom Powell was not immune to it. His breathing quickened. She stroked his cheek and it was burning. She murmured, 'You're so kind, *so* kind,' and then kissed him full on the lips, pushing him back onto the bed until he was stretched out beneath her.

Tom tried to protest, making groaning, gargling sounds, but when her body was stretched out on top of his, he was lost to the world.

Indeed, he could not help himself, being confused and overwhelmed, cast adrift on a tide of contradictory emotions compounded of rising guilt, growing fear and helpless desire. He hardly knew what was happening, was only dimly aware of it, consumed, as he was, in a heat that scorched all thought out of him.

He was crushed by Mai's body, trapped in her writhing limbs, deprived of will when her electric fingers stroked him, obliterated by feeling. He didn't know how they had managed it, could not even remember moving, yet somehow they had moved up onto the bed, his head near the pillow. Mai was still on top of him, her belly pressed on his belly, her breasts rubbing against his chest as she unbuttoned the top of his pyjamas and then tugged them open. Her tongue licked his bared skin, her teeth sank into his neck, and he heard someone groaning piteously – himself – as she pressed her groin against his throbbing erection and sucked the skin of his throat.

'Oh, God!' Tom groaned.

He had caught a glimpse of Molly somewhere out there in the ether, an accusing face floating in the cosmos of his disjointed, scattering thoughts. Guilt scorched him like a flame, making him open his eyes, and he saw Mai's hand groping across the crumpled bedsheet, as if searching for something. Her leather bag was lying there, not too far from Tom's head. Her fingers found it and managed to flip it open to grope deep inside it. Tom wondered what she was doing. That thought broke through his delirium. He saw something thin and glittering in her hand and then the room lights blinked out.

The sudden darkness was startling, a shock to his whole system, and then he heard a rush of wind, or what seemed like rushing wind, and an eerie light materialized out of the darkness and surrounded the bed.

'What . . . ?' Mai whispered, freezing on top of Tom and glancing about her. 'What the hell . . . ?'

The eerie light around them brightened, illuminating the whole bed, and the rushing wind became a distant humming that seemed almost physical. Tom thought he could *feel* the humming, a kind of pulsating infrasound, and then he saw that the brightening light was pulsating rhythmically as it filled up with . . . *stars*.

'What the hell . . . ?' Mai repeated in a whisper as she rolled off his body.

Even as Tom tried to sit upright, in which he was not successful – as some invisible force was now pressing upon him – featureless, slightly transparent, possibly feminine figures materialized magically out of that eerie, pulsating light, which now formed a dazzling, star-filled white haze. The figures seemed to be whispering, though no words could be heard, and they gradually encircled the bed and then moved right up to it. They were figures of silvery light, weaving slightly like windblown reeds. They had normal-shaped heads and an odd kind of face. They had no eyes, no nose and no lips . . . no facial features at all.

Mai screamed in terror.

That screaming lashed through Tom and also filled him with terror as the ghostly whispering turned into a roaring that made the bed shake and rattle. Tom tried again to sit upright, but he seemed to be paralysed, though Mai, who had stopped screaming, dropped something close to his head as she jumped off the bed. Instinctively grabbing her shoulder bag, she raced to the room door, running right through the ghostly, incorporeal figures and disappearing into the darkness beyond the dazzling light.

Tom was stunned and shaken. Mai had run straight *through* those ghostly, faceless figures as if they did not exist.

Suddenly, the roaring receded and the dazzling light dimmed. Tom heard the door being jerked open, followed by the sound of Mai's footsteps as she ran off down the corridor. Even as the footsteps receded, the light dimmed and shrank rapidly, as if sucked into a vacuum, taking the ghostly figures with it, and then the figures were totally swallowed up in the expanding darkness and the light shrank to the size of a coin. That tiny light floated briefly in the darkness and then it winked out completely.

The room lights came back on.

Tom sat upright and now had no problems in doing so. He was, however, sweating and shaking and the fear would not leave him. Eventually, when he felt that his senses had returned, he looked down to see what Mai had dropped on the bed. It was a hypodermic syringe.

Tom stared at it, terrified.

CHAPTER TWENTY-ONE

'So I had the hypodermic syringe checked by a friend in the Pathology Department of the Royal Free Hospital, Hampstead,' Tom informed Molly the next day while they were having lunch in the Museum Tavern, 'and he told me it contained a toxin that would induce a fatal heart arrhythmia without leaving any traces behind. In other words, that seemingly tragic young Thai lady was going to kill me!'

'Mmmm,' Molly murmured thoughtfully.

'And, of course,' Tom continued, perplexed by Molly's subdued response to this frightening news, 'when that strange light invaded the room, when those bizarre . . . *apparitions* materialized out of nowhere and moved in around the bed, forcing Miss Suphar to flee, they were obviously protecting me from her, just as that saucer-shaped light protected us on the road to the Mexico City airport.'

'Mmmm,' Molly murmured thoughtfully.

Frowning at her, wondering what was wrong with her, Tom continued doggedly, 'Then, just as you saw stars in the crystal skull and we both saw stars seemingly inside that great saucer-shaped light, I saw stars in the pulsating light in my room – *and* saw the stars either through, or inside, those incorporeal, faceless beings who surrounded the bed.'

'Mmmm,' Molly murmured.

Glancing in exasperation around the pleasant, old-fashioned pub, Tom was glad to see that it was busy with lunchtime diners and drinkers. Realizing that he was beginning to feel paranoid about being alone, he turned back to Molly's unusually thoughtful gaze.

'Finally,' he said, 'I don't suppose we have to speculate too wildly to reach the conclusion that the Miss Mai Suphar in my room and the Miss Anna Chow in that room of death in the Savoy Hotel are one and the same . . . Yes or no? Are you listening?'

As if startled out of a trance, Molly blinked repeatedly, glanced distractedly around her, then turned back to Tom and said, 'What *I*'d like to know is what you and the drop-down-dead gorgeous – according to you – Miss Suphar were doing together in your room.'

'I've just told you. She wanted me to fly to Bangkok and . . .'

'Yeah, yeah, I got all that,' Molly said impatiently. 'But what I want to know is what you were doing on your *bed* before all that other business began?'

'I beg your pardon?'

'You heard me.'

Tom smacked his own forehead in melodramatic frustration. 'I can't believe my ears! I'm telling you the most amazing things and you're sitting there being jealous of that woman. This is just too ridiculous!'

'That doesn't answer the question.'

'Molly, please!'

'Well? What the fuck were you doing on the bed? I mean, don't you have a *chair* in that room?'

'Yes, of course I have a chair and initially she sat in

it, but then she . . . Well, what I mean is . . . Nothing to it, really . . . She was distraught – or she acted distraught – and then, just before she left, she came to sit on the bed beside me and . . .'

'Yes?'

'Nothing happened, Molly! She just happened to sit down for a second on the edge of the bed . . . and . . .'

'But you said that when those manifestations materialized, you tried to sit upright but couldn't.'

'Well, yes, that's true, but . . .'

'So you were lying on the bed when it all happened.'

'Well, yes, but . . .'

'So why were you lying on the bed?'

'I don't know.' Tom was practically stuttering now. 'I just happened to fall back on the bed when . . .'

'And she got her hypodermic syringe out of her leather bag where it was lying on the bed near the pillow.'

'Agreed, but . . .'

'And then, if I recall correctly and I'm sure I do, she dropped the hypodermic syringe on the bed beside you, grabbed her leather bag from where it was lying near the pillow, and then ran right through the apparitions standin' around the bed, which means she had to be *on* the bed, right?'

'Right, but . . .'

'And to get the hypodermic syringe out of her bag and then drop it beside you and pick up the bag, she had to be *stretched out* on the bed, right?'

'Well, all right, you're right,' Tom said frantically, 'but you're grossly misinterpreting the situation. The woman . . .'

'Black widow spider, more like.'

'Pardon?'

'You know? The black widow spider. Has sex with its mate and then kills him.'

'Devours him, actually,' Tom automatically corrected her.

'Very fucking funny, I'm sure.'

'Molly, please . . .'

'So she was stretched out on the bed,' Molly went on relentlessly. 'Was she above you or beside you or below you? Answer me that, Tom.'

Tom was mortified with guilt and shame, knowing full well what had been about to happen between himself and Mai Suphar, but convinced that it hadn't been his fault, though he couldn't explain that to Molly. 'Listen, Molly, it wasn't what you think. She just . . . we just . . . Well, what I mean is that . . .'

'She seduced you, right?'

'Yes – *no!* I mean, nothing happened, Molly. She just sort of pushed me back on the bed and even before I had time to resist her, the lights went out and . . .'

'You dumb shit,' Molly said. She was really very angry. 'That bitch just has to give you a smile and you jump into her knickers. That's just fuckin' pitiful.'

'All right, it was pitiful.'

'As long as we're in agreement.'

'But I was thinking of *you*, Molly, believe me, and maybe that explains . . .'

'You thought of me and then you fucked that other woman. Well, that's—'

'*We didn't fuck, Molly!*'

'Stop shouting, Tom. Everyone's lookin' at us. Let's just change the subject. Okay?'

'All right.' Tom checked his wristwatch. 'It's time to leave anyway,' he said, 'so get up and let's go.'

They had finished their lunch and drinks, so they stood up and left the pub, aware that a lot of customers were staring at them, some of them smirking. Once out on the pavement, Tom turned left and let Molly fall in beside him. They walked along in silence for a moment, then Tom said, 'I just want you to know that what happened with Mai Suphar last night – and nothing sexual happened, Molly! – was not something that I planned or wanted to happen, though, I repeat, nothing sexual actually occurred. That's all I've got to say.'

'Fine, Tom. Go fuck yourself.'

Luckily, they did not have far to walk and soon came to the shop in Covent Garden. It was a very strange shop, filled with books on the occult, the paranormal, flying saucers and ancient civilizations, and adorned with hideous ritual masks, shrunken heads and other equally bizarre paraphernalia. Tom's friend was a very tall, barrel-chested, blond-haired man with a handsome face flushed by too much drink and enlivened by a quick, genuine smile. He embraced Tom emotionally when he walked in, then stepped back to examine him.

'Well,' he said, 'you don't look so bad after your trip to the Yucatán. Maybe a little tense from too much travelling, yes? But then you always *were* the nervous type. So who's this you've brought me?'

'Molly, this is my eccentric Dutchman, Paul van der Veer, who owns and runs this unique little shop. Paul, this is Molly.'

'Hi,' Molly said.

'Welcome,' Paul replied, kissing her on the cheek, then stepping back to add: 'So are you giving my friend

Tom what he needs? A regular helping of the good old in and—'

'We're here to get some information on the crystal skulls,' Tom interjected hastily, knowing that Paul enjoyed shocking the ladies.

'Then you've come to the right place, my friend. What would you like to know? Here . . . come back here.' He led them around his cash register and into a poky room in the back where, on an old card table, he kept a kettle, a bottle of milk, a box of sugar cubes and a well-attended bottle of Jameson's whiskey. When they were seated around the table, he filled three cups with the whiskey and passed them around. 'So,' he said, 'shoot.'

'Is that your knee pressing my knee?' Molly asked him.

'Sorry,' van der Veer said. 'I just couldn't resist it. So, Tom, the crystal skulls.'

'Well—' Tom began.

'What do you do?' Molly asked of van der Veer. 'I mean, what makes you an authority on the crystal skulls?'

'Didn't Tom tell you?'

'No.'

'He keeps my light under a bushel. This shop, which I own and manage, is the most famous of its kind in the world with an unsurpassed collection of esoteric books, old manuscripts, prints, and other items relating to the occult, the paranormal, UFOs and ancient civilizations. Apart from running the shop, I'm a practising white magician – we do good instead of bad – and an explorer of some note, having visited most of the major so-called lost cities of the world. Regarding this, I've contemplated my navel in a monastery in the mountains of Tibet, explored the interior of the Sphinx, lived and worshipped with the Dogon and discussed the Sirius mystery with them. I've searched for Atlantis and visited every possible location for it. I'm also the author of *Lost and Found Again*, the classic text on ancient civilizations. Last but not least, I'm a well-known, respected hypnotist who's placed many a young lady in a trance before screwing her until she was ecstatic. Is that enough for you?'

'That's fine,' Molly said, not impressed. 'Now if you'll get your elbow out of my tit, we can all proceed.'

'Molly!' Tom warned her. 'This is vengeance!'

'Damned right,' Molly said.

'Do I sense a little fissure?' van der Veer asked with a big, happy smile. 'Can I be of assistance?'

'Let's concentrate on the crystal skull,' Tom said. 'That's what we're here for.'

'Fire away, my good friend.' Van der Veer beamed at Molly while Tom, after clearing his throat by coughing into his clenched fist, said, 'We've been presented with the theory that the crystal skulls – the *genuine* crystal skulls—'

'Of which there are only two,' van der Veer interjected.

'Correct,' Tom said. 'Anyway, we've been told that they're the artefacts of an ancient, mysterious race, almost certainly pre-Mayan, which is believed to have made a great, centuries-long migration from west to east – a migration that took in the Yucatán peninsula and ended in Tiahuanaco, Peru, which of course you know well. Any truth to this theory?'

'What's your interest in this, Tom?' When Tom told him, van der Veer looked impressed. 'Sounds to me like you really *do* have the long-lost, priceless Rose Quartz Skull. That's some find, my friends.'

'We have it,' Tom said. 'So what about it – and the other skull? What about that mysterious race?'

Van der Veer threw Molly a smile like the beam of a lighthouse, then he turned back to Tom, looking thoughtful.

'Well now,' he said, 'Lady Barratt-White's contention that the source of the skulls is a city linked to the stars is certainly not strictly hypothetical. While not much is really known about the ancient city of Tiahuanaco, it *is* on record as having been a sanctuary, a holy city like Mecca or Jerusalem, and, I quote, *a city linked with mythic conceptions of the creation of the stars*, unquote. And certainly the records, scant though they may be, indicate that this ancient race of pre-Mayans emerged from somewhere in Asia, the cradle of civilization, and travelled restlessly for centuries, from the west to the east, stopping first in Angkor, then in Cambodia, where they built the so-called Forbidden City. Following an eastern trajectory, the next stop would certainly have been the Polynesian Islands, where the once sacred lagoon city of Ponape was located, then on to Easter Island, where they were almost certainly responsible for the fabulous monuments, then the Yucatán Peninsula and British Honduras where, of course, the two crystal skulls were found. The next stop, if we're to assume they continued east, or by now south-east, would have been Peru, where they constructed the holy city of Tiahuanaco.'

'How did they get there?' Molly asked sarcastically. 'Flying by Concorde?'

Van der Veer grinned at her and patted the back of

her delicate hand with his own enormous, indelicate mitt. 'No, my dear, by boat.'

'Are you trying to tell us,' Tom asked, glaring at Molly until she surreptitiously removed her hand from under that of the attentive van der Veer, 'that before recorded history there was a centuries-old *maritime* civilization?'

'Correct,' van der Veer said, shifting restlessly in his chair to make Molly also shift restlessly, fidgeting with her feet. 'As I stated in my book *Lost and Found Again*,' he continued, nodding to Molly to remind her that he was, among other things, a well-known author, 'when I was exploring Tiahuanaco, I uncovered sufficient evidence to prove conclusively that it had once been a port with vast docks – one big enough to hold hundreds of ships. While there, I also learned about the local legend of Viracocha, which is the name of the white god of the sea, though he's usually known in Peru as Thunupa. Also in Tiahuanaco is a seven-foot statue, carved out of red sandstone, and believed locally to be the statue of the same Thunupa. Finally, it's worth noting that above the Sun Gate itself, also known as the Gateway to the Sun, there's a figure holding a weapon in one hand and a thunderbolt in the other – another statue of Viracocha, or Thunupa, the white god of the sea. So certainly there's an abundance of evidence in Tiahuanaco that the ancient city was built and inhabited by a maritime civilization.'

'There's somethin' crawlin' up my leg,' Molly said, 'and I wish it would drop off.'

'Sorry,' van der Veer said, unperturbed, but placing his hand back on the table and studying his fingernails. 'I don't know how it got there.'

'What timescale are we talking about?' Tom asked,

being used to his eccentric friend's antics and so trying to keep his cool.

'I believe the civilization that built Tiahuanaco predated dynastic Egypt by many thousands of years.'

'Really?' Molly said sarcastically, working her chair sideways a little, inching it away from van der Veer and bringing it closer to Tom, who noticed the movement and was gratified.

'Really,' van der Veer said, also noticing Molly's surreptitious movement and smiling with amusement before giving Tom his most solemn, thoughtful gaze – his serious-author's gaze. 'The building blocks of Tiahuanaco weigh as much as four hundred and forty tons each – more than twice the weight of the blocks used in the construction of the Sphinx Temple at Giza in Egypt. Also, one of the friezes on the Sun Gate shows the rough form of an elephant, unknown on the South American continent, though a similar creature with tusks and trunk, the *Cuvieronius*, is known to have become extinct there about 10,000 BC. Another animal shown on the Sun Gate is a toxodon, a creature rather like a hippopotamus, which vanished from the Andes at about the same time as the *Cuvieronius*. Finally, mathematical calculations based on Tiahuanaco's astronomical enclosure, Kalasasaya, the Place of the Standing Stones, produced evidence indicating that the observatory could have been constructed approximately 15,000 BC, when, according to historians, man was still a primitive hunter, pursuing mammoths with spears. This date was later amended by more authoritative research to 10,500 BC, which, interestingly enough, would place the destruction of Tiahuanaco and the Sun Gate in line with the most widely accepted date for the destruction of Atlantis.'

'So how was it destroyed?' Molly asked, now sitting closer to Tom and no longer fidgeting.

'Almost certainly by some great natural catastrophe,' Van der Veer said.

'What makes you think that?'

'Located twelve miles south of Lake Titicaca and more than a hundred feet above it, the port of Tiahuanaco is surrounded by a great number of huge, chaotically scattered blocks of stone, indicating that it was destroyed in some great disturbance – an earthquake, most likely. Also, the available evidence indicates that the Sun Gate was split in two before it was actually completed and the scattering of the blocks around it indicates that this was caused by an earthquake. It is the opinion of Professor Arthur Posnansky, our foremost authority of Tiahuanaco, that this earthquake took place in the eleventh millennium BC, that it temporarily drowned the city of Tiahuanaco, and that it was followed by a series of seismic disturbances that lowered the level of the lake and made the climate colder. In short, if the ancient Aztec legend stating that Viracocha, the white god of the sea, landed on the east coast of Central America, his influence certainly travelled to the other side of the continent and he clearly came from a vast, possibly worldwide maritime civilization that may have been destroyed when the great agricultural revolution of Egypt was destroyed in a series of natural disasters, when Tiahuanaco was destroyed and when, according to the most widely accepted date, Atlantis vanished into the sea. The approximate date for all of those disasters is 11,000 to 10,000 BC.'

Having completed his lecture, the amiable van der Veer leaned back in his chair, sipped a little whisky, then smiled at Molly, his gaze clear and steady and inviting. Molly, who still trusted few men, merely stared stonily at him.

'That's all very interesting,' she said, 'but you still haven't explained why Tiahuanaco is supposed to be that ancient city linked to the stars.'

'Kalasasaya,' van der Veer responded unhesitatingly. 'The Place of the Standing Stones. That enclosure was an observatory with two observation points marking the summer and winter solstices.'

'The *what*?'

'The points at which the sun is directly overhead at the Tropic of Cancer or Capricorn.'

'So?'

'No matter what date we choose for the construction of that observatory – 15,000 BC, 10,500 BC, or even, as some would suggest, wrongly I believe, 4,000 BC – it was an extraordinary achievement for its day and almost certainly the only one of its kind. So given the existence of that observatory – our evidence that that ancient, mysterious race was, for religious reasons, observing the cosmos – we can take it as read that Tiahuanaco was indeed – and I quote again – *that majestic and long-hidden city that is linked to the stars*. Unquote. Case proven.'

'Think you're smart, don't ya?'

'Molly!' Tom warned her.

But van der Veer was merely amused. 'The question is, my dear, do *you?*'

'I don't fancy men who fancy themselves.'

'My loss,' van der Veer said.

'But,' Tom said, determined to keep this conversation on an even course and prevent his eccentric friend from exploiting his baser instincts, 'what makes so many believe that the crystal skulls originated there?'

'They did *not* originate there,' van der Veer said, 'but they may have been used there. Certainly they were used in esoteric rites and that ancient observatory would not have been used as you would naturally imagine – to study the cosmos scientifically – but to act as a link between ancient man and the stars or, in his view, the gods. So Lady Barratt-White's contention that the two crystal skulls must be returned to their source – to that long-hidden city linked to the stars – *could* suggest Tiahuanaco: the final step on that long migration, after Yucatán and British Honduras, now Belize, where the two skulls were actually found. However, Tiahuanaco was not the source of the skulls, but was, in fact, only the final resting place of that great, mysterious civilization.'

Ever more perplexed, Tom asked, 'So if Tiahuanaco wasn't the actual source of the skulls, where *did* they originate? And who, in fact, were those pre-Mayans? Were they Mayan at all?'

Van der Veer shrugged, now so lost in his thoughts that he had even stopped fooling around with Molly. 'The Mayas are a mystery. We don't know where they came from and, in a very real sense, we don't know where they went. All we really know is that they were an extraordinary race, that they built city-states in the jungles of Central America, and that in approximately AD 600, for reasons yet to be explained, they abruptly abandoned their cities, moved to new locations in the jungle and went into a slow decline, gradually drifting into virtual primitivism. However, given the content of Olmec and Mayan legends, we have strong grounds for believing that they evolved from that mysterious race that came to South America, probably under the leadership of Viracocha, or Thunupa, the so-called white god of the sea, and that they could have originated in Asia, possibly in Cambodia, where they built their first great city-state: the Forbidden City of Angkor.'

'So the skulls could have originated in Angkor,' Tom concluded.

'They could have – though this ain't necessarily so. Bear in mind that the journey from Angkor to Tiahuanaco took centuries with many lengthy stops along the way. So the skulls could have originated in any of those places: Ponape, Easter Island, or even where they were actually found: Yucatán and British Honduras.'

'Which gets us back where we started,' Molly said sardonically.

'My apologies,' van der Veer said, offering a sly smile. The door in the shop out front squeaked open and then closed again. 'Ah!' van der Veer said, cocking one ear and looking pleased. 'I hear the sound of a customer! I must leave you now, dear friends.'

They all pushed their chairs back and stood up. Van der Veer, after giving Tom another hug, kissed the back of Molly's hand.

'You're really *very* attractive,' he said. 'Should you ever tire of helping Tom to sleep peacefully, please give me a call.'

'You'll be lucky,' Molly said.

Van der Veer bellowed with laughter, then led Tom and Molly back into the shop where a lone customer, long-haired and wearing a brightly-beaded kaftan, with thongs on his bare feet, was perusing a row of occult books. Just as Tom and Molly were about to leave, Van der Veer called out to the former, saying, 'I've got something rattling about in the back of my head, but I can't quite dredge it up. Come and see me again.'

'I will,' Tom promised. Then he and Molly walked back out into the busy street where, unexpectedly, the sun shone warmly upon them and Molly, as mysterious as all women, shook her head slowly from side to side and smiled to herself.

CHAPTER TWENTY-TWO

'Let's go for another drink,' Tom said as they walked away from van der Veer's shop, warmed by the sunshine and, in Tom's case, pleased to be surrounded by the densely-packed pedestrians, many of whom were tourists heavily burdened with cameras and studying maps of London. Tom preferred to be in a crowd these days. He felt safer when not alone.

'You've already had two pints of that awful bitter,' Molly said. 'You should be drunk already.'

'Well, I'm not and I'm thirsty.'

'You're always thirsty when it comes to liquor, Tom. That stuff poisons your system.'

'You drink your Coca-Cola and I'll drink my beer. So why are you smiling?'

'Nothing.'

'You're not the kind to smile over nothing, so why are you smiling?'

'I was thinkin' of your friend van der Veer – what a card he is.'

'Liked him, did you?'

'Not at first, but then he kinda grew on me. He's not as bad as he acts.'

'He's a dreadful womanizer,' Tom said, feeling obscurely threatened, 'and can't understand why I'm not the same.'

'Yeah, I gathered that he'd like to corrupt you.'

'He's always trying,' Tom said.

'And of course he hasn't a hope of hell in succeeding.'

'What does that mean?' Tom was affronted. 'Are you suggesting that I'm some kind of puritan?'

'Well, you certainly weren't last night,' Molly reminded him.

'Don't bring that up again,' Tom said. 'Particularly not after the way you behaved with that insatiable womanizer back there.'

'Hey, hold on! I put the guy off!'

'He certainly didn't seem to think so. And now you have the cheek to tell me that you like him. Why not go back and ask him for a date? I'm sure he'll oblige.'

Molly smiled again. 'What's this I hear? Jealousy?'

'I'm merely putting matters straight. If I'm not allowed to complain about you and van der Veer, then you've no right to complain about me and that woman Mai Suphar. She could have killed me, for God's sake, and all *you* can think about is what we *might* have done on that bed. Now, after being groped by van der Veer, you have the cheek to tell me that you *like* him. Well, thanks very much!'

'You're jealous, Tom, that's why you're angry – and that's why I'm smiling. You're in love with me, Tom.'

'Please don't embarrass me, Molly.'

Grinning with delight and shaking her head ruefully, Molly stopped when they came to traffic lights and then turned to face him. 'Okay,' she said, 'let's change the subject.'

'Yes,' Tom said, 'let's do that.'

'I don't care what your friend says,' Molly told him.

'When I looked too deeply into that crystal skull, I saw stars inside it. Later, when we were rescued by that saucer-shaped light on the road to the airport in Mexico City, we *both* saw stars inside it. Finally, when you and that black widow spider—'

'Molly!' Tom interjected as a warning.

'When you and that Thai woman were surrounded in your room last night by that weird light, you saw stars either inside or through those ghostly creatures.'

'Correct,' Tom said. 'So?'

'*Stars*, Tom! The common denominator is *stars*! So I'm convinced more than ever that Lady Barratt-White was right and that the crystal skulls belong to that city linked to the stars. In other words, Tiahuanaco.'

'So?'

'So I say that we should try to get our hands on that other crystal skull and then make a tidy packet by taking both skulls to Tiahuanaco, as requested by Lady Barratt-White.'

Though the sun was shining, its light falling over the grey grandeur of the Victorian and Georgian buildings along the road, over the milling pedestrians, and over the jammed-up traffic that was belching acrid fumes, a chill, unseasonal wind was rising and Tom yearned more than ever for a cosy pub – for the warmth, if not the drink. Molly, however, was deeply engrossed in her thoughts and seemed extremely excited.

'And how, pray,' Tom asked, 'do we get our hands on the crystal skull stolen by Mai Suphar, aka Anna Chow?'

'Well, you *did* confirm that she was from Thailand and she said that she'd come from Bangkok at the behest – note the fancy word, Tom – of that criminal, Lu Thong. Now, given that she intended killing you anyway, to stop you repeating what she'd told you, my bet is that she told the truth about certain things and that Lu Thong is a real guy and that she *will* take the crystal skull back to him, in Bangkok, where both of them live.'

'So we fly to Bangkok and look up this Mr Lu Thong.'

'That's right,' Molly said.

Tom couldn't believe his ears, but he tried to be patient with her. 'So how do we *find* Mr Lu Thong once we get to Bangkok?'

'He's probably in the phone book.'

'You think so?'

'Yeah. Why not? Most criminals in America have phones and are listed. And if *they* are, Lu Thong probably is as well.'

'And if he happens to be a criminal who likes his privacy?'

'If he's as criminal as that bitch Mai Suphan says he is, then, even if he's not in the phone book, he's going to be known to everyone living around the Bangkok railway station and won't be hard to track down.'

'Thus spake the street-wise Brooklyn girl,' Tom said.

'You don't have to be sarcastic, Tom, but I *do* know more than you about certain things.'

'And if he's as criminal as Mai Suphar says, my dear Molly, he's unlikely to hand the crystal skull back – not without a fight.'

'So we fight 'im. We outwit the bastard and get it back somehow.'

'You really think we can do that, Molly?'

'Yeah, I think so.'

'I think you're mad, Molly, truly demented, and I don't want to hear another word. Come on, let's go for a drink.'

They started walking again, but only managed to cover a few yards before Molly tugged him to a standstill and looked grimly at him. 'So what do you suggest, buddy?'

Tom took a deep breath and let it out nervously. 'What I suggest, Molly, is that we accept that we're out of our depth, that we could be in serious danger, and that we get rid of our crystal skull by giving it to the Museum of Mankind in return for the one that was stolen. Then we forget this whole nightmarish business and return to our normal lives.'

'You're scared,' Molly accused him.

'Yes,' Tom confessed, 'I am. But for both of us, Molly. It's insane to think of flying to Bangkok to confront a notorious professional criminal who'd have no compunction about killing us. I'm not going. Forget it.'

'I'm not giving back my crystal skull,' Molly insisted, 'and if necessary, I'll fly to Bangkok alone.'

'Then you'll go without your crystal skull,' Tom said, 'because I've got it in the safe of my club and I'm going to give it to the Museum of Mankind.'

Molly was furious. 'You can't do that! I gave it to you in good faith. You've got to give it back, Tom!'

'No, Molly, I won't. I refuse to help you with this. I know that in this instance I'm betraying your trust, but believe me, I'm doing it for your own good and I won't change my mind.'

'You bastard!'

'Sticks and stones, Molly.'

'Okay,' Molly said, changing her tack. 'Then just let me remind you that the minute you enter that museum, even carrying the crystal skull, they'll have you arrested for the theft of *their* skull and probably thrown in jail. I hope to hell you rot there!'

With that, she turned away from him and stomped off along the busy street.

Tom watched her go, feeling indecisive, realizing that this situation was even more complicated and dangerous than he had previously imagined. He still felt like a drink, but did not want to drink alone, and then, recalling van der Veer's parting words, he turned back to see him. When he entered the shop again, the hippie-styled customer had left and only van der Veer was present, sitting behind his cash register and reading a book. When he saw Tom, he grinned.

'Back already!' he said. 'Where's the lovely Molly?'

'She said she couldn't stand any more of your groping and wanted to go straight back to her hotel.'

'She's waiting for my phone call,' van der Veer said, then he grinned again and spread his hands in the air as if pleading for mercy. 'I tried it on and was rejected,' he said. 'You should be proud of her, Tom.'

'I am,' Tom said decisively. 'You said something was rattling about in your head. Do you recall what it was?'

Van der Veer nodded. 'Yes,' he said. 'I think so.' He came around his desk and shoved the book he had been reading under Tom's nose. It was Carl Jung's *Flying Saucers: A Modern Myth of Things Seen in the Sky*.

'Know of him?' Van der Veer asked.

'Of course I do. The famous Swiss psychologist and psychiatrist, a disciple of Freud, who happened to have an interest in UFOs.'

'Correct. And in this book he speculates that UFOs may either be psychic projections resulting from our need to believe in a higher power or, failing that, manifestations from the racial memory of the whole of mankind.'

'Is that what was rattling about in your head when you weren't too busy making advances on Molly?'

'Not quite,' van der Veer said, acknowledging Tom's sarcastic comment with a grin but otherwise ignoring it. 'But it *is* part of it. Let's close the shop and go to the British Museum. I've got something to show you.'

Van der Veer put on his jacket, an old tweed with patched elbows, then locked up the shop and led Tom along the crowded pavement, talking as they walked.

'I have to confess,' he said, 'that I was pretty intrigued by those stories you told me about what Molly saw in the crystal skull, what both of you experienced on the road to the airport in Mexico City, and what happened to you in your room in the club.'

'The common denominator, as Molly has just pointed out, being stars.'

'Well, that's true enough,' van der Veer said. 'You two certainly see an awful lot of stars. You have stars in your eyes.'

'Does that mean we're in love?' Tom asked anxiously.

'I think so,' van der Veer said. 'However, what *really* fascinated me about the stories was that saucer-shaped light you saw on the road to the Mexico City airport and the ghostly figures, also seemingly made of light or some other incorporeal substance, in your room in the club. You said that the ghostly figures, though faceless, looked feminine.'

'That's right,' Tom said. 'I don't know why I thought that, because, as you reminded me, they had no features and their bodies were nothing more than thin blades of light. I had the impression that they had arms and maybe legs, but I can't even be sure of that. I only know that they struck me as being feminine. Something to do with them being so slim and the way they moved like reeds in a wind – it was graceful and sensual. Does that sound mad to you?'

'It intrigues me,' van der Veer said, 'and it jolted my memory. So I've something to show you. I phoned a friend in the museum when you left and he should have taken it off the shelves by now. I think *you*'ll be intrigued.'

They arrived at the museum in a matter of minutes and van der Veer led Tom straight to the manuscript department where he introduced him to his friend, William Claxton, the present head of the department. Claxton was small and portly, with a round, pink, kindly face, two tufts of snowy white hair above each big ear, and a bald head that shone like a polished eggshell in the bright strip-lighting. He was seated behind his desk with a finely bound antique book in front of him. When he had been introduced to Tom and shaken his hand, he pushed the book over to him and van der Veer, both seated at the other side of the desk.

'I've already been through it,' he said, 'and marked the pages you want with a slip of paper. Now I'm off for a quick cup of tea. I'll be back in five minutes. Is that enough?'

'That's enough,' van der Veer said. 'And thanks a hell of a lot.'

'My pleasure,' Mr Claxton said, then he stood up and walked out of the office.

Tom looked at the cover of the book. It was entitled *The Dresden Codex*. 'This is a finely bound reproduction,' van der Veer explained, 'of one of the only four surviving Mayan books. It is thus very rare and invaluable.' Sitting close to Tom, he opened the book where a paper slip had been inserted by Mr Claxton. Tom found himself staring down at the drawings and name glyphs of two women from ancient times. 'The young Moon Goddess and the Old Moon Goddess,' van der Veer informed him. 'The hieroglyphics on these pages suggest a Mayan belief that at some stage in their earliest history, in a place, quote, *where the sun always sets* – the west, possibly Angkor – a light – and I quote again – *brighter than the sun* – brought to Earth the Old and Young Moon Goddesses – the only gods in the whole Mayan pantheon ever to take human form.'

Looking at the drawings of the ancient goddesses, Tom recalled the ghostly figures in his room in the club and felt that he was now seeing their faces. A shiver ran down his spine and he felt very uneasy.

'Are you suggesting,' he began, hardly knowing where to begin, 'that those ghostly figures I mentioned are . . . ?'

'Wait!' van der Veer said, raising his index finger to indicate silence. Then he quickly flipped over more pages and scanned one intently. 'These hieroglyphics,' he said, pointing to the relevant place on the page, 'also indicate that the two goddesses, after inspiring the Mayans, or pre-Mayans, to their earliest great achievements, possibly including – I quote again – *that great migration toward where the sun rises*, unquote – pined to return to their spiritual state, but eventually died an Earthly death. The high priests then made replicas of their skulls in crystal in the belief that the crystal, containing magical properties, would retain their souls.'

Van der Veer closed the book and turned to look directly at Tom. 'Therefore,' he said, 'the two crystal skulls are almost certainly the magical replicas of the two Mayan goddesses, designed to house their souls and made either in Angkor, before the great migration commenced, or at some point during the centuries-long journey from Angkor to Tiahuanaco.'

Tom closed his eyes and tried imagining the two faces he had just seen as drawings in the *Dresden Codex* superimposed on the faceless creatures he had been haunted by in his room. When he did that, he then visualized arms and legs on those sensuously swaying, glowing, feminine forms. Shocked, he opened his eyes again.

'What are you saying?' he asked.

'What I'm saying,' van der Veer explained, 'is that flying saucers may indeed spring from a racial memory of mankind and that, as you and Molly were protected by a starfilled light shaped like a flying saucer, it could well have been a manifestation from the ancient past. What I'm saying is that the crystal skulls could have magical powers because they do indeed house the souls of those two Mayan goddesses and they're protecting you because you are, in a sense, protecting *them*. Finally, what I'm saying is that the ghostly figures you saw in your room, both filled with stars, struck you as being distinctly feminine, so they could have been the souls of the moon goddesses, incorporeal but made visible as star-filled light. Those crystal skulls, Tom, have magical properties and may form a bridge between Earth and the otherworld where the souls of the goddesses still reside. I don't know what this means – I can't speculate – but there's certainly a great mystery to be solved here and now you're part of it. You and Molly, of course.'

Reminded of Molly, Tom felt love and fear at once, but realized that he must now complete the journey that they had, accidentally, begun together. Given what he had just learned in this office – and what had he had experienced in his room the previous evening – he had little choice.

'I'd better find that other crystal skull,' he said.

'It might be worth it,' van der Veer said. 'All you can lose is your life.'

Grinning, he pushed the *Dresden Codex* back across to Mr Claxton's side of the desk just as the latter came back into the office. 'Finished?' he asked.

'Yes,' van der Veer replied, pushing his chair back and standing up. Tom did the same. 'Thanks a million for that.'

'That's an odd thing to be studying,' Mr Claxton said.

'I'm an odd man,' van der Veer replied, then he shook hands with Mr Claxton, as did Tom, and they both left the office and made their way back out of the museum.

'Fascinating,' Tom said when they were about to take their leave of one another on the pavement just outside the main gates. 'I suppose I'd better go and see Molly, tell her all about this, and let her know that I've changed my mind about Bangkok.'

'You do that,' van der Veer said, 'and also give her my warmest wishes and phone number.'

'No way,' Tom said.

'So what's she like in bed?' van der Veer asked.

'That's *my* business,' Tom said.

'You pitiful, inhibited English!' van der Veer exclaimed with a grin, then he gave Tom an affectionate hug, bade him goodbye and hurried across the road to disappear into the Museum Tavern.

Longing for a drink himself, but now feeling compelled to see Molly as soon as possible, Tom caught a taxi to her hotel. Entering the building, he went straight to her room, intending to knock on the door and, when she opened it, kiss her full on the lips and finally confess that he loved her.

Her room door was open.

Surprised, then instinctively feeling nervous, Tom timidly called out her name and received no response. Even more nervous, he opened the door further and entered the room.

The first thing he saw was that the bed was unmade and looked unusually rumpled – as if a struggle had taken place upon it or around it.

The second thing he saw was a glittering hypodermic syringe, lying on the rumpled sheets near the pillows.

Shocked, Tom picked the syringe up to examine it and saw instantly that the contents had been ejected, indicating that the syringe had been used.

And Molly had vanished.

CHAPTER TWENTY-THREE

Shattered and heartbroken, convinced that Molly had been killed by Mai Suphar using the same toxin that she had tried to inject into him, Tom hurried out of Molly's hotel and made his way back to his club.

Unable to bear the thought of being in his room alone, realizing that he was near to tears, and finding it impossible to shake from his head the thought that Molly had been murdered because Mai Suphar must have imagined that she still had the crystal skull, he asked the porter to conduct him to the communal safe in the basement, where he checked that the crystal skull was still there.

It was. Relieved to find this out, but trembling with grief and disbelief (the porter noticed his distress and asked if he felt all right), he still avoided his room and instead went into the bar for a drink, hoping that it would settle him down and enable him to think more clearly.

The drink didn't help much.

Tom had another. He couldn't think clearly at all. He kept recalling his own frightening experience with Mai Suphar and imagined Molly suffering the same experience, though without being rescued as he had been. All too vividly, he imagined Mai Suphar hiding in Molly's room (clearly as criminal as Lu Thong, she had probably picked the lock) and pouncing upon her as soon as she walked in. Drinking too quickly, aware that his heart was racing and seemed about to burst, he suffered shocking visions of Mai Suphar wrestling Molly to the bed and then plunging the needle of the hypodermic syringe into her neck.

Tom shuddered at the thought, felt revulsion and grief, but could not shake from his mind the ghastly vision of Molly quivering in the spasms of death as her heart raced too quickly. He even imagined Molly lying there, dead, before being spirited away by Mai Suphar, probably with the help of some equally vicious friends, all on Lu Thong's payroll.

The second drink did not help, so Tom had another. He was hiding in a quiet corner of the bar and at one point he broke down, shuddering helplessly and weeping profusely. When he dried his eyes, they were stinging and he had to close them again, but when he did so, he was haunted by more imaginings about what might have happened.

Mai Suphar was a murderer and obviously professional, almost certainly working for that Lu Thong and knowing just what to do. She would have used some of Lu Thong's men, all professionals as well, and Tom shuddered to think of how they might have disposed of Molly's body.

A body bag, probably. Tom saw it all too clearly. He saw Mai Suphar killing Molly, the men entering the room, their expert handling of Molly's body as they slipped it into the body bag and then their removal of that body in some ghastly, coldly professional way.

Tom had read about such things. Such things beggared

belief. He had read about psychopaths killing people and then cutting them into pieces and carrying the pieces out in suitcases and burying them somewhere. Of course, that meant a lot of blood. Tom sobbed and groaned at the very thought. Then he realized that there had been no blood in Molly's room and that the carpets had not been changed.

Perhaps Molly was still alive.

No, that wasn't possible. The toxin used had been poisonous. Molly had been killed by Mai Suphar and then her body disposed of. The question was: How?

Tom broke down in tears again and saw the barman staring at him. The barman was a long way away, but he could still see Tom crying. Tom tried to control himself. He wiped his eyes and took deep breaths. Closing his eyes, wanting peace, he visualized the whole scene again: Mai Suphar killing Molly, the dead body on the bed, Lu Thong's hoodlums coming into the room, pushing a wheeled laundry trolley. They slipped the dead body into a body bag, then shoved it into the trolley, then wheeled the trolley out of the room and took it down to the basement garage. Once there, they put it into their car and drove away from the hotel. They buried the body somewhere outside London and then went for a drink.

'Oh, Christ!' Tom sobbed.

The bar was filling up and people were starting to look at Tom, so he took himself up to his bedroom, despite his fear of being there. Feeling ill, he threw up into the toilet and then had a shower. Thus refreshed, though still feeling half demented, he lay down on the bed. He didn't think he could sleep – he was too tormented – but he fell asleep instantly.

In his dreams, he saw Molly being murdered, wrapped

up in a body bag, then lowered in ropes to a car waiting below at the back of the hotel. Mai Suphar and her henchmen clambered into that car and then drove away.

Tom groaned and awakened.

The room was very dark. Moonlight fell on the window. Tom's eyes adjusted to the darkness and he checked his wristwatch and saw that it was two o'clock in the morning. He thought of Molly and burst into tears and then fell asleep again.

Was hc asleep or awake? He couldn't be too sure. He recognized his room, understood that he was in bed, and then saw that familiar light materializing to surround him with stars. Then the eerie figures materialized too, slim and swaying like reeds, featureless, composed of light and stars, but definitely feminine. They closed in on the bed, looking upon him, though eyeless themselves, and he filled up instantly with fear and rapture. Then they faded away. There was a roaring for off in the cosmos, where the stars reigned, and then it turned into a sibilance that soon became a loud, nerve-shattering ringing.

Tom awoke to the ringing of the telephone on the cabinet beside his bed.

'Oh, my God!' he said. 'Christ!'

His heart was racing when he picked up the telephone and gasped his own name. He heard a soft, sensual voice.

'This is Mai Suphar, Mr Powell. I think you'll remember me.'

Shocked almost mindless, Tom just sat there, holding the telephone, aware that his hand was shaking, wondering if he was still in his dream or if this was for real.

'Are you still there?' Mai Suphar asked.

'Yes,' Tom said, 'I'm still here.' He reached across to the lamp on the cabinet and turned the light on. The room seemed perfectly normal. 'What do you want?' he asked.

'The question is: What do *you* want?'

'I want Molly,' Tom said.

Mai Suphar chuckled. 'What a sweet man!' she said, almost crooning. 'But what makes you think Molly's still alive?'

'Just tell me,' Tom said.

There was silence for a moment and he imagined that bitch smiling, taking her time to torment him a bit more, getting her kicks from his suffering. Eventually, after what seemed like an eternity, she said, 'Yes, she's still alive.'

'You injected her,' Tom said.

'That's correct,' Mai Suphar replied.

'I had that toxin checked out and it's lethal, so Molly must be dead.'

'Molly's still alive, Tom. I used a different toxin. The one I used on Molly was something else altogether and is widely used in the slave trade for the transportation of unfortunate kidnapped children who must, though they're being abducted and travelling under false passports, be seen to be perfectly normal and travelling willingly with adoring parents.'

'What does that mean?' Tom asked.

'It's a mesmerizing drug, affecting certain parts of the brain. Molly's still alive, her eyes are open and she can function, but she's in a deep trance and will only respond to my commands. When she does so, when she does what I tell her, she seems perfectly normal – certainly normal enough to travel to Bangkok, which is where I am taking her.'

'*What?*'

'I think you heard me correctly.'

'Yes,' Tom said, 'I did.'

Mai chuckled again, then went silent, though Tom knew she was smiling. He could almost feel her sadistic pleasure coming down the line as she drew the silence out to torment him. He wouldn't give her that satisfaction.

'Where are you?' he asked.

'I'm at Heathrow Airport, Tom. Molly's standing beside me. She's in a trance, she looks perfectly normal, and we've already been through passport control and are now in the departure lounge, preparing to board. We leave for Bangkok in fifteen minutes and that's why I'm calling you.'

'You want the crystal skull,' Tom said, anticipating her.

'What a bright man you are. I want you to bring it to Lu Thong's mansion in Bangkok. If you don't, we'll send your precious Molly back in a foul-smelling body bag.'

Tom winced at the very thought of that, but refused to rise to the bait. 'And what happens if I do? What guarantee do I have that you'll let Molly and *I* leave there alive?'

'You don't,' Mai Suphar said, sounding sensual and seductive. 'But what's love, if it isn't a gamble? Will you gamble for her, Tom?'

'Yes,' Tom said without any doubt in his heart.

'That's so touching,' Mai said. Then her soft, seductive voice turned as cold as ice. 'You'll find Lu Thong's phone number and address in your mail box downstairs. You have seven days to get to Bangkok. That's seven days, Mr Powell. We look forward to seeing you.

If we don't see you within a week, your beloved Molly will disappear. Is that understood?'

'Yes,' Tom said, 'I understand.'

Mai Suphar chuckled and then hung up, leaving Tom to fester in a silence that seemed to stretch out forever.

He was more frightened now than he had ever been in his life, yet despite this, his heart was filled with joy because Molly was still alive.

That thought gave him courage.

CHAPTER TWENTY-FOUR

Arriving in Bangkok, which should have terrified him, given what he had to do, Tom was more calm than he had ever been in his life. So calm, in fact, that he was able to relax in the back of the taxi taking him from the airport to the city centre and observe in fascination the exotic world passing by outside: first the jungle around the city, then the wide agricultural fields and industrial areas, then sprawling squatters, camps of wood-and-thatch shacks. The latter merged gradually into welfare housing estates and hundreds of Chinese shop-houses five or six storeys high, so crowded together that no motor traffic could pass between them, their linked alleyways like great cobwebs and filled with people wearing the diverse costumes of various Asian countries. However, only when the taxi was approaching the centre of the city, where the traffic was dense and chaotic, hemming in the three-wheeled *samlor* taxis, did Tom see the Bangkok he had imagined: Colonial-style and Thai-style office buildings, golden-spired temples and *wats* with bell towers, the many palm-shaded canals known as *khlongs*, sidewalk vendors with steaming bowls on their wheeled carts, and, on the crowded sidewalks, saffron-robed monks, ravishing Thai girls in local and Western clothes, a strikingly diverse mixture of Asiatics including Thais, Chinese, Indians, Burmese, Laotians, Vietnamese and, of course, many Europeans and Americans. Even given the high-rise buildings of steel, concrete and glass, Bangkok was an exotic city and Tom, now less nervous than he had ever been, was pleased to be here.

After checking into his hotel, a five-star monstrosity with every imaginable luxury and an almost total absence of human warmth, he decided to forget the latter and exploit the former by relaxing in his king-sized bath, stretching out on his king-sized bed, and enjoying a meal fit for a prince, even though delivered by room service. He then dressed in an open-necked shirt and light tropical suit, both purchased earlier in Bond Street, and poured himself an excellent whisky from his overpriced personal bar. Finally, feeling like a new man, he removed from his wallet the phone number and address of Lu Thong, which Mai Suphar had helpfully left for him in his mail box in his club in Mayfair. No longer frightened, he dialled Lu Thong and waited for a response.

'Hello, Mr Powell,' a familiar, very seductive voice said, 'this is Mai speaking. We saw you arriving at your hotel and were expecting your call. Do you wish to speak to Lu Thong?'

'Yes, please,' Tom said.

Mai chuckled, clearly amused by his politeness, and then there was silence. Tom waited patiently. He had nowhere else to go. He also knew that these people liked playing games and were probably testing him.

Well, as Molly would say, he found himself thinking, *fuck you. Fuck the whole damned lot of you. This time I won't bend.*

After an interminable silence (though he thought he heard Mai chuckling) there was the sound of hollow breathing on the phone. Then the walking dead spoke.

'Mr Powell?'

'Yes,' Tom said.

The voice he had just heard sent shivers down his spine because it sounded as ethereal as the whispering of the ghostly figures who had invaded his room in Mayfair. But this wasn't a ghostly voice: it was the voice of a living person – a male person, clearly not very old, and yet jaded beyond belief. It was the voice of despair, expressing dreams that could never be realized, and it came from the dark side of that moon where haunted souls languished. Tom could not put a face to that voice, but it reached deep inside him, resurrecting every lost dream of his childhood and somehow challenging him to make them come alive again. It was, in fact, the voice of a man who could never accept that there were things he could not have; the voice of a man who could not accept that God was actually greater than he was; the voice of a child, perhaps, who had refused to grow up. Tom listened and shivered.

'I am so pleased to meet you,' Lu Thong said, speaking perfect, though rather formal English in a dry, mocking manner. 'I've been dying to meet you. Of course, I'm dying anyway – we're all doomed from the day we are born – but I'm keen to meet a man who loves so much that he will give his life for it.'

'Is Molly all right?' Tom asked.

'Ah, the man proves my point! I practically tell him that he has come here to die and he still expresses concern for his true love. Tom, *I* love *you* already.'

'Just cut the crap,' Tom said.

It was a phrase he had learnt from Molly. She had taught him an awful lot. She had been teaching him all those things that he badly needed to know and he hadn't even had the sense to see it. Now he loved her even more.

'Come, come, Tom,' Lu Thong said. 'Such terminology does not suit you. It suits Molly – this much I have learnt already – but it trips with reluctance from your tongue. I fear that little Molly has corrupted you in the most dreadful way.'

'Is she all right?' Tom repeated.

'Of course,' Lu Thong said. 'What good would she be to me if she were not? While Molly's safe, you are mine.'

'I'm not yours,' Tom said.

'Give it time,' Lu Thong replied.

'I've come here to make a straight trade, Mr Thong. The crystal skull for Molly.'

'You brought it, then?'

'Yes.'

'You are wise as well as courageous. In my pitiful world, my cesspit, my hell on earth, I meet few like you. Alas, I have been jaded by past experience and cannot trust even a gentleman such as yourself. How did you get the skull into Bangkok? You must tell me this, Tom. If you don't, I won't believe that you have it and poor Molly will suffer.'

Tom thought he was hallucinating, hearing a voice from beyond the grave, but something in that eerie voice was calling to him, inviting him to find something in himself that otherwise he might never find. That voice was a siren call.

'You know an awful lot about me,' Tom said. 'I'm

surprised you know so much. You had me followed in Yucatán, you had me followed in Mexico, and you have the phone number and address of my club in London – so you know all about me.'

'How true,' Lu Thong said.

'So knowing all about me, you must know that I have friends in high places – my academic background, my good breeding – and therefore must also know that I could use those connections to bring the skull into Bangkok.'

'Diplomatic courier, Tom. Was that it?'

'Yes,' Tom said. 'It's now in the safe of the British Consulate, where even you can't get at it.'

Lu Thong chuckled and made an odd humming sound that tapered off into silence. At least, Tom thought at first that it was silence, but it wasn't: he could just hear Lu Thong breathing.

'Sublime,' Lu Thong finally said. 'What an artful creature you are, Tom.'

He was silent again, expecting Tom to say something, but Tom, knowing that he was being tormented, decided to hold his peace.

'But what's the point?' Lu Thong asked. 'You wish to trade the skull for Molly. If you come here, you must bring me the skull or poor Molly will suffer. Why the British Consulate?'

'You'll receive the skull,' Tom said, 'when I've personally met you and ascertained with my own eyes that Molly's safe.'

There was another long silence filled with Lu Thong's heavy breathing, then that voice, which had the ring of rattling bones, said, 'I'll send my car for you.'

The line went dead at Lu Thong's end.

Tom sat on at his desk, holding the telephone in his

hand, listening to the hollow buzzing of the dead line as if, in its eerie unsilent silence, he could still hear Lu Thong. He felt hypnotized, slightly divorced from himself, but eventually he managed to get his senses back and then he put the phone down.

Pouring himself another drink, he went to his window and looked out over the great curve of the Chao Phraya River, with its wide variety of boats and, beyond it, the railway station, located close to Wat Dusit where poor Mai had supposedly been born and raised. A likcly story, Tom thought. Before coming to Bangkok, he had done his homework – studied the maps and so forth – and now, given Lu Thong's address by Mai, he knew that far from running the sleazy district around the railway station, Lu Thong lived like a lord in the rich man's quarter of Bang Kapi. As for Mai, far from being Lu Thong's pitiful victim, she was almost certainly his willing accomplice and every bit as ruthless as her friend. Tom knew that they intended to kill him, but even that didn't worry him.

Lu Thong was prompt. Fifteen minutes after the phone call, Tom received a call from Reception, telling him that a lady was waiting for him downstairs in the lobby. Fully aware of who that lady was, Tom made his way down to the lobby where he saw Mai Suphar in all her glory, as dazzlingly beautiful as she had been in London and possibly even more so with her long black hair hanging to her perfect rump and her ravishing body encased tightly in a Malaysian-style *cheongsam* of silvery-white Thai silk. Taking a deep breath and letting it out slowly, Tom walked up to her and gazed steadily, fearlessly, at her.

'So,' he said.

Mai offered her most dazzling smile. 'How nice to see you again, Tom. It's been far too long.'

'Let's go,' Tom said.

Realizing that Tom was not as timid as he had been previously, but merely amused by this fact, Mai smiled at him and then turned away to lead him out of the hotel, her broad hips moving like a metronome under her slim waist and above those long, exquisite legs balanced neatly on high heels. A Chinese chauffeur wearing a black suit, black tie, white shirt and black peaked cap was standing by a silvery-grey Mercedes Benz and when Mai and Tom approached he bowed slightly and opened the rear door to let them get in.

Sitting in the rear beside the murderous Thai beauty as the Mercedes moved off, Tom was uncomfortably aware of her presence and of the fact that she had deliberately sat as close as possible to him, her shoulder pressing against his shoulder, her hip touching his hip, meanwhile crossing one golden leg over the other to let her *cheongsam*, slit up both sides, expose a teasing length of smooth thigh. Still dangerously seductive, she was clearly toying with him, but he wasn't about to fall for it this time and steeled himself to resist her.

'I'm glad you came, Tom,' she said, almost crooning, her voice like honey and yoghurt. 'Mr Thong is looking forward to meeting you. I've told him so much about you.'

'I'm looking forward to meeting him,' Tom responded. 'You've told me so much about him.'

Mai noted the sarcasm and smiled. 'Why, Tom, I think you're actually being wicked – and I *do* like wicked men.'

'Is Molly really all right?'

'Why wouldn't she be? Any bad that befalls her

will happen later, when she's no longer of use to us.'

'You told me that drug hypnotized her. What state is she in now?'

'She's perfectly normal, Tom. The effects of the drug have worn off. I only needed her pacified for the journey, which was made without incident. Now, though a prisoner, she's enjoying a life of luxury while pining to be rescued by her hero. Will you rescue her, Tom?'

'I'll certainly try,' Tom said.

Mai uncrossed her legs, crossed them the other way, then turned towards Tom to stare directly at him, breathing into his face. Her slight smile showed off her flawless white teeth and the pink of her wicked tongue. 'Why bother with a little frump like Molly when you can have a woman like me?'

'You're a black widow spider,' Tom said. 'I'd end up being breakfast.'

Mai chuckled at that and tickled Tom's chin with her index finger which had, he noted, a very long crimson-painted nail that could have slashed his face open. He pulled his chin back.

'So what happens to Molly if I don't get her out of there?'

'You won't get her out. When you hand over the crystal skull – and I'm sure you will in the end – your dear Molly will either die or end up as one of Lu Thong's playthings, to be used personally by him before being handed over to his goons and then sent into a brothel. She will just disappear, Tom.'

'You're an exceptionally nice crowd of people.'

'Survival is all, Tom. Life is hard in exotic Bangkok and we must do what we have to do. Would you like a kiss, Tom?'

'No, thanks,' Tom said.

Clearly admiring Tom's new-found courage and insolence, Mai continued to flirt with him, though without great success, until the Mercedes turned into the driveway that ran between expansive lawns and tropical foliage to the front door of Lu Thong's large but anonymous residence in Bang Kapi. As Tom emerged from the car, relieved to escape the close proximity of Mai Suphar, he noted that electrified gates had closed behind him and that the house was protected by high-tech surveillance systems and well-armed security guards who could be seen even now patrolling the grounds. This did not augur well for him.

'You like it?' Mai asked, coming up to stand beside him at the wide steps leading up to the front door.

'Very nice,' Tom said, taking note of the many palm trees, rainbow-coloured orchids, and other exotic flora and fauna that enhanced the broad smooth green lawns. 'More modest than I'd imagined it to be.'

'Lu Thong is a modest man.'

There was a big ape by the front door, Chinese, wearing a black suit, but he stepped aside when Mai and Tom approached to let the former press the door bell. When a tinny voice came out of the intercom, authorizing Mai's entry, the big ape opened the door with his personal key and then stepped aside to let them walk in. When the guard closed the door behind him, Tom heard the key turning in the lock and then being removed.

'Nice, isn't it?' Mai said.

'Very nice,' Tom replied.

Mai nodded and smiled, then led him across an expansive lobby with marble tiles, exotic carpets and wall hangings, as well as a proliferation of what clearly were very rare, doubtless stolen, Thai and Vietnamese antiques. Following Mai through a doorway off the lobby, Tom found himself in an equally expansive, vividly luxurious Oriental lounge with exquisite bamboo furniture, more exotic carpets and wall hangings, and a panoramic window that overlooked the high-rise buildings of the city.

In front of that window, a man wearing a dressing gown of Thai silk was seated on velvet cushions on the floor, his black-haired head bowed over a glass-topped bamboo table on which tiny piles of what looked like baking soda were laid out in a straight line along the edge.

The crystal skull stolen from the Museum of Mankind was resting on the glass-topped table close to the man's head.

The man sniffed some of the powder up through one nostril, then raised his head to gaze at the ceiling and take a deep breath before sighing with either relief or pleasure. The sigh turned into a loud gasp, then he lowered his head again to stare steadily at Tom, studying him at length.

'Well, well,' he said after a long silence, his voice as soft as a breeze on dry sand, suggesting vast desolation. 'Who have we here?'

'This is Tom Powell,' Mai said. 'He's just *dying* to meet you.'

Lu Thong smiled, but that smile was ice and fire, striking Tom as the grimace of a man who was yearning for death. Tom was shocked by what he saw, though he didn't quite know why, since Lu Thong was very much like the voice that he had heard on the telephone: disembodied, not quite real.

Lu Thong was handsome, certainly, in a rather

wan way, but his features, though unusually delicate, seemed oddly tormented, the face appearing to be stripped to the bone, all angles and flat planes. His brown eyes were beautiful, almost soulful, but also sleepy with drugs and imbued with that inner luminescence often seen in the dying. Undernourished, he seemed as insubstantial as a wisp of smoke. When he smiled again, the smile did not reach his eyes, which were focused elsewhere, almost certainly inward.

'And I'm dying to meet *you*,' he said to Tom, indicating with a wave of his hand that Tom should come to the table. 'Please, Mr Powell, be seated. We have so much to talk about.'

Tom sat on the velvet cushions that had been placed on the floor around the table. He sat directly facing Lu Thong and Mai then sat beside him, tugging the *cheongsam* up over her knees as she curled her legs beneath her. Lu Thong studied Mai's lovely legs at length and then smiled at Tom.

'May I just begin,' he said, 'by saying how much I admire your courage in coming all this way to rescue dear Molly.'

'Where is she?' Tom asked.

'She is here,' Lu Thong informed him, 'and perfectly safe. You will get to see her in due course.'

'That's why I'm here,' Tom said.

'And your crystal skull?'

'You'll get that when Molly's back in my hotel. We'll have to come to some kind of an arrangement.'

'What makes you think that when you give me the crystal skull I will not terminate you, not to mention dear Molly?'

'I'll worry about that when the time comes. Now let's discuss how to do this.'

Lu Thong smiled again. He seemed genuinely amused. 'Alas, Tom, we have to talk first. That's really why I blackmailed you into coming here.'

'What do we have to talk about?'

'We've tried to kill you before, Tom.' He nodded to indicate Mai Suphar. 'We tried to kill you in Mexico City, we tried again in London, and in both instances some very strange things happened and your life was miraculously saved. We are talking about the paranormal, Tom, and that's one of my interests. You're being protected by the magical powers of the crystal skulls and I'd like to know why. To understand it, or at least to attempt to do so, I have to talk with you.'

Tom shrugged. 'Talk away.'

Lu Thong sighed. 'You are being impertinent, Tom. But I admire that. It will not, I assure you, lengthen your life, but I still have to admire it.'

He bowed over the table, sniffed up some more cocaine, put his head back to breathe it in, then let his breath out with a long sigh and ended with another gasp of relief or pleasure. Lowering his head again, he stared at Tom with his sleepy, yet oddly intense gaze, looking out from somewhere deep within himself where his demons resided.

'Did you know, Tom?' he asked, 'that I have a particular interest in antiquity?'

'No,' Tom said, 'I didn't.'

'In fact,' Lu Thong continued in his quietly mesmerising manner, 'I possess one of the world's greatest collections of illegally-gained antiques – one that you, given your particular interests, would kill to have in your home.'

'I doubt that,' Tom said.

'There's nothing you would kill for?'

'No.'

'Not even Molly?'

'Perhaps for Molly,' Tom said.

Lu Thong smiled at Mai Suphar. 'Did you hear that, my dark beauty? Tom would kill for his little Molly. Such love is unknown to you and I and we may be the less for it.'

'We can live without it,' Mai said.

Nodding, still smiling, Lu Thong turned back to Tom and said, 'Anyway, dear Tom, to return to the subject at hand, one of my most prized possessions is an item so rare that even the specialists in this particular field have long argued as to whether or not it actually exists.' He waited for Tom to respond, but when Tom, wanting to slight him, refused to do so, he continued, unperturbed: 'It is the famous lost book of early Mayan history: the legendary *Mérida Codex*, a book of pre-Pleistocene Meso-American history which proves that the Mayans came from a mysterious, more ancient race. At the dawn of time, that particular race migrated over the centuries from their first holy city at Angkor, in what is now Cambodia, to Polynesia, the Easter Island, the Yucatán peninsula, including what is now British Honduras, and, finally, to the area that's now divided into Bolivia and Peru. There, by the shores of Lake Titicaca, they built Tiahuanaco, also known as the great city of the stars.'

'I know all that,' Tom said.

Ignoring Tom's deliberate rudeness, refusing to be baited, Lu Thong stood up, moving with possibly deliberate weariness, and went to the bookshelves lining one of the walls. It was clear to Tom, from one glimpse of those bookshelves, that they contained a magnificent collection of rare books and parchments, most of them almost certainly stolen. After removing one of the books, a superbly bound antique volume, from the top shelf, Lu Thong returned to his place at the far side of the table, sitting again on the velvet cushions and opening the volume to gaze down at certain pages. He studied the pages as if in a trance of quiet delight, then raised his head and returned his sleepily intense gaze to Tom, who noticed, for the first time, that Lu Thong appeared never to blink. Tom found this disconcerting.

'This,' Lu Thong said, tapping the opened book with a delicate finger, 'is the legendary *Mérida Codex*, so named because it was discovered in archaeological diggings in Mérida, which is, as you know, near Chichén Itzá. Now what this book tells us, Tom, is that at the dawn of Mayan history, when the Mayans were another race altogether, located mostly around the holy city of Angkor, disembodied alien beings materialized on or *in* Earth – *in* Earth in the sense that they may have accidentally tumbled out of another sphere of existence, or parallel universe, rather than from a distant galaxy.'

Lu Thong paused to let his words sink in and Tom did, indeed, take them in, though deliberately he offered no response. Gazing steadily at him, as if taking his measure and finding it worthy of consideration, Lu Thong smiled his diabolical smile and continued his monologue.

'These disembodied beings,' he said, speaking softly, calmly, as if this were the most normal conversation in the world, 'while being sexless as we know it, were of a female or, rather, feminine nature and could inhabit the material bodies of human beings. However, two of them were trapped accidentally inside some Earthlings:

priestesses of that ancient, mysterious race. Unable to escape from their physical prisons, the aliens turned their human hosts into the living embodiment of their formerly incorporeal selves. Which meant, in effect, that those two human beings, both female, looked perfectly normal, but had inherited the magical powers possessed by the aliens.'

'This is ridiculous,' Tom said.

'It's the truth,' Lu Thong insisted. 'Just think of what occurred on that road to the airport in Mexico City – yes, Tom, we learnt that from your bugged conversation with Lady Barratt-White – and then of what took place when you and Mai, a naughty twosome, were in the bedroom of your club in Mayfair. A saucer-shaped, star-filled light – that was on the road to the airport – and alien presences in the room in your club. Those were not hallucinations, Tom – you were protected – so please don't treat this as foolishness.'

'All right,' Tom said, vividly recalling both instances and shaken again at the recollections. 'I am all ears. Continue.'

'Oh, I will, Tom. I will . . .'

Lu Thong bowed his head to sniff up some more cocaine, to put his head back and breathe deeply and sigh and gasp loudly with pleasure or relief. This task completed, he returned his sleepy, eerily penetrating gaze to Tom. His brown eyes were unblinking.

'The two aliens in human form, being possessed of magical powers, were treated by the primitive pre-Mayans as goddesses and eventually, since they had come from the sky in – you know the quote, Tom – *a light brighter than the sun* – were named the Old Goddess of the Moon and the Young Goddess of the

Moon, both of whom are illustrated and annotated in the four rare Mayan Codexes.'

After staring steadily, thoughtfully at Tom, he studied his stolen *Mérida Codex* in a contemplative, dreamy manner, but eventually, with a sigh, looked up again.

'Though pining to return to their spiritual or, as we would have it, alien state of being,' he continued, speaking and looking like death warmed up, 'the two goddesses died a normal, Earthly death. Shocked by this great loss, the high priests of that ancient, pre-Mayan civilization made replicas of the skulls of the two goddesses. Believing that crystal possesses magical properties, they carved the skulls from quartz crystal, thereby hoping to retain, or imprison, the souls of the aliens and, incidentally, turn the skulls into magical objects of worship. In this, they succeeded.'

Lu Thong glanced at Mai Suphar, still sitting beside Tom, her long, golden legs curled beneath her and displaying much thigh. Lu Thong's sleepy gaze travelled the length of those legs, all the way up to the thighs, then he sighed, as if saddened by his base, earthly desires, and turned his gaze back on Tom.

'However,' Lu Thong said, as if sermonizing in a temple, 'the others in that essentially feminine, self-propagating alien species – whose consciousness, incidentally, forms a single entity – could not rest while the souls of their two lost sisters were missing. Thus, they tried repeatedly throughout the centuries – time is meaningless to the disembodied – to break through to the space called Earth – though solid to us, a mere space to them – and draw their lost sisters back to their own sphere of incorporeal existence. Those failed attempts to cross over into the material world have been witnessed throughout the centuries by many disbelieving human beings . . . in the shape of ghosts, UFOs and aliens – just like the ones seen by you and Molly and, indeed, by Mai here.' He nodded at Mai to let her know that he had not forgotten her. 'There the story ends, Tom.'

'Or begins,' Tom replied.

Lu Thong offered his deathly smile. 'How perceptive you are, Tom. Talking to you is certainly no loss. So where does this lead us?'

'You tell *me*,' Tom said.

'Please humour me, Tom.'

'The crystal skulls,' Tom said, 'must be returned to their source, that majestic and hidden city linked to the stars – namely, Tiahuanaco, in Peru – in order that their magical powers can be united. When that happens, the two alien beings trapped in space and time will be released back to their own incorporeal world, where space and time have no meaning.'

'Very good,' Lu Thong replied. 'You're close, Tom, but not quite right. Why do you think I still live here in Bangkok, which I loathe to the depths of my weary bones?'

'I don't know,' Tom said. 'Why?'

Lu Thong bowed his head to have another sniff of cocaine before, with eyes ever more intense yet far-away, he could reveal to Tom the secrets of his blighted soul. 'Because, dear Tom, I've always wanted to experience *everything* – money beyond counting, prestige beyond imagining, sex beyond all moral restraints, and limitless power on Earth. And now that I have it, which I do – believe me, Tom, I have it all – there is only one thing left to do . . . To unravel the ultimate mystery of what lies beyond this mortal, meaningless world.'

'Though the crystal skulls,' Tom said.

'Correct,' Lu Thong said. 'This is the knowledge that the crystal skulls will reveal if they're returned to their source.'

'Which isn't in Bangkok,' Powell said tartly.

'Nor in Peru, my insolent young friend. Tiahuanaco was the *end* of the pre-Mayans' journey from west to east; but the *beginning* of that journey – the origin of the crystal skulls – was the forbidden city of Angkor, in what is now Cambodia, bordering Thailand.'

He straightened his spine, raised his hands above his head, clasped his fingers together and cracked his knuckles. Tom imagined those fingers crushing human bones and, in so doing, was reminded of just how dangerous this extremely handsome, seemingly wasted man was.

As if reading Tom's mind, Lu Thong smiled, then lowered his arms and leaned forward with a tight, challenging smile.

'Look at me, Tom.'

Tom stared steadily at him, trying to stare him down, but he felt that he was being drawn into those brown eyes, which had the fires of hell in them. Tom had to forcibly shake himself out of this reverie and lower his gaze.

'Could I mesmerize you with my eyes?' Lu Thong asked him.

'I think you could,' Tom confessed.

'Yes, Tom, I could. Eyes can certainly mesmerize. Yet while Molly was mesmerized by the eye *sockets* of the crystal skulls, she was not mesmerized by its *eyes* – which are, of course, missing.' He pointed to the macabre crystal skull on the table to make this point clear, then he turned back to Tom. 'They are missing, but they are still there in spirit. So how can this be?'

'Just tell me,' Tom said.

'Ah, Tom, you are impatient. This I like very much. You need to solve this mystery as much as I do and this will make you my victim. But that's for later, of course.'

'Yes,' Tom said, 'of course. Now what about the missing eyes?'

'It is said that the skulls' eyes, which are also made of magically-endowed crystal, are located beneath a stone slab on the summit of Ta Keo, the first of the two great royal temples in the holy city of Angkor. Fearful that the power of the skulls would be exploited for evil, the high priests removed the eyes from the crystal skulls, which vastly reduced their powers, and buried them under a stone slab on top of Angkor's first great temple mountain. Only then did they begin their great eastward migration, taking the eyeless skulls with them, leaving behind not only their magnificent holy city, but also the seeds of that city's future magnificent Khmer civilization. Centuries later, near the end of their great journey, for reasons now lost in the mists of prehistory, they buried the two eyeless skulls in separate places in the Yucatán peninsula – one, as we now know, in Chichén Itzá, the other in British Honduras, now Belize – and then ventured forth to their final destination and ultimate destiny: to create the holy city of Tiahuanaco, Peru, and there, where the sun rises to mark the dawn, raise their great Sun Gate as a bridge between West and East, between the past and the future.'

'And the crystal skulls?'

'When the hidden crystal eyes are placed back in the

crystal skulls, another bridge between past and future, between the Here and the There, will be created, uniting the Earth to that other world of incorporeal, star-filled, alien life.' Lu Thong leaned forward again, to hold Tom's attention with his opaque, mesmeric gaze. 'Do you understand, Tom? That's why I still live in this cesspit. Because Bangkok is the gateway to Cambodia – and there, in the jungle, in the once holy city of Angkor . . . will be found the true meaning of existence.'

'You sound almost religious,' Tom said sarcastically, though he felt the return of a fear that went beyond fear of death.

'My religion is limitless power,' Lu Thong replied, 'and the crystal skulls could make me omnipotent.'

'Oh?' Tom was sceptical. 'How?'

Lu Thong was all too pleased to explain and did so, though still speaking softly, with unusual fervour. 'The lost souls of the two aliens can only be released and returned to their own world when the crystal eyes are placed back in the crystal skulls and laid to rest at their source – in Ta Keo, the first royal temple of Angkor. I cannot be sure, but I think it very likely that whoever does that will gain the powers possessed by the aliens . . . the ultimate power on Earth.'

Lu Thong leaned back again, releasing Tom, smiling thinly at him. 'So, my friend, you will die here in Bangkok while I go to Angkor with the crystal skulls, to either find unimaginable horror or become . . .'

His voice trailed off into a resonant, tingling silence and at last his drugged eyes blinked. Leaning forward, he sniffed up some more cocaine, then he sat straight again. He shrugged and smiled knowingly, shaking his head in a weary manner, as if to say that the answer, though put in the form of a question, could not be refuted.

'*God?*' he said softly.

CHAPTER TWENTY-FIVE

'Oh, dear,' Lu Thong said as if ashamed of himself. 'I am being a very bad host. Tom, you must eat!'

'Just let me see Molly,' Tom said.

'Well, of course, Tom. Of course! Molly must eat as well. In the excitement of our conversation, I simply forgot. Please attend to our lunch, Mai, and ensure that dear Molly is invited to join us.'

Clearly not a person to work herself to death, Mai performed her duties by picking a telephone off the glass-topped table and ringing the kitchen. When she had completed this task, she made another call, speaking in Siamese to the person at the other end of the line. When she had finished, she put the phone down and gave Tom a ravishing smile.

'I told the guard to inform Molly of your arrival,' she said, 'and tell her you wanted to see her. She should be here any minute now.'

'Thank you,' Tom said.

'Tom, Tom,' Lu Thong said, clearly enlivened by his cocaine, 'I can tell by your lack of conversation that you deeply resent us. You must not, Tom. Death comes to us all and yours will be quick, which is more than one can say of those unfortunates who die a natural, lingering death. Think of it this way, Tom. I am saving you from cancer or paralysis or multiple sclerosis or bloody incontinence related to painful bowel disorders – all the dreadful ailments that come to those who foolishly run their natural course. I should get an award, Tom.'

'I have none to give,' Tom said.

'Very good, Tom. Your wit fills my soul with warmth. Yet I sense that behind your little jokes, you still deeply resent me. This is truly unfair, Tom. I'm not a cruel man, after all. You will not die just yet – you and Molly will be reunited – and before I release you from this vale of sweat and tears, I will feed you and let you fuck Molly and perhaps have a good sleep. Life begins and ends there, Tom – in the bed and in the belly – and there are many right here in Bangkok who would sell their souls to the devil to have both. Why resent me for merely relieving you of the burden of living?'

'You don't have the crystal skull yet,' Tom reminded him.

'All in due course, my friend.'

Before Tom could ask Lu Thong what he meant by that, a door to his right opened and a Vietnamese waiter – white jacket, black bow tie, black trousers and black slippers – entered the room, wheeling a trolley the size of a coffin. Approaching the table, he bowed low to Lu Thong, then to Mai Suphar, and finally to Tom, then proceeded to transfer from the many shelves and swinging drawers of the trolley a great number of *Bencharong*, mother-of-pearl and lacquered bowls piled high with a variety of foods, some of which were steaming lightly and gave off a rich, mouth-watering aroma. When these bowls had been spread out on the glass-topped table, under the eyeless gaze of the macabre crystal skull, they made for a spectacular mosaic of various colours and composed of vegetables, peppers, noodles, rice, fruit, seafood, chicken and meats. Four eating bowls with spoons and forks – not chopsticks, Tom noted – and, of course, finger bowls and napkins, were placed around the table, with one place set, presumably for Molly, beside Lu Thong. When the table had been prepared, the Vietnamese waiter bowed again to everyone, then wheeled the trolley back out of the room. No sooner had he disappeared than Molly walked in.

Tom's heart skipped a beat.

Molly looked really very different, though certainly lovely, in a high-necked sleeveless Chinese-styled blouse of finely woven sky-blue Thai silk and matching pants, comfortably loose but not quite loose enough to hide her womanly figure which, though not as voluptuous as Mai Suphar's, was certainly womanly enough for Tom. She was wearing thongs on her bare feet which were, Tom noticed keenly, as white as snow and surprisingly delicate. Her blonde hair was hanging loose, tumbling over her bare shoulders and, although she was wearing no make-up, she looked, even with her prominent nose, as attractive as sin.

Tom's heart skipped another beat.

'You came,' Molly said to him with a smile. 'I always knew that you'd come. I knew you wouldn't desert me.'

'No, I wouldn't,' Tom said.

Lu Thong turned to Mai Suphar. 'Did you hear that, my dark angel? Have you ever witnessed such devotion? You and I could learn a lot from these two and we might be better for it.'

'I'm sure,' Mai replied.

'Come, Molly,' Lu Thong said, waving a tissue-paper

hand, beckoning her to him. 'Please come to the table and be seated. Tom is dying to talk with you.'

Molly glanced at the bowl placed beside Lu Thong and then turned to Tom. 'I don't wanna sit beside him,' she said. 'He gives me the creeps.'

'Come, come, Molly,' Lu Thong said. 'Don't hurt my feelings. If you do, I might have to hurt *you* and it would be unimaginable. So be a good girl and sit down. The food's getting cold.'

Molly glanced doubtfully at Tom, but when he nodded in a reassuring manner, she sat beside Lu Thong.

'Did you see that?' Lu Thong asked of Mai Suphar. 'He just nods and she does his bidding. It isn't fear, Mai – it's love and trust, which is something that you and I should learn about to enrich our poor souls.'

'Absolutely,' Mai said.

'Are you all right?' Tom asked of Molly.

'Yeah, Tom, I guess I'm okay. I can't remember comin' here – that bitch drugged me, so I'm told – but apart from making me take a bath and eat and sleep like a regular guy, they haven't really bothered me at all. They just wanted you here, Tom – that's all they wanted. I mean nothin' to them.'

'Untrue,' Lu Thong said. 'Unkind, my sweet Molly. It's been a pleasure to have you in my humble home, brightening up my stale life.'

'Hey, bitch,' Mai Suphar said.

'What?' Molly said.

'You ever call me a bitch again and I'll cut your tongue out.'

'And she'd do it,' Lu Thong said.

'Go—' Molly started to say.

'Molly!' Tom exclaimed fearfully. 'That's enough. Don't you dare say another word.'

Molly simply glared at him, then at Mai, but eventually she picked up her fork and spoon. 'Okay,' she said, 'let's eat.'

'That's the spirit,' Lu Thong said. Picking up his own spoon and fork, though holding them together between thumb and forefinger, he started pointing out the dishes one by one. 'This,' he said, 'is *Kuay Tiew*, or rice noddles, these are *Ba Mii*, which are noodles made from wheat flour, and this is, of course, simple boiled rice. Either dish goes well with the *Gaeng Khiao Waan Gai*, here, a chicken curry with chicken meat, coconut cream, eggplants and a variety of fragrant herbs; or the *Tom Kha Gai*, here, another chicken dish, but with boned chicken, coconut cream and lemon grass. This one, which tastes divine when poured over the rice – not the noodles – is the *Plaa Krapong Thawd Krathiem Prik Thai*, a local salt-water fish, fried until crisp and laced with garlic and black pepper. And this,' he continued, 'which looks like broccoli, which it is not, is *Phak Khanna Pha Nam Man Hoi Sai Hed Hawn*, a deliciously crunchy vegetable fried with oyster sauce and black Chinese mushrooms. The seasonings,' he droned on, 'are these small bowls of *phrik kii nuu*, known locally as *mouse-dropping chillies*, to be approached with caution unless you have a throat and stomach of cast iron. What more can I tell you?'

'You can tell me what's for afters,' Molly said, ''cause I can't eat this shit.'

'Come, come, Molly,' Lu Thong said, 'be a little more adventurous. This is *Bangkok*, my dear, not Brooklyn, and we do not have hamburgers.'

'What's for afters?' Molly asked again, looking stubborn.

'We have papaya and watermelon and pineapple

and banana and pomelo and sapodilla and lichee and mango, but, alas, no ice cream.'

'I'll start with the afters,' Molly said, picking up a piece of peeled, cut pineapple and looking at it suspiciously. 'At least I won't get the runs.'

'You darling girl,' Lu Thong said.

They ate the magnificent repast in a silence only broken by the tinkling of forks and spoons against bowls. As the meal went on – and it certainly took a long time – Tom studied Lu Thong and realized that although he was only in his mid-thirties and had skin as smooth as butter, he looked truly ancient in some indescribable way, as if decadence and a surfeit of self-satisfaction had prematurely aged him. Nevertheless, Lu Thong's eyes, though sleepy with drugs, possessed a glittering intensity contradicting the sleepiness, and they sometimes wandered up and down Mai Suphar, crawling like spiders over her golden limbs, but dispassionately, with academic curiosity. Seeing this, Tom realized that he was looking at the only man he could possibly imagine could be immune to Mai's deadly charms. Lu Thong also studied Molly, again with no more than academic curiosity, as though she were some kind of insect under his microscope. Tom knew then, without a doubt, that Lu Thong was beyond the pale, that he had done too much too soon, that he'd had too much too early, and had prematurely reached that point in life where he had nothing to live for. Only danger, the ultimate gamble, the throwing of dice with God to perhaps find the devil, would recharge his batteries. He was as frightened of the crystal skulls as was Tom, but his fear gave him life. Lu Thong would willingly go to hell if it offered that – and he was, Tom sincerely believed, on the dark road to that very hell.

Finally, when they had finished the meal and caught up with Molly, still on her afters, making short shrift of the fruit, Lu Thong fastidiously dabbed his thin lips with his napkin and said, 'So, Tom, to the business at hand. Make me tremble with fear.'

'The deal is . . .' Tom began.

'I do not deal, Tom. I dictate.'

'The deal is,' Tom repeated, 'that I'll walk out of here unharmed with Molly. Once we're back in my hotel – and your men can follow us there – I'll phone you with details concerning where the crystal skull can be picked up.'

'That's all there is to it?'

'Yes.'

'And how am I to know, Tom, that once you are back in that hotel you won't break your part of the bargain and fly off with the crystal skull?'

'Because I know that if I try to do that, you'll simply send your men around to pick me up.'

'Which indeed I would, Tom.' Lu Thong leaned forward to pick a red-hot *phrik kii nuu* chilli out of the bowl, pop it into his mouth and chew it as if it were as harmless as a green bean. When he had swallowed it, he dabbed fastidiously at his thin lips with his napkin, then sat back and smiled. 'Very good, Tom. I admire your little display of chutzpa. Unfortunately for you, no matter what we agree, I cannot let you or Molly live. You know about the crystal skull, about Angkor, about me, and for those reasons you must both disappear.'

'Then I can't let you have the crystal skull.'

'You can't *stop* me from having it.' Placing his napkin back on the glass-topped table, right beside the crystal skull, which gazed upon Tom out of hollow eye sockets, Lu Thong raised his hands above his head, cracked his knuckles, thus making Molly wince, then lowered his hands to the table and offered Tom his most diabolical, deadly smile. 'Ah, Tom,' he said as if speaking to a child to whom he had to give bad news, 'I can't decide if you're heroically courageous or simply naive. Have you ever wondered, my dear friend, why, in this pestilent city of Bangkok, which is a veritable hotch-potch of nations and religions, the Thais and Chinese and Indians and Burmese and Laotians and Vietnamese and white expatriates manage to live and work together without strife? Do you know why that is, Tom?'

'No,' Tom said, 'I don't.'

'It's because we're all so deliciously corrupt, Tom, and I, being more corrupt than most, have exploited it beautifully. Bangkok is a heap of excrement and I squat on top of it, my tentacles reaching out to root about in even the smallest dark hole. I have people everywhere, Tom, and they all live in fear of me, and one of them works in the British Consulate as my mole and general fixer. He lets me know what's happening, Tom. He gets me false passports and visas. He slips items into diplomatic pouches and has them transported worldwide. He has the key to their safe, Tom.'

Even before Lu Thong spoke again, Tom knew what was coming, and it sent a sliver of fear shivering through him, convinced, as he was at that moment, that he and Molly were doomed.

'Yes, Tom,' Lu Thong continued, 'unfortunately for you, you have told me little that I didn't already know – you have simply confirmed what I suspected all along. There are only two ways you could have brought your crystal skull into Bangkok: either as an artefact hidden in a consignment of other, legal artefacts being transported from one museum to another – as you did when you had it transported from Mexico City to London – or in a protected diplomatic pouch. However, I know Bangkok, Tom, and it has no museum of the kind that would have use for such an artefact, so clearly it was not shipped in that way. Which left only the diplomatic pouch, Tom, and so that's what I bet on. You have simply confirmed what I suspected and now the skull will be mine. I will now phone my man in the British Consulate and ask him to confirm that the skull is there. When I receive that confirmation, I will tell him to steal it and then I will terminate you and Molly. Poor Tom. What a fool you've been.'

He turned to Molly, reaching out to pat the back of her wrist, but she jerked her hand away and glared at him. Lu Thong just smiled at her.

'Tom loves you, Molly,' Lu Thong said with dry, sly mockery, 'but, alas, love is not enough when it comes to living or dying. He failed you, Molly, and now you will pay the price, but I trust that this will not destroy your love for him, which is surely worth dying for.' He then turned to Mai Suphar. 'Let this be a lesson to both of us, my dark angel. The love which you and I have never known would not have taken us too far. This is a sad fact of life.' Finally, he turned his glittering cocaine gaze upon Tom, whom he clearly admired and would sorely miss. 'Do you know what it is, Tom, that Mai likes more than anything else in the world?'

'Killing,' Tom said.

'No, Tom, not just killing. She likes inflicting pain. Indeed, she likes it so much that she's devised countless highly inventive ways of doing it, all of them slow. I will now, with great reluctance, hand you over to my dark angel and observe what diabolical torture she comes up with. Then, as she is demonstrating her dark and cruel talents, I will hope to learn from your suffering whether or not the love that you and Molly share can withstand hell on earth. If it cannot, then I'll be sorely disappointed and shall shed a tear for my lost hopes.' He turned to Mai Suphar, who was smiling grimly at Molly. 'Make it exquisitely slow,' he told Mai. 'Let their pain become music.'

'That's guaranteed,' Mai replied, smiling and rising to her feet to advance upon Molly.

'No!' Tom bawled.

That instinctive cry of love and defiance seemed to move the whole heavens.

Tom heard a fierce rushing of air that quickly turned into a roaring, then the panoramic window behind Lu Thong exploded inward, showering him in shards of broken glass, and a dazzling, silvery light filled the room to temporarily blind them all.

Battered by the fierce wind, closing his eyes against the light, Tom threw himself onto the floor and then opened his eyes again. The dazzling light still filled the room, but it was not a normal light; it pulsated and flickered and filled up with streams of darkness and there, between the light and the darkness, Tom saw ribbons of stars.

He crawled towards Molly. She seemed immune to the whole disturbance. She was still sitting upright, staring about her with big eyes, as Lu Thong and Mai Suphar, both being battered by the maelstrom, were picked up and slammed into the bookshelves before crumpling to the floor. Mai screamed and Lu Thong cursed, both silhouetted in the unreal light, while around them ghostly figures materialized to look down upon them. The figures gazed down by lowering their heads, but their faces contained no features – no eyes, no nose and no lips – and they formed a circle around Mai and Lu Thong, then seemed to reach down to touch them.

Yes, they had arms and hands, though those appendages were formed by light, and as their hands touched Lu Thong and Mai, streams of light darted out of them, surrounding Lu Thong and Mai in an eerily glowing cocoon in which more stars could be seen. As if electrified, Lu Thong and Mai went into spasms and screamed like stuck pigs.

Tom crawled up to Molly, took her hand and tugged her towards him. She was on her knees and she fell into his arms and let him give her a hug.

'Let's get out of here!' Tom bawled.

The roaring wind was like a tornado, devastating the whole room, as Molly picked the crystal skull off the table and then ran with Tom to the door, carrying the skull in the crook of her arm. Tom stopped briefly in the doorway, looking back, disbelieving, to see books and bowls and forks and spoons and wall hangings and rare paintings swirling in a great circle around the room as if caught in a whirlpool. The whole room was filled with stars which glowed even in that bright light and in that light, which was still pulsating and flickering rapidly, creating a slow-motion strobing effect on everything within it, Tom saw the eerie, silvery figures of the faceless aliens still surrounding Lu Thong and Mai Suphar. The latter were still on the floor, trapped in that glowing cocoon of light, and they were being jolted repeatedly by the small bolts of lightning that exploded from the hands of the aliens and shot into their bodies. Tom saw it, hardly believing his own eyes, then he turned away and tugged at Molly's free hand and they fled from the room.

'We won't get out of this building,' Molly said.

'I think we will,' Tom replied.

And, indeed, he was right. Hurrying across the broad hallway, they found the front door open, its scorched and battered lock lying on the floor in a pile of smouldering wood splinters. Rushing outside, expecting to see the Chinese guard, they were dazzled by more light and almost deafened by another roaring wind.

Squinting into the light, Tom saw that the guard had vanished, though his Browning 9mm High Power handgun was lying on the top step of the porch. Instinctively reaching down to pick up the gun, Tom shoved it into his jacket pocket and then, aware that something was very strange, he hurried down the steps with Molly, both leaning into the wind, and glanced upwards as they hurried along the driveway.

Hovering directly above the house, about a hundred feet above it, was an enormous, saucer-shaped, pulsating silvery light with stars gleaming out of its dark, swirling base. The swirling base, which was like a whirlpool viewed from the bottom, like an inverted funnel, was creating the tornado now devastating the house while filling the air around it with flying foliage, swirling soil and other debris.

'Good God!' Tom exclaimed, slowing down and almost coming to a halt. 'What on earth . . . ?'

'There's a car!' Molly bawled. 'The door's open! Come on, Tom, let's go!'

She tugged Tom towards a red Ford Cortina that was parked by the edge of the driveway, down near the electronically controlled gates. Those gates, Tom noticed, had either been opened by one of the fleeing guards or had been opened in a miraculous manner by that immense, saucer-shaped light still hovering above the house. The driver's door of the Ford Cortina was hanging open and the key was still in the ignition, indicating that the driver had fled at the appearance of the saucer-shaped light and the sudden, unnatural storm. Realizing that he and Molly were being protected again, Tom slipped in behind the steering wheel and waited until Molly had taken the seat beside him, holding the crystal skull firmly on her lap. Then, after carefully fastening his safety-belt, he turned the ignition on, drove the car out through the gate, and turned into the road that led back towards the centre of the city and the Chao Phraya River.

'Look!' Molly exclaimed.

Glancing sideways at the house, then raising his gaze to look above it, Tom saw that great whirlpool of light ascending vertically at high speed, shrinking rapidly as it ascended, taking the roaring wind with it. Within seconds, when it was the size of a single star, though clearly visible in broad daylight, in that vast sheer blue sky, it abruptly blinked out, letting the fierce wind die away altogether.

The debris that had been swirling around the house suddenly fell to the ground.

Lu Thong and Mai Suphar rushed out of the house to glance wildly about them, obviously trying to ascertain what had happened while, at the same time, looking about desperately for Tom and Molly.

Tom laughed and kept driving.

CHAPTER TWENTY-SIX

Checking repeatedly that he was not being followed, Tom drove through the achingly slow traffic of the city until he reached the British Consulate, located in the government district near the Grand Palace and Ratchadamnoen Boulevard. Parking a good distance from the building, he checked again that they were not being followed, saw no cars slowing down and no one approaching, so indicated to Molly that she should get out of the car and come with him.

'What about this?' Molly asked, indicating the crystal skull on her lap.

'We can't take it into the Consulate,' Tom said, 'so we'll just have to take a chance that we haven't been followed and leave it in the boot of the car.'

'Lu Thong will know that we've come here to collect that other crystal skull and his hoods might recognize their own car.'

'That's why I parked so far away,' Tom explained patiently. 'They'll either look for their car in the Consulate car park or in the streets immediately around the building. They won't find it tucked in here.'

'Gee, you're so clever,' Molly said with genuine admiration.

'I have my virtues,' Tom said.

'Why don't I wait here?' Molly asked. 'I'd feel better not leaving this skull behind.'

'I'd rather lose the skull than lose you,' Tom replied, 'and if Lu Thong's men *do* find this car, there's no way you could protect the crystal skull and those bastards would kill you.'

'That's the nicest thing I ever heard, Tom.'

'My pleasure. Now let's go.'

Almost tearful with joy, Molly slipped out of the car and joined Tom as he was raising the lid of the boot. The car's boot was cluttered with various tools, an old canvas bag and a white sheet covered in dirt and what looked like blood stains.

'Jesus!' Molly exclaimed softly.

'They must use it for the transportation of their unfortunate victims,' Tom said. 'That sheet might have been meant for us, Molly, so you're *definitely* coming with me.' He checked the canvas bag and found it empty except for some spent cartridge shells. 'They obviously used this for carrying weapons in,' he said, 'but we can put the skull in it.' Molly carefully placed the crystal skull in the canvas bag and Tom zipped it shut. Then he closed the lid of the boot and said, 'Now to the Consulate.'

The walk to the consulate took about five minutes. Tom had to identify himself in reception and ask for his friend Leonard Clarke-Smith. Shown up to Mr Clarke-Smith's office, they entered to find a tall, slim, impeccably dressed Englishman – pinstripe suit, striped shirt and old-school tie – with a lean, pale face, thick auburn hair, and a rather languid way of moving, as they could see when he arose from his chair. He came around the desk to take hold of Tom's shoulders and shake him affectionately. Then he looked inquiringly at Molly.

'Molly Beale,' Tom said by way of introduction. 'A dear friend of mine.'

'Pleased to meet you,' Clarke-Smith said. 'Any friend of Tom's is a friend of mine, particularly when she's as attractive as you are.'

'Gee, thanks,' Molly said, obviously meaning it this time.

Clarke-Smith turned to Tom. 'I trust you've come to take that bloody awful artefact off my hands.'

'Yes, Leonard, I have.'

'Thank God. That thing gave me the shivers when I opened the package and saw those gleaming, empty eye sockets. What on earth is it?'

'A crystal skull,' Tom said.

'I gathered *that* much,' Clarke-Smith retorted. 'But what *is* it, Tom? I mean, what's its significance?'

'It's just an old Mayan artefact,' Tom said. 'Quite rare and valuable.'

'So where did you get it?'

'Don't ask,' Tom replied.

'So why did you have it brought here – to Bangkok of all places?'

'Don't ask,' Tom repeated.

Clarke-Smith gazed thoughtfully at him, then offered a slight, sardonic grin. 'Well, Tom,' he said, 'you are surely a dear old friend, but don't ever ask this of me again. The next time, I'll want to know what I'm dealing with.'

'There won't be a next time.'

'Good,' Clarke-Smith said. 'So let me get the damned thing brought up and then take it out of here.'

He started to pick up the phone, but Tom placed his hand on his wrist. 'Wait,' Tom said. 'Are you phoning the man in charge of the basement safe?'

'Of course,' Clarke-Smith replied.

'What nationality is he?'

'Siamese . . . Thai. Why?'

'Have you ever heard of a criminal called Lu Thong?'

'God, yes. Who hasn't? He's the worst of a very bad bunch and certainly the most powerful of them all. Why, Tom? What is this?'

'I've strong reason to believe that the man in charge of your safe is working for Lu Thong, acting as a mole, gathering confidential information and also supplying Lu Thong with false passports and visas, using, or misusing, the Consulate facilities. You'd better check him out, Leonard, and in the meantime, I'd rather that you personally went down there and brought the skull up yourself.'

Clarke-Smith had stopped smiling and was wrinkling his high forehead in disbelief. 'Are you sure about this?' he asked.

'Yes, I'm sure.'

'From whom did you obtain your information?'

'Directly from Lu Thong.'

'*Pardon?*'

'You heard me.'

'You've had *personal* contact with Lu Thong?'

'Yes, Leonard. Exactly.'

Exasperated, Clarke-Smith ran his fingers through his thick thatch of hair and said, 'I have to tell you, Tom, that while I appreciate this information, I'm seriously concerned about how you came by it. What on earth is your connection to the notorious, possibly insane and certainly criminal Lu Thong?'

'I've only met him once and it wasn't pleasant. Now, given the contents of our conversation, I have to flee from Bangkok.'

'Tom, this sounds wretched.'

'Just fetch the crystal skull and I'll be out of here. When I'm gone, have your Thai friend investigated and I'm sure you'll discover that I'm right.'

'Wait here,' Clarke-Smith said.

He walked out of the office and Tom sank into the chair in front of the desk. Molly walked up to him, placed her hands around his face, turned his head up and kissed him full on the lips. When she straightened up to look down upon him, she was wet-eyed and smiling.

'You're not an English wimp at all,' she said. 'You're the man of my dreams.'

'I truly hope so,' Tom said.

'What are you like in bed?'

'Not very good.'

'I'll have to do somethin' about that when we have the right time and place.'

'And where might that be?' Tom asked.

'God knows,' Molly said. 'So what happens when he brings us the crystal skull?'

'We return to my hotel, pick up my suitcase, buy you some clothes, and then go on to the railway station and catch a train to Ubon Ratachathani, which is deep in Thailand. From there, we'll make our way to Angkor in Cambodia. Have you got your passport?'

'As a matter of fact, I have,' Molly said, looking triumphant. 'That bitch Mai Suphar was so busy making fun of me when I came out of my trance and was being told where I was, that she didn't notice me taking my passport out of my travelling bag and slipping into the top of these pants, just over my ass. I can feel it there right now.'

'You're a very bright girl, Molly Beale.'

'Not as bright as you, Tom, but I know how to survive. I learnt that on the streets of New York and I won't ever forget it.'

'I think you've a lot to teach me, Molly.'

'And you, me,' Molly said.

They fell silent after that, feeling comfortable with each other, united by love and mutual respect, taking confidence from it. Ten minutes later, Clarke-Smith walked back in, carrying a cardboard box under one arm. He placed the box on his desk and then turned to face them.

'I've already checked the box,' he said, 'and the crystal skull is in it. My Thai friend wasn't there when I collected it, so he doesn't know that it's missing. I'll have him checked out as you suggest, but now please take that gruesome object out of here.'

Tom walked to the desk and opened the flaps of the cardboard box. He looked into it and saw the gleaming dome of the crystal skull. Satisfied, though feeling a little paranoid, he closed the box again. 'Yes,' he said, 'that's it.' He picked the cardboard box off the desk, tucked it under one arm, shook Clarke-Smith's hand with his free hand and said, 'Thanks a lot for this, Leonard.' When he started for the door, Molly rushed ahead to open it for him, but then Clarke-Smith called out to him. Tom glanced back over his shoulder.

'Where are you going,' Clarke-Smith asked, 'when you leave Bangkok?'

'It's best that you don't know that,' Tom said.

'Does that mean that what you're doing is dangerous?'

'I think so,' Tom said.

'Is Lu Thong involved?'

'Yes, Leonard, he is.'

'Then the best of luck to both of you. You'll need it.'

'Thanks, Leonard. Goodbye.'

'Goodbye, Tom.'

Molly closed the office door, then she and Tom made their way back downstairs and out of the building. The sun was high in the sky when they emerged, the air hot and humid, and as they made their way along the palm-lined street they both started sweating. Five minutes later, they reached the car, placed the cardboard box in the boot, beside the other crystal skull, then climbed into the vehicle and drove off, heading for Tom's hotel.

Tom drove carefully, nervously, inching along in the dense traffic, trying to avoid the thrust-and-parry of the expert *samlor* drivers, the crazy motor-cyclists, the scu-rrying, ignored pedestrians, and constantly checking his rear-view mirror for any car that might be following him, even though he knew that in this kind of chaos it would be hard to spot such. The journey seemed to take forever, though in fact it took only twenty minutes, but eventually they arrived at Tom's hotel, which event made them both sigh with relief. Tom drove down into the basement car park and, after circling around for another five minutes, he finally found an empty space.

When he and Molly clambered out of the car, they both looked about them, automatically searching for Lu Thong's men, though they didn't see anyone. Relieved, they removed the crystal skulls from the boot, each taking one, and then made their way up to the lobby. Stopping at the reception desk, Tom collected his key, informed them that he was checking out, and asked for his bill to be prepared. This done, he and Molly took the lift up to the fifth floor, then walked along the corridor to Tom's room.

Even there, Tom did not relax for a second. He opened the door very slowly, stepped tentatively inside, saw nothing, heard nothing, but still went, treading carefully, to check the bathroom. Only when he had fully accepted that there was no one in the room did he finally place the cardboard box on the bed and turn to face Molly. She had placed the canvas bag on the floor and was gazing lovingly at him.

'So what now?' she asked of him.

'Now I pack,' Tom said, going straight to the chest of drawers facing the bed and pulling open the top drawer.

'Immediately?' Molly asked.

'Yes,' Tom said, transferring the clothes from the top drawer into the suitcase still lying open on the lushly carpeted floor.

'Maybe we should sleep first,' Molly said. 'You know? Get some rest.'

'I don't think so,' Tom said, opening the other drawers and continuing to transfer his clothes from them to the suitcase on the floor. Molly watched him in silence until he was finished and had snapped the locks on the case. Then, before he could pick up the suitcase, she walked up to him and placed her hands on his shoulders and nodded towards the big double bed.

'Let's go to bed, Tom,' she said. 'We might never get the chance again. We don't know what's going to happen after this, so let's at least have our moment together. To hell with all the rest of it. Let's snatch this while we can. If you're bad in bed, I wanna teach you to be good and we'll both feel better for it. So come on, Tom, let's use the bed.'

Tom choked up with emotion, with embarrassment

and love and fear, but what moved him at that moment wasn't his fear, but his need to protect her.

'No, Molly,' he said, 'we can't. We simply don't have the time. Lu Thong or Mai Suphar or their hooligans will come here sooner or later and I'd judge that to be sooner rather than later. In fact, they're probably on their way here right now. We have to leave straight away, Molly.'

'Damn it, Tom, that's an excuse.'

'No, Molly, it isn't. It's my declaration of love. I don't want us to be caught in that bed when those bastards burst through the door. I don't want you humiliated or killed. What I want is a future for both of us, which we won't have if we don't get out quickly. So please pick up one of those crystal skulls and let's get the hell out of here.'

'Okay,' Molly said. 'Right.'

Molly grabbed the canvas bag, Tom picked up the cardboard box and the suitcase and, when Molly had opened the door for him, they both left the room. Making their way downstairs, Tom went straight to Reception, telling Molly to go to the shop off the lobby and pick out some clothes. After paying his bill, Tom made his way to the shop where he found Molly with sensible clothing hung over one arm: denims and shirts and underclothes. She was also holding a pair of rubber-soled canvas boots and scouting for something to put them in. After settling on another canvas bag, a well-designed travelling bag, they went to the counter, paid for the goods with Tom's credit card, then packed the clothes in the bag and, still carrying the crystal skulls, made their way back down to the underground garage.

Tom looked around the garage, checking for Lu Thong's men. Seeing no one, he opened the boot of the Ford Cortina, placed his suitcase, Molly's travelling bag and the two crystal skulls in it, then closed the boot and clambered into the car. When Molly was strapped in beside him, he started the car and drove out of the garage, back into the chaotic traffic and bedlam of the city.

It was now late afternoon, but the light was still bright, burning down through the fumes of car exhausts that were belching out on all sides. Tom turned left, intending to head for the Pracha Thipok Road, which would take him across the river, but no sooner had he straightened the car out than he saw, in his rear-view mirror, a silvery-grey Mercedes Benz – the same one used earlier by Mai Suphar – pulling out from the kerb to slip in directly behind him.

'Oh, Christ,' he said, 'they're right behind us, Molly. *Now* what do we do?'

'Just keep drivin',' Molly said. 'They can't do much in this fuckin' traffic jam, so just head for the station. We'll decide what to do when we get there. There's nothing else we *can* do.'

Tom took her advice, not really having any choice, and just followed the flow of the slow-moving traffic while keeping his eye on his rear-view mirror and trying not to evacuate in his pants. Fighting to control the fear that he had thought was well behind him, but taking faith from the knowledge that he was more concerned for Molly than he was for himself, he checked out the car behind, Mai Suphar's Mercedes Benz, and saw enough to know that it was packed with passengers. All of those passengers, he knew, would be armed to the teeth and gunning for him. His heart started racing too quickly and he felt himself sweating.

'Can you see them?' he asked Molly.

In fact, she had twisted around in her seat to look through the rear window. Turning back to her normal position, she said, 'No, I can't make 'em out, but I'd say they're his goons, 'cause Lu Thong's too smart to be caught in a firefight in the streets. I don't think he or Mai Suphar are there. It's just the goons with the guns.'

'*Just?*' Tom exclaimed. 'What will we do if they attack us? We can't *fight* them, Molly!'

'Yes, we can,' Molly said. 'I don't have my handgun – Mai Suphar took that off me before we got to Heathrow Airport – but you've still got the Browning you picked up from Lu Thong's driveway. I can use it, believe me.'

'This isn't a movie, Molly! We can't have a shoot-out. We have to think of something else. Think, Molly! *Think!*'

'We dive into the river and drown ourselves. That's my thought for today. Now give me that handgun.'

Feeling that he was dreaming or, more accurately, having a nightmare, Tom handed her the weapon and then concentrated on making his way around the roundabout, chaotic and dangerous, to reach the bridge that spanned the Chao Phraya River. Surviving the roundabout, he turned onto the bridge and looked down on the river which was, as usual, crammed with boats of all kinds and seemed more than a little inviting. Though possessed with the sudden urge to jump out of the car and dive into those muddy waters, Tom concentrated instead on his driving and saw two parallel lines of traffic, heading in both directions across the bridge in a cloud of exhaust fumes. Confident that even Lu Thong's men would attempt nothing here, he tried to relax enough to think straight . . .

then he saw a jet-black Honda Accord pulling out from the line of oncoming traffic, causing many horns to hoot angrily, and careening across the road to come between him and the cars crawling, bumper to bumper, in front of him.

Shocked, Tom braked to a halt.

'Jesus Christ!' Molly exclaimed, having been thrown forward by the sudden braking and then pulled back by her safety belt, but now raising the Browning 9mm High Power in her right hand and releasing the safety catch.

'Oh, my God!' Tom exclaimed.

Glancing in his rear-view mirror, he saw that the traffic had banked up behind him, the drivers angrily tooting their horns, and that Lu Thong's hoodlums were emerging from the silvery-grey Mercedes Benz, now directly behind him, and were armed with a variety of weapons, including handguns and sub-machine guns. Appalled to see this, he looked straight ahead and saw more hoodlums pouring out of the jet-black Honda Accord, all of them also well armed.

'Sonsofbitches!' Molly exploded, winding her window down in order to lean out and fire her handgun.

'Molly, don't!' Tom shouted, then he glanced in the rearview mirror and saw that Lu Thong's hoodlums were taking up firing positions behind the open doors of their car and taking aim with their weapons. As they did so, the drivers behind them, perhaps used to this kind of situation, started reversing or attempting impossible three-point turns to save their own skins.

'Oh, God!' Tom exclaimed without thinking, then he turned to the front again and saw that the hoodlums who had poured out of the Honda Accord were also taking up firing positions behind the open doors of their vehicle and that the drivers in front of them, on both sides of the bridge, were doing exactly the same as the drivers behind, either reversing or making impossible three-point turns that only led to them crashing into other cars.

'Molly!' Tom screamed as he twisted around in his seat, grabbed her by the shoulders, pulled her back from the open window and then forced her down onto the seat and threw himself on top of her, intending to use himself as her shield. 'Stay down!' he screamed. '*Stay down!*'

As Molly wriggled frantically beneath him, he heard the simultaneous sounds of gunshots and bullets smashing the front and rear windows of the car and ricocheting noisily off the metalwork. Shards of glass rained down upon him as the weapons continued firing – quickly repeated single shots from the handguns, sustained bursts from the sub-machine guns – and then he heard another sound, an ethereal bass humming, unreal, almost *physical*, an almost palpable sound that seemed to press down upon him, tightening his skull as it gradually turned into a distant roaring – it seemed distant, but it was *here*, all around him – and then the gunfire tapered off and was replaced by shouts and screams, men and women in panic, and he raised himself off Molly and looked out and saw what he had clearly seen before but could still not believe.

His car was surrounded by light – not sunlight: an unearthly light – and that light was spreading out in great striations that formed an enormous fan across the bridge. Within that light were stars – their light was brighter than the other light – and within the stars, between the stars, where the light had made daylight darken, he saw a host of ghostly forms, with arms and legs, though faceless, not walking but somehow *drifting* across the road of the bridge, alighting here and there, touching the cars with fingerless hands, sending tiny bolts of lightning from those hands into whatever they touched.

The whole bridge was in chaos. Cars were swerving and crashing. Lu Thong's hoodlums, front and rear, were throwing down their weapons and either falling to their knees, hands up to their chins in prayer, or running away in both directions, some vaulting over cars in their determination to escape, others throwing themselves off the bridge to fall into the river far below, preferring death to the unknown.

'Hold me, Tom!' Molly screamed.

Seeing Molly's fear and wonder, both unfamiliar to him, Tom pulled her into his arms and buried her face in his chest. In doing this, he felt ennobled, raised above his weaker self, and he looked out at what was happening on the bridge and understood, beyond a shadow of doubt, that it had been preordained. Released from fear, blessed with wonder, taken back to his childhood, to the dreams that he had lost and finally found again, he leaned forward to look out through the open window of the car and cast his gaze upwards, to the sky, knowing what he would see there.

An enormous, saucer-shaped, pulsating light, limned with a silvery-white haze and filled with brilliant stars, was descending slowly, inexorably, unstoppably, over the whole bridge. When it was mere feet above the bridge, its dazzling, unearthly brilliance obscuring the structure itself, making it melt into infinity, sending it back where it belonged – to Bangkok, in the present – the gently weaving, sensuous forms, those faceless beings of no substance, surrounded Tom's car and closed in upon it to carry him off.

'Hold me, Tom!' Molly cried.

Tom fell upon Molly, kissing the back of her neck, holding her head with loving hands, and then he felt the world turning – turning him inside out – and then time shrank, sucking space into itself, and sent him winging past suns and moons and all the stars of eternity. He saw himself, past and present, young and old, here and there, and then he returned, dazed, to a present that he could never have imagined.

When he opened his eyes again, raising his head, which required great courage, he realized that he had passed in an instant from childhood to manhood, regaining faith in himself.

He raised his head and looked out of the car, wondering what he would find there.

White light.

Jungle mist.

CHAPTER TWENTY-SEVEN

Tom blinked repeatedly, bewildered. Molly was in his arms. They were still in the Ford Cortina, but it was parked at an unusual angle, practically turned over on its side, caught in a tangle of enormous branches and leaves at the foot of the soaring trees of an Oriental jungle.

And there, outside the car, stretching away for miles, was the once holy, now forbidden, city of Angkor. It was immense, magnificent and covered in the rot of centuries. The mist drifted around the soaring trees and great mountain temples. The silence was frightening.

'Oh, my God!' Tom whispered.

Molly yawned and opened her eyes, then sat upright herself to look out of the weirdly angled car. Her eyes went as wide as two spoons when she saw what was out there.

'What the . . . ?'

'That's Angkor,' Tom said. 'We're in Cambodia. How on earth did we get here?'

'I dreamt about stars,' Molly said. 'The same stars and moons – double moons – that I saw when I looked into the crystal skull. So maybe it wasn't a dream, after all. Maybe . . .'

She didn't complete her sentence, because what she was thinking defied reason and could not have happened.

'I dreamt about stars as well,' Tom said. 'Stars too large to be our stars and surrounding double moons. I remember us on the bridge that spanned the Chao Phraya River in Bangkok, the light descending, the aliens, and then I lay across you and closed my eyes and the world, either outside or inside my head, seemed to turn inside out. Then I fell asleep, or at least I think I fell asleep, and saw space, the cosmos, stars I couldn't recognize, double moons, and then I opened my eyes, or I woke up, and this is what I found. We're still in the damned car, the car seems fine, but here we are in Cambodia.'

'I'm scared, Tom,' Molly said. 'I'm really scared. Is that ruined city, that Angkor place, in Cambodia or is it someplace else? Where are we, Tom? What *year* is this?'

'We're in Angkor,' Tom insisted. 'I know it intimately from books I've studied. We're in Angkor, Cambodia – that's Cambodian jungle out there – but *when*, whether in the past or the future, well, I haven't a clue.' He checked his wristwatch. It said five in the morning. He saw striations of weak sunlight breaking through the dark clouds, a hint of dawn light, and assumed that his wristwatch was now set to local time. He could not imagine how he had come to be here, still in one piece, his wristwatch set to local time, but he was certain that this was Angkor in Cambodia and it was just before dawn.

'Come on,' he said. 'Let's clamber down.'

Overwhelmed, he and Molly lowered themselves out of the car and clambered down through the thick branches to the ground. Suddenly panicking, realizing that they had both forgotten what had actually caused them to be here, Tom climbed back up and, to his immense relief, found the two crystal skulls still in the boot of the Ford Cortina, one in the cardboard box, the other in the canvas bag once used to hold weapons. He lowered both to Molly, then clambered back down until he was standing beside her.

'I don't really believe we're here,' he said, 'but I think we'll be all right.'

'Let's hope so,' Molly said.

They embraced and kissed, then, carrying their separate packages, walked through the jungle's mist, toward the soaring towers and minarets of Angkor. As they advanced carefully into the great complex, still surrounded by dense jungle wreathed in morning mist, Tom wondered if he and Molly were really alive, still in their mortal bodies, in the same year or time-frame, because the city was totally deserted, with neither tourists nor guards, and it gave off no sound other than the cry of a distant bird or the eerie call of some unseen forest animal. Nevertheless, he kept walking, side by side with Molly, taking his faith from her love and trust, determined still to protect her.

As they advanced into the complex, heading north, Tom constantly looked about him, trying to take in what it was he was seeing and make some sense of it. Though struck by the chilling lack of humanity in the ancient temples, reservoirs and canals, their bleakly imposing profusion of almost identical grey sandstone gods, dancing girls and various animals, some unrecognizable, he was awed at the very thought of how this great complex, formerly the centre of one of the largest kingdoms in South-east Asia, had been sacked and abandoned by Thai armies over five hundred years ago. He was awed, too, by the knowledge that although this 'forbidden city' was known to have been the centre of the magnificent Khmer dynasty, then extending from the tip of the Indochinese peninsula northward to Yunnan and, from Vietnam, westward to the Bay of Bengal, it was believed to have existed long before that, beyond the veils of recorded history, way back in the mists of prehistory when it could, indeed, have been built by that ancient, mysterious race that had travelled from here to Meso-America.

'Tom, I'm scared,' Molly repeated.

'Don't be,' Tom said. 'Hold my hand. That should make you feel real again.'

Molly took hold of his hand and squeezed it. 'Yeah, right,' she said. 'I feel real again. You and me, we're an item.'

'Aren't we ever?' Tom said.

He wanted to make her smile, but he was just as scared as she was and did not feel any better when they completed the five-kilometre walk that eventually brought them to Angkor Wat, the greatest of all the sites, located about three kilometres west of what he was looking for: Ta Keo, the first of the two great royal temples, where, hopefully, the crystal eyes of the crystal skulls were hidden. As they made their way through the labyrinthine pathways of the complex, walking under the towering walls, along the sides of the empty canals and moats, embalmed in deathly silence, Tom thought of how history had constantly been rewritten and of how, before recorded history, the only constant was mystery. Angkor was itself a mystery, raised to foil time, widely believed to have been constructed as a symbolic universe based on imported Indian cosmology, but designed to concentrate the potency of the soil upon which the prosperity of that ancient kingdom depended. Yet before that, before its history could be recorded and, thus, rewritten, it had existed, either in reality or as a dream, as the living centre of the cosmological, star-filled universe, beyond Earth, beyond time; and its great pyramid temples, some still standing, foiling time, might have been raised, or conceived, as repositories for the hidden powers of that universe and all it contained: other worlds, alien beings. Tom thought of this with wonder and awe until he and Molly, after hiking another three kilometres to the east, reached Ta Keo, the first of the pyramidal royal temples.

'This is it,' Tom said.

'We have to climb to the top of it?' Molly asked.

'Yes,' Tom said. 'Don't you want to?'

'It looks creepy,' Molly said doubtfully.

'Just keep holding my hand.'

Ta Keo was indeed imposing, being over a hundred metres wide at its base and rising over twenty metres, on three separate levels, one containing a continuous, sealed-in gallery, to a forty-six-metre-square terrace surmounted by five ornate sanctuary towers. Though the walls of each of the lower terraces were broken up with open doorways, each framing the darkness inside the unfinished temple, a flight of broad stone stairs led upwards from the base of the building to the high terrace with the sanctuary towers.

'I'm convinced that the crystal eyes for the skulls are hidden in one of those sanctuary towers,' Tom said. 'So take a deep breath and let's start climbing.'

Still carrying their crystal skulls, one in its canvas bag, the other in a cardboard box, Tom and Molly commenced the arduous climb up to the top terrace, taking the broad stairs carefully, one by one, advancing from one terrace to the next, passing friezes of gods and the vague outlines of figures that might or might not have been girls, who might or might not have been dancing, might or might not have been human – indeed, as Tom noticed, who seemed not quite like girls, though they *were* distinctly feminine, reminding him of the alien figures formed out of light and swaying gently, sensuously, like windblown reeds.

Eventually, breathless, they found themselves on the top terrace, overlooking the vast complex of Angkor and the jungle surrounding it. The terrace was over forty metres square and grass was sprouting between the stone slabs. A tall sanctuary tower, raised to the sun, moon and stars, stood at each corner of the terrace, with a fifth tower, the tallest, in the middle.

'That's it,' Tom said, pointing to the central, and highest, sanctuary tower. 'The eyes of the crystal skulls, if they're here at all, will be hidden in the central, the highest, tower. There are doorways around the base of the tower, so let's see what's inside.'

They entered to find a square-shaped room of grey sandstone walls and dust-covered stone slabs, gloomily illuminated by the weak morning light bleeding in from outside. The place was completely empty, offering not the slightest hint of where the crystal eyes might be hidden.

'Now what?' Molly asked, her voice reverberating eerily in that enclosed space.

Tom didn't know what to say. He felt unreal and disorientated. Looking out through the doorway, at the other pyramid temples of the vast, jungle-enshrouded complex, trying to work out what time it really was –

even what year it was or what planet he was on – he saw only a somnolent, cloudy sky, a vast anonymity. Then, just as he was about to look away, the sun broke through the clouds, one curved yellow rim sliding free. Striations of light fell upon the ruins and reached out to the temple.

Squinting, turning away, looking back down at the stone-slab floor, Tom saw a single ray of light beaming in across his shoulder to illuminate a slab fixed into the far corner. That finger of light made Tom remember the aliens and the beams of sparkling light, some unknown form of energy, that had darted from their fingerless hands when they reached out to anything material. He knew then, without a shadow of doubt, where the hidden eyes of the crystal skulls were hidden.

'Put your bag down,' he said to Molly. 'We're in the right place.'

As Molly did his bidding, Tom knelt on the floor near the illuminated stone slab and placed the cardboard box by his side. He studied the stone slab and was instantly elated to note that although it had supposedly been there for centuries, the cement surrounding its two sides, where it was not fixed tight against the two walls forming the corner, had turned to powder and those two sides of the slab seemed to be loose. When he looked around him, he saw that the other stone slabs were still firmly embedded.

'This is it,' he said with absolute conviction.

Molly knelt beside him, studied the stone slab, ran her finger around it and then, as practical as always, said, 'The cement may be loose on those two sides, but there's still no way to lift that damned thing out. We don't have any tools, we have nothin', so we don't have a prayer.'

'Let's unpack the crystal skulls,' Tom said. 'Let's just see what happens. We'll unpack them and place them beside the stone slab, one on each of those two sides where the cement has been loosened.'

'And then?'

'Then we simply sit back and see what happens.'

'Oh, my hero,' Molly said with affectionate sarcasm, then she opened her canvas bag and pulled out her crystal skull while Tom removed his from its card-board box. They placed the crystal skulls, as Tom had suggested, one to each of the two free sides of the slab forming the corner.

'Move back,' Tom said.

They sat together in the opposite corner, beneath the finger of light beaming in and now falling over – and eerily illuminating – the two macabre, eyeless crystal skulls.

Nothing happened for some time. The only sound was their nervous breathing. Molly reached out to take hold of Tom's hand and tug it onto her lap, where she squeezed it repeatedly. She didn't say a word and he didn't speak to her, but both of them were mesmerized by the crystal skulls which, illuminated in that eerie light, seemed to take on a magical sheen and odd, shadowy features.

The finger of light brightened, then it moved as the sun moved, and eventually it fell directly upon the eye sockets of the two skulls and those eye sockets reflected the light to fill the gloom with criss-crossing, constantly shifting striations. Those striations of light, in their turn, fell upon Tom and Molly, forming a dazzling mosaic, distorting what they were seeing, making them both imagine that the stone slab was moving, rising out of the floor.

They both blinked and rubbed their eyes, then squinted into the dazzling light. They heard a muffled rumbling, a louder grinding sound, and then, though they could hardly believe it, they saw that the stone slab was, indeed, rising out of the floor, as if being pushed up by an unseen hand. Eventually, when its base was level with the floor, it fell over at an angle, falling between the two crystal skulls without actually touching them. When it hit the floor with a dull, reverberating thud, the finger of light blinked out.

'Jesus Christ!' Molly whispered.

Without thinking twice, Tom jumped to his feet and raced across the floor to look down into the hole in the corner.

Four eyes of clear crystal, embedded in loose soil, were staring up through the gloom.

'Oh, Christ!' Tom whispered.

He dropped to his knees and just stared down upon those awful eyes as Molly also jumped to her feet and raced over to join him. When she, too, looked down into the hole, she let out a soft gasp. They both stared at the crystal eyes for a long time, both too shocked and thrilled to speak, then Tom reached down and picked them up carefully, one by one, and, just as carefully, placed them in the eye sockets of the two crystal skulls.

The four eyes fitted perfectly and the skulls, with their crystal eyes back in place, looked even more frightening.

'What now?' Molly said.

'We just sit back and wait again.'

At first nothing happened and Tom began to feel uneasy, turning numb with disappointment, but then, just as he was thinking that this whole venture had been in vain, he heard a distant throbbing sound, growing louder, coming closer, and finally, when the throbbing sound had turned into a roaring, the floor of the temple shook slightly, making small clouds of dust boil up.

Realizing that the noise was not coming from the floor or walls of the sanctuary tower, Tom turned his head to look to the side, out over the spires of the other temples, that vast web of ancient ruins, the maze of canals and moats, the lush green jungle beyond. The noise was coming from over there . . . not from the ground . . . from the sky . . . and as it grew louder it became more familiar and then Tom saw what it was.

A helicopter descending.

Even as he saw it, hardly believing his own eyes, feeling crushed by disappointment, the helicopter dropped below the high canopy of the trees into a clearing not far away, and Mai Suphar jumped out, wearing figure-enhancing lime-green coveralls and holding a pistol in her right hand. She glanced up at the temple, obviously knowing just what it was, then she ran across the clearing and disappeared from Tom's line of vision. He heard her boots clattering up the broad stone stairs that led to the terrace.

'Damn!' he exclaimed, turning to Molly. 'Where's the handgun?'

'I don't know. It must be back in the car. I probably dropped it when we both blacked out.'

'Damn!' Tom exclaimed again. He glanced desperately left and right, across the broad expanse of the temple roof, but clearly there was no place to go apart from one of the other sanctuary towers, where Mai would surely find them. 'What's happened to those bloody crystal skulls?' he said as he heard Mai's footsteps clattering up the stone stairs and nearing the summit. 'Now we *really* need their magical powers!'

'Oh, fuck!' Molly exclaimed.

By now, the sun had moved out from behind the clouds and its light suddenly flared brilliantly in great striations that fell over the temple. At that moment, Mai Suphar emerged onto the roof and advanced carefully on the central sanctuary tower, holding her pistol at the ready. The wind was whipping her long black hair across her golden, gorgeous face and her figure, emphasized in the tight, lime-green coveralls, was truly something to see.

Shocked to realize that even in these circumstances he could not ignore Mai's beauty and was, indeed, helplessly dazzled by it, in danger of becoming its victim, of being *devoured* by it – by the salivating jaws of the black widow spider – Tom rescued himself by taking hold of Molly's hand and squeezing it reassuringly, thus reassuring himself. Then, heartened, though certainly not out of danger, he led her outside as the sunlight, growing brighter by the second, dazzled his eyes.

Squinting into that light, he saw Mai coming towards him, smiling with triumph, raising the pistol in her hand, first aiming it at him, then, grinning even more broadly, turning the weapon on Molly. She stopped when she was mere feet away, keeping the weapon aimed at Molly.

'I'm rather fond of shy English gentlemen,' she said to Molly, 'and I need this particular one to play with, so you have to go first.'

With a fearful, choked sob, Molly turned to Tom and wrapped her arms around him. Disgusted with this display of unseemly emotion, not realizing that it was calculated, Mai stepped forward to pull Tom and Molly apart. But when she grasped Molly's shoulder, the latter spun around, springing out of Tom's embrace, and chopped the side of Mai's neck with the edge of her open palm, a brutal, expert blow that made Mai stagger backwards and drop her pistol. When the weapon clattered noisily onto the stone-flagged floor, Tom picked it up and stared at it, bewildered, not knowing how to use it, then looked helplessly at Molly as she kicked and chopped at the stunned Mai, using the skills that she had resolutely picked up in the rough streets of New York.

'Shoot her, Tom!' she bawled. *'Shoot the bitch!'*

But Tom, being a gentleman and having led a sheltered life, didn't know how to cock the weapon, let alone fire it, and he just stood there, wondering what to do with it, as Molly took one final kick at Mai, then threw herself to the floor, rolled away and jumped to her feet again.

Looking impossibly beautiful and absolutely deadly, her eyes flaring with rage in the brightening sunlight, Mai whipped a dagger out of the belt around her waist and lunged viciously at Molly.

Molly ducked and cried, 'Dammit, Tom, just fire it!'

'I can't!'

Mai slashed again. Molly ducked again. 'Here!' she shouted, waving her hand for the pistol.

Mai slashed and Molly feinted. Mai slashed again and Molly weaved. 'God damn it, Tom, throw me that pistol!' Tom threw the pistol. Molly ducked, caught the pistol, turned towards Mai and fired. The bullet hit Mai in the chest, hurling her backwards, soaking the front of her lime-green coveralls with a bright stain of crimson. She stopped staggering backwards, stared at Molly with surprise, managed to croak, 'Beginner's luck, bitch!' then sank to the floor, her lovely legs bending slowly, as in a dance, but tantalizing no more. Eventually, she fell onto her back, legs and arms akimbo, to stare up into the dazzling sunlight with wide-open, dead eyes.

Shocked by what she had done, Molly dropped the pistol and Tom instantly bent low to pick it up. Before he could do so, however, Lu Thong's voice rang out behind him: 'Don't bother, Tom!'

Tom straightened up as Lu Thong stepped onto the terrace and walked languidly across the grass-covered stone slabs, holding his own pistol at the ready.

'Nice try, my friend,' he said, stopping mere feet away, still aiming his pistol at them while glancing down at Mai, who lay lifeless and bloody at his feet. Raising his gaze again, he shook his head from side to side, saying, 'Dear, dear, what a dreadful thing to do! How *could* you, Tom?'

'He didn't. I did it,' Molly said.

'I might have known,' Lu Thong said. 'So, Tom, where are the crystal skulls? Inside that sanctuary tower behind you?'

'Yes,' Tom said. 'Where else?'

'And have you found the missing eyes?'

'Yes,' Tom said, sweating in the humidity and realizing that the sunlight was becoming so bright that it seemed unnatural.

'And did you, dear Tom, place them back where they belong?'

'Yes,' Tom said, 'I did.'

'So what happened, Tom?'

'Nothing,' Tom said.

Lu Thong looked disappointed, then confused and disbelieving. He glanced past them to the tower, his eyes narrowed against the brightening light, the dazzling light, an unreal light, then he nodded and waved his pistol up and down, indicating the tower. 'Get back in there, the pair of you.'

Entering the base of the central tower, Tom noticed immediately that the dawn sunlight was falling upon the crystal skulls, directly onto their crystal eyes, making them reflect that same light in a fan of dazzling striations that cast eerie shadows on the walls. Temporarily blinded, he blinked a few times, letting his eyes adjust to the light, though this did not prevent the feeling of unreality that was creeping up over him.

'Sit down in that corner,' Lu Thong ordered. 'The pair of you, back to back. And don't try any nonsense.'

As Tom lowered himself to the floor, back to back with Molly, he heard the sound of more footsteps advancing across the terrace outside. Glancing sideways, he saw four of Lu Thong's hoodlums, all armed with pistols, coming up behind Lu Thong. While one took up a position beside Lu Thong, holding a coiled rope in one big fist, the others spread out around the base of the tower to ensure that Tom and Molly could not escape.

'Tie them up,' Lu Thong said.

While Lu Thong kept them covered, his hoodlum tied them back to back with the thick rope, pulling it tight and knotting it with a double loop. This task completed, he stepped back to let Lu Thong, attentive as always, kneel in front of Tom. He stared at Tom with eyes no longer sleepy, but now glittering with cocaine-induced intensity. Though smiling, he seemed slightly deranged, adrift in his secret world, unreal in the dazzling light.

'We've both been fooled,' he said. 'We both pursued a vain dream. We've both gone to great lengths to find the lost eyes of the skulls and now that they're back where they belong, the world remains unchanged. I'm deeply disappointed, Tom. I'm also angry beyond belief. I came here to find revelation and now you tell me I can't. I could hate you for that, Tom, for building up my hopes, but unlike Mai, I'm not a vindictive person and I seek no revenge. Nevertheless, you two must die. Alas, you know too much about me. Besides, I saw what happened in my house and on that bridge in Bangkok and I know that though nothing has happened here, those crystal skulls still have magical powers. How do we release those powers? Clearly not as we had imagined. We now have the crystal eyes in the crystal skulls and the world, which is a meaningless cesspit, remains as it always was. Yet the skulls have magical powers. We have both seen that, Tom. We have seen it and so I must still have the skulls and you two must die because I cannot have witnesses to my vile transgressions against God and man. The skulls are still priceless, Tom, they have powers that *can* be released, so I'll take them back with me to examine them at great length and sooner or later, preferably sooner rather than later, I'll unravel their secrets. You and Molly, my dear Tom, must stay here and watch the sunset with sightless eyes. The caretakers, when they come later, will find you, both as dead as these ancient stones.'

'What caretakers?' Tom asked out of some deep intuition that temporarily dampened his fear and led his nose to sniff the wind of truth.

'The ones who work here every day,' Lu Thong replied. 'It's very early, Tom, it's not yet full daybreak, but they will come in due course.'

'It's not full daybreak yet?'

'No.'

'Then why is it so bright?'

Lu Thong stared at him, looking confused again, then he glanced around him with widening, disbelieving eyes and finally stared at the crystal skulls. The skulls were shimmering in a radiant, unreal light, their crystal eyes reflecting other rays of light that illuminated Lu Thong's wasted face and made it seem like a death mask.

'Good God, Tom, you're right!'

'How did you get here?' Tom asked.

'You saw that – by helicopter.'

'It was a perfectly normal flight?'

'More or less,' Lu Thong said. 'Though, come to think of it, maybe not. We flew through the night and at first it was dark and cloudy, the sky threatening rain, but then suddenly there was turbulence, a very strange kind of lightning – not lightning, sheets of light – we were surrounded by dazzling light – and then, where there should have been clouds, we saw only the stars. We thought we were lost. The stars seemed to be all around us – above and below and cascading on both sides – and then the engine of the helicopter cut out and we thought we were going to die. Then suddenly it came back on and the stars disappeared and abruptly we were back in black clouds. Shortly after, much sooner than we had expected, we were looking down upon Angkor. Why do you ask, Tom?'

'Because I think the skulls are working,' Tom said, 'and they've transported us here.'

'Where's *here*, Tom?'

'I don't know.'

Frowning, Lu Thong crossed to the crystal skulls and reached down to pick one of them up.

When he touched it, his world turned inside out and at last he found what he had been seeking.

Eternal life.

Hell.

CHAPTER TWENTY-EIGHT

The instant Lu Thong touched the first skull, its crystal dome flared into life, its mouth gave forth with a roar, and daggers of fierce, dazzling light shot out of its crystal eyes. Even as Lu Thong staggered backwards, temporarily blinded, his face scorched, the second skull, as if triggered by the first, also roared and exploded with light, sending the beams from its bulging crystal eyes in the opposite direction. The beams were hot and phosphorescent, pulsating, filled with sparks, and they fanned out to criss-cross each other and cast their light on the walls and floor, creating flickering mosaics of white and black that had a life of their own. The skulls themselves now seemed alive, being illuminated from within, that light reducing the normal light to darkness while burning in the depths of the skulls like globes of silvery fire. Darkness swirled around the skulls, a black whirlpool filled with more light and, as Lu Thong recovered, opening his eyes, staring downwards, that light broke up and turned into streaming stars that seemed, in their extraordinary brilliance, to be here and faraway at the same time, defying all reasoning.

Lu Thong stood there, transfixed, mesmerized by what he was seeing, as the beams of light around him, the ones forming two great fans, first started bending in an unnatural manner, then, making whipping, whooshing sounds, arched and coiled through one another like snakes, rising up and coiling back down, sweeping around to form circles that imprisoned him and closed in upon him.

Startled, not expecting this, feeling fear for the first time, Lu Thong struck out at the beams of light with his pistol and saw the weapon go through them. He tried to step out of his prison, to escape the encircling snakes of light, but when he touched them, he was scorched by a fierce heat that sent electric shocks through his body and made his every nerve sing.

The crystal skulls roared again and streams of stars shot from their mouths. Surrounded by those stars, losing all sense of direction, of space and dimension, confused between what was up and what was down, what was left and what was right, Lu Thong became disorientated and staggered this way and that, repeatedly striking the encircling streams of light with his body and limbs, being scorched and electrified repeatedly.

'No!' he cried out. *'Not this!'*

Tom saw this dreadful spectacle from where he sat on the floor, still tied back-to-back with Molly, who was wriggling and gasping in frustration. Yet he and Molly remained untouched, bearing witness, not involved, the swirling light streaming above them and past them, before, without touching them, rushing away to explode over the hoodlums outside and cocoon them in a phosphorescent glowing that grew ever brighter. The hoodlums all screamed at once, dropped their weapons, went into spasms, and then the glowing cocoons exploded with a mighty roaring and set fire to those trapped inside. The hooligans, screaming dreadfully, suddenly burst into flames and within seconds were separate balls of fire that gave off a black, billowing smoke. Three collapsed and one tried to run away, still in flames, but then he, too, collapsed and was still, becoming no more than a heap of smouldering rags.

'Christ!' Molly said. 'Jesus!'

Tom was trying to wriggle free, but his bonds were too tight, and as he struggled, refusing to give in, Lu Thong, still trapped in swirling coils of phosphorescence, screamed out in terror – yes, even Lu Thong was terrified – and raised his pistol to fire upon the crystal skulls and blow them to pieces.

He never fired a shot. The crystal skulls roared again. Their mouths spewed twin streams of sparks that exploded against Lu Thong's hands, burning them instantly, turning the pistol into a piece of red-hot metal that forced his scorched fingers to release it. The pistol clattered to the floor where the light was drawn to it, spreading out to fall over it, covering it like translucent lava, and the gun, after turning red-hot again, melted into the stone.

'Push, Molly!' Tom shouted, trying to make himself heard about the roaring of the crystal skulls, above the whipping and whooshing of the swirling streams of light, as he struggled to loosen their bonds and set them both free. 'Push as hard as you can against the ropes. We might be able to break them!'

'It's impossible!' Molly replied, though she did as she was told, leaning forward, away from Tom, as the light swirled above her, just past her, streaming outside, and Tom continued wriggling frantically to loosen the ropes, refusing to give in.

'Don't stop, Molly! Try it!'

Yet even as he was struggling, he saw the crystal skulls changing, taking on ghostly features, turning into female faces, oddly beautiful, ageless, their full lips smiling ethereally, dark eyes radiant with the growing awareness that they were being released from their Earthly prison. They found freedom in that instant, flaring up and fading away, and then the crystal skulls dissolved, sucked back into their own light, becoming mere clouds of dust that, when it settled, released an even greater light, a veritable explosion of silvery-whiteness, that swept away the streams of light that were swirling around the room and then consumed them as it filled the whole tower and seemed to make the walls melt.

Tom saw stars on all sides, above and below, as Lu Thong, who could not see the floor, lost his balance and twisted wildly this way and that, then fell screaming disbelievingly into darkness. That darkness was below, where the floor should have been, and it looked like a bottomless pit with stars in its deepest depths. Lu Thong screamed as he gazed down – obviously he was lying on *something* solid – 'The floor's still here!' Tom bawled, hoping to ease Molly's fear – and then, looking down, Tom saw exactly what Lu Thong was seeing and was equally petrified.

Pools of lava glowed down there, illuminating banks of mud, and men and women, all naked, were either waist-deep in the lava, waving arms, wailing dementedly, or writhing in the mud, trying in vain to stand upright, their blistered bodies covered in serpents and spiders and scorpions and vermin. They, too, were wailing dementedly, or sobbing or groaning, and around them, in the putrefaction of eternal decay, wandered other members of the dead and the damned.

Lu Thong screamed in mortal terror, seeing what he would soon become. When he looked down, as did Tom, through that swooping, depthless darkness, seeing the damned and then seeing through them, he perceived, even farther down, in those depths beyond time and space, a mountain of bones covered in maggots, dismembered limbs filled with worms, wide-eyed faces, so far away and yet so near, wrapped in cobwebs and covered in slime, wailing throughout eternity for God's mercy.

Lu Thong also screamed for mercy, trying to raise himself from the darkness, but as he broke free, jerking upright, gasping painfully for breath, a great roaring emanated from the dark pit beneath him, from the very bowels of the Earth, from the basements of hell, and a blast of hot air enveloped him, sucking the breath from his lungs, and he was dragged down, protesting hysterically, wriggling frantically, screaming insanely, into a vortex of swirling flame and boiling blood and tripe and slime, into the belly of the beast created by him in his wild cocaine dreams.

Tom saw him down there, being offered what he had sought, but now that Lu Thong had what he had always wanted – eternal life – he was horrified by the price he would have to pay and screamed blasphemous insults. Thus, he was spewed back out, carried up on a bed of smoke, and reached where he had been before – that mere sliver of time – only to fall back into the darkness that still covered the stone-flagged floor.

Realizing that the floor was still there, he stood up and ran outside.

Tom broke free from his bonds – at least, he thought that he had done so – but as the rope was torn apart and he felt the bonds around him loosening, he saw more streams of light pouring out of the far corner, rising from the hole where the stone slab had formerly been, covering up the crystal eyes, forming a triangle with two sides for the crystal skulls to be positioned by – the skulls that had vaporized, turning back into crystal powder, into the dust of centuries – and then he saw those familiar figures materializing out of the light, slim, faceless, swaying sensuously, in silence, to surround him and bathe him in their light and lean down to touch him.

In fact, they could not touch him, but their power reached out to him: minute bolts of lightning filled with sparks that shot out of their fingerless hands to burn and sever his bonds.

Tom spread his hands in the air, free at last, and cast the severed ropes aside.

'Yes!' he cried. '*Yes!*'

'Christ, let's go!' Molly snapped.

They jumped to their feet and ran outside, then stopped, seeing Lu Thong.

He looked like all hell, face blistered, hands scorched, but when he saw them, his cocaine eyes were brightened with fury and fear. Reaching down to the ground, he picked up a pistol dropped by one of his dead hoodlums and aimed it at Tom.

'It's all over for me,' he said. 'My life no longer has meaning. As it is for me, so it is for you, but you will go to hell sooner. First that tart and then you.'

He turned the pistol on Molly and cocked the hammer, preparing to fire, but Tom, without thinking, dived at him and crashed into him, sending him bowling backwards to the ground.

They struck the ground together, a tangle of arms and legs, but Tom pushed himself away and jumped back to his feet and then, as Lu Thong also jumped to his feet, mere feet away from the edge of the broad terrace, Tom rushed at him and brought him down with a rugby tackle and, once more crashing to the stone slabs, rolled sideways as Lu Thong fell backwards over the edge.

Lu Thong offered his last sound on Earth – a long, drawn-out scream.

That scream seemed to reverberate for an exceptionally long time – it was not abruptly cut off by Lu Thong's contact with the ground – and as a great, saucer-shaped light materialized directly above Ta Keo – a dazzling light filled with stars – and descended over the temple to obscure the five sanctuary towers in its pulsating, silvery haze, offering Tom and Molly protection, Tom crawled to the edge of the roof and looked down nervously.

He saw a maelstrom of light and sound.

Lu Thong was down there, a mere puppet on a string, a silhouette in pools of light, being turned this way and that, raised on high and cast down again, before finally being turned inside-out, his soul released from his mortal body; and that soul, long corrupted beyond all measure, turned back, like a black widow spider, to devour its own mate.

Lu Thong saw it coming – the monstrous beast of his own creation; his mirror image, his dominant dark side – and he screamed with the collective terror of all the damned of eternity as he was sucked again into the maelstrom, into the jaws of eternal hell, finally this time, and then, his fate decreed, the unholy fires awaiting him, his Earthly body was allowed to continue its journey to the hard, unforgiving ground far below. He thudded into the timeless soil of the ancient city of Angkor, obliterated by its indifference, and remained there, his features crushed and erased, to make manure for the future.

'Well, well,' Tom whispered.

The maelstrom settled down, becoming a harsh wind, then a mere breeze, letting the normal light return, and Tom rolled away from the edge of the roof and looked directly above him. The great saucer-shaped light was dimming and shrinking as it ascended vertically, serenely to the clouds, where it abruptly winked out. Tom climbed back to his feet.

'Day's work done,' he said.

Molly was staring at him. Though shell-shocked, she recovered quickly. Walking up to him, she cupped his face in her hands and then kissed him full on the lips. Her lips felt very nice.

'To hell with the money,' she said. 'To hell with it all. Why not marry me, Tom?'

'That would make you a respectable woman.'

'I can live with that,' Molly said. 'Come on, let's get out of here.'

They took the steps down to the bottom of the mountain temple, then made their way back across the ancient city, past the dried-out canals and moats, the ruins shrouded in jungle mist, which had mysteriously returned, and on to where the Ford Cortina was still resting where they had left it, oddly angled over the tangled undergrowth around the base of the soaring trees. Without thinking, not speaking, they clambered up over the tangled roots, the rot of centuries, and climbed back into their respective sides of the car, where they sat side by side, in tingling silence, not fastening their safety belts.

When Tom glanced out of the car, he saw the caretakers of the site, all moon-faced Cambodians, piling out of an old wreck of a van and advancing into the complex, obviously assuming that this was just another day, not worth thinking about.

'We're in the real Angkor,' Tom said to break the silence. 'In Cambodia and clearly in the present.' He checked his wristwatch. It still said five in the morning. Time had stopped for him and Molly, though not for the real world, and the caretakers would get on with their work, not knowing what had taken place here. Tom and Molly were safe.

'So how do we get home?' Molly asked.

'Don't ask me,' Tom replied.

Molly turned into him, resting her hands on his shoulders, and looked steadily into his eyes while smiling mischievously.

'Tom?'

'Yes?'

'We might not get another chance like this. Have you ever fooled around in a car, Tom?'

'I don't believe so,' Tom said.

'Gimme your hand, Tom.'

Tom let her hold his hand. She unbuttoned her Chinese blouse and pulled it off her shoulder, then placed Tom's hand upon her bare breast and sighed with deep pleasure. Tom closed his eyes.

'Do you like the feel of me, Tom?'

'God, yes, Molly, I do.'

'There's an awful lot more of me, Tom, and you're a born explorer. Go exploring, Tom. Live a life.'

Tom kept his eyes closed. He let Molly be his guide. Together, they went to places that he had never been before and the experience lifted him out of himself and offered transcendence. There were stars in his head. The cosmos unfurled before him. He was released from the inhibitions that had constrained him and he felt resurrected. Good spirits surrounded him. Though faceless, they smiled upon him. He felt their warmth and it poured down to his loins and let him melt into Molly. Entering Molly, he found a new life, a world beyond time and space; and he sensed that the world he had left behind, if still there at all, had been changed in some way he could not imagine; though the changes, he was convinced, were for the better and might bring peace on Earth.

Not that it mattered. Nothing mattered but his new feelings. He saw more stars and was raised on high by angels and surrounded by white light. The white light was benevolent.

'God, I love you,' Tom said.